T0305030

SWEET NIGHTMARE

THE CALDER
ACADEMY SERIES

ALSO BY TRACY WOLFF

SWEET NIGHTMARE

THE CALDER
ACADEMY SERIES

TRACY WOLFF

PIATKUS

PIATKUS

First published in the US in 2024 by Entangled Teen,
An imprint of Entangled Publishing, LLC.
Published in Great Britain in 2024 by Piatkus

1 3 5 7 9 10 8 6 4 2

A CIP catalogue record for this book
is available from the British Library.

HB ISBN: 978-0-349-43918-1
TPB ISBN: 978-0-349-43919-8

Printed and bound in Great Britain by
Clays Ltd, Elcograf S.p.A.

Papers used by Piatkus are from well-managed forests
and other responsible sources.

Piatkus
An imprint of
Little, Brown Book Group
Carmelite House
50 Victoria Embankment
London EC4Y 0DZ

An Hachette UK Company
www.hachette.co.uk

www.littlebrown.co.uk

To everyone who's faced their worst nightmare and come out stronger on the other side.

This book is for you.

Sweet Nightmare is a fast-paced, paranormal romance with horror elements set at a school for rogue paranormals. As such, the story includes elements that might not be suitable for all readers. Graphic violence, gore, death, blood, vomit, fire and burning, drowning, venom and poisoning, bullying, hallucinations, profanity, monster attacks that relate to common phobias, and natural disasters are depicted. Death of family members is discussed. Readers who may be sensitive to these elements, please take note.

NIGHT AFTER NIGHT-MARE

- *JUDE* -

I know your worst nightmare.

No, not that one. The other one.

The one you don't trot out at parties.

The one you don't whisper to your best friend late at night.

The one you don't even acknowledge to yourself until it's three a.m. and the lights are out and you're too paralyzed with fear to even reach your arm out and flick on the bedside lamp. So you lay there, heart racing, blood pumping, ears straining for the slide of the window, the creak of the door, the footstep on the stairs.

The monster under the bed.

The monster inside your head.

Don't be ashamed. Everyone has one—even me.

Mine always starts out the same.

Full moon. Hot, sticky air. Moss hanging low enough to brush your face on a late-night walk. Waves crashing against the shore. A cottage—a girl—a storm—a dream, forever out of reach.

I know it doesn't sound like much, but the story isn't in the setup. It's in the blood and the betrayal.

So fall asleep if you dare. But don't say I didn't warn you. Because the only thing I can promise is that my nightmares are worse than yours.

CHAPTER ONE

NO SUCH THING
AS A QUICK ESCAPE

- *CLEMENTINE* -

Of all the punishments this school for misfits and fuckups could throw at a person, I can't believe I'm stuck with this one. Just last week, one of the new vamps nearly drained a witch and all she got was dish duty.

Ironic? Absolutely.

Fair? Not even close.

Then again, here at Calder Academy, fair is pretty much a nebulous concept, right up there with safety and good judgment. Hence the reason my mother—aka the headmaster not-so-extraordinaire of this not-so-extraordinary establishment—thinks assigning me to chrickler duty is actually a reasonable thing for an administrator to do.

Spoiler alert: it's not. It is, however, absolutely miserable. Not to mention dangerous as hell.

Still, nearly three years of this nightmare have taught me a few tricks—chief among them, to walk softly—and slowly—and carry a really big bag of kibble.

A quick scan of the large, shadowy enclosure shows me the food has once again done its job. The little monsters are actually distracted—at least for now.

With that thought in mind, I take a small, calculated step back toward the door. When none of the chricklers raises so much as a furry eyebrow, let alone actually looks up from their long troughs full of kibble, I take another. And another. The old, wooden door that separates me from the basement hallway is almost in reach. A couple more steps and I might actually make it out of here without losing any blood.

Hope, like assholery, springs eternal.

A drop of sweat slides down my spine as I take another cautious step backward. Then I hold my breath as I reach behind me for the old-fashioned latch that keeps the chricklers—and me—locked in this cool, dark pen.

But the moment my fingers touch the lock, a huge clap of thunder rumbles across the sky.

Shit, shit, shit.

Hundreds of heads lift at the same exact time—and every single one of them turns straight toward me. Eyes narrow. Teeth flash. Growls echo off the rough stone walls.

And just like that, I'm totally fucked.

Nails skitter across the floor as they race toward me as one.

Fuck slow and steady. I whirl around and dive for the door just as the first wave reaches me.

Nails rake down my calves as I fumble for the door. I shake off the first few then gasp as teeth tear into my thigh and hip. Reaching down with one hand, I rip several more of the little bastards off of me.

But one enterprising chrickler manages to hang tight as it climbs up my back. It's got long, pointy teeth that scrape a gash across my shoulder while its longer, even pointier claws drag straight down my right biceps as it tries to hang on. I muffle a yelp as fresh blood—my blood—hits the toe of my battered but beloved Adidas Gazelles, but I don't bother trying to pull it off a second time. Freedom is right here. I just have to reach out and take it…and avoid getting swarmed yet again while I do. I flounder around trying to flip the iron latch. The lever is ancient and likes to jam—but I've done this enough to know all the tricks. I push the left side in, jimmy the right side up, and pull as hard as I can. The latch gives way just as another chrickler—or maybe the same one, who can tell at this point—bites down hard on my ankle.

To shake it off, I kick straight back as hard as I can and wildly thrash my leg around while simultaneously yanking on the door, also as hard as I can. It's heavy and my shoulder is throbbing, but I ignore the pain as the door finally moves. I rip the last chrickler off my shoulder and dive through an opening barely wider than my hips before slamming the door close behind me.

To make sure nothing follows me out—chricklers are sneaky like that—I throw my back against the old wood as hard as I can. Just as I do, my best friend, Luis, saunters into the dim light of the basement hallway. "Looking for something?" He holds up my first aid kit, then stops short as he finally gets a good look at me. "Damn, Clementine. Has anyone ever told you that you really know how to make an entrance?"

"Don't you mean an exit?" I rasp, ignoring the horrified look on his face. "The incoming storm must have riled up the chricklers more than usual today."

"'Riled up'? Is that what you want to call it?" he shoots back but is nearly drowned out by a loud, animalistic crying coming from behind the door. "What is that godawful noise?"

"I don't know." I glance around, but I don't see anything. Then again, this entire hallway is lit up by exactly one sad, bare lightbulb hanging from the ceiling, so it's not like I've got a fantastic view. Like the rest of this school, darkness is definitely the basement's friend.

But the crying is definitely getting louder...and now I can tell it's coming from inside the pen.

"Oh, shit." As I slide the last lock into place, I see a small chrickler paw caught between the door and the frame.

Luis follows my stare. "Fuck, no. Clementine, don't even think about it!"

I know he's right, but— "I can't just leave the poor thing like that."

"That 'poor thing' just tried to eat your entrails!" he shoots back.

"I know! Believe me, I know!" Considering how many parts of my body are currently throbbing, it would be impossible for me to forget about it.

He rolls his silver wolf eyes so hard I'm a little surprised they don't actually disappear into his skull.

By now the crying has turned into muffled little yelps and I can't just leave the thing like that, monster or not. "I have to open the door, Luis."

"Damn it, Clementine!" But even as he says it, he's moving behind me to back me up. "I want the record to state that I oppose this decision."

"The record shall so reflect," I tell him as I take a deep breath and reluctantly flip open the lock I just closed. "Here goes nothing."

CHAPTER TWO

AT YOUR BECK AND CALDER

"Keep your hand on the door!" Luis urges as he leans over my shoulder to micromanage, something he tries to do in so many areas of my life.

"I'm planning on it," I answer, wrapping one hand around the handle and bracing the second one directly above it so I can push the door shut as soon as the chrickler's paw slips free.

I pull what I'm hoping is just hard enough, and the second the paw slips back through the opening, I throw all my weight behind the door and slam it shut again as hard as I can. By some miracle, I actually manage not to create a new disaster.

A chorus of outraged yowls arises from the enclosure, but nothing escapes.

I'm safe...at least until the next time.

Exhausted now that the last burst of adrenaline has left my body, I lean back against the door, slide down until my butt hits the floor, and then breathe. Just breathe.

Luis sinks down next to me, nodding to the first aid kit he's dropped a few feet away. He's taken to bringing it down here for me every day that I have chrickler duty—and, unfortunately, I've rarely not needed it. "We might want to get started patching you up. The bell's going to ring in a few minutes."

I groan. "I thought I was getting faster at this."

"There's faster and then there's fast," he says with a rueful grin. "You really don't have to make sure every single one of the little monsters' bowls is filled with perfectly cold ice water. Room temp will suffice."

"It's September. In Texas. Cold water is a necessity."

"And what thanks do you get for your concern?" His black hair flops over his left eye as he looks at the shredded sleeve of my T-shirt—and the deep scratches below.

It's my turn to roll my eyes as I reach for the first aid kit. "The headmaster stays off my back?"

"I'm sure *your mother* would understand you giving them room-temperature water if it means saving yourself copious amounts of blood loss. She is the one who insists on boarding these damn things, after all." He eyes the large Band-Aid I've extracted from the kit as we've been talking. "Want help with that?"

"Maybe," I answer grudgingly. "Just do the one on my back, okay? And I think the whole point of chrickler duty is that it's a punishment, so I am not sure my mother has my feelings at the top of her list."

He snorts in acknowledgment of this truth as he drags the collar of my red uniform shirt down just enough so that he can slap the bandage on my scratched and still-bleeding shoulder. "But it's not like you got yourself sent to this school for some nefarious deed or big, bad behavior like the rest of us."

"And yet here I am. The joys of being a Calder…"

"Yeah, well, Calder or not, you've got to lay off chrickler duty or I don't think you'll actually make it to graduation."

"Oh, I'm making it to graduation," I tell him as I slap on a few more bandages, "if for no other reason than I can finally, finally, get the hell off this island."

I've been counting down the days since freshman year. Now that I'm finally a senior, I'm not about to let anything stand in the way of me getting out of this hellhole and actually starting a life somewhere where I don't have to watch my back—and every other part of myself—every second of every day.

"One more year," Luis says as he holds out a hand for the first aid kit. "Then we're both out of here."

"More like two hundred and sixty-one days." I shove the box of bandages back in the first aid kit and hand it to him. Then I push to my feet, ignoring all the places that hurt.

As we start down the depressingly dank hallway, the lightbulb starts to sway and sizzle in the completely still corridor. "What the hell is that?" asks Luis.

"A strong suggestion that we get a move on," I answer, because lingering in the Calder Academy basement/dungeon is never a good idea. But before we can take more than a few steps, the bulb makes a popping sound. Seconds later, a bunch of sparks explode out of it—right before the hallway is plunged into darkness.

"Well, this certainly isn't eerie at all," Luis deadpans, coming to a complete stop to peer hesitantly into the black.

"You can't honestly be afraid of the dark, can you?" I can't resist goading him as I pull my phone out of my pocket.

"Of course not. I *am* a wolf, you know. I do have night vision."

"Doesn't make you less of a chicken," I tease.

I swipe my thumb across the flashlight app on my phone and shine the light straight down the hallway.

After all, the chricklers aren't the only monsters down here—just the smallest and the nicest.

As if on cue, the door directly in front of Luis shakes violently on its hinges.

We don't need any additional motivation. We both take off running, the beam of the phone flashlight bouncing along with my strides. As I look behind me to make sure that nothing is following us, the beam catches what looks like a hulking shadow in the adjacent corridor. I swing the light in its direction, but nothing's there.

My stomach clenches because I know I saw something. But then a loud thump comes from the room on the left, followed by a clatter of chains and a high-pitched, animalistic screech that doesn't seem muffled—at all—by the thick wooden door between us.

Luis picks up the pace, and I join him as we pass several more doors before the one in front of us starts to vibrate so violently that I'm afraid it could shake off its hinges at any second.

I ignore it, forcing myself to stay calm. One more turn, a mad dash, and we'll be at the staircase. Home free.

Apparently, I'm not running fast enough for Luis, because he grabs my hand and pulls me along with him as a loud, furious shriek follows us around the corner.

"Move, Clementine!" he shouts, throwing me into the stairwell in front of him.

We pound up the stairs and burst through the double doors at the top just as the warning bell rings.

CHAPTER THREE

ANOTHER ONE BITES
THE PIXIE DUST

"**Y**ou have the power to defeat the monsters inside of you," a soothing voice says over the intercom. The affirmation that doubles as the bell fills the hallway as Luis and I pause to catch our breaths.

"No offense to your aunt Claudia and her daily affirmations," he gasps out, "but I don't think it's the monsters inside of us that we've got to be worried about."

"No shit," I agree, even as I fire off a text to Uncle Carter to let him know that he needs to double-check the locks on the monster enclosures.

My uncle Carter is in charge of the basement menagerie. Back in the day, Calder Academy Island started out as a sanatorium where rich paranormals would ship off family members to "convalesce." But rumor has it that the basement was actually reserved for the criminally insane—which explains the giant, eighty-pound doors on each of the cells. Not great for humans, but the setup comes in handy when you need to keep creatures from wreaking total and complete havoc.

"Remind me again why your mother thinks it's a good idea to board some of the most fucked-up monsters in existence?" Luis asks as he finishes tucking his red polo shirt into his black uniform shorts.

"Apparently, the school needs the money to 'keep the students in the style to which they've become accustomed,'" I quote.

We take a moment to admire that supposed style before we're forced to duck as a loose ceiling tile falls to the floor. After the sanatorium closed, it didn't take much work to convert the ornate Victorian buildings into a luxury hotel for paranormals, which occupied the island until my family bought it eighty years ago.

The buildings themselves were commissioned back in the day when they built beautiful buildings for architecture's sake, even if those buildings were part of a hospital. The remnants of that bygone era still peek through the years' wear and tear. Like the carved marble staircases now worn with steps and age, the large arched turrets, the bay windows, or the intricate brickwork that adorns the entrance to the Admin Building, where we have most of our classes. But all of that potential charm has been overshadowed by the institutional green paint that has been slathered on every wall and the drop ceilings that are surely covering up some pretty cool moldings.

Luis snickers and shakes his head as my phone buzzes with a text from my roommate, Eva.

Eva: Where are you?

Eva: I can't be late to anger management. Danson's a dick

Eva: If he gives me shit again, I swear I'm going to totally throat punch him

I fire off a quick reply letting her know I'm on my way.

"You okay?" Luis checks as we walk quickly in an attempt to avoid getting yelled at by the hall trolls.

"Thanks to you, I am," I answer, giving him a quick hug before I push the door open to the girls' bathroom in the center of the hall. "Love you, Luis."

He brushes off my moment of tenderness with a snarky, "You'd better," just before the door closes behind me.

"Damn, Clementine. You're supposed to feed the chricklers, not be their feed," Eva tells me as she straightens from where she's leaning against one of the old-fashioned bucket sinks.

I snap my fingers. "I knew I was doing something wrong."

"I brought you coffee." Her long, black curls bounce as she leans forward to hand me a turquoise-and-pink string backpack.

Joy floods me as I see the two go-cups of what I know is Eva's famous café con leche, a recipe from her Puerto Rican family that includes just a pinch of a special spice blend. It's practically legendary among the seniors. I reach out a greedy hand for it. "Give me."

She nods to the backpack. "Time is ticking. Change first, coffee later."

I groan, but I'm already ripping off my shirt and tossing it into the trash can. I pull out the fresh polo she's brought me and—after a quick glance at the mirror—add the red hoodie she's packed on top of it.

Even though it's over a hundred degrees of pure humidity outside, it's still better than walking around for the rest of the day looking like open season has just been declared on my ass. Even the smallest sign of weakness tends to bring out the predator in the other students. Despite the fact that every student's powers are locked down, they still have fists—and teeth—and are more than happy to use them.

Thirty seconds later, I've got my face washed, my hair pulled into a ponytail, and a long sip of café con leche in my belly.

"You ready?" Eva asks, her concerned brown eyes doing a final sweep of me from head to toe.

"As I'll ever be," I answer, holding up the coffee cup in silent thanks as we head back out into the hall.

A quick glance at my phone shows a text from Uncle Carter, saying that he's on his way to check the basement. I wave goodbye to Eva before taking off down the hall toward my British Lit class.

A small pack of leopard shifters is loitering in the hall near the door to the science lab. One eyes me like I'm his post-lunch snack as a glimmer of ivory fang flashes at me. The girl next to him senses his excitement and starts prowling toward me. I keep my eyes averted— the last thing I need right now is a dominance challenge.

That's when I see a freshman—I think she's a witch—look directly at me and the shifters. Bad move, kid. They immediately smell chum in the water and turn their sights on her. If you want to survive here, direct eye contact is usually not the way to do it.

I pause, unsure of what to do next, when the girl suddenly lets out an ear-piercing scream that rings out through the hallway. It reverberates off every hard surface as it makes its way to my protesting eardrums. *Not a witch, a banshee*, I mentally note, as the leopards scatter to class.

Saved by the scream.

I quickly walk to my locker. I grab my backpack and slip through the door into my seat about one second before the final affirmation sounds.

"I am stronger than all of the problems and challenges I encounter. I just have to believe in myself."

A groan goes up from the class even before Ms. Aguilar chirps, "And there's the bell! Let's dig deep today, shall we?" in a voice that is way more bubbly than the affirmation bell or this school warrants.

Then again, everything about Ms. Aguilar is too bright and shiny for Calder Academy. From her electric-yellow hair and her bright-blue eyes to her manic smile and frighteningly upbeat attitude, everything shouts that the pixie doesn't belong here. And if that wasn't enough, the snickers coming from the asshole fae currently taking up the last row warn that they're about to make sure she, and everyone else in this classroom, knows it.

"Fuck, teach, did you snort too much pixie dust at lunch?" Jean-Luc calls, swishing his deliberately messy blond hair out of his eyes.

"And you didn't even bring us any." His friend and henchman Jean-Claude sneers. As he laughs, his green eyes glow with the unnatural electricity common to the dark magic fae. "Don't you know, sharing *is* caring."

The fact that the two of them—as well as the other two members of their little coterie of immaturity and evil, Jean-Paul and Jean-Jacques—start cackling tells everyone in the room that they've got something planned.

Sure enough, the second she turns her back to write on the board, Jean-Jacques sends a handful of Skittles soaring straight toward her.

I swear, these guys couldn't get more annoying if they tried.

Ms. Aguilar stiffens as the Skittles hit her. But instead of reprimanding the obnoxious fae, she ignores them and keeps writing on the board.

Her silence just eggs them on, and they throw another whole round of Skittles at her—but this time, they've sucked on them first, so that when they hit her white blouse, they leave a rainbow streak of goo. And that doesn't even count the ones that get caught in her spiky hair.

When she continues facing the board in what I'm pretty sure is an effort to hide tears, Jean-Luc flashes to the front of the room—fae are still preternaturally fast, even without their powers—and stands right in front of her, making crude faces and flipping her off.

Most of the class bursts out laughing, though some look down uncomfortably. Ms. Aguilar whirls around, but Jean-Luc is back in his seat by this point, smiling innocently and leaning on an elbow. Before she can figure out what happened, yet another handful of Skittles flies at her. Most hit her in the chest, but a couple strike her right between the eyes.

She squeaks a little, her chest heaving, but still doesn't say a word. I don't know if it's because she's a new teacher and has no classroom management skills or if she's just afraid of shutting down the Jean-Jerks because they come from some of the most powerful—and dangerous—mafia families in the paranormal world. Then again, it's probably both.

As spitballs soar toward her, I start to speak up like I usually do, but I stop myself. If she doesn't learn to stand up for herself and fast, this school is going to eat her alive. I've already saved Ms. Aguilar's butt three times this week—and have the bruises to prove it. After all, you don't cross members of the fae court with the darkest magic in existence and not expect to get the shit kicked out of you. Plus I'm still shaky from all of the chricklers I spent the last hour fighting off. I'm not sure I have it in me to take on a whole different group of monsters after class.

She doesn't say anything, though. Instead, she just turns back around and starts writing something in a flowery script on the board again. It's the absolute worst thing she could do, because the Jean-Jerks—and a few other less-than-enterprising souls—take it as a sign that it really is open season.

A new round of spitballs soars straight at her, getting caught in the tips of her pointy hair.

More Skittles are launched at her ass.

And Jean-Claude—jackass that he is—decides now is the time to shout a bunch of suggestive comments.

And that's it. That's just it. Fuck the pain. It's one thing when the Jean-Jerks were just being their regular asshole selves, but they've crossed the line. No one, not even the sons of fae mafia dons, gets to sexually harass a woman and get away with it. Screw that.

I clear my throat, resigning myself to another beatdown by the Jean-Jerks after class, but before I can figure out an insult devastating enough to shut their mouths, a rustling sound comes from the left of me.

It's quiet, so quiet that most people in the class don't even register it. But I've heard the slow, deliberate rhythm of that slide from stillness to action before, and though it's been a while, it still makes every hair on my body stand straight up even as an unwitting relief sweeps through me.

Apparently, I'm not the only one in this class who thinks their foray into sexual harassment is worse than their usual bad behavior and has to be stopped.

I shift slightly to my left just in time to see all six-foot-seven, gorgeous, grim-faced, broad-shouldered inches of Jude Abernathy-Lee turn around in his seat. For one second, my eyes clash with his swirling, mismatched gaze, but then he's looking straight through me to the members of the Jean-Jerk club.

I wait for him to say something to the fae, but it turns out he doesn't have to. One look from him has their words, and laughter, crumbling like dust around us.

For several seconds, silence—long, taut, jagged-edged silence— hangs in the air as the whole class holds its breath and waits to see what happens next. Because the Jean-Jerks' unstoppable assholery is about to meet Jude's immovable everything.

CHAPTER FOUR

A FAE WORSE
THAN DEATH

Lightning flashes outside the room's lone Queen Anne–style window, slicing through the sudden, unnatural darkness of the early afternoon sky.

As if to underscore the seriousness of the upcoming storm—not to mention the current atmosphere in this classroom—thunder booms seconds later. It's loud enough to rattle that same window *and* shake the ground around us. Half the class gasps as the lights flicker, but instead of breaking the tension in the room, Mother Nature's temper tantrum only ratchets it up higher.

Maybe we'll get lucky and lightning will strike a Jean-Jerk. Right now, fae flambé really doesn't sound so bad.

Ms. Aguilar glances uneasily out the window. "With all this lightning, I certainly hope someone remembered to check the fire extinguishers."

Thunder booms again, and more students shift uneasily. Normally the threat of a September storm wouldn't so much as get a second look. They're a way of life here on this Gulf Coast island—especially during hurricane season.

But this one didn't grow and build the way they usually do. It pretty much came out of nowhere, and its intensity seems to mimic the explosive energy in the room even before Jean-Paul and his band of not-so-merry losers shift forward in their desks like they've been waiting for this moment their whole lives.

My stomach tightens, and I slide my legs out from beneath my desktop, preparing for the worst.

"Don't even *think* about getting in the middle of that," the new girl behind me—Izzy, I think her name is—hisses. "I've been waiting for them to get their asses kicked from the first day. Yours, not so much."

"Thanks?" I whisper back even as I tell myself to listen to her.

But before Izzy can say anything else, Jean-Luc half coughs, half laughs as he runs a hand through his long blond hair. "You got a problem, Abernathy-Lee?"

Jude doesn't answer, just raises one dark, slashing brow as he continues to stare Jean-Luc and the others down. Jean-Luc doesn't look away, but there's a sudden glimmer of doubt in his eyes.

The glimmer grows into a whole lot of concern as Jude continues to watch them, the unease in the room becoming so palpable it hangs in the air along with the humidity. But Jean-Jacques must be too self-absorbed to notice as he sneers, "Yeah, that's what we thought. You're fucking wi—"

He breaks off as—out of nowhere—Jean-Luc's hand flashes out, slamming into the back of Jean-Jacques's head and shoving his face straight into his desk before he can spew any more vitriol.

"What did you do that for?" Jean-Jacques whines as he wipes one dark hand across the small trickle of blood now coming from his nose.

"Shut the fuck up," Jean-Luc snarls back, but his eyes continue to stay locked on Jude, who still hasn't moved more than that one, lone eyebrow. But his stillness doesn't seem to matter to Jean-Luc, at least not judging by the belligerent look on his face. "We were just fucking around, man. We don't have a problem here."

Jude's second brow goes up, as if to query, *Don't we?*

When no one else answers—or so much as breathes, to be fair—his gaze shifts from Jean-Luc to Jean-Claude, who is squirming uneasily in his seat. The moment their eyes meet, Jean-Claude suddenly develops a deep and abiding fascination with his phone—one the other three Jean-Jerks mimic with their own phones in short order.

Suddenly, none of them will look Jude in the eye.

And just like that, the danger passes, tension leaking out of the air like helium from an old balloon. At least for now.

Ms. Aguilar must sense it, too, because she lets out a relieved puff of air before pointing to the flowery quote she wrote across the board in bright-pink Expo marker. "'The only means of strengthening one's intellect is to make up one's mind about nothing.'" Her voice rises and falls with the words, like she's singing a song. She then gestures to the line written below it in teal blue. "'To let the mind be a thoroughfare for all thoughts.'"

Looks like we're just skipping straight over the elephant-sized fae problem in the room and going with a quote from a dead white guy. Then again, at the moment I don't actually hate that decision.

After she's given what I assume must be a dramatic pause, Ms. Aguilar continues. "That, my friends, is a quote from my favorite Romantic poet. Can any of you hazard a guess who it is?"

No one immediately volunteers the answer. In fact, we all just kind of sit there, staring at her in a combination of disbelief and surprise.

Her face falls as she looks around the room. "No one even has a guess?"

Still no response.

When she lets out a heartbroken sigh, one of the witches in the second to last row ventures, "Lord Byron?" in a tentative voice.

"*Byron*?" Somehow Ms. Aguilar looks even more disappointed. "Certainly not. He's much more wicked, Veronica.

"Still no guesses?" She shakes her head sadly. "I suppose I could give another quote."

She taps one cotton candy–colored fingernail against her chin. "Now, which one should I use? Maybe…"

"For fuck's sake," Izzy bursts out from behind me. "It's John fucking Keats."

Ms. Aguilar jerks back in surprise, but it quickly turns to joy. "You know him!" she crows, clapping her hands.

"Of course I bloody well know him. I'm from bloody Britain, aren't I?" Izzy snaps.

"That. Is. *Wonderful!*" Ms. Aguilar practically dances over to her desk to retrieve a pile of packets. "I'm so glad you've read him before! Isn't he just divine? 'Heard melodies are—'"

"He's an egotistical blowhard," Izzy interrupts before the teacher can once again flit from one end of the room to the other. "Just like the rest of the Romantic poets."

Ms. Aguilar pauses mid-flounder in horror. "Isadora! John Keats is one of the most brilliant poets—nay, one of the most brilliant *people*— to ever walk the face of the Earth, which I am sure you will all come to understand as we study him for our next unit."

Oh, sure. *Him* she stands up for. Maybe if the Jean-Jerks threw Skittles at the pictures of the poets she has up all over the walls, she could actually talk back to them, too.

She walks over to me and dumps the stack of packets on my desk. "Clementine, be a darling and pass these out for me, will you?"

I say, "Sure," even though my abused body would much rather go with, "Hell, no."

The Jean-Jerks barely look up when I toss a packet on each of their desks. I expect Jude to do the same when I get to him—but instead he looks straight at me.

The moment our gazes collide, it's as if everything inside me freezes and burns all at the same time. My heart speeds up, my brain slows down, and my lungs tighten until it hurts to breathe.

It's the first time he's looked directly at me—the first time we've looked at each other—since freshman year, and I don't know what to do...or how to feel.

But then his disgustingly gorgeous face goes dark right in front of me.

His razor-sharp jaw tightens.

His light-brown skin pulls taut over slashing cheekbones.

And his eyes—one so brown it's nearly black and the other a swirling, silvery green—go completely blank.

I've spent three years building a wall inside me just for this very moment, and one glance from him takes a stick of dynamite to it. I've never felt more pathetic in my life.

Determined to get away as fast as possible, I all but throw his packet at him.

The rest of the class passes in a blur as I beat myself up, furious that I wasn't the one to shut it down first. That, even after everything that happened between us, *he* was the one who got to ice *me* out instead of the other way around.

But as the bell is about to ring and we all start packing up, Ms. Aguilar claps her hands to get our attention. "There's never enough time, is there?" she laments. "But to combat that problem for next class, I'm going to assign your partners now."

"Partners?" one of the dragon shifters calls out. "For what?"

"For your Keats project, silly. I'll assign each of you a partner today, and when you come into class tomorrow, you can start on your projects right away."

Instead of going down a pre-planned list based on proximity or even alphabetical order like a normal teacher would, she starts looking around the room and pairing people up according to "the vibe she's currently feeling from them."

I don't know what kind of vibe I'm giving off, and honestly, I couldn't care less. Now that the adrenaline from the chrickler cage has worn off, the pain is kicking in. Add that to the weird shit that just went down with Jude, and I just want to get through my next class so I can head to the dorm to take some painkillers.

Not to mention a hot shower.

I tune Ms. Aguilar out and spend the next couple of minutes daydreaming about copious amounts of hot water, but I jerk back to attention the moment she calls out my name...followed by Jude's.

Oh, fuck no.

CHAPTER FIVE

BETTER LATE THAN CALDER

M s. Aguilar continues pairing people up until everyone has a partner, completely oblivious to the fact that she's just blown my shit straight up.

The bell finally rings less than a minute later. "You are on the right path for you. Stay the course."

Geez, Aunt Claudia. On the nose much?

The rest of the class heads for the door, but I hang back. Once everyone has cleared out, I head toward Ms. Aguilar, who is watching me expectantly.

"No need to thank me, Clementine," she says with a conspiratorial grin.

"Huh?" I ask, bewildered.

"For pairing you up with Jude. I could tell there's something going on between you two."

"There is *nothing* going on between me and Jude—"

"Oh, come now, you don't have to hide it. I do have a poet's soul, after all."

"I'm not hiding anything. Jude and I have a...very strong mutual dislike of each other." Or at least that's the vibe he's been throwing my way since he ditched me with no warning and absolutely no explanation.

"Oh." She looks startled. "Well, then, maybe you can use this time to mend fences—"

Mend fences? There's no *mending fences* with Jude Abernathy-Lee. How can there be when he obliterated the fence and the entire plot of land it was built on a long time ago? "Actually, I was hoping I could swap partners."

"Swap partners?" Her eyes go wide, and she bats her naturally sparkly eyelashes like the idea of changing out of her assigned groups has never occurred to her. "Oh, I don't think that's a very good idea, do you?"

"I absolutely do!" I give her my most winning smile. Or at least I try to. But judging by the way she rears back, I'm certain the day's trauma has turned it into a frightening grimace. "That's why I brought it up."

"Yes, well, I can't very well swap your partner around, Clementine. If I do that, then everyone will expect a change as well. And if I don't do it for them, then I'll be accused of favoritism toward the headmaster's daughter, and I can't afford that. I just got here."

"No one has to know!"

"I assigned the groups in front of the whole class. Everyone will know." She shakes her head. "You'll just have to make the best of it. And maybe you'll find out the two of you have more in common than you think. Now get to class. You'll be late."

She pivots to her computer to let me know the conversation is over. I give her a half-hearted goodbye and slink, defeated, out of the classroom.

I make it to my last class of the day, Anger Management with Danson the Dick, just as the affirmation bell sounds. I spend a miserable hour listening to him explain to us how much we suck and how we'll never amount to anything if we don't get our powers under control. I'm tempted to ask how anyone can be expected to learn how to control their magic if the school locks down every student's powers from the second they land on this damn island to the second the graduation boat leaves, but I don't have the fight in me today.

After class, I race for the stairs. This afternoon is Calder Conclave, and showing up in anything but a dress uniform is "completely unacceptable." Only being late is worse—well, that and missing it completely. But I'm pretty sure you'd have to be dead for that to happen—although I'm not certain that would stop my mother from requiring my attendance.

Thunder booms overhead as I book it toward the dorms, but the rain that has been threatening all day still doesn't fall. That only makes the heat and humidity worse—September in Texas is just another word for Hell—and by the time I reach the huge fence that separates the classroom buildings from the dorms, my uniform shirt is sticking to my back. Built by Giant blacksmiths, the two fences that surround the whole island and separate the academic buildings from the dorms ensure that every Calder Academy student is powerless with a combination of magic-dampening spells and paranormal technology. Eva and I like to call it the *lack* of honor system.

And I'm subjected to the same draconian rules.

Even if I didn't philosophically disagree with my mother on absolutely everything, I'd be angry with her for that alone. She grew up with her magic. My aunts and uncles grew up with theirs. A special spell keeps them exempt from the dampening and lets the adults access their power while on the island. They even renew the spell every year, whenever it's weakened. But, when it comes to my cousins and me, we can't be trusted to have access to ours.

It's what makes Danson the Dick's lecture so infuriating and unfair. I've never abused my power, never lost control of my magic, never hurt anyone—how could I when I've never, even for a second, known what it's like to *have* magic?

I'm in pain and annoyed as I head down the buckled sidewalk that leads to the dorms. On either side of the path, haphazardly placed live oak trees cast eerie shadows while the Spanish moss hanging from their branches rustles and chatters as it blows wildly in the wind. I speed up as I pass beneath them, their nefarious conversation sending chills down my spine until I can finally turn onto the long center mall that leads to the senior "cottages."

Freshmen through juniors have to stay in the primary dorm, which was once the resort's main accommodations—while the seniors get the privilege of staying in the now run-down guest cottages. The little New Orleans–style bungalows have front porches, storm shutters, and gingerbreading, though the pastel paint is now faded and peeling.

Eva's and mine has two cracked windows and a family of mice

in the pantry, but at least the air conditioning works, so we don't complain. It's part of that style to which we've become accustomed.

Eva's not home yet, so I strip off my disgustingly sweaty uniform the second I hit the door before running for the shower. A quick soap and scrub of the chrickler bites is all I have time for—the luxurious shower of my daydreams will have to wait for later. Then I towel off, throw my wet hair up into a bun, and grab my dress uniform from the basket of unfolded laundry at the bottom of my closet.

One white button-down blouse and red plaid skirt later and I'm almost ready to go. I pull on socks, slide my feet into the black loafers my mother *insists* on, and grab my phone before making a mad dash back toward the admin building.

Conclave starts in five minutes, and unfortunately, it's a ten-minute jog, so I lay on the speed. The one time I was late I ended up with chrickler duty until graduation. I definitely don't want to level up to the bigger monster enclosures.

I'm sweating profusely—*fuck humidity*—and gasping for air by the time I make it to the conference room on the fourth floor of the admin building, but I've got ten seconds to spare, so I call it a win. At least until my phone rings as I slip into the room and all twelve members of my extended family turn to stare at me in obvious disapproval.

CHAPTER SIX

GASLIGHT AT THE END OF THE TUNNEL

My phone keeps ringing in the total silence of the room. To spare further familial humiliation, I pull it out of my pocket to decline the call. It's my friend Serena, who graduated last year and is now living in Phoenix, so I fire off a text telling her it's Conclave and I'll call her when it's over. Then I slide into my seat—third from the left on the far side of the table, same as always.

"Nice of you to join us, Clementine," my mother says coolly, brows raised and crimson-painted lips pinched. "Perhaps next time you'll make sure your uniform is clean before you do so."

She's staring at my chest, so I follow her gaze only to find a large brown stain directly over my left boob. I must have pulled this uniform out of the dirty clothes basket and not the clean one.

Because that's just the kind of day I'm having.

"I'd offer you some tea," my cousin Carlotta snickers, "but it looks like you've already had some." She's in tenth grade this year and is downright sophomoric about it.

"Don't listen to them, Sugar," my grandmother tells me in her syrupy-sweet Southern accent. "The nice boys like a girl who doesn't put too much stock in her appearance."

"Don't be talking to my sweet girl about boys now, Viola," my grandfather scolds her with a wave of his hairy-knuckled hand. "You know she's too young for all that business."

"Yes, Claude," my grandmother replies even as she winks at me.

I give them both a grateful smile—it's nice to have someone in my corner. Sometimes I wonder if things would be different if my dad hadn't left before I was born. But he did, and now my mother has made it her mission to punish him by taking his fuck-ups out on me— whether she realizes it or not.

"Now that Clementine is here, I hereby call this Conclave to order," my uncle Christopher says, banging the gavel on the table hard enough to rattle all the tiny porcelain tea cups my mother insists we drink out of. "Beatrice, please serve the tea."

Within seconds, the conference room is filled with kitchen witches pushing tea carts. One is loaded down with tea pots and all the accoutrements. Another is piled high with finger sandwiches, while a third has a variety of scones and elaborate pastries.

We all sit in silence as everything is perfectly arranged on my mother's favorite floral tablecloth.

Flavia, one of the youngest kitchen witches, smiles as she puts a plate of small cupcakes on the table next to me. "I made your favorite cream cheese pineapple icing for the carrot cakes, Clementine," she whispers.

"Thank you so much," I whisper back with a large smile, drawing an annoyed frown from my mom.

I ignore her.

Flavia is just being kind—something that's not exactly prized here at Calder. Not to mention she makes a crazy good carrot cake.

Once the oh-so-pretentious Calder family Wednesday afternoon tea is served and everyone has filled their plates, my mother ceremonially takes the gavel from Uncle Christopher. She's the oldest of the five siblings currently gathered around the table. It's a position she takes very seriously since she inherited it from their oldest sister when she died, sometime before I was born...and something she doesn't let any of her brothers or sisters—or their families—forget.

Though she has the gavel in hand, she doesn't do anything as gauche as bang it. Instead, she just holds it as she waits for the table to fall silent around her. It only takes a second—I'm not the only one in the room who has suffered one of my mother's endless lectures or diabolical punishments—although I still maintain that chrickler duty is *way* better than when she made my cousin Carolina clean the monster fish tank for a month...from the inside.

"We have a full agenda today," my mother begins, "so I'd like to break protocol and start the business part of the meeting before we finish eating, if no one objects."

No one objects—though my favorite aunt, Claudia, looks like she wants to. Her bright-red topknot is quivering with either indignation or nerves, but she's so shy and introverted that it's hard for me to tell.

My mom, Uncle Christopher, and Aunt Carmen definitely like to be the center of attention at these meetings, while Uncle Carter spends most of his time trying, and failing, to focus the spotlight on himself. It's a manticore trait, one that only Aunt Claudia and I seem to be lacking. Everyone else fights for center stage like it's the only thing standing between them and certain demise.

"The first two weeks of classes have gone exceptionally well," my mother intones. "The new traffic patterns that the hall trolls have instituted appear to be keeping the flow of students orderly in between classes as well as keeping fights from breaking out in the hallways, just as we'd hoped. We've had no injuries."

"Actually," Aunt Claudia speaks up in a breathless voice that's little more than a whisper, "I've dealt with several fight injuries in the healer's office. But they were all minor, so—"

"As I was saying, no *major* injuries," my mother interrupts, narrowing her eyes at her sister. "Which is the same thing."

One glare from my mother and Aunt Claudia knows this is a losing battle. Uncle Brandt reaches over to pat her knee, and she gives him a grateful smile.

"There's a storm watch in the Gulf right now, but we should be fine," Uncle Christopher manages to interject even without the gavel. "Our protections should hold, and if it does develop further, it should pass us right by."

"Do I need to talk to Vivian and Victoria?" Aunt Carmen asks, jumping in—as she always does—at the first opportunity. "Have them cast another protection spell?"

Uncle Christopher twists the end of his auburn mustache around his finger as he contemplates her suggestion. "I suppose it couldn't hurt. What do you think, Camilla?"

My mother shrugs. "I think it's unnecessary, but if it makes you feel better, Carmen, who am I to stop you?"

"Then I'll have the witches take care of it." Aunt Carmen's voice is nearly as stiff and cold as my mother's. There is no love lost between my mother and Aunt Carmen, who is the sibling closest to her in age.

She's tried several times to launch a coup to replace my mother as headmaster. They've never worked, but they *have* made family conclaves extra entertaining.

"What about the, um"—Aunt Claudia lowers her voice like she's about to tell a secret—"the matter in the, umm, lower level...?"

"You mean the dungeon?" my grandmother corrects with a shake of her head. "At least call it what you people have turned it into."

I'm with her. That dank, dark area definitely qualifies as a dungeon.

"The matter in the *basement*," Uncle Carter says, steely-voiced, "is well in hand."

"I'm not so sure about that. Something almost got out of its cage while I was down there earlier." The words slip out before I know I'm going to say them. Everyone turns to stare at me like I'm some kind of particularly nasty bug.

I know I should regret saying anything, but stirring the family pot is the only thing that makes Conclave bearable.

"Everything is perfectly secure, Clementine," my mother tells me, eyes narrowed so much that all I can see now is a sliver of blue as she looks at me. "You need to stop making false reports."

"It wasn't a false report," I say as I defiantly swipe some icing from my cake with my finger and lick it off. "Ask Uncle Carter."

All eyes turn silently toward my uncle, who turns Calder Academy red.

"That's simply not true. Our security is top-notch. There is nothing to worry about, Camilla," he blusters, his goatee quivering in affront.

I think about pulling out my phone and blowing up the whole charade, but it's not worth the detention I'll surely get.

So instead, I duck my head and lean back in my chair. This time, it's my shoulder Uncle Brandt pats, and for a second, I want to cry. Not because of my mom, but because his smile reminds me so much of his daughter's—my cousin, Carolina, who died a couple months ago after escaping the scariest prison in the paranormal world.

She was sent there when we were both in ninth grade, and not a day goes by that I don't miss her. But knowing she's gone forever has made that ache so much worse.

My mother continues the meeting per her agenda, but after a couple more minutes, I tune her out.

Finally, just when I can taste freedom, she hands the gavel back to Uncle Christopher.

"Our last order of business tonight is a little more family oriented." He grins with pride, and so does my aunt Lucinda, who is practically squirming in her seat with excitement.

The suspense lasts mere seconds before Uncle Christopher announces, "I'd like us all to take this opportunity to congratulate Caspian on getting early acceptance into the University of Salem's prestigious Paranormal Studies program!"

The whole table erupts in cheers while I just sit there, feeling like I've been shoved off a cliff.

CHAPTER SEVEN

LET THE PICKLE CHIPS FALL WHERE THEY MAY

"Congratulations, Caspian!" Aunt Carmen tells him, lifting her tea cup in salute.

"That's fantastic news!" Uncle Carter jumps up, knocking over his chair in an effort to be the first one to clap Caspian on the back.

The others quickly follow, and it isn't long before my cousin is preening under all the attention and well-wishes.

I force myself to walk over to him and give him a hug. After all, it's not his fault I'm reeling. Any more than it's his fault that my mother won't so much as glance my way.

She refused to let me apply.

She told me I couldn't go—that none of us fourth gens could leave the island for college.

She even asked why I couldn't be more like Caspian and be happy to stay on the island after graduation—take over the academy like we're meant to do.

And now I find out that he's been applying to schools all along? That his parents have been supportive of him?

Anger rips through me as I give Caspian a hug.

He may be a bit of a tool, but I don't blame him for finding a way off this island and taking it.

My mother, on the other hand? I definitely blame her.

"Congratulations!" I tell my cousin when he finally lets me go.

He beams at me, his bright-blue eyes shining against his copper skin. "Thanks, Clementine! I can't wait to hear where you've been accepted."

My stomach sinks, because what can I say?

Why didn't Caspian and I talk about college before now? Why did I just trust my mother when she's been known to play fast and loose with the truth?

My smile is forced as I try to figure out what to say when Carlotta elbows me out of the way to congratulate Caspian.

I try to calm down, try to tell myself there's still time to apply anywhere I want to go. I'm not stuck here after I graduate. I can still leave this place in my rearview.

Her control over me is almost over.

It's that thought that gets me through the rest of the Conclave. It gets me through Caspian's ridiculously pompous speech and Uncle Christopher's proud bragging. It even gets me through my mother's continued refusal to meet my gaze.

But the second the meeting is adjourned, I race for the door.

I'll confront my mother tomorrow. Tonight, I just need to get far away from her and the rest of my family.

Grandma calls after me as I book it down the hall, but I don't turn back. If I do, I'll end up bursting into tears. Tears are emotion, and any emotion is weakness. My mother doesn't respect weakness. So, to keep the tears from falling, I just keep running.

My phone vibrates just as I make it back to the cottage. Part of me expects it to be my mom demanding that I come talk to her, but it's all quiet on that front. Instead, it's Serena.

Serena: I hope Flavia's carrot cake made it more bearable. I want to hear all of the gory details

Me: It helped, but there's not enough carrot cake in the world

Serena: I'm finally going to do it

Me: Do what?

Serena: My first spell

Serena: It's going to be a full moon tonight. I've gathered all the ingredients I need. Once it gets dark, I'm going to cast a circle, channel the moon, and go for it

I send her a celebratory gif.

Me: What kind of spell is it?

Serena: It's for luck. I still haven't found a new job, and rent is coming due

Me: Why don't you just cast a prosperity spell? Then you can take your time finding something

Serena: All the books say not to do that. Prosperity spells always backfire. But I've got an interview tomorrow, so I'm hoping the luck will help me get the job

Me: You'll do great, with or without the spell. Send me pics of the circle you cast!

Serena: I will! Wish me luck!

Me: Always <3

I think about calling Serena and telling her about what happened with my mom, but she sounds so happy that I don't want to kill her mood.

The front porch light comes on, and the moths immediately flock to it. A second later, Eva sticks her head out the door. "You coming in?" she asks. Then she takes one look at my face and says, "Uh-oh. Bad Conclave?"

"Bad everything," I answer, heading inside.

She's watching *Wednesday* on Netflix, and there's a half-eaten bowl of M&M's on the coffee table. "Apparently I'm not the only one who had a bad day."

"Guys are dicks," she answers.

"So are mothers." I flop face down on the blue velvet sofa that takes up most of our sitting area and bury my face in one of the bright-purple pillows.

"And English teachers."

She settles down at the end of the sofa, and a few seconds later, I hear her rattling the bowl of M&M's next to my ear. "Chocolate makes everything better."

"I'm not so sure it can fix this," I groan. But I reach out and take a few anyway. "What'd Amari do?"

She snorts. "Cheated on me with a mermaid."

"What an asshole!"

"It's not like it was true love or anything," she says with a shrug.

"But I did like the big jerk."

The leopard shifter does have a reputation for being a fuck boy, unfortunately. "How did you find out?"

"She was in the theater, bragging to her friends about their hookup and how I 'didn't have a clue.' She didn't know I was painting sets backstage." She picks through the candy bowl until she has a handful of green M&M's, then starts popping them in her mouth one by one. "For a minute, I really wished I had access to my magic."

"I can punch her for you," I offer. "I know it's not the same, but it could be satisfying."

Eva shrugs again. "She's not worth it. Though I did think about punching Amari when I confronted him and he tried blaming it on me."

"On you? Why?"

"Because I don't 'understand him.' And because he thinks with his dick, obviously." She reaches for the bowl of M&M's again and this time starts picking out all the orange ones. "Now tell me what happened to you?"

"Caspian got into U of S."

"What? I thought you couldn't—"

"Apparently that rule only applies to me. Caspian is free to do whatever he wants."

"Wow. That's not cool." She hands the bowl back to me. "So what'd your mom say?"

"Nothing. She wouldn't even look at me." I flop back down on the sofa.

Eva looks concerned. "Why not? You need to talk to her and—"

"Aguilar paired me up with Jude for a class project," I interrupt.

Her eyes go wide. "Holy shit." Then she stands up.

"Where are you going?"

"M&M's aren't going to cut it for this." She opens the pantry and coos, "Oh, hi, Squeaky! Good to see you're okay. We missed you yesterday."

I roll my eyes. "I can't believe you named the mouse."

"Hey, mice need love, too."

Seconds later, she's back with a bag of our favorite dill pickle chips.

"Where'd you get those?" I ask, making grabby hands.

"I have my ways. I was keeping them for an emergency, and this is definitely an emergency." She opens the bag of chips before handing it to me. "Now spill."

So I do, telling her everything that happened in class today. She stares at me in rapt silence until the end.

"I can't believe she wouldn't change your partner," she says when I'm finally finished. "Everyone knows not to pair you with Jude."

"I am so unbelievably screwed." I shove another chip in my mouth as a knock sounds at the door. "If it's my mom, tell her I'm dead," I snark as I toss the furry blanket over my head.

I need time to figure out what I'm going to say to her. Right now, I feel like I can't even be rational when it comes to all her lies.

"It's not," Eva says, going to answer it.

I raise my brows. "So you've got x-ray vision now?"

"No. But I did call in reinforcements." She throws the door open and reveals Luis standing there, carrying Korean face masks in one hand and a bottle of cyanide-green nail polish in the other.

"Green?" Eva asks, brows arched.

"You've heard of fuck-me red? This is fuck-you green, perfect for breakups." He hands it to her, then turns to me. "You look awful. Tell me everything."

"I can't do it again," I say, shoving a handful of chips in my mouth so I don't have to talk.

He turns to Eva. "What did Jude do?"

"How do you know it's Jude?" I squawk.

"Please." He waves a dismissive hand. "The last time you looked like this was when I first got to the island and that boy had just broken your heart. It took forever to mend you, so tell me what that jerk did this time so I can go kick his ass."

I put the chips away before I'm tempted to eat the entire bag. Then I say, sulkily, "He never actually broke my heart."

"Oh, please." He rolls his eyes. "You cried yourself to sleep every night for six months."

"Because I'd just lost my two best friends. Jude ditched me for no reason, and Carolina—" I break off because I don't want to think about her right now.

Luis sighs as he settles himself on the couch and pulls me in for a hug. "I didn't mean to bring her up. I'm just saying, you've got two new best friends who are totally willing to kick Jude Abernathy-Lee's ass if we need to. Right, Eva?"

"I mean, I'm willing to try," she agrees doubtfully. "But I don't know how well it's going to go. That boy is tough as hell."

"True." Luis contemplates for a second, then holds up the packets in his hands. "How about face masks, then? Looking good *is* the best revenge."

I laugh, exactly as he intended. Then I say, "Only if I get the watermelon one."

"Please, do you think you're dealing with an amateur here?" He snorts. "They're *all* watermelon."

"Okay, then." I hold out my hand for one. Because Luis is right. I do have two new best friends, which is a rare thing to find here. While neither of them will ever replace Carolina, they don't have to. Because they really are the best, just the way they are.

Even before Luis—in typical guy fashion—says, "I still think we can take Jude."

Eva considers it. "Maybe if we pepper spray him first?"

"You know what they say, baby." Luis makes a little clicking noise with the corner of his mouth. "First the face, then the mace."

"Literally nobody says that," I tell him when I finally stop laughing.

"Not where you're from," he says slyly.

I roll my eyes at him, lean back on the couch, rest my head on his shoulder, and kick my feet up just as the next episode of *Wednesday* comes on the TV.

Tomorrow's going to suck, but that's Tomorrow Clementine's problem. Because tonight, it's all about us, and that's more than enough.

CHAPTER EIGHT

RAIN, RAIN GHOST AWAY

"So what happens if you call in sick to chrickler duty?" Luis asks the next day at lunch as we make our way down to what is very definitely a dungeon. He insisted on accompanying me today because "yesterday was rough."

He isn't wrong.

"I have to say, after your mom's bad behavior, I think she should have to do it instead."

"No shit," I agree. I stopped by her office this morning to talk to her before my first class. I figured I'd be calmer before I had to take on the chricklers and Jude in the same afternoon—but she blew me off. Told me she'd try to make time for us to "chat" after school.

Also, that damn storm that was brewing yesterday is moving in fast—which means the chricklers should be in extra nasty moods today. I'm a little terrified that I'm going to be longing for yesterday's level of roughness before the next hour is over.

"I think you should let me go in with you," Luis suggests for the fourteenth time today as we continue down the hallway. "It's clear you need help."

"Yeah, but if my mother catches you helping me—" I start, but Luis cuts me off.

"It's not like I'm going to tell anyone," he says, making a face at me. "And it's not like your mother is going to be setting so much as a toe down here any time soon. No one has to know."

"Yeah, until one of the chricklers takes a chunk out of you."

He rolls his eyes. "Claudia seems good at keeping secrets."

"You really want to test that theory?" I shoot back as I pull out my phone to turn on the flashlight. Before I swipe it on, I fire off another text to Serena, asking how the spell and the interview went. I really hope she gets the job.

"I can't believe your uncle didn't replace the lightb—" Luis breaks off as I stop dead. "What's wrong?"

"Nothing." My stomach clenches a little, but I ignore it. Just like I ignore the fact that the closer we get to the end of this hallway, the more I notice a strange glow coming from the vestibule at the end.

"Your face doesn't look like it's nothing." He glances at me, concerned.

"It's probably just the storm. No big deal."

But then a low, rasping moan creeps its way around the corner and stops me in my tracks.

"What?" Luis demands, skidding to a halt beside me. "What did you see?"

"It's not what I saw. It's what I heard." The sound comes again, lower and more desperate this time, as unease slithers along my skin.

Luis, on the other hand, jumps straight past panic into full-blown terror. "I didn't hear anything. Did something actually get out?" He squints his eyes, surveying the hallway with his diminished but still excellent wolf vision.

"It's not the menagerie." I try to force my feet to start moving again, but they don't budge.

His eyes widen as he finally figures out why he isn't hearing—or seeing—what I am. "Oh, fuck."

I look down at the floor, focus on the cracks running through the cement, and force myself to get my shit together.

"Let's go," I tell him.

"Go?" Luis looks wild eyed. "Don't we need a plan? The last thing I want is for them to hurt you again."

"They won't." I blow out a breath. "And I have a plan."

"Oh yeah?" His brows go up.

"Get in front of me and run like hell. We'll take the long way to the chricklers and hope they don't follow us."

"That's it? That's the whole plan?" he demands.

I nod. "That's the whole plan."

"I should have made it clear I meant a *good* plan." Still, he starts backing up. "Okay, tell me when to run."

Another eerie wail makes every one of my pores prickle. The sounds are getting closer.

One more deep breath before I force myself to shout, "Now!"

We book it all the way back down the hallway, but I skid to a stop a few feet before we have to turn because the eerie light is leaking around that corner, too.

"Why are we stopping?" Luis demands. "Shouldn't we—"

"We need to get to the stairwell." I grab his arm and start tugging him backward.

"The stairwell? What about the chricklers?"

"They'll have to wait." But the second I turn around, I know it's too late.

"What do we do?" Luis yells.

"I don't know," I answer. Because everywhere I turn is suddenly filled with ghosts.

Hundreds and *hundreds* of ghosts.

CHAPTER NINE

TIME TO GET THE HALL OUT OF HERE

The ghosts hover just a few inches off the floor, and they all have three things in common. They're all translucent, they all have a strange, misty glow that radiates from inside them, and they all emit a musty smell that reminds me of old, dusty books.

Right now, the hallway smells like a dim, ancient library even though it's lit up like a fireworks show.

"Shit, there are a lot today," I mutter. I try to draw a mental map around them to the stairwell, but it's so crowded right now that I don't know how I'm supposed to get past them all unscathed.

Because of Calder Academy's long and not-so-illustrious past, a lengthy, spectral legacy has remained. One that is distinctly uncomfortable for me, since I've been able to see them my entire life.

I don't know *why* I can see them when no one else in my family can. And I definitely don't know why the same spell and equipment that inhibit my manticore magic, that keep me from being able to shift or create venom, don't also tamp down this weird ability. Maybe it's not a power at all. Maybe it's something extra the fates decided to curse me with, as if being born on this damn island wasn't curse enough.

Whatever it is, it's led me here, to staring at a sea of the dead.

I take a few tentative steps, then really wish I hadn't because hundreds of milky gray eyes turn toward me. Seconds later, they all start slowly floating in my direction—which, I decide, is an invitation to get the hell out of dodge.

I take off at a sprint, with Luis right behind me. I sidestep a couple of giant hoop skirts and a rolling head right off the bat and even manage to juke my way around a conductor waving his cane in the air as he leads a symphony none of us can hear.

Confidence fills me—maybe I'll actually make it to the end without getting stopped—but then, out of nowhere, something flickers directly in front of me. I have one moment to recognize it as a teenage girl—one with waist-length hair and a septum piercing—and then I'm running straight through her.

Pain slams into me, taking hold of my insides and shaking them until I feel like I'm about to explode. Like the very molecules that make up every part of me are spinning faster and faster, bouncing off each other before hurtling themselves at the inside of my skin. I clamp my teeth together to stop an instinctive whimper from escaping, but I stumble regardless. Luis makes a dive for me, but his hand glances off my shoulder, and I fall flat on my face. What the hell was that? It didn't feel like a ghost—or at least, not like any ghost I've ever touched before.

Luis reaches down and pulls me up, but I barely take more than a step or two before I come face-to-face with Finnegan, one of the ghosts I've known the longest.

"Clementine." His low rasp fills the hallway, along with the clank of his manacles as he lumbers toward me, dragging his left leg behind him through the mist. One of his eyes is hanging halfway down his cheek, attached through the eye socket by a thin, barely visible silver thread.

As he makes his way to me, I catch a streak of red out of the corner of my eye.

I turn my head, try to figure out what other student would be foolish enough to risk it down here if they didn't have to. But before I can figure it out, Finnegan reaches for me and snaps me back to my oh-so-painful reality.

"Clementine, please," he mumbles, his dislocated jaw popping and clicking as one translucent hand tries to touch my shoulder. I dodge it just in time and start running.

"I can't help you, Finnegan," I tell him, but as usual, he can't hear me.

I don't slow down, just keep racing toward the stairwell. Something else flickers to my right, and I jerk backward, whirling away so as not to get caught by whatever that is again.

It works, and I even manage to avoid a small group of ghosts dressed in shorts and bathing suits...only to plow through yet another flicker-like being that materializes directly in front of me.

The thing is huge—dressed in what looks, alarmingly, like a spacesuit—and trailing the same kind of shimmery material the teenage girl was. It appears totally different from the usual mist. But before I can even wonder why that is, I run headfirst into what feels like a million fragments of glass.

They slice through me, burrowing beneath my skin, cutting into my flesh, my bones, my heart. They shred every part of me and send the pieces crashing against each other until I can't breathe, can't think, can't stand.

I scream as I start to fall, and I throw my arms out in a futile effort to catch myself. It doesn't work, and I stumble several more steps before falling to my knees.

Behind me, Luis shouts, "Get up, Clementine!" as he grabs my arm and starts to pull.

The spirits are closing in on me from all directions now—the weird flickers *and* full-blown ghosts—and there's nothing I can do to stop them.

Luis positions himself in front of me, trying to protect me as best he can from the unprotectable. He even raises his fists like he's ready for a fight, though I have no idea what defense he thinks *that* will be against a bunch of ghosts he can't even see.

I scramble for purchase as I try to get upright. But then a spectral chest crashes into my shoulder from behind, and a thousand needles prick my skin. Another ghost grabs my arm, sending ice-cold razor blades slicing through me.

My stomach rolls and pitches at the agony.

I stagger away in a desperate attempt to escape the pain...only to run into another flicker.

And not just any flicker. This one is a small toddler wearing dragon pajamas and carrying an oversize looking glass.

"Hold me!" he wails, his little fingers clutching at my hip. The pain is so intense that it burns straight through my skin to the flesh—and bones—below.

Instinctively, I start to jerk away, but tears are pouring down his little face. He's no more than three or four, and flicker or not, pain or not, I can't just leave him like this.

And so I crouch down until our faces are level, ignoring Luis's startled, "Clementine! What are you doing?"

I know he can't hear me, can't feel me, but I reach out a finger to wipe a few of the boy's tears away anyway. The weird, fiery feeling spreads to my fingertips and my palms.

His only response is to throw his ghostly arms around me and sob harder as he presses his little face into my neck. I can't feel his weight in my arms, but agony swamps me at the contact anyway, pain flowing over me from all sides. But I don't let go—how can I when he's got no one else to hold him?

"What's wrong? Are you okay?" I say instinctively, even though I know an answer won't come.

But he shakes his head, sending new, deeper waves of pain through me, even as he whimpers, "I don't like snakes."

"Me either," I answer with a shudder. But then it dawns on me that he's not just talking to me—he's *answering* me.

Which means he can *hear* me, even though none of the other spirits have ever been able to.

I only have a second to wonder how that's possible before he asks, "Why not?" His teary eyes are wide, and his little hands burn my cheeks where he cups them.

"I was bit by one when I was your age, and I haven't gone near a snake since."

He nods like that makes sense before whispering, "Then you should run."

CHAPTER TEN

SPILLING ALL
THE TEE(TH)

I still can't believe he's replying to me. But then his words register, and a sick trepidation grows inside of me. "What does that mean? What—"

I break off as a sudden *bang* echoes down the hallway, followed by a loud, bone-chilling roar. One that doesn't sound nearly as muffled as it should.

"What the fuck is that?" Luis demands, his silver eyes wide and more than a little wild.

Before I can answer, a massive shadow lumbers into view that renders both me and Luis speechless. It's like nothing I've ever seen or heard of in my life. Its unnaturally large, wolf-like body has a serpentine head covered in fiery amber eyes. Hissing snakes, ready to strike, have replaced its upper extremities, and when it opens its mouth, its palate, gums, and tongue are covered in giant, knifelike teeth.

It gives a low, ominous growl, and I watch in horror as all of those teeth clatter to the floor, some of them hitting us, slicing us open, as they fall. And much to our horror, new ones immediately grow back in their place, turning its gaping maw into a brand new horror-show.

"Run, Clementine!" Luis screams as he scrambles backward. But I'm already moving, his terrified yelps adding to the frigid terror inside me as we race for the staircase at the end of the hall.

Fuck the chricklers. Screw the ghosts.

Because it seems like Uncle Carter didn't exactly do a great job securing that loose door. Because the monster behind us is nothing short of all my worst nightmares. And right now, it has all of its many, glowing eyes currently fixated on us.

We start to run, and I'm too terrified to look behind me, but the creepy clattering sound its teeth make as they hit the floor keeps getting closer. How many times a day can one creature lose its teeth anyway?

I push harder, run faster, but I'm still not fast enough. Something strikes my shoulder, and a weird, tingling numbness flows down my arm. I glance back just in time to see one of the dozen snakes that make up the monster's "arms" retracting—and another one coiling as it gets ready to strike at me again.

"What the fuck is that thing?" Luis yells over to me. "Besides something straight out of a horror movie?"

I'm running so hard that I don't even have enough breath to answer as I weave to the left, trying to get out of the strike zone. It doesn't work—the snakes are too damn long. Another one catches me on my lower back, its teeth sinking in fast and hard. I twist to the right to dislodge it and keep going.

The rattling sound that comes with every step it takes tells me that even though it managed to get free of its pen, it *is* still chained. But it seems like the chain is long enough to reach most, if not all, of the way down the hall. Because that seems like a really banner decision on Uncle Carter's part.

"Run faster!" I urge Luis, just as one of the snakes grabs him by the ankle and brings him down. Luis manages to kick himself free and keeps sprinting.

One of the snake hands comes flashing toward my head. I duck to avoid it. But then the creature releases all of its teeth again in a hailstorm of sharp blades. I try to shield myself, but it's futile. The teeth, acting as natural daggers, make quick work slicing at my skin.

Luis reaches over to pull me out of the danger zone.

I shoot him a grateful look even as I yell, "Keep going!"

The monster shrieks again, and suddenly it's going for my best friend instead of me, its long snake-fingers wrapping around Luis's forearm.

Luis whirls around and lets out a long, low snarl that might be the most terrifying sound I've ever heard him make. The monster must think so, too, because it rears back for a moment before responding in kind.

But a moment is all Luis needs to free himself. We take off one last time, aiming for the staircase. We even make it to the second step before the beast grabs onto me again. It wraps the snakes around my waist and starts pulling me backward.

A scream sticks in my throat as I desperately try to pull myself from its grasp. But it's got a hold of me now, and it's not letting go.

Luis positions himself on the next step and tries grabbing the snakes from around my waist, two at a time. But every time he pries two off, two more take their place in a Sisyphean nightmare.

"Just go!" I tell Luis as the creature bares its teeth again. "Get out of here."

"Hell no." Luis looks beyond insulted at my words.

But now I'm too busy trying to squirm away to care. Desperate, terrified, with my heart slamming against my ribs, I do the only thing I can think of. I lift my left leg and kick backward as hard as I can.

I may not have my powers, but I'm manticore strong, and when my heel connects with its knee, it does so with a sickening crunch. The monster bellows in rage, swaying violently, and the snakes hiss miserably as they unwind themselves from around my arms, their fangs catching me in several places and raking through my skin.

"Move!" Luis yells.

I surge forward, racing for the steps like my life depends on it— because it probably does.

Behind us, the creature has recovered, too. It extends all four twisted, slithering hands toward us just as it reaches the end of its tether.

It lets out a sound that is half hiss, half roar, and *all* terrifying, but I don't look back as Luis and I pound up the stairs. We get to the top, all but collapsing into the hallway as the doors close behind us.

Before either of us can so much as catch our breaths, Roman, a hall troll, pops up, demerit book in hand. "Clementine, you know you're not supposed to run on the stairs. This is your second offense this week. I'm going to have to write the two of you up."

"Are you serious?" Luis snarls indignantly.

The troll just tsk-tsks. He rips off our demerit slips and hands them to us.

"Have a nice rest of your day," he tells us. "Oh, and get that bleeding under control, will you? You know it's against the student safety code, and I'd really hate to have to write you up again today."

As he turns and stomps his way back up the hallway, a loud burst of thunder shakes the whole building. Roman lets out a loud squeal as he jumps about three feet in the air and drops his clipboard.

"If all it takes is a little thunder to freak him out," Luis snarks, "I'd hate to see what he'd do if that thing made it up the stairs."

"Drop more than his clipboard, probably."

Luis turns to look at me blankly. And then we both crack up, because it's either that or cry. And there's no way in hell I'm facing Jude with red, puffy eyes.

CHAPTER ELEVEN

HOW TO SPELL DISASTER

O nce Luis and I pull ourselves together—which takes a few
minutes—I text Uncle Christopher. This time, I tell him that if I
die, he'll have my mother to answer to, so fix the goddamn lock.

It's amazing how a near-death experience helps you stand your
ground.

"I'm going to go try and get cleaned up before class," Luis tells me.
"I've already texted Eva and let her know we're done early."

"You're the best, Luis." We both know I'm talking about more
than the text.

But he just rolls his eyes before heading down the hall. "Can we at
least *try* for an uneventful afternoon?"

"No promises!" I call back with the last ounce of snark I have
inside me.

"No shit!" Luis *must* be tired, because he doesn't even bother to
flip me off.

When I get to the bathroom, I have to spend a few minutes calming
Eva down when she catches sight of me before I can clean myself up. A
few dabs of her concealer help my face look presentable—as long as no
one looks too closely—and a bun does the same for my hair. As for the
rest of me, a new uniform shirt isn't going to cover half the damage, so
instead I slip on a hoodie again despite the steaming-hot weather and

hope my many injuries don't bleed through their bandages.

"You're sure you're okay?" Eva asks for like the thousandth time as the bathroom door slams shut behind us.

"I'm good," I assure her. Which is a stretch, but that has more to do with the fact that I'm about to sit down with Jude than it does with the fact I just faced some freakish monster.

Eva looks doubtful, but she gives me a little hug and whispers, "Give him hell," before heading to her anger management class.

I've got about ten minutes before class starts, so I text Serena again to see how her interview went. Surely, she's done by now. I also make a mental note to call her tonight so I can hear the whole story. If things are good, we can celebrate, and if they aren't, I can listen to her cry.

But she still hasn't answered by the time I get to Brit Lit, so I shove my phone in my pocket and take a few deep breaths to calm the overactive butterflies that have suddenly taken up residence in my stomach.

A couple of vamps walk by as I do, eyeing me like they're contemplating what I taste like. I'm sure they can smell my bleeding wounds, but I have absolutely no energy for dealing with their shit today, so I keep my gaze on the ground as I start into my class.

But before I can walk inside, someone calls my name.

I turn to see Caspian coming up behind me, a concerned look on his face.

His dark-brown hair is tucked into a black baseball cap with Calder Academy spelled out in the same bright red as his polo shirt, shoes, and backpack. Basically, he looks like a walking billboard for this damn school. Which—now that I think about it—is exactly what he is.

Then again, if I knew I was getting out of here in nine months, I might like the place more myself.

"Oh, God!" He runs a hand over the back of his neck as he looks me up and down. "You already heard."

"Heard what?" I ask as I start to brush past him. I'm not in the mood for Caspian's over-the-top drama today. Plus, I'm still pretty bitter over the college announcement, even if it's not his fault.

But he blocks the door, and the second my eyes meet his, I realize something is actually very wrong. His eyes are wide and dark with concern, even before he throws his arms around my shoulders and says, "I'm so sorry."

Instinctively, I go onto tiptoes to wrap him in a hug. "Sorry about what?" I ask, completely confused. He looks—and sounds—like he's about to cry.

"What happened?" I demand even as a dark, restless feeling invades my chest. "Tell me."

It's not a request, and the look on my cousin's face says he knows that. But he still presses his lips together in a show of reluctance that is totally unlike him. Usually, Caspian loves nothing more than to prove he's more in the know than everyone around him.

Which is why his hesitance has a chill running down my spine—one that directly belies the fact that the humidity from the incoming storm has completely overwhelmed the building's ancient air conditioning.

He sighs, then—in an even more alarming gesture—takes my hand in his. "There's no good way to tell you. It's about Serena."

"Serena? What's wrong with Serena?"

Terror strikes like the lightning outside at the sound of my friend's name, eviscerating my insides and sending shocks through every part of my body as I wait for him to say what I so desperately don't want to hear.

Not Serena. Not Serena. Not Serena.

Please, not Serena with her laughing brown eyes and too-big smile and even bigger heart.

But all I can think about is being stuck on "Read" since last night.

Please, please, please, not Serena.

My cousin shakes his head sadly. "We just got the news this morning. She died last night. She was conjuring a spell and lost control. By the time the authorities could get to her, she was…"

My knees go liquid at his words, and for one, terrifying second, I'm afraid I'm going to hit the cracked tile floor. But then I manage to lock them in place.

No weakness, I remind myself.

I curl my hands into fists, dig my fingernails into my palms, and let the tiny pricks of pain keep me from spinning completely out of control as Caspian's voice trails off before he even finishes the story.

But then, he doesn't need to finish it. I already know what happened. The same thing that happens to so many Calder Academy graduates when their magic comes flooding back, unchecked, and more powerful than ever for being suppressed for so long.

The same thing I've been fearing since she graduated and went off on her own—determined to learn everything about her magic and make up for the four years she lost on the island. But a good luck spell? It doesn't get much more ironic—much more cruel—than that.

The thought has tears clogging up my throat, but I shove down the urge to cry. Then I lock my shoulders and my jaw as tightly and emotionlessly as I can.

Caspian searches my face for several seconds.

I try to tell myself it's because he's concerned, not because he's looking for a reaction to report back to my mother, like the good soldier that he is. We've always been close because we're cousins—because we're *Calders*—but loyalty? I don't really know how far that goes. I do know that I don't have any desire to test it right now. Especially not when everything inside of me feels like a crystal vase that's already hit the ground.

"It was bound to happen eventually. It almost always does," I say. "Anyway, we should really get to class."

"That's kind of an exaggeration, isn't—" Caspian starts, but he breaks off abruptly because even he can't stomach the lie right now. Or is it just because he can't speak the truth?

It's what we do here at Calder Academy—what we *have* to do. Squirrel everything soft and hopeful and vulnerable away deep inside, where no one can see it—not even us.

It usually even works...until it doesn't.

CHAPTER TWELVE

KISS MY FANNY

'm still working on swallowing down a tidal wave of grief as I walk into the classroom...only to find Jude *sitting at my usual desk*.

Grief turns to rage in an instant. Because fuck this. And fuck him. Fuck all of them.

I square my shoulders and march over to him. He's the one who stopped talking to me, and after I got over that trauma, I swore that if we ever spoke again, he'd have to be the one to break the silence.

I've kept that vow, and there's no way I'm going to break it now... over a desk.

I slide into the desk beside him and keep my head down, but I can feel the weight of his eyes on me the whole time. Who cares? Let him look.

The angry part of me wants to stare back. But my grief over Serena is too fresh for me to be playing power games with Jude, no matter how much he deserves it.

I also notice Jean-Luc staring at me from across the room. He's wearing the same shit-eating grin he had on when I caught him burning ants under a magnifying glass freshman year. My stomach clenches, because I've dealt with him long enough to know that it's never good if he thinks you're one of those ants. Too bad I don't have enough fight left in me today to disabuse him of the notion.

Whatever's up with him, Jude seems to notice it, too. He keeps glancing warily between Jean-Luc and me.

Ms. Aguilar flits to the front of the room, yellow hair bouncing and skin glittering with pixie dust. "'I find I cannot exist without poetry.'"

She clutches her hands to her chest, whirling around and coming to a stop right in front of my new desk before continuing, "'I will imagine you Venus tonight and pray, pray, pray to your star like a Heathen!'"

She gives another spin...only to get a fist full of Hot Tamales flung at her face.

They bounce off with an audible thump, causing the Jean-Jerks to snicker. "Hey, teach!" Jean-Luc starts, but before he can get very far, Izzy slides into the desk next to mine.

She toys with the ends of her long, red hair as she leans over to me and says—loud enough for the entire class to hear—"So what's the penalty in this place for slicing off the fingers of fellow students?"

Her gaze slides over to the Jean-Jerks as she says it.

"Pretty sure that'd count toward your community service hours," I tell her as my anger over Serena—my anger over all of this—continues to build inside me.

"That's exactly what *I* was thinking." Her fangs flash in what I'm pretty sure is her version of a smile.

"You really think you can take us?" Jean-Luc snarls. Seconds later, a handful of Hot Tamales hits Izzy in the face, too. "Come at us."

She fades across the room and back so fast that barely a second goes by. But as she settles back into her desk, Jean-Luc lets out a screech. Both his hands are now spread on his desk, and there are daggers jammed into the desk between each of his fingers and another two longer knives bent and wrapped around his wrists like cuffs, pinning him to the desk.

"What the fuck?" he snarls as he tries to lift his hands and fails.

Izzy shrugs as she crosses her arms over her chest. "Next time, I won't be so careful."

"You'll pay for this, vamp!" Jean-Jacques threatens. "Do you know who our fathers are?"

Izzy yawns. "Here's a tip. No one ever sounds threatening when they feel the need to bring their daddy into the conversation. If you want to be taken seriously, what you should ask is, *Do you know who I am?*"

The answer to that is clearly someone not to be fucked with. Which is why everyone in the class is currently busy looking anywhere *but* at Izzy. Well, everyone but Jude, who gives her a little chin nod of respect. Izzy turns back to Ms. Aguilar and says, "Go on."

Ms. Aguilar doesn't answer for a few seconds, just stares at Izzy with her mouth agape. I can see her mind working behind her big blue eyes, trying to decide if she needs to report Izzy for bringing contraband knives into the classroom and then using them against another student.

She's either too scared or too impressed to do it, though, because in the end, she doesn't say anything at all. Instead, she just clears her throat and says, "So, with no further ado, here are your Keats poetry assignments."

She grabs the ends of the pink cloth that's covering the front board and yanks it off to reveal our groups written out in exaggerated script, a poem listed next to each one. "There are questions in the back of the packet. This portion of the assignment must be finished today or you'll fall behind, since we have more to do next class." She claps her hands. "So get to work! And have fun!"

Fun, my ass. To stall, I stare at the list of questions—but all I can think about is Serena.

Still, once I get my brain to actually process them, they're fairly straightforward, and a person can only read questions about rhyme schemes and meter so many times before they end up looking ridiculous. Though not as ridiculous as the Jean-Jerks, who are currently grunting and sweating as they work to free Jean-Luc from Izzy's little knife trick.

Apparently fae don't have the same upper body strength as vampires. What a pity.

I flip to our poem—"To Fanny"—and then, with no further excuses as to why I can't look at Jude, I turn around. And end up staring straight at his very broad, very muscly chest.

Not that it matters, because it absolutely, positively, does not. None of it does.

Not his carved-out jaw.

Not his perfectly chiseled cheekbones.

And definitely not the ridiculously long eyelashes that frame the most interesting and arresting eyes I've ever seen.

Nope, none of it matters *at all*. Because what does matter is that he's a total jackass who used to be my best friend until he kissed me out of the blue—which I refuse to think about anymore—and then unceremoniously cut me out of his life with no explanation. That's what I need to focus on right now and not how good he looks...or smells.

Seconds roll into minutes, and my stomach churns as I wait for Jude to say something. Anything.

Not that there's anything he *can* say to justify what he did, but I am curious about how he'll start. An apology? An explanation? Just because there's no explanation good enough doesn't mean I don't want to hear one.

Several more seconds pass before Jude clears his throat, and I brace myself for anything. Anything, that is, except, "Keats was in love with Fanny for most of his adult life."

"Excuse me?" I try to bite the exclamation back, but I'm so shocked it practically falls out of my mouth. Jude hasn't spoken to me in three years, and that's what he leads with?

"The poem, Clementine," he prompts after a second, and his use of my real name feels like a low blow.

He doesn't seem to recognize the gut punch, as he continues, "It's called 'To Fanny.' He fell in love with her soon after they met when he was twenty-two." Jude holds up his phone—open to a literature site—like it's his knowledge of John Keats I'm questioning and not the giant elephant in the room.

But fine. Just...fine. Two can play at this game. He's not the only one who can google, so I take a moment to do just that before holding up my own phone to him. "And she was seventeen, which is a little gross if you ask me."

I know it was a different time, one where people routinely died at twenty-five, like Keats. But if arguing about a dead Romantic's problematic love life keeps us from actually discussing the disgustingly sappy love poem, I'm all for it.

Except Jude doesn't seem to be in the mood to argue. "Agreed," he answers, raking a casual hand through his chin-length black hair.

I try really hard not to notice the way it falls perfectly to one side, like it has a mind of its own—one that's determined to make him look as good as paranormally possible. I also ignore the way the razor-cut tips of it brush against his chin, accenting the ridiculously perfect light-brown skin that he inherited from his Korean dad.

Then again, most oneiroi are gorgeous, I remind myself. Jude's not special. It's just that being a dream daimon makes him a member of the most beautiful paranormal species in existence. Which is totally not fair.

Despite being a manticore, I feel downright boring in comparison—everyone is when they're sitting next to him. Even Izzy looks a little blah, and she's the most striking vampire I've ever seen.

But it doesn't matter what he looks like. Because Jude may look like a dream on the outside, but he's an absolute nightmare on the inside. I didn't know that when we became friends all those years ago, but I know it now, and there's no way I'm forgetting it.

"John Keats was complicated," he continues in that deep, musical voice that I don't think I'll ever get used to. When we were friends, his voice hadn't yet become this dark, rhythmic thing that fills the air around me.

An unwitting shiver slides down my spine, but I ignore it. It must be the air-conditioning vent I'm sitting under.

"And by complicated, you mean an asshole, right?" I snark, gesturing to the poem in front of me. "What gave it away? The fact that he abandoned the self-proclaimed love of his life to die alone and penniless in Italy?"

"You think that makes him an asshole?" He looks outraged. "Even though he had to leave?"

"He didn't have to do anything but die," I snap. "It's awful that he left her when they needed each other most. Nearly as awful as her just letting him leave without a fight."

He lifts one dark brow, taps his pen against the edge of the desk. "You wouldn't have?"

"If I loved him the way she says she did in this letter?" It's my turn to wave my phone. "I would never have let him run off to basically die alone. And if he loved her, he wouldn't have just walked away and left her wondering."

"Maybe he thought distancing himself would keep her safe." His pen is tapping faster now.

"From what? Tuberculosis? He didn't seem to mind infecting everyone else. It says here Fanny wrote letters to him almost daily. But he didn't even open them because he couldn't 'bear to read them.' So he never wrote back. He didn't leave to keep her safe. He left for his own vanity. That's fucking selfish."

"You don't know that. She could have moved on, forgotten all about him—"

"Yeah, because all of those letters she wrote scream, 'I've moved on.'" I roll my eyes.

"He was probably trying to help her move on—"

"By leaving her wondering if he ever thought about her the way she thought about him?" My voice is getting louder now, indignation tearing through me as I throw up my hands. "That's bullshit and you know it."

"What's bullshit is expecting him to stick around and ruin her life," he shoots back, sounding almost as annoyed as I feel. "Especially when he knew things could only end one way."

And just like that, I've had enough. Of Jude. Of this poem. Of this school that sends its graduates out to die like lambs to the paranormal slaughter. "Are we really going to do this?"

The words practically explode out of me, so loud that Ms. Aguilar lets out a little squeak from the front of the room.

I ignore her, and so does Jude.

To his very small credit, he doesn't try to pretend my question is about the assignment. But he doesn't answer, either. He just watches me out of eyes that seem much older than his years, eyes that have always seen way more than I want to show.

But this time, I stare back. I've spent too many months— too many years—looking away, trying to hide the maelstrom of emotions inside of me. But Serena's death, my mom's betrayal, and Jude's latest bullshit have collided to make me feel as volatile as the storm that's building outside. Screw keeping a low profile. I'm done pretending.

"Is everything okay over here?" Ms. Aguilar asks nervously, and I glance up only to realize that Jude and I have been staring at each other long enough for her to cross the whole room.

"Everything's okay," Jude tells her, but his intense gaze never leaves mine.

I don't even try to disguise the harsh laugh that comes from my throat. Because nothing is okay. Not with Jude. Not with Serena. Not with anyone or anything in this whole messed-up school.

"Are you—" She breaks off as the classroom door opens. She pivots, clearly grateful for the distraction.

"How can I help you, young man?"

"My schedule changed, and I just got transferred to this class," answers a voice with a slow, thick New Orleans accent that has my blood freezing in my veins.

No. Just no.

Because there is only one person in the whole of Calder Academy who has that accent—and I've done my best to stay as far away from it, and him, as I can since he showed up here a few weeks ago.

But apparently the universe has other plans for me today. First Serena, then Jude, and now this?

Ms. Aguilar walks to the front of the classroom and takes the slip of paper from the office that he holds out to her. "Remy Villanova Boudreax. Welcome to Brit Lit. We're currently working on analyzing one of the greatest poets of all time."

Her eyes scan the classroom, quickly darting past the Jean-Jerks before coming to rest on Jude and me. "Why don't you go join Clementine and Jude's group? I'm sure they'd love the...help."

CHAPTER THIRTEEN

DOESN'T METER TO ME

Ms. Aguilar's words knock the breath out of me, leave me gasping for air as tears bloom in my eyes. I curse the fact that I put my hair up, ensuring that I can't hide behind it even though I really, really want to right now.

Instead, I pull my hood over my head, and duck deep inside it in a desperate effort to mask my tears—and the momentary weakness they signify. But I wasn't prepared for this today, had told myself that I'd just be able to avoid Remy for the rest of the year. Just because he's a senior, doesn't mean he has to be in *my* Brit Lit class. Not when I've been so careful to turn around and go the other way every time I so much as see him in the halls.

But I can't do that now. I'm stuck here as he walks straight toward me.

"Hey. You okay?" Jude's voice, low and surprisingly gentle, comes from what feels like a million miles away. "I can tell her to put him in another group."

He shouldn't know about Remy, shouldn't know about everything that happened. He gave up that privilege a long time ago. But he does know, and all I can think is that Caspian told him everything. The jerk.

I know they were friends, too. I know that they still talk in the hall sometimes. But everything inside me is screaming that Caspian had no right to talk to Jude about this. About *her.*

I don't want to answer him, but Jude continues to watch me with concern until I finally shake my head—though I don't even know what question I'm answering at this point. Maybe both at the same time, because no, I am definitely *not* okay. But last I checked Ms. Aguilar isn't really interested in how I feel about my group members. Just one more "perk" of being the headmaster's daughter that I am very much hating right now.

"I'm fine," I snap at him seconds before Remy comes to a stop next to our desks.

Remy, my cousin Carolina's closest friend in prison—not to mention the boy she wrote to me about after she finally broke out of the Aethereum. The boy she loved.

Remy, the same guy who came to the island three months ago to tell us she was dead—and that she'd sacrificed herself to *save him,* that her death wa*s his fault.* My aunt Claudia—Carolina's mother—told him not to blame himself, that we all know there was no stopping her when she set her mind to something.

And while I might agree with that in theory, I still never want to see him again. And I definitely never want to talk to him.

Because something broke in me the night I found out about Carolina's death, and no matter how hard I try, I haven't been able to put the jagged pieces of my heart—my soul—back together again. She was my best friend in the entire world. My ride or die, even before she got shipped off to the Aethereum with no warning and no real explanation. Three years later and I still don't know why.

Part of the reason I've been so hell-bent to get off this island the last few years was because I was determined to go find and rescue her from that hideous prison.

And now I'm supposed to do a poetry project with the boy she loved? The boy who just let her die?

A shudder tries to work its way through me, but I tamp it down as ruthlessly as I tamped down the tears.

Weakness isn't an option—showing it or having it.

And still rage burns inside me, even before Remy's slow amble across the room finally ends—exactly two feet from my desk. All I know is that there's no way I'm actually going to last my entire senior year in this place. It's just taken too much from me.

I need a fresh start.

"Do you mind if I sit here?" Remy asks quietly, nodding toward the empty desk across from Jude. His dark, shaggy hair bounces a little with the nod, the intense look in his forest-green eyes belying the casualness of the question.

I glance at Jude, but his face is blank—a surefire sign that there's more going on under the surface than he wants anyone to know. And I get it. I don't want to admit it, but I know that losing Carolina hurt him, too. That what he did to me—to us—didn't erase all those years of hide-and-seek in the forest, of scraped knees and truth-or-dare and endless troublemaking. Being in a group with Remy must be a gut punch to him, too.

Knowing that doesn't make it any easier for me to bear, though. But before I can think of an appropriate answer to Remy's question, a massive lightning bolt shoots through the sky. It's followed immediately by a boom of thunder so loud it shakes the entire building, and seconds later, one of the two fluorescent lightbulbs in the room explodes.

Glass goes everywhere, including all over the floor in front of Ms. Aguilar's desk.

She jumps—God, she really is a candyass—then trills, "No one move until I can get this cleaned up. Just focus on your projects and don't worry about me."

Like anybody is? In the grand scheme of bad shit that happens at this school, exploding lightbulbs don't even make the chart.

She crosses to the closet at the back of the room and pulls out a small hand broom and dustpan. I ignore her in favor of looking down at my desk, unable to bring myself to speak to Remy. Jude doesn't say anything, either. He just watches me with those all-seeing eyes.

When it becomes obvious that Hell will freeze over before Jude invites Remy to join us—and that the rest of the class is suddenly much more interested in what's going on in our little corner of the room than they are in Ms. Aguilar—I shrug and nod toward the empty desk. It's not exactly the friendliest invitation, but it's more than I thought I had in me.

"Thank you, Clementine," Remy tells me, his tone formal and a sad smile on his handsome face.

Despite the niceties, my stomach does a three-sixty. We've only met once, briefly, yet he knows exactly who I am. Then a sickening realization dawns on me—he probably knows way more about me than I want to imagine. He and Carolina were super close. Does that mean she told him my secrets, too? The ones we only dared to share in the dark?

All of a sudden, I can't help but feel violated. But it's way too late to do anything about it.

Just because I let Remy join our already messed-up group doesn't mean I have to talk to him or have anything to do with him. Jude may not care about making a scene—no one is stupid enough to mess with him—but I don't have that luxury.

So I give up arguing with Jude about John Keats's relationship with Fanny Brawne and concentrate on getting the questions about figurative language and meter answered. The sooner we finish the assignment, the sooner I can get out of this hellscape.

Remy tries to help at first, but after I deliberately ignore him a few times, he gives up.

On the plus side, Jude isn't uncooperative for once.

Maybe it's because he's too busy watching Remy with narrowed, suspicious eyes. Or maybe it's because he senses how close I am to the edge. For the first seven years he was on the island, we were inseparable, and he knows me better than anyone ever has—except for Carolina—and there's definitely no "enemy of my enemy is my friend" stuff going on here.

After what feels like an eternity of avoiding both Jude's and Remy's eyes in the tensest atmosphere imaginable, the bell sounds.

"Today, I am going to be my best, most positive self."

"And that's it for today, students!" Ms. Aguilar cheerfully exclaims from her own desk in the corner of the classroom, shaking her head. "I hope you felt your spirits come alive reading and dissecting these luscious poems!"

No one answers her as we all spring up like jack-in-the-boxes and start shoving our stuff into our backpacks.

"I'll hold on to this," Jude says, reaching for the notes still sitting on my desk.

I nod my thanks but don't trust myself to say anything around the giant lump in my throat as grief presses down on me. Instead, I slide the zipper closed on my backpack and all but run for the door.

I push my way into the now-crowded hall, desperate to put as much distance between Jude, Remy, and myself as I possibly can. My brain's on overload, and the rest of me feels like it's going to shake apart any second now.

I weave around a pissed-off warlock with an attitude problem before slipping between two dragon shifters who look more than a little high. I have one second to wonder what they've been sniffing and how they got the contraband before someone calls my name from behind me.

I turn instinctively, only to find Remy jogging down the hallway toward me, an intent look in his eyes that says he's done letting me ignore him. He's tall—even taller than Jude—and between his height and the beeline he's making for me, we've definitely begun to attract attention.

This isn't where or when I would have chosen to have a showdown with Remy, but if that's what he wants, so be it.

My knees are wobbling because I'm hungry—the granola bar I grabbed for breakfast was a long time ago—not because I'm the least bit nervous.

Except Remy apparently doesn't want a showdown after all. Because he stops in front of me with that sad smile of his and murmurs, "I'm sorry about that."

"Sorry about what?" I ask, much more belligerently than his approach warrants.

He shakes his head, gives me a look that says he knows I'm lying. "I can do the rest of the project on my own." His languid New Orleans accent softens the words—and his approach.

"Do whatever you want," I answer with a shrug. "It doesn't matter to me."

It does matter, so much, but now isn't the time—and this definitely isn't the place—to have that discussion.

Remy looks like he wants to call my bluff, but instead he just shakes his head. "You're going to be okay, Clementine."

I give him a cool look. "You can't possibly know that." For the first time since he walked into English class, his eyes twinkle.

"I know a lot of things people don't think I can know."

"Except when you don't," I shoot back. And though I don't mention her name, suddenly Carolina is there between us, clear as day.

The light goes out of his eyes, and his handsome face turns dark. I brace for him to lash out at me—it's no less than I deserve considering what I just said to him—but it only takes a moment for me to realize the darkness isn't directed at me at all. It's directed inward, a tornado of grief and rage that's wrecking him from the inside out.

Apparently, I won't need to beat him up for Carolina's death. It looks like he's doing a good enough job of that all on his own. Even if it's only visible if you look closely.

Maybe it should bother me that his suffering makes me feel better, but it doesn't. Carolina deserves his pain. And mine. And so much more.

Still, the fact that he's suffering, too—that he's not just glossing over her death like my family has—makes me like him more than I expected to. It also makes me feel bad for him, because I know just how much it hurts to lose her.

Perhaps that's why I extend the tiniest of olive branches—or maybe it's because he's the only person I can share her with. The only person who might actually want to hear what I have to say. Most days even Aunt Claudia acts like she just wants to forget.

Either way, I whisper, "She made really good cookies."

He grins cautiously, and the darkness slowly fades a little from his gaze. "She told really great stories."

"Yeah." The fist around my heart eases just a little, and somehow, I find myself smiling, too. "She really did."

The warning affirmation sounds—this little exchange has eaten up our passing period—and I glance toward the group therapy room. Last class of the day.

But before I can head that way, my gaze snags on Jude, who is walking down the hall with his friend, Ember. She's a lot shorter than he is, so he's leaning down a little to hear her in the noisy halls as he nods along with whatever she's saying.

But his eyes aren't on her—they're on me and Remy. And he doesn't look happy.

Not that he has the right to look any way about me or what I'm doing—we aren't friends, no matter how he acted toward the end of English class today. I start to look away as the lights flicker yet again—this storm is really doing a number on our power grid—but then Ember screams.

The sound—loud, high-pitched, nerve-shattering—rips through the hallways as she bursts into flames.

CHAPTER FOURTEEN

WHERE THERE'S SMOKE THERE'S A PHOENIX

It starts with her tight, red-tipped curls, so for a second, I think I'm imagining it. But within seconds, her whole head is engulfed in flames, followed by her shoulders, her arms, her entire torso, her legs.

"What the fuck?" Luis exclaims as he comes rushing up to me, eyes wide and freaked out as Jude jumps into action.

Not that I blame him. Ember burning is absolutely the most terrifying thing I've ever seen, bar none. And that's not even counting her pain-filled screams, which have my throat closing up in horror.

Judging by the way other students start yelling and scrambling out of the way, I'm not the only one who feels like that. Not Jude, though. Instead of fleeing, he rips the huge water canteen from his backpack and dumps the whole thing over Ember's head.

It doesn't make a dent as she continues to scream. And as every part of her continues to burn—her long curly hair, her dark-brown skin, even her deep black eyes. The flames are everywhere.

Desperate to help her, Jude rips off his red Calder Academy hoodie and starts slapping at the flames, trying to smother them as Ember turns into a column of fire and the sickening scent of singed hair and clothing fills the hallway.

"What do we do?" Remy demands, scooting toward her even as the wave of retreating students continues to push its way toward us.

"I don't know," I answer, trying to avoid getting trampled as I move with him. "She's a phoenix."

But she shouldn't be burning. We've had dozens of phoenixes come through here, and *none* of them have ever caught fire. Like theirs, her magic should be tamped down by the school's power-dampening shields, her ability to flame out completely gone.

And yet here she is, burning and burning and burning, and there doesn't seem to be anything that can stop it. Not the water Jude dumped on her. Not his sweatshirt, which has long since gone up in flames. And not the hands he's now using to continue to swat, fruitlessly, at the flames.

"It's okay, Jude!" My uncle Carter runs out of his classroom, his blond hair flopping with each step as he grabs onto Jude and uses every ounce of his manticore strength to try to pull him away. When that doesn't budge Jude even an inch, he tries to slide between them instead. "She's a phoenix! She's supposed to burn like this."

But Jude doesn't look convinced—probably because Ember is still screaming—and he continues to try to put out the flames, his hands blistering a little more with every second they're in contact with her fiery body.

That's what finally shakes me out of my terror, the knowledge that he won't stop trying to help her anytime soon. He's getting burned, badly, and I'm terrified that if the damage gets much worse, even the healers won't be able to help him.

Ms. Aguilar's offhand comment from yesterday's class plays through my mind as I race three doors down to the chem lab and grab the fire extinguisher off the wall. Then I run back to Jude and Ember and spray them both with the potassium carbonate inside it.

The flames on Jude's shirt and hands go out instantly, but Ember continues to burn. When he tries to dive back in, I wrap my hand around his upper arm and hold him as tightly as I can.

"Jude, it's okay!" I tell him as I try to pull him away. "Ember's going to be okay."

It's like he doesn't even hear me, like he's so focused on trying to save her that he doesn't realize what I'm saying—or what's really going on here. "I can't let her die, too," he whispers. "I just can't."

I don't know what that means, but now isn't exactly the time to ask.

Thankfully, Uncle Carter has backed off, so I take the opportunity to put myself between them. "Look at her, Jude," I whisper, ignoring the blaze of heat on my back. "Look inside the flames. Really look at Ember. She's burning, but she's not actually getting burned. She's okay."

It takes a few more seconds, but my words finally get through. He drops his hands and pulls back just a little.

Now that I'm past my initial terror that he's going to burn up right alongside her, I move back and watch Ember burn, too. Engulfed in flames so hot they're white and blue, she is absolutely mesmerizing. And now that she's finally stopped screaming and the pain seems to be over, the knot in my throat relaxes.

For the first time in my life, I understand the relationship between fire and rebirth.

After what may be the longest ninety seconds of my life, Ember's fire finally goes out as quickly and efficiently as it started. One second, she's on fire, and then the next, she isn't.

She is, however, shivering, naked, and more than a little out of it, if her vacant stare is any reflection of her state of mind. Her fire burned so hot it turned everything to ash but her actual hair and body. Even her piercings melted away in the flames, turning into hot piles of gold and silver on the hallway floor beside her.

As she drops to the ground, my uncle Carter turns away immediately, calling for a blanket even as he moves to block her from view with his body. She's kneeling, and her arms are wrapped around herself, covering almost everything, but she's still so out of it that leaving her like this for even a moment feels wrong.

Following my uncle's lead, I move closer to Ember, too, blocking as much of her from view as I can.

But Jude isn't waiting for a blanket. Instead, he rips off his partially burned shirt and pulls it over her head. It's got several coin-size holes in it, but the size difference between them is so huge that it dwarfs her, covering everything important and then some.

Then he leans down like he's going to help her up, but I can see the singed skin on his hands and know he must be in absolute agony.

So I beat him to it, bending down and wrapping an arm around Ember's shoulders as I ease her to her feet. "You're okay," I whisper softly in her ear. "You're just fine."

Her eyes meet mine, and for a moment, I can still see the flames burning deep inside of them. But then she blinks, and the fire and the fogginess are gone.

Eva comes forward, carrying the blanket Uncle Carter called for. Her normally rosy-brown complexion has turned ashen, and she looks as shaken as I feel.

"Are you okay?" she murmurs to me as she waits for my uncle to take the blanket from her.

I nod as Ember shakes her head and whispers, "You should check on Jude," in a voice gone gravelly from screaming.

"I'm fine," he tells her, but he's swaying a little on his feet, and nothing about him looks fine—especially not his hands, which are red and blistered in some places and look charred in others.

"You're not fine," Uncle Carter says, scanning the crowd until his gaze meets mine. "Clementine, take him to the healer, please."

Then he wraps the blanket around Jude's shoulders.

His words have Eva's brown eyes going wide and darting between us. I know she's waiting for me to argue, but after everything that's happened today, I've got no fight left in me. Besides, just because I'm taking Jude to Aunt Claudia's office doesn't mean I have to stick around and hold his hand—figuratively speaking.

"It's okay," I tell her, because what else am I supposed to say?

My roommate looks like she wants to argue, but before she can figure out how to respond, my uncle turns to her.

"Eva, please escort Ember back to her room so she can change clothes. Everyone else, get to class, please. The show's over."

And just like that, we have our assignments. I just hope this one goes better than the last...

CHAPTER FIFTEEN

THAT'S JUST F.I.N.E. BY ME

I turn to Jude, suddenly feeling uncomfortable with him now that the crisis has passed. Especially since the only thing covering his naked torso is the blanket Uncle Carter draped over him, letting his chiseled chest peek out. We stare at each other for a moment before I finally clear my throat and ask, "Do you think you can make it to the healer?"

"I'm fine," he says again.

I roll my eyes as I brush past him. "There's a really old Aerosmith song called 'F.I.N.E.' You know what they say it stands for?"

"Fabulous, Intelligent, Noble, and Endearing?" His eyes dare me to contradict him.

I won't give him the satisfaction. "Your knowledge of old music is appalling."

"Oh, I know the song," he tells me. "I just don't agree that I'm insecure or emotional."

He's right. Jude is a guy who contains multitudes, but insecurity definitely isn't one of those multitudes. Even as a child—lost, broken, devastated—he knew who he was. And what he wanted. Or, to be more specific, what he *didn't* want. As far as I can tell, none of that has changed in the ensuing years.

I notice he doesn't say anything about the fucked-up or the neurotic parts of the acronym. Then again, what can he say? He's pretty much the poster child for both and has been for as long as I've known him.

I don't point that out, though.

Jude doesn't say anything else as we climb the three flights of stairs to Aunt Claudia's office, and neither do I. But more thunder booms above us, and a glance out the window shows the nearby trees nearly bending in half with the wind.

A tremor of unease works its way through my body at the sight, and for the first time, I start to wonder if this storm is going to be even worse than I thought.

Even though the door is half open, I think about knocking, but the room itself is dark, and Aunt Claudia is nowhere to be found.

"There's no one here," Jude says, whirling around like he can't get away from the place fast enough. "I'll come back later."

But that just brings us face-to-face—or, more accurately, my face to his very large, very powerful, *very naked* chest. His warm, dark scent—cardamom, leather, and rich, hot honey—overwhelms my senses immediately. It makes my knees tremble and my heart beat way too fast. Even as I tell myself to move back, to get away from him as quickly as I can, I don't move. I can't.

Lost in memories, I breathe him in, breathe him deep. In that moment, it's just like it used to be—when I actually wanted to be close to him.

And for a second that feels like a whole eternity, Jude lets me. He doesn't move, doesn't breathe, doesn't blink—just stands there and lets me remember.

But then he pulls away abruptly, and hot humiliation sweeps through me. I've had three years to build my defenses, to forget the ridiculous crush I used to have on him, yet one whiff of him has me all but melting at his feet again. It's disgusting.

Especially since it's obvious he has no such problem when it comes to me.

"I don't think that's a good idea," I answer, striving for a normal tone as I pull out my phone and text my aunt Claudia. "Those burns have to be treated before they get infected. Plus, I can't even imagine how painful they are."

"I can handle the pain."

"Stop trying to be stoic," I tell him.

He shrugs, like there comes a time when a person is in so much pain that more—no matter how small or great—barely registers, let alone matters.

But I'm done caring about his pseudo-martyr attitude. If he wants out of here before he's taken care of himself, he's going to have to get through me.

So I position my body directly in front of his, crossing my arms over my chest in a very obvious dare for him to try to get past me.

"Cleaning those burns with some shower gel isn't going to cut it, and you know it."

Normally, it wouldn't work with him—the attitude or the dare—but Jude is swaying on his feet, so I press on.

"You need calendula and probably some aloe elixir. Maybe some curcumin ointment, too."

He tries to slip past me again, but this time when he moves, his hand brushes against his pants. He lets slip the most infinitesimal flinch at what I know must be excruciating pain, and his voice is strained when he says, "Fine, whatever. But I can get it."

"It's cute that you think so." I shoot a pointed look toward his *very* messed-up hands before crossing to one of the large, glass-front cabinets straight out of the 1950s that houses the magic-infused herbal remedies.

As I reach for the cupboard handle, my phone buzzes with a series of messages from my aunt.

"Claudia's in the middle of helping Ember." Jude immediately looks concerned, so I clarify, "Ember's okay, but Claudia will be here as soon as she can." Jude's shoulders immediately fall with relief as I pull out the long, skinny bottle filled with calendula. "She wants me to soak your hands while we wait for her. She told me what to use to take the pain away and speed up the healing process."

Jude sighs like my helping him is the biggest inconvenience in the world, but he doesn't say anything else as I pull out a bowl and fill it with the mixture of water and herbal elixirs my aunt told me to combine for him.

When I'm done, I put the bowl on the old, scarred table in the corner of the room and gesture for him to sit in the battle-worn chair. As he moves to comply, the blanket slips from his shoulders, and I get my first good look at his back. I have to bite back my gasp of surprise. Because his entire back is *covered* in tattoos.

Like *covered* covered. Barely any of his skin pokes through the feathery, black, rope-like swirls that twist and turn in every direction as they curve their way over his shoulders and down his biceps.

Like Jude himself, the tattoos are beautiful but sinister, powerful but just as ethereal, and I can't help staring. Any more than I can help the sudden urge I have to trace a finger over them—over *him.*

Just the thought has my cheeks burning, and I slide my hands into my pockets. Because they're cold, obviously, not because I don't trust myself not to touch Jude Abernathy-Lee.

But not touching him doesn't stop me from wondering where he got the tattoos—and when. Because unlike most of the students at Calder Academy who come here sometime during their high school years, Jude has been here since he was seven. And—like me—he hasn't left the island since. Not once.

Yet I've never once noticed them before. Not even when he ripped his shirt off in the chaos of the hallway just minutes earlier.

Is this why he always wears long sleeves?

Why he would never go swimming with us in the mermaid pool when we were little?

As far as I know, I've never actually seen him shirtless, even when we were kids. Back when I had a crush on him—eons ago—I used to imagine the very sexy washboard abs I was sure he was hiding under his Calder Academy polo. But I never once imagined what else he was hiding.

But how could he have had the tattoos that long? He's grown a lot since he was seven, and they would be distorted, stretched out, faded even, if they had grown along with him. Yet these are none of those things. In fact, I've never seen any tattoo as defined and richly saturated as his are. They don't look like drawings at all—they look real, like they could come to life at any second.

Again, my fingers itch with the need to trace one. But I keep them where they belong, curling my hands into fists as I very deliberately walk around to the other side of the table.

Of course, once on that side, I'm faced with the sculpted abs that are even better than I ever imagined. Not to mention the implacable, mismatched eyes that always seem to know exactly what I'm thinking.

Jude watches me as he slides into the chair, and it's obvious he's figured out that I've seen the tattoos. And just as obvious that he has no intention of saying anything about them.

I start to ask, but then he's slipping his hands into the bowl. His shoulders stiffen the second the raw burns come into contact with the healing elixirs. He doesn't say a word, though, just sits completely still through what must be a nightmare of agony.

Nervous sweat rolls down my back. I hate seeing other people in pain, hate even more the fact that I can't do anything to ease it. The fact that it's Jude in such pain makes it even worse.

I used to think I wanted him to suffer for hurting me the way he did, but this isn't the kind of suffering I was thinking about.

To combat the nervous energy, I take my time straightening up the rest of the room—there isn't much to do, but it keeps me from staring at Jude.

I'm sweating by the time that's done—the incoming storm has turned the already sticky air into glue—so I pull off my hoodie and look around for something, anything, else to do. I pick up the medicine bottles and gather them up to put them away. I've barely gotten the cabinet open when a woman comes flying out and fills me with a vicious, terrible pain that slices across every nerve ending.

CHAPTER SIXTEEN

UNSTEADY AS SHE GHOSTS

I scream, stumbling backward as jars fall out of the cabinet and slam into my body on their way down. A whooshing fills my ears—along with the tinkling sound of breaking glass—and I trip over my own feet, nearly going down amid the broken shards.

Tears make diluted tracks in the blood that covers her face. But it's her eyes that pull me in. They're moving with unnatural speed, darting from side to side, up and down, as if they're seeing a thousand images all at once. And each one is breaking her heart.

Her trembling hand reaches for me and I don't move. I can't move. Fear has me in its grip even before she runs one single, bone-chillingly cold finger down my cheek.

It hurts, pain cracking into a thousand different tendrils that wind their way through me. I gasp, try to jerk away, but she has me in her thrall. As do the images that start flashing in my head—tiny vignettes blazing across my eyelids in a million bursts of light.

I see her sweat-drenched body splayed on a bed.

I see blood—so much blood.

I see a handshake, hear high-pitched crying.

She's despair personified, her sadness an endless, black blanket that smothers me and makes it impossible to breathe.

But as she pulls back, I see a flash of bright-blue eyes beneath the blood and I know I've seen her once before—when I was in ninth grade, just before everything went to shit. "What is it?" Jude demands, rushing toward me.

But I can't speak as her face gets closer and closer to mine. The physical pain and the mental anguish are too great.

"Clementine, talk to me," he orders, jaw grim and eyes narrowed as he puts himself in front of me.

The moment he does, she disappears as quickly as she emerged, leaving me trembling and drenched in sweat.

"It's nothing," I gasp even as I know that's not true on some primal level. But I double down anyway. "There's nothing there," I say firmly.

Jude's not buying it, though. Why should he? There was a time when I told him all my secrets. "But there was something there before?"

"Nothing important," I say as I try to herd him back toward the table—and the healing bowl of elixirs.

But Jude's never been one to go where he doesn't want to, and he stands his ground, refusing to budge as his gaze sweeps over me. "Did it hurt you?" he asks.

"I'm fine." He lifts a brow, and I know he's thinking about our earlier conversation, so I change it to, "I'm *okay*. It's long gone."

"Good." He only deigns to acknowledge the last part of what I said as he looks me over from head to toe. As he does, his eyes narrow even more. "For someone who insists they're okay, you certainly look like hell."

I stiffen at the insult. I know I look rough—it's been a shit day. Just like I know it shouldn't matter what he thinks. But for some reason it does. "Yeah, well, we can't all be oneiroi, can we?"

He rolls his eyes. "I meant, there's blood on your shirt. And a bruise on your face." He leans forward, strokes his thumb over my jaw.

I jerk back, startled. But he looks just as surprised—like he's as shocked as I am that he touched me like that.

"We really should take care of those cuts." He nods toward my arm.

I glance down and realize he's right. I must have bled through the bandages Eva and I applied earlier. Now that my hoodie is off, there's nothing to hide all the damage that disgusting snake monster did.

"How did this happen?" he asks gruffly.

"I had a run-in with one of the monsters in the menagerie before class."

He looks far more horrified than a few cuts, even nasty ones, warrant.

I laugh—or try to—around the sudden tightness in my throat. On the plus side, my galloping heart rate has finally returned to normal. "The storm seems to have put a lot of things in a bad mood today."

Jude doesn't answer, but his gaze is downright stony as he scans my body, cataloging the damage. My stomach jumps a little at the scrutiny. At *his* scrutiny.

I tell myself to turn away, tell myself that after everything that's happened, he doesn't have the right to look at me like that. But I can't move. Can't think. Can't *breathe*—at least until he says, "You really need to take care of those wounds."

And just like that, my stomach goes from flipping to sinking. How can I be so pathetic that one slide of his eyes over my body makes my defenses crumble like dust?

"I have to go," I say as I all but flee to the corner of the room where I dropped my backpack. "Claudia will be here in a little while—"

"Clementine." His voice rumbles through the space between us.

I ignore the way it makes my stomach jump and my cheeks burn hotter as I gather up my sweatshirt. "Just keep soaking your hands and she'll—"

"Clementine." This time there's a warning in the three little syllables that make up my name, but I ignore it the same way I ignore him. Badly.

"Bandage them up or whatever needs to be done. You know how good she is with—"

"Clementine!" The warning has turned to an ultimatum, and this time it comes from much closer. So much closer that my heart—and my feet—stutter over themselves at the exact same moment.

"What are you doing?" I demand, whirling around. "You need to get back to soaking your hands!"

"My hands are doing just fine." He holds them up to prove his point. And while fine is a stretch—they are still very red and angry looking—the elixir worked fast to close up all the open wounds. "I need to take care of *you* now."

Suddenly, he sounds so sad I just can't bear it.

"I'm okay. The bites are no big deal." I stumble backward toward the door.

But he's moving with me, his steps outpacing mine until he's closer—so much closer—than I'm comfortable with.

"Stop fighting me," he insists again.

"Fine." I whirl around to find I'm back at the cupboard. Caught between the door I'm a little terrified to open and the guy I'm even more terrified to let touch me. "But I can do it."

I don't need magic to know Jude doesn't so much as budge an inch. His gaze blazes like a brand between my shoulder blades even as the heat rolls in waves off his big, powerful body. So close that I can feel the burn. So intense that I can feel the weight of those three long years pressing down on me like an off-kilter scale, one that will be off-balance forever.

Desperate for some distance now, a chance to think—to breathe—I start to reach for the handle. But Jude gets there first, moving me gently aside in what I'm pretty sure is an effort to protect me as he opens the door.

This time, though, nothing comes out. *Thank God.*

"Okay?" Jude asks, and I know he's talking about what happened earlier, not my injuries.

"Okay," I answer, reaching in and pulling out the first bottle my fingers come in contact with. "But I can take care of myself." I infuse the words with as much power as I can manage.

Which, admittedly, isn't nearly as much as I'd like.

"That's peppermint elixir," is his answer. "Unless you're planning on puking, I don't think it will do you any good."

Jude pries the bottle out of my numb hand before grabbing another one off the shelf. I try to take it from him, but he holds it out of my reach. "Turn around."

"I don't need your help." But even I can hear the lack of conviction in my voice.

"Give me your arm, Clementine." This time, his voice brooks no argument. Neither does his unyielding gaze.

For one long, interminable moment, our eyes lock, my heart beating too fast and my breath coming in jagged little pants I can no longer control.

I longingly wish for the floor to open up and swallow me whole, but when that doesn't happen—when *nothing* happens save Jude making an impatient sound deep in his throat—I finally give in. Ungraciously.

"Whatever," I mutter and extend my arm.

When he finally takes a small step, I consider the fact that I don't immediately run out of the room a small sign of personal growth.

"Thank you." Jude's words are so low and growling that I can't say for sure that I haven't imagined them over the pounding of my heart.

Several awkward seconds pass as he shakes the bottle and flips the cap open. But then his fingers are on my skin.

A shiver works its way down my spine, but I ruthlessly control it. I've already embarrassed myself in front of Jude enough today. No way in hell am I doing it again.

My resolve lasts until he starts rubbing my cuts with the antiseptic-soaked cotton ball like he's trying to work out a stain.

"Ouch!" I yelp, pulling away to glare at him. "There are nerve endings attached to that, you know." I hold out a hand. "Just give it to me."

"I've got it," he says, and the hands he places on my arm are so soft that his touch is like a whisper.

This time when he starts to clean my wounds, he's so gentle I barely feel the cotton ball at all. Which is a new problem altogether, because now all I can think about is the brush of his skin over mine as he moves from wound to wound.

It feels good—dangerously good—and it takes every ounce of willpower I have not to pull away. Not to run away. But I refuse to give him the satisfaction of knowing how much he still affects me.

So I stay exactly where I am, forcing myself to concentrate on the sting of the antiseptic, on the physical pain of it all instead of the empty ache deep inside me.

It's no big deal. It's no big deal. It's no big deal. The four words become my mantra, and repeating them over and over again becomes my salvation. My breathing levels out. My knees stop trembling. My heart remembers how to beat properly.

I take a deep breath and blow it out slowly. Tell myself one more time that this really is no big deal. And I almost believe it…right up until Jude releases my arm and places a hand on my shoulder to spin me around so that my back is facing him. My shirt looks like Swiss cheese, so I know he sees the myriad of bites that pepper my skin. His fingers move to the wound on my lower back as he says, "I think you're going to have to take your shirt off for this one."

CHAPTER SEVENTEEN

CLEAN CUTS
AND RUN

Of all the things I've ever imagined Jude would say to me, that honestly has never been one of them. At least not since freshman year, when I let myself dream—

I cut the thought off abruptly and focus, instead, on the here and now. And mainly on the fact that Jude just suggested that I *undress in the middle of my aunt's office.* I will not make myself even more vulnerable than I already am. "What did you just say?" I demand, turning to him with incredulous eyes.

For what might very well be the first time in Jude Abernathy-Lee history, there's a faint pink blush across his high, stubbled cheekbones. "Or maybe just pull it up? There's a cut on your lower back and you don't want it getting infected."

"Excuse me?" Somehow, he's made the request sound even worse.

The faint pink turns to a dusty rose, and he looks more and more flummoxed as I continue to stare at him, his normally fathomless eyes more than a little wild as they focus anywhere but on me. But I'm not giving in this time, not filling up the quiet between us with soothing words to make things more comfortable for him. I used to do that all the time when we were friends, but he forfeited that courtesy a long time ago.

So now I just watch him as the silence stretches on, becoming more awkward and uncomfortable with every moment that passes until finally he throws his hands up and says, "Do you want me to clean your back or not?"

"I'm pretty sure I told you I could do it myself."

For a second, it looks like he wants nothing more than to hand me the echinacea tonic, but in the end, he just shakes his head. "Lift the back of your shirt up, will you? I'm not going to look at anything."

The way he says it—like it's ridiculous for me to even imagine he would *want* to look at me—leaves me feeling like a total fool. Of course, his only interest in getting my shirt off is purely medicinal. This is Jude, after all, the boy who for years has treated me like I have the plague.

"Fine." I grab the top of my shirt in the back and tug it up so that my entire back is exposed. "Just don't hurt me again, okay?"

Because I'm suddenly afraid I'm referring to a lot more than just my back, I close my eyes and try to pretend I'm anywhere but here. With anyone but him.

Jude, of course, doesn't even bother to answer.

But his giant hands start out gentle this time as he uses a piece of gauze to wipe away what I can only assume is blood before cleaning the large cut in the center of my lower back. The antiseptic burns more than I expect it to, but I just press my lips together and don't say a word. Partly because I don't want to show any weakness and partly because I'm afraid he'll stop if I do.

I don't have time to wait on Aunt Claudia to get here—not if I want to get to my next class before it's over. Or at least that's the story I'm telling myself.

It's a good story, too, right up until the moment Jude finishes bandaging my wounds. I expect him to step back right away, but instead he lingers for just a moment, his calloused fingertips trailing across my lower back so softly that I'm not sure if I'm imagining it.

Except his fingers feel like fire as they slide across my skin, leaving enough heat in their wake to rival the thick, muggy air currently surrounding our little island. Shivers work their way down my spine, and the hair on the back of my neck stands straight up—in warning or something else, something I'm too afraid to acknowledge. I just know that I'm not pulling away, even though I really, really should.

"You should have your aunt look at them tomorrow." The words come out stilted.

"I will." My mouth is a desert, and I barely get the words out as I turn to face him. "Thank you."

"Here. You can reach the rest." He thrusts the tonic and ointment at me.

"What about you?" I reach for his hand, run a finger over the tender-looking skin. "We're not done—"

Something flashes in his eyes at my touch, something dark and hungry—almost feral—as he quickly pulls his hand away.

"Did I hurt you?" I ask, worried.

"I'm okay, Kumquat." He breathes the words more than says them, and for a moment they hang in the air between us.

It's been a long time since he's called me that, and it momentarily soothes the hurt from class earlier when he called me by my real name.

For a second, he doesn't move. Doesn't breathe. He just stands there watching me through blown-out pupils, his jaw clenched and throat working double time.

Overwhelmed by the intensity of the look—of the moment—I close my eyes. Take a breath.

Unconsciously, I reach for him again, but this time my fingers meet only air. Startled, I open my eyes. And realize that—once again—Jude has left me.

CHAPTER EIGHTEEN

WE ARE NEVER EVER EVER GETTING OFF THIS ISLAND

Jude is gone. Not just stepped back gone, which would be embarrassing enough. But gone gone. Like *Elvis has left the building* gone.

What the actual hell?

My stomach plummets and humiliation burns my cheeks as I start cleaning up the last of the mess we've made of my aunt's office. And by we, I mean *him*.

A bitter anger simmers in my heart as I clean. Anger at him for doing this to me again. And even more anger at myself for letting him.

When he ditched me freshman year to hang out with Ember and their other two friends—Simon and Mozart—I promised myself I'd never trust him again. And now, the first time he so much as looks at me in years, I let him pull me back in like the last three years never happened.

Like I didn't spend the first half of my freshman year crying myself to sleep, reeling from loneliness and confusion at being discarded by my best friend the same day my favorite cousin, and only other real friend, got sent to the Aethereum.

I'm not sure who's worse—Jude for being such a jerk or me for being so incredibly gullible. But even as I ask myself the question, I know the answer.

It's definitely me.

Jude's just being Jude, horrible as that is. I'm the one who knows better than to trust him, but I slipped up and did it anyway. And now I'm the one left standing here, totally mortified.

Instinct has me reaching for my phone to text Serena and tell her about this latest disgrace. But then I remember. I'll never text her again, never talk to her again. *Never see her again.*

A scream wells up inside me, and this time it's a million times harder to swallow it down. But somehow I manage it, even as grief rocks me to my core. Pulling me down. Pulling me under.

I fight my way back up, grabbing antiseptic and a few cotton balls to treat the last of my wounds. I focus on the pain, use it to beat back the sorrow for at least a little while longer.

When I can breathe again, I bandage up the bites and put the first-aid supplies away before closing the cabinet door. Then, after sending a text to my aunt Claudia letting her know that all is well, I grab my backpack from the ground and head for the door.

But I've barely made it into the hallway before I catch sight of my mother striding down the hallway, a very unhappy look on her very pinched face.

She catches sight of me and pauses for a moment before arrowing straight toward me. Her Calder-blue eyes are locked on my face like a heat-seeking missile while her red stiletto heels click out her displeasure with each commanding step she takes. Normally I'd be glancing around, looking for an escape route—dealing with my mother when she's dressed in her red Chanel pantsuit is *never* a good idea.

But right now, I couldn't care less about how this ends. I'm too angry, too sad, too *hurt* to run away. Serena's death is a gaping wound inside me, while Caspian's acceptance at my first-choice college is lemon juice poured straight into that wound.

So instead of running, I stand my ground, eyes locked with hers as I wait for her to unload so that I can do the same.

But instead of launching into what's bothering her right away, she stops in front of me.

And waits.

And watches.

And watches.

And waits, until I feel like I'm about to jump out of my skin.

Which is exactly how she wants me to feel—not only is she a master strategist, she's also a master manipulator. Plus, she's in the wrong here and she knows it, which means she'll wait forever to talk.

But knowing all of that doesn't make it any easier for me to wait her out. It definitely doesn't make it any easier to stand here like I'm some kind of lab specimen while she studies me with her signature narrowed gaze, her head cocked to one side.

But whoever makes the first move dies—my mother taught me that long before *Squid Game* ever could—so I keep my mouth shut and my eyes open as I wait some more.

Finally, she sighs—a long, slow exhalation that has skitters of anxiety racing along the back of my neck. I ignore them, and eventually she says, "Your shirt has several holes in it."

"The monsters were—"

She cuts me off before I can go further. "I'm not sure why you're presenting that as a valid excuse." She shakes her head, and for the first time a touch of exasperation creeps into her tone. "You know prevaricating is not acceptable. The menagerie is perfectly safe."

I stare at her for a second, not really sure what I'm supposed to say to that. I suppose I could argue with her. But instead, I settle on classic old avoidance.

"Fine," I say shortly. "I'll change after class."

"You represent this school, Clementine. You're a *Calder*. You need to be above reproach at all times, and that includes following the dress code." She throws up a hand. "How many times do I have to tell you? If you don't follow the rules, how can we expect any of the other students to do so?!"

"Yes, because me having a messy uniform is going to lead to total anarchy in the rest of the school." I start to brush past her, but her red-tipped fingers reach out and grab my arm, aggravating the fresh cuts and keeping me from walking away.

"You don't *know* what will lead to anarchy," she insists. "And neither do I. These students have had difficult lives. They've made some pretty terrible mistakes. A dress code may seem trivial to you, but keeping *things* regimented, orderly, *uniform*, is how we keep them on an even keel."

Ah, now I get why she's so worked up.

Nothing gets my mother more on edge than when a strange power surge happens and one of the students manifests their magic despite the school's most stringent efforts. Today it was Ember bursting into flames, but it's been other students and their magic in the past. We may have state-of-the-art technology combined with some really strong spells to lock powers down, but accidents *do* happen. Especially during power surges.

This makes me think of Serena and her powers and how she died because she never learned to control them.

Another wave of grief knocks the air out of me. This one nearly flattens me, and I slap back at my mother and her ridiculous words before I even make the conscious decision to do so. "And here I thought keeping them *alive* was the way to keep them—and the school—on an even keel."

The moment my words hit, she reels back like I've physically slapped her, but I'm not sorry for saying them. Not in the slightest. Because focusing on dress codes and rules and the status quo seems pretty ridiculous to me when the status quo isn't preparing Calder Academy graduates for the real world—it's getting them killed, again and again and again.

My mom, however, doesn't see things the same way I do—not if the way her jaw snaps shut is any indication. And though the look she shoots me warns me that now would be a really good time to close my mouth, I can't do it. Not now. Not this time.

But I do lower my voice, making it more conciliatory than accusatory as I continue, "Is it really any wonder so many students die when they graduate from here when we give them absolutely no life skills?"

At first my mother looks like she wants to just ignore my attempt at actual discussion, but then she just sighs heavily. "I assume this little tirade means you've heard about Serena."

"You make it sound like she's a weather report. 'I assume you've heard about the storm moving in?'" An extra-loud burst of thunder picks that moment to rumble across the sky, as if underscoring my words—and anger.

"That isn't my intention."

"Maybe not, but it feels like it is—not just with Serena, but with all of them," I tell her.

She shakes her head, sighs again. "We did the best we could to turn their lives around. We kept them safe while they were here. But what happens after they graduate is totally out of our control, Clementine. Do I feel bad that Serena's dead? Of course I do. Do I feel bad about the other former students who have died? *Of course I do.* But you have to understand that their deaths are what they are—sad, unfortunate accidents."

"And that doesn't bother you? How can you possibly think it's okay that students from this school that you're in charge of, this school that you keep reminding me is our family's legacy, can't live outside its walls?"

"Now you're being overly dramatic." Another round of thunder— this one low and long—shakes the building, but my mother ignores it. "First of all, many of our students go on to live very fulfilling lives. And secondly, you're putting words in my mouth. I have never discounted the sadness nor the import of their deaths—"

"You just said their deaths 'are what they are,' just another unpleasant fact of life we have to accept. What is that if not discounting it?"

"It's being realistic!" she snaps. "The students who come here are troubled, Clementine. Very, very troubled. They have burned down buildings. They have blown things up. They have *killed* people in terrible, terrible ways. We do our absolute best to rehabilitate and help them while they're here. We give them a place away from some of the darker consequences of their powers. We give them a chance to avoid prison, a chance to breathe, to heal—if they take us up on it—as they come to grips with who they are and what they can do. We give them anger management and therapy *and* choice mitigation. But none of it negates the fact that when they leave here, away from our close supervision, bad things can happen to them no matter how much we try to prevent it."

"Dying is a little more than just bad, don't you think?" I ask incredulously. "There has to be a better way to help these kids than what we're doing. You know Grandma and Grandpa wouldn't want this to—"

"Don't you dare try to tell me what my mother and father would want when you've never even met them!" The reasonableness has left her tone, and all that's left is cold fury. "You think because you were born on this island that you know how things work here. But the truth is you don't have a damn clue."

I don't argue with her about having met my grandparents— there are some things I know better than to bring up, and my ability to see ghosts is one of them—so I focus on the rest instead.

"If I don't know, tell me!" I implore. "Explain to me why you think this is the only way—"

"It is the only way! If you'd stop daydreaming for a second about leaving the island, you might just figure that out."

"And why do you think I'm so desperate to leave, Mom? Could it be because you keep me prisoner here, too, just like everyone else? I've never even been off the island! Do you know how bizarre that is? And then you tell me I can't go to college, that none of us fourth gens can. And I find out that's a lie, too, that Caspian's getting out of here as soon as he possibly can. And going to my dream college. How do you expect me not to be frustrated?"

Her face, already closed, shuts down completely. "I'm not going to discuss this with you right now, Clementine."

"Because you don't have an answer?" I ask caustically. "Because you know you're wrong?"

"I am not wrong!"

"But you are. What's so wrong with me wanting to see what it's like out there? To feel what it is to actually be a manticore? The students are all missing out on that experience, that core part of who they are, and it's literally killing them, Mom."

"We've tried it your way, Clementine. We did. And it didn't work. You think things are scary now? You should have seen it before. Students died regularly while under our care, and we couldn't stop it until we tried this. It works. They're safe, and that's what matters."

"You mean they're safe for now. That's not the same thing."

"You—" She breaks off as her phone notifications suddenly go wild. "I need to go handle this. And you need to drop all this talk of changing things here. It's not going to happen. Things are the way they are because they have to be, whether you like it or not. We already had several students get hurt today in that power surge. There's no way we can let them have their powers back permanently."

"I don't believe that—"

"It doesn't matter what you believe!" Her voice snaps like a rubber band that's been stretched too far. "It only matters what *is*. Now knock it off, Clementine!"

But she's not the only one who's been stretched past her breaking point. "Or what?" I shoot back. "You'll ship me off to prison—off to *die*—like you did Carolina?"

Quick as a snake, her hand shoots out and connects with my cheek. Hard.

I gasp, stumbling backward under the onslaught even as my gaze slams into hers. "You're not leaving this island, Clementine. Not to go to the Aethereum, not to go to college. Not for any reason. The sooner you get that through your head, the better off you'll be."

My cheek throbs hotly, but I fight the urge to press a hand to it. That would be a weakness, and I don't show weakness—not even in front of my mother. *Especially* not in front of my mother.

"You can say that all you want," I tell her. "And you might even believe it. But once I graduate, I'm leaving this nightmare behind me as far and as fast as I can."

"You're not listening. When I say you're never getting off this island, I mean you're *never getting off this island*." She smiles thinly. "But don't get too upset about that. Nightmares aren't nearly as bad as everyone thinks they are—I would have thought you'd have figured that out by now."

Fear rolls through me at her words, drowning out the anger and the pain and the horror and leaving nothing but a cold terror in their place. "You can't mean that," I whisper.

"Try me." And just like that, she turns and walks away, her bloodred stilettos tap-tap-tapping out the sound and the fury of her withdrawal from the field of battle. At least until she gets to the end of the hall and calls, "Just remember, Clementine, dreams can be prisons, too. And that's worse, because—unlike with nightmares—you don't see the trap coming until it's far too late."

CHAPTER NINETEEN

RAIN DROP
A PIN

I stare after my mother in shock and dismay. Even as the true horror of her words slowly, steadily, sinks in, there's a part of my brain that's still focused on the mundane. It's urging me to get moving, to go to class, to avoid getting on Dr. Fitzhugh's radar.

But even as I tell myself to at least make an effort to get to the second half of group therapy, I can't move. It's like my feet have grown roots as the things my mother said reverberate in my mind over and over again.

Nightmares aren't so bad.

Calder Academy students will never have their powers.

I will never have my powers because I'm never—

I cut that last one off before it can fully form, pretty sure if I let myself think it—let alone believe it—I'll start screaming and never, ever stop. As it is, I feel like I'm holding on to control by a very thin, very nebulous thread.

Outside, the storm continues to build. It's raining full-out now, water pouring down in torrents from a sky turned black and oppressive. Wind howls through the oak trees, the leaves chittering and branches bowing to its force.

I step closer to the window, and now that I'm alone I allow myself the weakness of pressing my throbbing, burning cheek against the coolness of the glass. The physical relief is instant, if not the mental. For several seconds, I let myself sink into the chill, and into the strength of the wall, as my knees finally turn to nothing. Just like the rest of me.

Tears burn against the backs of my eyes, and for once I don't bother to blink them away. Instead, I stare out into the raging storm—and the restless ocean just beyond the fence—and tell myself that she doesn't mean what she said.

We did this to Serena. Calder Academy, with its power dampening and its affirmations and its focus on anything and everything but how to use our magic. *We* did this to her. We did this to all of them.

We spend four years keeping our students from shifting or performing even the most basic spell, and then we shove them back out into the world as adult paranormals, with all the power that comes with that. Then we say that it's not our fault they can't function. That it's not our fault they keep dying in magical accidents. That it's not our fault they keep blowing themselves up with a potion or shifting incorrectly or any of the million other ways there are for paranormals to hurt themselves.

And then we just go on about our lives like nothing happened. And in some ways, it hasn't. People graduate and leave the island, basically disappearing from existence for those of us who are stuck here. So when they die—which so many of them have recently—it doesn't feel real because it's no different than them just leaving.

But it is different. It does matter.

Serena matters.

Jaqueline matters.

Blythe and Draven and Marcus matter.

All dead now, and they're not the only ones.

Carolina matters. My beautiful, self-absorbed, larger-than-life cousin matters. So much.

At least to me. I'm not sure if she matters to anyone else, except my aunt Claudia and uncle Brandt. And even they seem to be moving on. She was their daughter and they loved her, but from the minute she got sent away, it's like she ceased to exist…long before she actually died.

And now to find out that my mom seems to think this is the best we can do… It's mind-blowing.

Totally and completely soul-destroying.

How can I be the only one who sees that? And how can I be the only one who wants to do something about it?

Outside, a huge crack of lightning splits the sky. Instinctively, I jump back, but as I do, I see a flash on the path at the very edge of the gym. I lean forward, trying to see it again. But the darkness is back despite the fact that it's barely mid-afternoon, and I can't get a clear look at anything that's much beyond the borders of the quad in front of the building.

Still, I strain my eyes trying to get another glimpse of whatever it is I saw. Because, storm or not, what I caught sight of looked an awful lot like a *person*.

But who would voluntarily be out in this mess right now—especially since all the other students should be in class? And where could they possibly be going?

I watch the area for several more seconds, willing myself to see another flash of…something. But the rain and the gray have made everything too muddled. I give up, start to turn away, but as I do, another flash of lightning illuminates the sky as thunder booms at practically the same second, and I catch another look at what is, indeed, a person.

A very tall, very broad, very shirtless person, with dark hair plastered to his neck and bold, black tattoos climbing up his back.

Jude.

What the actual hell?

Where could he possibly be going, still shirtless, and covered in still-healing burns?

And what could he possibly have to do that is so important it can't wait for this storm to be over?

He should be in class right now. Or, if he's ditching, he should at least be heading back to the dorm to get a shirt and jacket instead of jogging, half naked, toward a huge thicket of trees in the middle of a violent rainstorm.

What if lightning strikes one of the trees and a branch falls on him?

Or worse, what if lightning strikes *him*?

Not that I care, because I don't.

But still, sneaking off into the woods during a storm this wild is not normal behavior. He's obviously up to something, and whatever that something is, I'm betting it's not good.

A quick glance at my phone tells me I've got about forty minutes before class ends. If I hustle, I can probably get away with talking Fitzhugh into a detention that doesn't involve getting bitten by anything...

But I'm barely halfway down the stairs when my mother's voice comes over the PA. "Attention, students. Due to the storm, all after-school activities will be canceled for this afternoon. Please report directly to the dorms after the final bell. I repeat, all after-school activities will be canceled for today, and dinner will be served in the dorm common areas instead of the cafeteria. Thank you for your cooperation."

Dinner at the dorms? I can count on one hand the number of times she's ordered that in my entire life. Just how bad is this storm supposed to get? And how fast?

I take the last of the stairs two at a time, then glance out a window as soon as I'm in the hallway. As luck would have it, lightning chooses that moment to illuminate the sky, but it doesn't matter. Jude is already gone.

Damn it.

I pull out my phone and swipe open the weather app. And shit. Just...shit.

It looks like the tropical depression we've been watching has moved straight through tropical storm into hurricane. Because of course it has.

And Jude is out in it.

One part of me says that he'll be fine. Surely Jude won't actually *stay* out in this mess for any length of time. And if he does, well... that's on him.

But the logical part of me is screaming that something is off. That he's out there doing something he shouldn't be. And that whatever it is just might get him killed.

Let it go, I tell myself. *He's made it very clear that nothing about him is your business. Let* him *go.*

I try. I really do. But then I think about that Keats poem, and I realize I wasn't just mad at Keats for ghosting Fanny but at Fanny for letting it happen. I realize I'm mad at her because she didn't fight for what was important to her.

This has nothing to do with love.

But still, something isn't right with him. And I just can't let it go. The rain starts falling harder, and I find myself pulling up his number. I can at least text him, tell him about the orders to get back to the dorm. Right?

But when I pull up our conversation, the last few texts jump out at me.

Jude: Meet me outside the gym.

Me: I can't. The assembly is mandatory

Jude: Come on, Mandarin. Live a little

Me: Easy for you to say, Sgt. Pepper

Me: We're going to get in trouble

Jude: I'll protect you from the big, bad wolves

Me: So you say

Me: But it's not you they like to chew on

Jude: That's because you taste better

Me: How do you know what I taste like?

There's a lapse, and then two minutes later, he wrote:

Jude: Maybe I'd like to know

Needless to say, the conversation ends there. I hightailed it out of the assembly so fast it's embarrassing to think about. Especially knowing how that night turned out.

Even worse, there are a few more texts after that—all from me, sent at different times over the following few days.

Me: Hey, Bungalow Bill! You weren't in class this morning. You good?

Me: Should I be worried about you?

Me: Hey, what's up?

Me: Where are you? Please answer me. I just found out they took Carolina and I'm freaking out

Me: No one will tell me what happened with Carolina. How could they just send her away in the middle of the night?

Me: WHERE ARE YOU?

Me: What's going on?

Me: Seriously, you're just going to walk right by me in the hall like I don't exist?

Me: I don't understand what's happening here

And then a couple of days later:

Me: I really miss you

And then, that's it. Not another text from either of us for the last three years. Until now.

Humiliation churns in my stomach, but I type a quick message.

Me: The storm's turning into a hurricane. My mom says everyone needs to report to the dorms as soon as school is out

I reread it and start to second-guess what I wrote. Somewhere around the fourth time I read it, I force myself to hit send.

Almost immediately it shows that it can't be delivered.

Damn it, damn it, damn it.

Go to class, Clementine, I tell myself even as I head back into the stairwell and race down the stairs.

Go to group therapy. You only have it once a week, and if you miss it, it's a big deal.

Tomorrow when you're in some kind of detention hell, you'll regret not going to class. Especially since Jude will be just fine, enjoying lunch with Ember and their other friends while you risk life and limb.

Go to class.

But even as I exit the stairwell into the hallway that leads to Dr. Fitzhugh's class, I know I'm not going to go. Instead, I turn in the other direction, and—after glancing to make sure the hall trolls are nowhere to be seen—I race toward the huge double doors at the end of the building.

Don't do this, Clementine, I tell myself once more. *This isn't your business. You need to go to class.*

Go to class.

Go to class.

Go to class.

But no matter what I tell myself, it's already too late. The truth is it was too late the second I saw Jude walking through the storm.

When I get to the end of the hall, I burst through the double doors without a second thought—that damned Fanny running through my head again—and race straight into the dark, steamy wet.

CHAPTER TWENTY

RAIN, RAIN AS
FAST AS YOU CAN

The rain pelts my face as I race down the slippery, moss-laden rock path toward the edge of the bald cypress trees where I last saw Jude. It's coming down so hard and fast that I can barely see, but a lifetime spent on this island—spent at this school—has me swerving to the left just in time to miss a hole on the right side of the path.

Exactly twenty-seven steps later, I leap right over a giant tree root and the raised, broken stones it's caused. Forty-one steps after that, I veer back to the right and miss a ten-inch-wide crack that crisscrosses the path.

When your whole life is narrowed down to a practically five-square-foot island, you learn every inch of it. Partly because there's nothing else to do—even when the humidity is oppressive—and partly because you never know when you'll be running for your life from a pack of pissed-off wolves or a vampire literally out for blood. Strange things happen on the daily here, and knowing the ins and outs of your prison just makes good sense.

Apparently, I'm finally putting my knowledge to the test.

The rain continues to crash through the towering trees, slapping hard against me as I run past what once was a student garden experiment but is now just a home for weeds. I weave around the gym and a ramshackle old building that used to be a ballroom back when people voluntarily paid a lot of money to come to this island during its days as a resort.

I take a left and sprint between the art studio—which is really more of a graffiti park—and the library, making sure to avoid the flock of geese and ducks that have found shelter under the bushes.

I follow the path around the corner, then brace for the two-foot dip that's been there as long as I can remember. I slide down the muddy slope without twisting an ankle, then immediately jump over another gnarled root that's poked through the stones.

A couple more minutes of running and I finally make it to the fence that separates the academic buildings from the dorms. And while I can get through it easily when classes aren't in session, it's a lot harder during school hours. But that just means I have to get creative...

The gate is programmed to keep each student in the academic area of the island during their classes, using a combination of a pin code and eye scan biometrics. But I've watched my mother enter her code a million times, and no matter how sneaky she thinks she is, I'm sneakier. Plus, I've learned that all manticore eyes have the same signature. So I can fool the system into believing I'm her.

It's a trick I don't use often—if she checks the logs, the last thing I want is for her to notice that she exited the academic area when she actually didn't—but I do pull it out in case of emergencies. And I definitely think this qualifies.

Which begs the question—how did Jude get past the fence when I *know* he has a class right now? There's no way the system should have let him pass.

Just then, one of the trees on the other side of the fence makes an ominous crack. Seconds later, a giant branch falls right onto the top of the fence. I watch sparks fly in all directions as it scrapes its way down the chain links—charred and smoking, despite the rain—before finally falling to the ground.

Because fencing us in isn't enough—they've actually electrified the damn things as well. Had I been touching the key pad, I would have ended up looking a lot like that tree branch...

I punch in the code, let the system scan my eye, then wait impatiently for the gate to swing open.

The second it does, I race through it and down the central path.

But when I get to the fork in the road that separates the student side of the island from the forest and abandoned remains of the sanatorium, I veer off the heavily used part of the path and straight into the large copse of trees that marks the other side. I mean, sure, Jude and I explored it when we were kids alongside Caspian and Carolina. But there's not much out there—a few old buildings, an old well we used to toss quarters down, and a root cellar from the days before regular refrigeration, when people had to store vegetables underground to keep them fresh.

All of which fascinated us when we were kids, but none of which would be of any interest to Jude now.

Still, the Jude I used to know never did anything without purpose. Which means he has a very definite reason for being out here. If I could just figure out what it is, maybe I'd actually have a chance of figuring out *where* he is.

Deciding I might as well start at the decrepit old buildings that were part of the former sanatorium, I veer off the main path as soon as I get to the small, manmade lake they used for rowing boats. Unlike everything else in this area, it's still in half-decent shape—mostly because the resident mermaids and sirens adopted it about a decade ago and cleaned it up for their own personal use. They can't shift, but they obviously still love the water.

It's the only part of this side of the island that students actually come to regularly. Plus, the admins don't mind because it means they don't have to maintain the swimming pool anymore.

I pass the lake and head to the old doctor's office and "daily constitutional" hut. They're shrouded by looming bald cypress trees, needles blanketing the roofs. But the doors are all padlocked with rusty chains that look like they haven't been touched in decades—because they haven't.

But I still remember how we used to get in when we were kids. So I slip around the side to find the small, second-story window with the faulty lock. The rickety trellis we used to climb to reach it is still there, but there's no way it would support my weight now, let alone Jude's.

Deciding the huts are a bust, I head farther down the path to the root cellar. But I'm barely halfway there when I see a flash of red.

When I look closer, I realize someone is cutting through the rocky ground to my right, but it's definitely not Jude. Whoever is out there is shorter and much scrawnier—but it's definitely a student.

I try to wipe the rain out of my eyes to get a closer look, but it's no use. It's coming down in sheets now, and there's nothing to do but suffer through it. Still, the odds that this person—whoever they are—is out here for a reason that isn't connected to Jude is pretty much non-existent in my mind. Especially considering they're risking a major storm and my mother's ire.

So what the hell is going on? And how much trouble is Jude going to be in if he gets caught? Or, conversely, how much trouble is he already in?

It's that thought that spurs me forward, that has me falling into step behind the person in the red shorts and hoodie. I tail close enough that I don't lose them in the storm but also stay far enough away not to call attention to myself.

But unlike Jude, they're definitely not in stealth mode, so they don't seem focused on anything but getting to their goal. Which, apparently, is the root cellar they're leading me straight to.

What the hell?

There was nothing there the last time I was in that place. Just some old shelves, a few empty burlap bags, and a few broken jars. So what on earth could this person want—

I freeze as they bend down and throw open the door buried in the ground. Because as they do, I get my first good look at their face. And realize that I've been following Jean-Luc, self-appointed leader of the Jean-Jerks and asshole extraordinaire.

CHAPTER TWENTY-ONE

TIME TO GET TO THE ROOT CELLAR OF THE PROBLEM

What is he doing out here?

And what could it possibly have to do with Jude? They *hate* each other. I saw proof of that in class yesterday. And yet they're both out here in the middle of this storm doing God knows what... It makes no sense.

Something definitely isn't right here—and while I'm the first to acknowledge that can be said for all manner of things at Calder Academy, there's something about this that really freaks me out.

Curiosity—and more than a little worry—is burning inside me as I take off running toward Jean-Luc, no longer caring if he or Jude see me. Something very not okay is going on out here, and I may be pissed off at Jude, but I still have trouble believing he's somehow mixed up with the Jean-Jerks.

I watch as Jean-Luc disappears inside the root cellar. The thought of him in there with Jude has me sprinting toward it—or as close to sprinting as I can get over the slick, rocky ground. As I run through the low bushes and weeds, sand gives way to mud that sucks at my shoes and makes it impossible for me to move quickly.

But Jean-Luc is long gone—and the root cellar doors closed behind him—before I even make it to the structure.

A frisson of unease skitters down my arms, has goose bumps

rising all over my body. Nothing about this place feels like it used to—nothing about it feels right—and every cell in my body is suddenly screaming at me not to touch anything.

To back away.

To run away.

But what if Jude isn't involved? What if he's in some kind of trouble? If he's in there, I can't just leave him, can I? I don't know a lot about what got the Jean-Jerks sent to Calder Academy—there are a million stories circulating, most of which I'm pretty sure were started by them—but I do know who they are.

Or, more specifically, who their parents are—major players in the biggest underground criminal organization in our world. And while that doesn't stop me from standing up to them when I need to, it does stop me from ever turning my back on them. And Jude may have done just that.

Whatever may be going on here, fear and truth are suddenly propelling me forward.

To hell with the trepidation currently sweeping through every part of me. Instead, I throw open the doors and plunge straight down the long, decrepit staircase into the dark to try and figure out exactly what's happening here.

CHAPTER TWENTY-TWO

HIDE AND
SNEAK

I'm halfway down the broken, rickety steps when I remember my phone. I take a second to shake the excess water off my hands before pulling it out of my soggy pocket and swiping on the flashlight app. Thankfully it still works, despite being soaked, and the entire storeroom is suddenly illuminated below me.

The entire *empty* storeroom...which makes absolutely no sense.

I sweep the flashlight around the room as I continue to descend the stairs, checking out every nook and cranny for some kind of clue. But there's nothing.

No Jean-Luc.

No Jude.

And absolutely no explanation of what they might have been up to.

To be honest, there's not even any sign that they *were* here.

The room looks like it probably did a century ago—some old shelves line three of the walls while an ancient tapestry covers the back wall of the cellar from corner to corner. Directly in the center of the room sits a wooden table with exactly one chair tucked under it. The table is covered in decades of dust, as is the old canning press that rests on top of it, and there are a bunch of closed, empty jars on the shelves.

Other than that, the room is completely empty.

I *saw* Jean-Luc open the doors. I *saw* him disappear down the stairs. I *know* I did.

But he's definitely not in here.

I do another pass with the flashlight, just to be sure. Nope, no fae hiding in one of the shadowy corners. But as the light swings around the room, I notice wet footsteps winding in a strange pattern around the whole room.

I see them just about the same time I notice something else strange—namely that there is absolutely no dust on the old, wooden floor. The shelves are *covered* in years' worth of the stuff, and so are the table and chair. But the floor doesn't have so much as one speck of dust on it.

Which is impossible, unless someone—or lots of someones—have been coming in here regularly for who knows what reason. Nothing good, I'm sure.

I try to follow the footsteps around the table, but I didn't close the cellar doors—trapping myself in here with a pissed-off fae didn't seem like the best idea at the time. So rain is blowing in, soaking the ground near the ladder and obliterating some of the footsteps. And what the rain isn't destroying, I am, as I drip all over everything.

I do one more circle of the room, checking for some sign that there's a secret room or a subcellar, anything that might account for the disappearing footsteps. But I find absolutely nothing.

Nothing behind the shelves. Nothing under the table. Nothing in the corners of the room. And nothing behind the tapestry—except enough dust to send me into a sneezing and coughing fit after I pull it away from the wall to check.

As I struggle to catch my breath—and stop sneezing for the millionth time—my flashlight shines on the tapestry itself. It's a typical Galveston beach scene from the early nineteen hundreds. A cheery-looking ocean is in the background, along with a multihued sky as the sun sets on the horizon. In the foreground, I recognize the large, circular hotel with its wraparound balconies. An umbrella is set up on the beach in front of the hotel, and underneath it is a wooden lounge chair with an open book resting on its seat.

Beside the chair is an inner tube along with a bucket of champagne, and on the small table beside the chair is a crystal champagne flute.

Several yards away is a large, circular pile of sticks, like someone is planning to start a bonfire.

It looks completely ridiculous and as anathema to the Calder Academy I know now as anything I've ever seen here. No wonder it's been relegated to an old root cellar—I can't imagine my mother letting anything like this hang in the halls of our school. There's too much cheerfulness in its bright colors, too much hope in that bonfire just waiting to be lit.

Still, it's strange what you pay attention to when you're a kid, because I remember there being a tapestry here before, but I didn't remember it looking like this—so fun and whimsical and bright. I guess when I was young, it seemed normal, while now it just seems too happy for a place like this. An island like this.

Still, time is ticking down, and if I don't check in at the dorm after class, there'll be hell to pay. Plus, I can already hear the storm getting worse.

The idea of leaving Jude, and even Jean-Luc, out here in the middle of this is starting to not sit well with me—despite my suspicions. I need to find them or head back to the dorms on my own.

I cross back to the staircase and, after shoving my phone back in my pocket, climb out of the root cellar. Lightning flashes above me as I go up the stairs, and thunder rumbles continuously. I've never been afraid of storms, but this seems extra, even for the Gulf.

I try to climb faster—the sooner I get out of here, the better—but the rain is pounding down and my shoes are slipping on the narrow steps, so I take it slow. At least until I pop my head above ground and find myself staring straight up into Jude's wet, angry face.

I'm not sure which one of us is more surprised. Maybe him, judging by the way his eyes go wide before he demands, "What the hell are you doing here?"

CHAPTER TWENTY-THREE

LOVE, LOVE ME DON'T

Is he seriously growling at me right now? "I'm pretty sure I should be asking you that question," I shoot back as I finally make it out of the cellar.

Instead of answering me, he busies himself closing the doors behind me. "You need to go back to school."

"*We* need to go back to school," I correct. "What are you even *doing* out here, anyway? And why is Jean-Luc out here?"

"Jean-Luc's here? Where?" He looks around like he thinks the fae is going to materialize out of thin air.

"I have no idea. I thought I saw him go into the root cellar, but by the time I caught up, he was gone." I eye him suspiciously. "Are you going to try to tell me that you know nothing about this?"

He doesn't answer. Instead, he says, "Go back to the dorm, Clementine," and turns away, as if to underscore that he's done with me. Like his use of my real name isn't enough to make that clear.

And that's all it takes for something to snap inside of me. I don't know if it's the blatant dismissal or the way he thinks he can order me around or the fact that he is once again walking away from me. But whatever it is, something just breaks inside of me, and I end up snarling, "You don't really think that's how this is going to play out, do you, Bungalow Bill?"

He pauses for a second at my reference to the classic Beatles song—and the ever-changing nicknames we used to give each other as kids. He used to call me different citrus fruits, popular and obscure, instead of Clementine. And since he shares a name with one of the most famous Beatles songs of all time, I called him by all the others instead.

I know he remembers—he's already slipped once today and called me Kumquat—and I think maybe this is it. Maybe, here in the pouring rain, is where we finally have it out.

But then he just keeps walking, and it pisses me off. I follow behind him and grab his arm, trying to spin him around. When that doesn't work, I scramble to get in front of him and block his path.

He looks at me with eyes that have gone completely blank. "What are you doing?"

"What are *you* doing?" I answer, wiping my hands over my face in a futile effort to sluice the water away. "You haven't talked to me for three years—three years, Jude—and then, today, you finally break that silence and—"

"I didn't have a choice. We were in a group together."

I'm expecting the words—hell, I know the truth of them very well—but that doesn't keep them from hurting as they hit. All the pain and anger from earlier combines with the pain and anger I've been nursing since freshman year, and I end up hurling a whole bunch of my own words at him. Words that at any other time, in any other place, would never have left my mouth.

"That's seriously all you've got to say to me?" I demand. "After cutting me off completely, after ignoring every message I sent, after pretending Carolina didn't just disappear from our lives, '*we were in a group*' is the best you've got?"

His jaw works, his too-full lips pressing together as he stares down at me through the pounding rain.

Long, storm-drenched seconds pass, and I know he's waiting for me to look away, waiting for me to just give up. That's what the old Clementine would have done, the one he knew—and ditched.

But I've grown since then. I've gone through a lot. And I've waited too long for this moment just to let the matter drop—especially when I know him well enough to know that if I walk away now, I'll never get the answers I'm looking for.

So instead of backing away—backing down—I hold my ground. I keep my gaze locked with his until, finally, *finally*, he replies, "It's the truth."

"It's a cop-out, and you know it," I toss back as anger jets through me. "Just like you know I'm not asking why you finally talked to me today. I'm asking why you haven't talked to me in three years. I'm asking why you kissed me, why you made me think you cared about me and then discarded me like I was garbage. Worse than garbage—at least you give trash a second thought when you pick it up to throw it away. I didn't even warrant that much attention from you."

"You think it was easy for me?" he whispers, and somehow, I hear his words even over the storm. But maybe that's just because they're echoing inside me, scraping against my skin and hollowing me out like a pumpkin waiting to be carved up.

"You really believe that walking away from you wasn't the hardest thing I've ever done?" He closes his eyes, and when he opens them, there's something in their depths that looks an awful lot like pain. "You were my best friend."

"But you *did* walk away! And you've got other best friends now, so no harm, no foul, right?" I take an unsteady breath, for once grateful for the rain because he can't see the tears burning in my eyes. "But it's all okay, I guess, because so do I."

He looks away, and I watch his throat work for several seconds before he turns back and says, "I know it's hard without Carolina."

"You know it's hard?" I squeak out, shock practically stopping my heart as I stare at him wide and wild-eyed. *"You know it's hard? That's what you've got to say to me right now?"*

Jude lets out a frustrated roar, one that any other time would have chills careening down my spine. Right now, though, it just pisses me off even more. As does his demand of, "What do you want from me, Clementine? What the ever-loving fuck do you want from me?"

"The same thing I've wanted from you since freshman year!" I shout back at him. "The truth. Why'd you have to go and change everything? We were fine as friends—better than fine. So why did you have to kiss me? Why'd you have to make me feel something good for the first time in my life just to tear it away? Was I that bad of a kisser?

Or did you regret it? Did you just figure out that you didn't like me like that and, instead of telling me, you took the easy way out and ghosted me? What was it, Jude?"

I'm breathing heavily by the time I'm done hurling questions—and accusations—at him. There's a part of me that's horrified—that can't believe I actually said all of those things that have run through my head countless times in the last few years. But there's another part of me, a bigger part, that feels liberated for finally having my worries out in the open.

Is it embarrassing? Yes. But is a little embarrassment worth finally having my questions answered? You're damn straight it is.

At least until Jude looks me straight in the eye and says, "We go to the same school. It's impossible for me to ghost you."

It's my turn to roar with frustration, though mine comes out sounding more like a scream.

"Again, that's what you focus on? The mundane details instead of the question I'm all but begging you to answer?"

"Clementine—"

"Don't you dare Clementine me," I grit out. "Not when you're so pathetic that you can't even answer a simple question. Or maybe it's not that you're pathetic. Maybe it's just that you're an asshole."

I've laid myself bare. Furious, and more hurt than I want to admit, I turn away. Fuck it. Just fuck it. And fuck him. He's not worth—

Jude stops me with a hand on my elbow. One gentle tug and he's whirling me back around to face him. "You were an amazing kisser!" he yells into my face. "Your lips tasted like pineapple. I wanted to hold you forever. And I never wanted anything more in my life than to know that you were *mine*."

I stare at him, shocked, as his words hang in the air between us. Even the storm dies down for his confession, the wind calming and the rain drying up between one breath and the next so that the two of us are left, staring at each other with nothing but a few scant inches of air between his mouth and mine.

"So why?" I whisper when I can finally get the words out. "Why did you walk away? Why did you cut me out of your life so completely? So cruelly?"

"Because—" he answers, his voice breaking a little on the last syllable.

"Because," I echo, breath held and heart beating like a riot inside my chest as I wait for him to be able to speak.

"Because I'm not good for you." He swallows convulsively. "If we were together, *I'd* be your worst nightmare."

CHAPTER TWENTY-FOUR

MAKING
KISS-TORY

The wind lets loose a giant howl at his pronouncement, one that shakes the leaves and rattles the door of the root cellar.

I barely notice.

I'm too busy staring at Jude and turning his words over and over in my head to pay attention to something as commonplace as a storm—even one as wild as this one.

He shifts uncomfortably under my stare. "Clementine—"

"I don't understand."

"I know, but—"

"I. Don't. Understand."

"I can't explain it to you." He reaches for me. "You have to trust me—"

"Trust you!" I laugh, yanking my arm out of his grasp. No matter how gentle he is, I don't want him touching me right now. Not when confusion and rage are bubbling up inside of me, just waiting for a chance to explode. "Don't talk to me in vague puzzles if you want me to trust you. And don't be completely illogical."

I force myself to keep my voice low now that I don't have to shout over a bunch of thunder and lightning. But it's hard when I'm so confused, so angry, so *raw*. I don't know what I thought he would say when he finally gave me an answer, but "I'd be your worst nightmare" isn't it.

Jude, in the meantime, just looks disappointed. He takes a step back from me and lets his hand fall. I can see it in his eyes—can see him taking a giant mental step back at the same time as he takes the physical.

My heart kicks against my ribs in protest and panic, but I tamp it down. The old Clementine would try to tear down his emotional wall brick by brick. Terrified to lose him to his own darkness.

Not just would. Did. Over and over again until that wall became a permanent fixture.

No way am I doing it again.

No matter how hot he looks with droplets of water running down his firm, sculpted chest, with those wisps of tattoos creeping across the canvas of his warm, brown skin.

And he does look hot. Very, very hot. But I don't care right now. More, I won't let myself care. Not when he just admitted that he upended my whole world because he doesn't think we'll work, even though he never gave us a chance. And somehow that makes everything so much worse than it already was.

"What makes you so sure we wouldn't work?" I'm on a roll now, and there's no stopping me. "Did you read it in a magazine? Did some witch riding on the back of a newt tell you? Or did you just make it up?"

Jude's full lips thin out. It's an old, familiar sign that he's getting annoyed, but I don't give a shit. I'm *glad* he's annoyed. If he ratchets that up about two million percent, maybe he'll get on my level. Because I left annoyed in the rearview mirror about five questions ago, and I don't think I'll be going back to it anytime soon.

"'I'd be your worst nightmare,'" I parrot. "A little on the nose for an oneiroi, don't you think? And a magicless one, come to—"

But it's his turn to interrupt. "I'm not m—"

Too bad, I'm not having it. "You think that's supposed to scare me away like I'm some wilting flower? Big, bad Jude Abernathy-Lee is my worst nightmare," I mock. "If you didn't want to date me, you just had to tell me! That's all you've ever had to—"

"Enough, Clementine!" Jude's voice fills the air around us. He doesn't yell, but then, he doesn't have to. His voice is deep and rich and commanding enough to get even my attention—though not my acquiescence.

"Enough?" I fire back. "I'm just getting started. In fact—"

This time when he takes hold of my arm, he doesn't give me a chance to pull away. Instead, he tugs me just hard enough to have me tumbling against his chest.

I have one second to recognize that my body is pressed against his, one second for my mind to conjure words like hot, hard, strong, and then his hands are cupping my cheeks and his mouth is slamming down on mine.

It's been three long years since I've felt Jude's lips touch my own, but I remember it as clearly as if it happened an hour ago.

The tentative brush of his lips against mine.

The soft tickle of his hair brushing against my cheek.

The warmth of his arms around me as he gently pulled me closer.

It was barely more than a peck, but still I used to lay in bed at night, replaying that moment—that kiss—in my head, over and over and over again as I tried to figure out what went wrong. Every tiny detail of it is ingrained in my mind *forever*.

So when I say this kiss is nothing like its predecessor, I really mean it. More, it's like nothing I've ever experienced before. Like nothing I ever dreamed was even possible.

There's heat. So much heat, radiating from his body to mine.

There's power. So much power in the hands that cradle my face.

And then there's need. So, so, *so* much need in the mouth—in the lips and tongue and teeth—that ravage my own.

And I'm here for all of it. Because if I have to live on this kiss for the rest of my life—I'm not going to miss one tiny second of it.

More, I'm going to memorize every single one of them.

I'll remember the way one of Jude's hands slides over my shoulder, down my arm, and across my waist to the small of my back as he presses my body closer...closer...closer to his.

I'll remember the way his fingers smooth over my shoulders and tangle in my wet hair as he holds the back of my head in his palm.

And I'll remember—oh my God, will I ever remember—the way his warm, lemon-scented breath feels on my cheek just before his lips cover mine.

And this time, it's no soft brush of lip against lip.

No, this time, there are three years of pain and loneliness and betrayal between us. Three years of denied heat, and need, and an all-encompassing desperation that boils up from a place deep inside me—a place I didn't even know existed before this moment. This kiss.

And there's Jude—always Jude—guiding me through the maelstrom and the magic with his sweetness and his strength.

His mouth is soft and warm, his body is wonderful and wicked. And his kiss...his kiss is everything.

Magic and mystery.

Power and persuasion.

Right and oh so wrong in all the best, most important ways.

It's every escape I've ever dreamed of. Every wish I've ever made. Every crash of the deep and endless ocean against the shore.

I gasp at the intensity of it, the all-consuming command that pulls me in and drags me down, over and over and over again. It bathes me in its perfection, overwhelms me with its power, threatens to break me into a million tiny pieces all over again. And I. Don't. Care.

I can't, not when every beat of my heart is his name and every breath in my body is the call of my soul to his.

The world we live in may be a nightmare, but this moment—this kiss—is a dream come true. One I never ever want to end.

I gasp out his name, and though it's just a broken whisper on the sweet, wild wind whipping through the air around us, Jude hears me. More, he feels me and takes instant, desperate, glorious advantage.

He nibbles his way across my lower lip, licks his way into my mouth, strokes his tongue against my own until I'm drowning in the wicked, wonderful heat of him sliding through my veins and into every single part of me.

He feels like the ocean and tastes like the sun breaking across the early morning sky—and nothing in my life has ever felt this good.

My hands clutch at his shoulders, my fingers twist in the wet, untamed strands of his hair, and my body opens to him like a flower to that sun, arms tightening, body arching, everything inside of me reaching for more.

More of him.

More of us.

And more—definitely more—of this, of the sensations Jude calls forth so effortlessly from inside of me with every squeeze of his fingers on my hip and every slide of his body against my own.

I pull him closer, relishing the way he wraps himself around me, the way his warm honey-and-cardamom scent envelops me. But before I can take the kiss even deeper, before I can take *him* even deeper, the lull in the storm ends.

The sky opens up once more, and rain comes crashing down around us.

And Jude slowly lets me go.

I clutch at him with desperate fingers, determined to hold on to him. And for a second—when he buries his face in my hair and whispers, "I've always been crazy about you, Tangelo"—I even think it's going to work.

I pull him back to me, so tight that I can feel the deep, fast beat of his heart against my own. "Then why?" I whisper through the storm. "Why did you just let me go?"

CHAPTER TWENTY-FIVE

THE OLD KISS AND RUN

"Because it's the only way to keep you safe." I feel Jude's words—on my skin, in my soul—more than I actually hear them. "And no matter what, that will always be the most important thing to me."

"It's not your job to keep me safe," I tell him.

The look he gives me says he disagrees. "Go back to the dorm, Clementine. There's nothing for you out here."

I reach a hand out for him before I can stop myself. "Jude, don't just—"

But he's already pulling away—already running away—head bent and shoulders hunched against the wind.

And no. Just no.

I'm not fourteen years old anymore, and neither is he. He doesn't get to say shit like that and walk away from me. Not this time.

So instead of just letting him go, I chase after him, plunging through the underbrush and into the forest like an animal running for its life. And maybe I am—or at least, running for my sanity, because I can't spend the next three years the same way I spent the last three, wondering what I could have done to make things turn out differently.

But Jude's already gone, slipping through my fingers like the raindrops that fall so steadily around me. And still I run, still I chase after him, determined not to let this shred of hope disappear as easily, as completely, as he has.

But no matter where I look—the old huts, the boarded-up wishing well, the surrounding forest—I can't find him. My heart settles heavily in my chest as I realize he really is gone. Again.

In the distance, I can hear sirens going off. The storm must be getting bad if my mom is resorting to the old hurricane sirens that she keeps locked up in the groundskeeper's hut to call everyone back to the dorms. This is only the third time I've ever heard them in my life.

I really do need to get back. Maybe Jude is already heading there—hell, for all I know, he's already changed into dry clothes while I continue to run around like a girl who can't take a hint.

Shoving my hair out of my face for what feels like the millionth time since this wild goose chase began, I glance around and try to get my bearings. I'm close to the edge of the forest on the east side of the island now, which clears at the back of the dorms.

It's a shortcut, one I don't normally take because it involves going through the teachers' quarters. But dry clothes are calling—and so is my bed—so shortcut it is. Besides, most of the faculty is probably at the dorms anyway, making sure the students don't get into any trouble now that they're all penned up.

As soon as I get close enough to the forest to get some cover from the trees, I pull out my phone and fire off a text to Eva.

Me: What's going on? I hear the siren
Eva: Where are you???????
Me: Other side of the island
Eva: What?!?!
Me: Long story
Eva: Well, get your ass back here
Eva: There's a mandatory meeting in the dorm common area in twenty minutes. If you're not there, you're going to end up living in that damn menagerie
Eva: Or getting blown away by this category-five hurricane
Me: It's category five now?
Eva: Want to stay out there and find out?
Me: omw

I shove my phone back in my pocket and start moving again just as the loudest clap of thunder I've ever heard rumbles through the air. Wind whips through the trees with an eerie howl, sending leaves and sand into a frenzied dance as lightning spears the sky. Moments later, the ground beneath my feet shudders from the force of the strike.

I really need to get out of this mess.

I start jogging now, weaving in between the old, stooped trees as I head straight for the dorms. When Jude, Carolina, and I were young, we used to explore this forest all the time, so I know all the shortcuts. I turn left as soon as I get to the huge, ancient live oak tree at the center of the dirt path, and then I make a right at the tree blackened and split down the middle from a long-ago lightning strike.

It's a straight shot between here and the dorms, and I start to run faster, determined to get back before my family notices I'm missing.

But as I weave between the trees, my stomach starts to feel funny. It doesn't hurt, per se, just feels hollow and a little uneasy, which makes my whole body feel a little shaky all over. It's probably just running around in the heat without any water—normally the rain cools the steamy September air off a little, but today's storm just seems to be packing it on, turning the air more dense with each passing minute.

Add in the fact that the granola bar I grabbed for breakfast is the only thing I've eaten all day and it's no wonder I'm feeling off. I'm sure it's nothing a bottle of water and a sandwich can't cure.

I weave around a couple more trees, the low-hanging moss tickling my arms, and then pass the therapy circle. The psychiatric faculty likes to lead hikes and group discussions through here sometimes. Apparently, they think walking through trees is much better than walking next to a giant wall that reminds people that there really is no getting off this island.

I don't think it actually matters, though. Prison is prison, no matter what it looks like.

I'm in the deepest part of the forest now, where the tree canopy is so dense and moss so heavy that barely any rain penetrates the leaves. But that means that very little light filters through them, either, so I once again use my flashlight to illuminate the way as I wind through the thick expanse of trees. Despite the light, shivers work their way down my spine as the leaves rustle around me.

It's just birds taking shelter from the rain, I tell myself. *Maybe even a few bats discombobulated by the preternaturally dark sky. Either way, it's just nature. Nothing to get freaked out about.*

But my heart rate picks up a little anyway.

I speed up a bit more, but before I can go more than a few steps, a wild gust of wind sweeps through the trees above me. It's so hard and fast that I swear I can hear branches cracking. My stomach flips sickly. That strange hollowness spreads out from my midsection to my limbs, and even though I tell myself I'm being ridiculous, I can't help but glance over my shoulder.

There's nothing there but tree trunks and shadows. Absolutely nothing to worry about.

And still unease dances around me like the wind.

I skirt the tree that Caspian, Jude, Carolina, and I built a treehouse in when we were little. The treehouse is long gone, but the blocks of wood we'd hammered into the tree trunk for a ladder are still there.

I let my fingers run over one of them as I walk by, memories of my cousin welling up inside me. Her face dances in front of my eyes, and I finally admit to myself that she's the real reason I don't like coming through this forest anymore—not the fact that it borders teacher housing. Carolina and I spent so much of our childhood playing together in this forest that walking through it is filled with the ghosts of what used to be.

Sometimes I miss her so much I can barely stand it. Not getting to say goodbye, not even knowing she was dead until Remy came to tell us... Some days it really is unbearable.

A sob wells up in my throat, but I swallow it. I've already shown way too much weakness today. It stops now.

I weave around the large rock in the middle of the path—and totally ignore the fact that it's got all of our initials carved into it. Three sets of C.C.s and a J.A. from that day we were playing hide-and-seek and all got lost in the forest for hours.

All of a sudden, the picture of the four of us shimmers in front of me like a movie. Nine-year-old Carolina crouches down to carve her initials first while the three of us wait excitedly for our turn. But then something nebulous and icy dances across the nape of my neck, and the image dissipates like mist.

I turn away, jumping over the large hole in the path that's been there as long as I've been alive. As I do, I refuse to think about the way Jude used to swear it was made by a meteor.

Old memories are just that—old. They don't have any bearing on—

Something suddenly whooshes by my face, so close that I can feel the chill of it brush against the hot skin of my cheek.

At first, I think it's a ghost, but when I look around, no one is there.

I shrug it off—probably just the wind—and keep going. But I've barely made it twenty yards before another one slides by on the right, its coldness slicing my biceps like a knife.

I whirl around to see what it is—and where it went—but it's gone, too.

What the actual fuck?

Every hair on the back of my neck is standing straight up now, and I spin in a circle, flashlight lifted, as I scan the darkness.

But there's nothing in front of me but inky blackness and the crooked oaks.

Maybe it was some freaked-out bird, I tell myself as I keep walking. *Or perhaps a ghost?*

Definitely nothing to worry about.

But that doesn't stop a bead of sweat from rolling down my spine any more than it keeps my heart from hammering in my chest. Still, I keep moving, a little slower now that I'm sweeping the flashlight all around the forest in front of me, but moving all the same.

It's just a little bit farther, I remind myself. *Just a half mile or so more and I'll be out of here.*

Not a big deal.

At least not until a strange, staticky sound fills the air around me.

CHAPTER TWENTY-SIX

DIS-ASSEMBLY

I whirl around again, trying desperately to figure out where the sound is coming from. But, again, there's nothing but trees. Nothing but shadows.

Until something else darts by my face, so close that the cold of it burns against my temple.

The static buzz gets worse, more discordant, as an ancillary sound tries to break through it. I listen closely, hoping something will help me figure out what's going on. But then the extra sound disappears just as quickly as it came, and it's plain static again.

My jog turns into a full-blown sprint through the piney undergrowth, my breath coming in choppy pants and pure adrenaline rushing through my veins. But I'm still not fast enough, because moments later there's a quick flicker by my left ear.

It disappears as quickly as it comes, trailing that strange sparkly substance I saw in the dungeon. I give the glimmer a wide berth, but another flicker flashes right in front of me.

I have one second to register a large guy in a suit before I'm running through him.

I brace for the icicles, but they don't come. Instead, that weird feeling happens again, where everything inside of me feels like it's speeding up and slamming against the inside of my skin.

I jerk my arms close to my body, wrapping them around me as I force myself to keep moving, keep running as another sound breaks through the static.

This time it's loud enough for me to realize it's a scream before the static swallows it again.

My stomach is jumping now, and cold sweat mingles with the rain on my skin as I push forward. I'm almost there.

This time it's a laugh that breaks through, a full-blown cackle that feels like it's directed straight at me—and mocking my hopes of safely getting out of this hellscape.

When an entity moves past me now, it does more than just slide across my arm or face. It wraps itself around me, spinning me around—once, twice—before undulating away, trailing more of the stardust.

I swallow a scream, but that doesn't matter because the whole forest suddenly fills with screams breaking through the static all around me, until the sticky air turns into a cacophony of pain and terror that I pull deeper inside my lungs with every inhalation.

The moans turn to laughs—fast and high-pitched and terrifying in a way that has my already upset stomach pitching and rolling inside me.

It's just the ghosts, Clementine. No big deal. They won't hurt you, not really.

Another eerie wail, another screeching laugh, break through the discordant buzz that fills the air. Another slither of something—this time against my bare knee.

Cold, followed by more agony. Bigger needles this time, jabbing into me over and over again.

This cut and run is something new and absolutely terrifying.

The pain is worse, yes, but it's so much more than that.

It's the constant static creeping inside my head.

The tortured screams that come from nowhere and disappear the same way.

The targeted attacks I can't run away from no matter how hard I try.

All I can do is push through and try not to falter. But it's easier said than done.

This time, when the cackles break through the noise, they're a chorus instead of a single vocalization. They echo around me, filling the air—and my head—as they reach inside me and grab on with razor-sharp claws.

Agony explodes inside me at the first scrape, and that's it. That's. It.

Ghosts, flickers, whatever the hell these things are, I'm getting the fuck out of here. Now.

I race through the forest, my feet flying over the uneven terrain as terror turns into a wild beast within me. Only the faster I run, the louder the static—and the shrieks—get. Soon they're all I can hear as my feet hit the ground over and over again. But then the cold comes back, and so does the strange feeling that I'm ruthlessly being turned inside out. Pain blossoming wherever they touch as the edge of the forest beckons.

I push forward, determined to make it through the sensory assault, determined to make it to—

I scream as pain—bitter and cold—slams into my back like a fist. I have one second of shocked disbelief as the subsequent agony ripples from the back of my head to my heels. And then it's punching right through me, swallowing every ounce of me for one second, two—turning me into something that doesn't even feel human anymore—before exploding out the front of me.

I stumble, my breath bellowing in and out like a train whistle. I bend over to brace my hands on my knees as I try to catch my breath and figure out what just happened to me.

But what's left of my fight-or-flight instinct takes over, and my body propels itself toward the last line of trees in front of me. The moans turn to high-pitched screams all around me, but I don't stop. I can't.

I run as hard and as fast as I can, throwing myself out of the trees like a running back throws himself at the goal line, desperate for a win. As I do, one last flicker appears in front of me. I arch backward, determined to avoid it, but it's too late. I fall straight through a tall, scary woman dressed in black lace. As soon as I touch her, she wraps herself around me, holding me tight as she somehow turns my insides into a vibrating mass of knife-edged molecules.

Desperate, terrified, I wrench myself through—and away from her.

Then I use the last burst of strength I've got to twist in midair before slamming to the ground and rolling, just as I finally break through the tree line.

The moment I clear the forest, there's silence. The static stops, as do the screams, the laughs, and the strange vibrations inside of me. The pain vanishes with them, so quickly that everything feels like nothing more than the product of my overactive imagination.

I'm trembling as I push to my feet, stumbling several steps away from the forest while my breath lodges in my throat and my heart continues to beat like a metronome at high speed. I shine my flashlight at the forest, but I can't see anything move—not even the leaves or branches. The rain has stopped, and even the wind has died down for the moment.

Weird. Very, very, *very* weird.

I turn the light on myself, searching my chest, my hands, my legs—everywhere I felt pain slice through me—but there's nothing new there. No blood, no bruises, not even any new tears to my shirt. Nothing that wasn't already there from before. It's as if everything that just happened...didn't.

But it *did* happen. I know it did. I heard it. I felt it, on my skin and deep inside myself. Something was in that forest, something I've never felt or heard or seen before.

I suck air into my lungs and tell myself that it's over. That whatever just attacked me isn't going to come after me again. But saying that and believing it are two different things, and I keep glancing over my shoulder at the trees as I suck in huge, noisy gulps of oxygen.

Determined to get myself as far away from here as I can, before whatever *that* was comes back, I turn left and half run, half stumble along the rocky path that borders the teachers' quarters. And I don't stop until I finally make it to the round, six-story-tall former hotel annex that is now the residence hall for underclassmen.

I take a few seconds to get my breath back, then scan my eye and head inside, bracing myself for whatever I'm going to find.

"There you are!" Luis pounces on me the second I walk through the door, his silver eyes flashing. "Where have you been?"

"Later," I answer out of the corner of my mouth, because he's not the only one whose attention I've attracted. My mother is watching me from her spot at the center of the common room…and she doesn't look happy.

Then again, neither does anyone else in the building.

The hallway finally ends in the center of the building, where the main floor common room is located. Because the building itself is circular—a common design in hurricane-prone areas in the late 1800s—each of the six floors is built around a central room, with the student dorm rooms forming a full circle around it.   .

On the upper floors, that central room is divided into study rooms, a small library, a TV room—though the TVs have long ago been stolen out of all of them—and a small snack kitchen. But down here, on the first floor, the room has pretty much been left alone since it functioned as a room for guests who actually paid for the privilege of being here.

The pale-blue paint from its heyday is chipped and peeling.

The lobby chairs and sofas are stained and torn in some places, lopsided in others.

And, like the rest of the school, half of the lightbulbs are burned out. Here, the dead bulbs are ensconced with stained glass lampshades depicting sea creatures. Somehow the remnants of over-the-top resort decorations just make the building look even sadder and more neglected.

A vibe that's only helped along by the eerie dimness that fills the place, along with the strange darkness from outside leaking in through the hallways that bisect the circle.

In preparation for the meeting, my uncle Christopher has had the furniture moved against the walls and filled the center of the room with enough chairs to fit the whole student body. Most of the chairs are full by now—I'm definitely late to the party—and the whole place is filled with a restless energy that has my nerves on high alert.

Because this kind of energy almost always leads to trouble, even without the threat of a major storm hanging over the island. Something that is proven out by the harried way my aunts and uncles are running between groups of students, trying to catch things at the skirmish level before they develop into full-blown wars. My mom—who has changed into a tracksuit the same bright red as my uniform shorts—stands in the center of the room watching the clock and waiting for it to count down to the exact second she can begin the meeting.

Apparently, keeping the peace while also crowding a couple hundred paranormals with control issues, bad attitudes, and a penchant for violence into a tight space isn't as easy as it sounds. Not to mention it's a full moon tonight, which always makes the student body act wilder than usual.

"I got us seats over here," Luis hisses, handing me a towel to dry off as he leads the way to two chairs that are as far from my mother—and the other students—as we can get.

But before I can take more than a few steps in that direction, my aunt Claudia comes rushing toward me. "Clementine, thank goodness you're here!" she calls, her normally high-pitched voice made even more so by the stress of the situation.

Her blue eyes are twice their normal size, and her towering red bun quivers a little more with each second that passes. But before I can say anything, Caspian appears out of nowhere, in full-blown super helpful nephew mode. "What can we do, Aunt Claudia?" he asks.

"Oh, you dear sweet boy." She pats his cheek, then points to Uncle Christopher, who is currently standing in front of a pissed-off mermaid who is shouting at two even more pissed-off fae. And while they're currently keeping their cool—barely—Uncle Christopher is trapped. Because the second he walks away, someone is getting punched. And once that happens, anything goes. "Why don't you go see what can be done with that...situation?"

But Caspian's already gone, racing toward his father to see how he can help. He weaves through the crowd like someone who's been doing it his whole life...because he has.

On the other side of the room, Uncle Carter is locked in a battle of his own—with what looks like a newly formed pack of wolf shifters, all of whom are circling him like they're about to go for his jugular.

"Clementine, sweetheart—"

I sigh. "On it, Aunt Claudia."

"You aren't really getting in the middle of that, are you?" Luis asks, alarmed, as I head toward my uncle. "Those guys are bad news."

"What am I supposed to do? Let them eat him?"

"One bite and they'll spit him out," he says with a shrug. "Plus, if they nibble on him a little, maybe he'll figure out that it's not a lot of fun and think twice about sending you into the menagerie again." Part of me agrees with Luis, but still, responsibility—and my mother's eyes—rest heavy on me, so I make my way to Uncle Carter. But by the time I get close to him, he's got one wolf on the ground and has already set his sights on a second. Wolves may be tough, but my money is on a pissed-off manticore any day. Especially when the wolves can't shift...

I head back toward Luis, but before I can get there, my grandparents float in.

"Someone's got to help with this mess. These kids are looking feral." Grandpa Claude drifts by me. "Look out for the angry vamp at four o'clock. She's spoiling for a fight."

A glance over my shoulder tells me he's talking about Izzy and, well, he's not wrong.

"I'm more worried about the dragons in the corner," Grandma says as she hovers beside me. "When I went by there earlier, they looked like they were up to no good."

"I don't know why Camilla thought an assembly was a good idea right now." My grandfather shakes his head.

"I'm going to go check on those leopards," my grandmother answers. "They look like they're going to be a problem."

I jump out of the way as she passes to avoid the painful chill that accompanies any ghost's touch—even hers. After what just happened in the forest, that's the last thing I need.

And end up crashing straight into someone's back.

"Sorry," I start, automatically looking up. "I wasn't..."

My voice trails off as I realize that I'm not going to have to find Jude after all. Because he's just found me.

CHAPTER TWENTY-SEVEN

THE NOT SO CALM
BEFORE THE STORM

For a moment, I don't say anything. I can't. I know I chased after him in the storm, know I had a million different things to say to him when he walked away from me, but right now I can't remember any of them. And maybe that's for the best—it's not like I want to have this conversation in the middle of the common room anyway.

So I settle for saying, "Excuse me," and then stepping to the side to pass.

Except Jude doesn't take the out. Instead, he sidesteps with me, so that we stay face-to-face. Exactly where I don't want to be right now.

"What are you doing?" I ask, and this time I try to shoulder him aside.

But Jude is immovable at the best of times. When he's actively attempting to hold his ground, nothing short of a forklift could budge him.

"What happened?" he asks.

"Besides your standard kiss-and-ditch?"

He shoves a frustrated hand through his hair. "That's not what I mean. You look—"

"Pissed?" I interrupt.

"Shaken," he answers, scanning my face. "What happened after I left?"

"Nothing." Again, I try to move past him. And again, I have

absolutely no success. I swear, it feels like he's grown even larger, though I don't know how that's possible.

"Kumquat."

For the second time in as many minutes, my eyes meet his swirling, multicolored gaze. And though the last thing I want is to feel something right now, what I want doesn't seem to matter. Because the moment our eyes connect, a shiver of something I refuse to give any more credence to works its way through me.

But I shove it back down.

He kissed me and blew me off…again. No way am I letting my guard down a third time.

"Get out of my way, Dear Prudence."

His eyes darken, but he stands his ground. "Tell me what has you looking so freaked out and I will."

My heart—and my breathing—speed up, and my fingers suddenly itch with the need to reach out and smooth away the crease by the side of his mouth. It's a little bit dimple and mostly worry line, and it's been there since he was a kid.

The more concerned he is about something, the deeper that little groove gets. And right now, it's looking really deep.

Not that I care, I remind myself as I shove my hands into my sodden pockets.

"I'm *fine*," I tell him.

"Remind me." He lifts a brow. "What does fine stand for again?"

I roll my eyes at him, mostly because he's right. At the moment, I feel exactly like Aerosmith described in that song. But considering Jude's the one who's caused a lot of those feelings, I'm not exactly in the mood to share with him.

"It stands for okay," I shoot back. "Which I am. Or I will be, if you would get the hell out of my way."

Jude's jaw tightens, but before he can say anything else, my mother blows three times on the gold whistle she wears whenever she's on headmaster duty—which is the signal here at Calder Academy for everyone to sit down and shut up.

"I need to go," I tell Jude, and this time when I try to push past him, he lets me. But I can feel his eyes following me as Luis slides up beside me and steers me toward our seats.

"What was *that*?" Luis asks, brows arched.

But I just shake my head—partly because I don't want to talk about Jude and partly because I don't actually know *what* that was.

What I do know is that having Jude look at me like that makes me feel all kinds of things I'm better off not feeling—especially since I'm pretty sure he doesn't want to reciprocate them. I can't help wishing we could go back to the way things were, when we just ignored each other.

At least I knew where we stood.

"All right, everyone." My mother's voice booms through every corner of the round, cavernous room as she takes hold of the microphone my uncle Carter holds out to her. "I have some updates on the current storm as well as some instructions I'm going to need you to follow. I know the conditions aren't ideal, but if we stick together, we can get through this."

She pauses for a moment, and Luis leans over to me. "Updates?" he repeats, brows raised. "It's going to rain a lot. What else is there to say?"

"I'm assuming she didn't get the hurricane sirens out for nothing."

He shrugs, waves a hand. "Hurricane, shmurricane. Sounds like a tempest in a teapot to me."

"Yeah, until your cottage is underwater."

"Hey, I know how to doggy paddle." He grins.

Before I can think up a suitable response to that ridiculous quip, the room around us grows quiet and my mom continues.

"The storm we're getting right now is just foreshadowing of bigger things to come. I've spent the afternoon communicating with several expert meteorologists and paranormal weather services, and they have all determined the same thing. This island and Calder Academy are directly in the path of a major, category-five hurricane—one whose current circumference is about two hundred and fifty miles wide. Normally, we would just ride it out and not worry—our safeguards are the best there are. But there is concern that this storm is too powerful for our regular protection spells—or any spells, for that matter."

A frisson of unease runs through me as the room once again erupts into dozens of side conversations. Category-five hurricanes are bad—really bad. And being sitting ducks on an island in the middle of one usually means a whole lot of destruction.

I hate being here—hate the rules and the regulations, the unfairness of basically being born into a juvenile detention center—but that doesn't mean I want the whole place to be leveled.

I see genuine panic on more than a few faces. They're whispering uneasily to each other instead of joking around or gearing up for a fight, as they were a few minutes ago. And like me, they're staying relatively quiet so they can hear whatever Mom says next before totally and completely freaking out.

This time my mom doesn't wait for the conversations to die down before continuing. Instead, she plows straight ahead, steely eyed and confident as she spins to face each part of the circle in turn. "Right now, we're experiencing the outer rainbands of this very large storm, but this is just the beginning. It will move ashore, and it will bring with it what we are afraid are catastrophic rain and wind—as well as some dangerous rogue waves."

She holds a hand up to stall the inevitable explosion her words are going to cause, and it works. Every student in the room, though tense and on the edge of their seat, holds their tongue. And as the whole room watches her, as close to spellbound as this group gets, I can't help but feel a tiny spurt of pride.

My mother is impossible in a lot of ways. She is hard to talk to, hard to understand, hard to...well, just hard. There's very little give in her, and that makes being her daughter exceptionally difficult at times. But it's that same hardness that has her standing up in the middle of this room, completely calm and in control as she delivers devastating news. And it is that same hardness that keeps everyone in the room calm, because they know that somehow—she's got this.

More, she's got us.

In a school like this, where trust is in short supply and a huge percentage of the student body has been screwed over by what feels like the entire world, that kind of trust is impossible to buy. They might not trust her to give them a fair shake if they act up, but they trust her with their lives. And in our world, that's a hell of a lot more important—even if there isn't a giant hurricane on the horizon.

"Surprisingly, the storm has come up very fast, which is why we haven't had news for you sooner," she continues, sweeping the room with her gaze so she can look as many students in the eye as possible. "But the emergency response team and I have spent the last two hours putting together a plan to get us all through this safely."

My uncles Carter and Christopher step forward at her words, along with my aunts Carmen and Claudia. "We're actually very lucky," she continues once they're standing beside her. "Because the storm has stalled out in the southern Gulf of Mexico. Now we don't know how long it will stay there before it begins moving forward again, but it gives us the hours we need to prepare the island." She pauses. "And to evacuate."

CHAPTER TWENTY-EIGHT

WHEN LIFE HANDS YOU MONSTERS, DON'T STOP TO DRINK LEMONADE

For a second, I'm certain that I've heard wrong. My mother could not possibly have said that we're going to evacuate. In its entire eighty-year history, Calder Academy has *never* evacuated.

Not through Carla or Camille.

Not through Gilbert or Andrew.

Not even through Harvey or Rita.

All of them devastating hurricanes. All of them barely a blip on Calder Academy's radar.

It's one of the many perks of being magic, my aunt Claudia always says. The students may be banned from accessing our powers, but we have enough witches, warlocks, and other powerful paranormals on staff to create barriers that withstand even the toughest storms...and other situations.

So what does it say about this particular hurricane that even my mother actually thinks we need to evacuate? Especially since it's only been a couple of hours since she told me she'd never let me off this island?

For one moment, pure, unadulterated joy sweeps through me at the thought of finally—finally—getting out of here. But then I have to wonder what kind of disaster would actually drive my mother to take such a drastic step...

As the decibel level in the room starts to rise, I pull out my phone to look up information on the storm myself. I'm not surprised when a quick glance tells me most of the people around me are doing the exact same thing.

What is surprising is there isn't much out there on the storm yet. It's named Gianna, it's in the Gulf of Mexico, and it's huge, but that's about all there is to find. Maybe because it's so new?

I don't actually buy that excuse, but I can't find a better one before my uncle Carter leans his nearly seven-foot frame down to speak into the microphone my mother is still holding.

"It's going to be okay," he says in the deep, reassuring voice I remember from my childhood. But then I remember him using this same voice—this same tone—the day they took Carolina away, and it turns into nails on a chalkboard. "I know this is unusual, but this is only a precaution, and we will protect you and the island the way we always have. But this storm is strong enough that we don't want to take any chances. Your safety is our highest priority, and right now, that means evacuating you to a large installation about a hundred miles from Galveston, where we can guarantee you'll be safe."

"Holy shit," Luis mutters as he slouches down farther in his chair. "That doesn't sound ideal."

"None of this sounds ideal," I answer, slouching down with him. Because while there's a part of me that is overjoyed at the idea of actually getting off this island for the first time in my life—it's what I've wanted for as long as I can remember—there's another, bigger part that's waiting for the catch. Because with my family, there's always a catch.

And if anyone thinks they're just going to take a bunch of dangerous paranormals off this isolated, very protected island and plop us down in the middle of a hotel somewhere, then they don't know my family— especially my mother—very well.

It's much more likely that she'll ship us all off to the Aethereum itself for the foreseeable future.

Just the thought of ending up at the same deadly prison where my vibrant, beautiful cousin spent the last years of her too-short life has my blood running cold. A glance across the room to where Remy is sitting with, but definitely not talking to, a very annoyed-looking

Izzy tells me I'm not the only one whose thoughts are running in this direction.

A feeling that's made even more abundantly clear when his voice—with his New Orleans accent out in full, Cajun force—rings through the rotunda. "Installation?" He looks as skeptical as he sounds. "Exactly what kind of installation are we talking about here?"

Before my uncle can answer, a violent howl of wind sends the trees outside the dorm into an absolute frenzy.

Their branches shake.

Their leaves skitter against each other, causing a creepy rustling to fill the air around us.

And their trunks bend so far over that I can't help wondering if they'll just give up and break in half.

As I watch them through one of the room's large picture windows, a feeling of foreboding creeps over me, sliding over the hair on the back of my neck and slithering slowly, steadily, into my very pores. I try to figure it out, to put my finger on exactly what it is that's making me so uneasy, but I don't have words for the feeling.

I just know I don't like it—even before a woman in a long, pink nightgown walks by the window. She's barefoot, and her long hair is hanging in wet clumps around her face as she lifts her hands in a futile effort to keep the rain out of her eyes.

My mind starts to race with questions like who is she and what is she doing out there in this weather before she turns and I realize she's very, very pregnant.

I jump to my feet, start to race across the room toward her. But she disappears before I've taken more than a couple of steps, and I realize she wasn't real about the same time I realize everyone is staring at me.

Luis reaches out and grabs my hand before gently tugging me back into my seat. But not before my mother's annoyed gaze slams into me.

I have no doubt I'm going to pay for my little outburst later.

"Are you okay?" Luis asks, concerned. "Are you sick or something?"

"It's fine. I just saw a—" I break off as I realize the woman I saw had brown hair. And she was wearing a pink nightgown. Which means she couldn't have been a ghost—they're always gray. But how did she disappear like that, then? And who is she? It's not like strangers randomly wander on to our little island at the best of times, let alone during a hurricane.

Before I can figure out what's going on, my mother's confident voice fills the room. "We've found a warehouse to rent in Huntsville, Texas. We've already contacted a local coven who has begun setting it up for us." She pauses and once again attempts to look as many of us in the eye as she can. "Of course, things will be a little different there, but that's a bridge we'll cross when we get to it. The important thing to remember is that your safety and security are of the utmost importance to us. I assure you every precaution is being taken to make sure things go exactly as planned."

I've had seventeen years to grow fluent in mom speak, and I know what she's actually saying is, *We don't trust any of you, even in the middle of a massive storm, and we're going to lock your asses up nice and tight to make sure no one escapes or does anything else that we deem unacceptable.*

The feeling of trepidation inside me grows, even as I continue to stare out the window, trying to catch another glimpse of the pink-nightgowned woman.

My worry must show, though, because Luis's eyebrows shoot up when I glance at him. "Why do you look so freaked out? I thought you'd be jumping for joy."

Me too. I've been waiting my entire life for an opportunity like this. A chance to see someplace, anyplace, else. More, a chance to never, ever come back. So why am I so inexplicably nervous?

"I don't know," I tell him. "But something feels...off."

"It's Calder Academy." He rolls his eyes. "Something always feels off."

"Because something always *is* off," I shoot back. "And I'm pretty sure this is no exception."

"What do you mean?" he asks.

Before I can figure out an answer, my mother continues, "I need the cooperation of each and every one of you for the next few hours."

She pauses, holding up a hand to stave off the expected objections— but for once, none are forthcoming. Instead, every student in the place just stares at her, waiting for whatever comes next. Which is more than a little terrifying in its own way, considering cooperation isn't exactly our strong suit.

My mom looks as surprised as I feel, but she recovers quickly. "After things are set up in the warehouse, the coven there is going to join with our security team here and create a portal that we can evacuate through at six a.m. tomorrow morning. We should all be safely at the warehouse by seven a.m. at the latest."

"Why are we waiting so long?" someone calls from my left. A quick glance identifies her as Jude's friend, Mozart. The dragon shifter shoves a hand through her silky dark hair as she continues, "If the hurricane is as bad as you say it is, shouldn't we get out of here now?"

My mother's blue eyes flash dangerously at her words, but I know it's not the actual question that pissed her off. It's the fact that Mozart— that anyone—has the audacity to inquire about her plan.

"As I said," she starts, her voice as dry as ice, "the storm has stalled out, and that buys us several hours. The best projections say that the storm won't reach us for another eighteen to thirty hours, so that gets us out of here in plenty of time. But we need to make sure the warehouse is ready so you are safe there as well. It's no use taking you from one dangerous situation to another."

Mozart raises a dark brow. "You could just give us our powers back and let us find our own ways out of here."

One of the new wolf shifters—a blond guy that I haven't met yet— shoots her a fuck-you look. "We can't all fly, jackass."

Mozart returns the look with interest. "I'm not exactly sure that's a downside to my plan."

"No one is flying out of here. Or swimming. Or doing anything besides following the plan." My mother's annoyed voice booms through the microphone. "The portal will be ready by six tomorrow morning. Until then, we have some tasks we need each of you to accomplish."

She hands the microphone to my aunt Carmen, who takes over with a huge smile that doesn't quite meet her blue eyes. I'm not sure if it's because she disagreed with my mother's plan and lost like she usually does or if she's more worried than she wants to let on. But something's not right.

"I know this is a lot to take in," she tells us in her low, soothing voice. "But everything is going to be okay. We'll evacuate, let the storm pass, and be back here in just a few days."

"If there's anything left standing." Jean-Jacques snickers from his spot right in front of her. "Maybe the storm will blow this whole damn place apart."

"It won't," she assures him before turning to look at the rest of us. "And to that end, the tasks we have for you will ensure that remains the case. We'd like all of you to pitch in to help get the school ready to withstand the hurricane. We need sandbags filled and lined up to create a barrier against storm surge, windows covered with plywood, trees and bushes trimmed so they won't go through any roofs or windows, as well as a few other tasks."

Groans fill the room at her words, but they're half-hearted at best, and steely looks from my mom and Uncle Christopher shut them down quickly.

"There are tables on each floor of the dorm, manned by faculty members, who will help you with the next steps," my aunt Carmen continues. "Seniors, stay where you are for a few more minutes. Underclassmen, head up to your rooms and pack a small bag for the evacuation. Then report to the table on your floor to receive your group assignment. When complete, report back here and check in to receive a box dinner that the kitchen witches have prepared." She scans the room. "Any questions?"

There aren't any, so she finishes with a quick thank-you for our help before dismissing us.

"So what exciting task do you think we'll get stuck with?" Luis mutters as we wait for the ninth through eleventh graders to file out, and I swear, if he slinks down any farther in his chair, the boy will be on the floor.

"As long as it's not stocking up the chricklers' food supply, I couldn't care less." The scratch on my shoulder twinges at the thought, and part of me can't believe I just got it yesterday. It feels like days have passed since then.

"No shit," Luis replies with a snort. "Even your mom couldn't be that cruel."

"I think we both know that's not true."

"Okay, seniors, thank you for your patience." Uncle Christopher takes the microphone. "Since you're all out at the cottages, we've centralized your task tables in here." He points to four tables stationed around the room, each with letters corresponding with a range of last names. "Report to your table and get your group assignment. Once it's completed, you can come back here to pick up your dinner before heading back to your room to pack a bag and get some sleep before we portal out of here. Any questions?"

A few queries get called out, but the rest of us are already moving. The faster we get this done, the higher our chances of beating the next rainband.

I don't mind boarding up windows or trimming trees, but I'd prefer to not do it in the pouring rain. Despite the beach towel Luis handed me earlier, my clothes and hair are still really wet from the last round.

Except, when I get my assignment, I realize it doesn't matter if it's still raining or not. Because it turns out I was right and Luis was wrong.

My mother really can be that cruel.

CHAPTER TWENTY-NINE

FEELING DOWN IN THE DUNGEONS

"You can't be serious." Luis looks pissed as we walk over to the east door, where my assignment says to meet the rest of the admin building group.

"At least I won't be by myself for once," I answer. "More people equals less of a chance I get bit."

"By the chricklers, maybe." He snorts. "What about the rest of the creatures?"

"I feel like the theory still stands."

"Even the ones that get riled up with more people around?" he shoots back. "I can't believe they gave you the menagerie. Does your family hate you or something?"

"I think so, yes." But my answer has nothing to do with the task I've been assigned and everything to do with who is standing next to the east door, where we're supposed to meet everyone else assigned to the admin building. Because, as the crowd thins out, I can very clearly see Jude, Mozart, Ember, and their other friend, Simon.

This has disaster written all over it.

"Ready to hammer some stuff?" Eva asks as she comes up from behind me and drapes an arm over my shoulders. "We can take some of our angst from last night out on those boards."

"*We* can take it out on the boards," Luis tells her. "Clementine has menagerie duty. Again."

She looks astonished. "For fuck's sake. You've really got to stop pissing in your mom's cornflakes," she tells me with a shake of her head.

"To be fair, Aunt Carmen said she assigned two of us down there. I figure it's got to be Caspian." He's the only other student they let into the menagerie cages, though he almost never has to do anything because I'm always in trouble. "Maybe they'll bite him instead."

"Currently the consensus is it's because Clementine's mother is evil and heinous," Luis volunteers.

"True story," I mutter as I shove my hands in my pockets and stare at the ground. I can feel the weight of Jude's eyes on me, but I refuse to give him the satisfaction of looking up.

I'm ignoring Jude. I'm ignoring Jude. I'm IGNORING Jude.

I'm not looking at him.

I'm not touching him, even by accident.

And I'm damn sure not kissing him. Ever again.

"Hold up. Is *Simon* in our group?" Her voice turns into a squeak as she stops dead. "I can't be in a group with Simon!"

"It's fine," I tell her, putting a hand in the center of her back and propelling her forward. "I'm sure he doesn't even remember what happened."

She shoots me a get-real look. "Everyone remembers."

"It *was* pretty memorable," Luis agrees.

"You're not helping," I hiss before turning back to my roommate. "It's fine, Eva."

"It's so not fine." She shudders. "I still blame it on the fact that he's a siren. I don't even sing normally!"

"That's for sure," Luis snarks.

"Everyone knows it's because he's a siren," I soothe. "I'm sure things like that happen to him all the time."

"Things like that don't happen to *anyone* all the time," she moans.

Luis opens his mouth, but I shoot him a warning look. He snaps it closed with a roll of his eyes.

"It's going to be fine," I tell her again. "I swear. Let's just get over there and get it over with. The sooner we start—"

"The only way it's going to be fine is if you trade places with me and one of the monsters in that damn menagerie eats me."

"You could feed yourself to one of them," Luis recommends. "There's a snake one that would probably do the trick."

Before I can even begin to come up with a response to *that* suggestion, Jude glances over at us. His silver-green and black eyes meet mine, and every word in my head suddenly disappears. All that's left is a cacophony of mismatched emotions swirling around inside me, tangled up so tightly that there's no way I could separate them, even if I wanted to.

Which I don't—at least not here.

Determined not to get caught up in his bullshit yet again today—twice is more than enough to be humiliated by the same guy in a twenty-four-hour period—I force myself to look away. But not before I note the current tumult in Jude's normally inscrutable eyes, all the colors swirling together into a gorgeous puzzle I'm desperate to solve.

Too bad that puzzle is currently missing several important pieces—pieces I want but am beginning to think are lost forever.

Hands still safely in my pockets, I move past Jude without so much as nodding hello. I'm still beyond pissed he kissed me and then walked away like it was nothing. Again. I'm even more pissed that I can't corner him now and demand the answers I spent so much time chasing after him to get.

"Clementine—" he starts, but his use of my real name just annoys me more. It's like he's trying to piss me off all over again.

"Hey, you," Simon says, smiling at me as I walk toward him, his eyes the same shade as the ocean under a full moon. They're as clear as Jude's are tortured.

"Hey." I surreptitiously hold my breath as I move past him—you can never be too careful with sirens—but that just makes him grin more wildly. He knows exactly what effect he has on all of us, and he likes it, no matter what he pretends to the contrary.

As I get closer, he winks at me, but I just roll my eyes in response... and *still* don't take a breath until I'm several yards away from him. That doesn't stop his scent from lingering in the air around me, though—clean and warm and provocative in that way only a siren's can be. Is it any wonder Eva lost her head the last time she had a group project with him?

"Hi, Eva." Simon's voice is innocent as he greets my friend, but there's an amused look in his eyes that says he does, indeed, remember. Even before Mozart starts humming "Kiss the Girl" from *The Little Mermaid*.

Eva's normally bronze cheeks turn the color of our uniform shorts, and she does an abrupt about-face on the heel of her prized red-checkered Vans. "I need a new group!" she calls out to my uncle Carter as he walks by.

"No changes," he tells her sternly, his goatee quivering with resolve. "We have to have a record of where everyone is at all times as the storm moves in."

"She's fine with us," I tell him as I start herding her back toward the others.

He gives me a serious look. "Just make sure you both stay with Jude while you're in the menagerie, Clementine."

Yeah, I'm *so* not doing that. "What about the keys? I only have one to the chrickler enclosure."

"I gave them to Jude," he answers. It looks like he wants to say more, but then my aunt Carmen calls to him, and he starts walking away. But he only takes a few steps before turning back to remind me, "Stay with Jude. He'll keep you safe."

I want to ask why he gave him the keys and not me, but he's already halfway to my aunt.

"Did you hear what Mozart was humming?" Eva whispers once my uncle walks away.

"If it's any consolation, it's not the first time someone has serenaded him with that song," Ember comments from where she's lounging against the wall, arms crossed and legs kicked out in front of her. "And probably not the last."

"I loved it," Simon adds with another smile so sexy it gets my own heart pounding even though I have absolutely no interest in the guy.

He moves closer, and I go back to breathing through my mouth as Luis makes a little choking sound deep in his throat. "Sirens really don't play fair," he growls.

Eva, in the meantime, looks like she's about one second from breaking into song *again*. Her lower lip quivers, and she turns desperate eyes to me.

"Help," she whispers. "I'm begging you."

Jude interrupts with a growl. "Knock it off, Simon."

"I'm just having a conversation," Simon answers, all innocence—as long as you don't pay attention to the wicked gleam in his eyes or the twin spots of color on his own dark-brown cheeks. The guy really is diabolical.

"And this damn hurricane is just a rainstorm." Luis snorts.

"Look, can we get on with it? The sooner we get started with this assignment, the sooner we'll be done," Ember comments as she pushes off the wall.

"I already told you guys I can handle it," Jude tells her, fiddling with the large key ring that will open every pen in the menagerie. "Stay outside like your assignments say, and I'll run down and take care of the menagerie. It won't take me that long."

As if. The guy really is a piece of work.

"To get eaten, maybe," I scoff. "No way are you going into some of those cages alone."

"What cages are these exactly?" Izzy asks as she and Remy walk up to us. Like almost everybody else, he's dressed in fresh, non-uniform clothes—not that I'm jealous over here in my wet, clingy shirt or anything—while her miles of red hair are somehow tucked up into a purple New Orleans Saints cap.

"In the menagerie." Mozart shoots them both a mischievous grin. "Are you guys on admin building duty, too?"

"We are." Remy's dark brows hit his hairline. "But I thought we were just boarding up some windows. We're on petting zoo duty, too?"

"I guess you can call it a zoo, but petting is highly discouraged," Luis tells him.

"Oh, I don't know. You can pet whatever you want down there," Ember tells him as she heads for the nearest door. "As long as you don't mind losing a few fingers."

"More like an entire arm." The smile Simon sends Remy and Izzy is so warm that I get residual tingles, and I'm nowhere near the line of fire.

"For fuck's sake," Jude mutters with an annoyed shake of his head. But he steps between Simon and me, blocking out the siren's glowing smile with his very broad shoulders.

I'd thank him for the rescue, but I'm still too annoyed over what happened between us in the forest. So I just make a face at him before following Ember toward the door.

Besides, Izzy looks more than capable of handling one little siren. Since I'm not so sure about Remy, I hook my arm through his as I pass and tug him along with me. After talking to him in the hallway today, I can't help thinking that I probably shouldn't be heinous to the only other person on the planet who misses Carolina as much as I do.

"I appreciate it," he murmurs in his thick New Orleans accent. "Sirens are trippy as hell."

"I think you mean tricky as hell," I answer as we walk down the hall. A glance over my shoulder—not to mention the heavy weight of his stare burning into the back of my head—tells me Jude is following close behind us, a sour look on his face.

I have no idea what he's got to be sour about, but considering I'm feeling pretty sour myself right now—at least when it comes to him, thanks to his latest kiss and run—I'm more than fine with it.

Eva is walking several feet away, earbuds in and sunglasses on, clearly a ploy to block out Simon. I start to call her over, but before I can, Mozart falls into step on my other side. "Don't worry. You'll get used to him."

"Before or after I serenade him with a Disney love song?" Remy asks dryly.

Mozart shrugs, her sleek black ponytail bouncing with each step. "I'd say the odds are fifty-fifty."

"I feel like I could do a pretty good rendition of 'You've Got a Friend in Me.'" He clears his throat like he's getting ready to practice.

"Hey, I thought Eva's 'Kiss the Girl' was brilliant," Mozart says with a grin that only adds to the wildness in her black ice eyes.

"I've heard better," Ember says with a sniff. "She was a little flat."

"Wow," I say. "Judgy much?"

"I just call it like I hear it," she says with a shrug, then falls back so she can join Jude.

Remy lifts his brows in silent question, but Mozart just shakes her head as we walk outside where it, thankfully, has momentarily stopped raining. "Phoenixes can be...temperamental. I've learned it's better not to ask."

"You're just a coward," Ember shoots back, proving she's still listening even if she doesn't want to be anywhere near us.

"Coward. Genius." Mozart holds her hands in front of her, palms facing the sky, and moves them up and down like weights on a scale. "Pretty sure it's genius."

Ember flips her off as she and Jude pass us.

"See?" She shrugs. "Temperamental."

"One of these days she's going to set you on fire," Jude comments as we make our way through the gate.

"Please," Mozart retorts. "I'm a dragon. *That makes me* the fire, baby! I can take anything she tries to dish out."

"That's pretty big talk considering we don't have any powers right now," Ember calls back to her.

"See?" She makes a face behind Ember's back. "I'm always thinking ahead. Genius."

She's so ridiculous that I can't help cracking up. I try to stop—I don't know her well enough to figure out if it will offend her—but she just grins at me, so I decide it's okay.

It's kind of weird that we've been in school together for three years now and this is definitely the most words she's ever said to me. I'm not sure if that's her choice or mine—from the day I finally figured out he was ditching me, I've given Jude, and his new friends, a wide berth.

They've always seemed a little intimidating, and my years at Calder have taught me that unless you know someone's story, it's always better to let them come to you. But Mozart actually seems pretty cool. So does Simon, as long as I don't look him in the eye or breathe when he's around.

And yes, I am precisely aware of how ridiculous that sounds. But Mozart's comment about getting used to him notwithstanding, sirens aren't easy to be friends with.

"So what exactly *is* a monster menagerie?" Izzy asks. She's the last one through the gate. She doesn't look worried so much as intrigued as it slams shut behind her.

CHAPTER THIRTY

WHY YOU GOTTA BE SO JUDE

"The admins keep a bunch of creatures in the school dungeon," I tell her as we walk toward the admin building. "Most of them aren't exactly what I'd call friendly."

My shoulder picks that exact moment to twinge, as if calling me out on my understatement.

"What kind of creatures are we talking about?" Remy asks, and he doesn't look any more concerned than Izzy. Then again, he did spend almost all of his life in the Aethereum, the scariest prison in the paranormal world. He probably figures a few monsters can't touch what he's already been through. And who knows? Maybe he's right.

Besides, it's not like he's doing anything but nailing plywood over windows. Why should he be concerned?

"We've got chricklers," Jude tells him matter-of-factly. "Along with a bunch of creatures so unusual I don't actually think they have names."

"That's an interesting choice to populate a menagerie with," Remy comments. "I thought I'd heard of everything, so I can't imagine creatures *more* obscure than chricklers." He lifts a brow. "What are chricklers anyway?"

Luis and I exchange a look. "They're special," he says.

"Probably not the kind of project you want to take on," I add.

"I already told you, I've got this," Jude interjects.

"Have you ever even been to the menagerie?" I ask incredulously. "Hearing about what's down there isn't the same as actually being in the cages with them."

He doesn't answer—big surprise—just widens his stride so that he effortlessly pulls several feet ahead of the rest of us.

I start to try to keep up but decide there's no point. It's not a contest—and even if it were, I'd lose. Partly because he's nearly ten inches taller than my own five-foot, nine-inch frame. And partly because I always do when it comes to Jude.

It's pretty much the blueprint of our relationship.

By the time we get to the base of the admin building, my trepidation is sky high. Not just because some of these people actually seem to think they're going into the menagerie with Jude and me—which they definitely should not—and partly because I'm terrified the hallway will have filled back up with ghosts—or, worse, those strange flicker things. And while it's one thing to let Luis or Eva see me trying to deal with them, it's another thing to let Jude and a bunch of people who are pretty much strangers see me that vulnerable.

I mean, it's not like I exactly shout out to everyone on campus that I can see ghosts. I told my mom a few times when I was younger, but she insisted that there are no such things as ghosts. Years on this island have taught me differently, however, and the escalating negativity of her reaction has taught me to keep my weird ability to myself.

A glance at the sky tells me the storm must still be stalled, because the weird lull between rainbands is still holding. The sky is a strange shade of greenish gray that I've never seen before, and while an occasional burst of wind comes through and shakes the hell out of the trees, it disappears almost as suddenly as it showed up.

Maybe, just maybe, I'll get lucky and the ghosts will have decided the creepy snake monster escape from earlier makes the hallway too risky of a hangout.

Hope springs eternal, after all...

"The instructions say to grab wood, hammers, and nails from the station set up next to the groundskeeper's hut," Simon says, looking at the instruction sheet we were all given. "We're supposed to use them to board up the dungeon and first-floor windows from the outside. Then we need to make sure everything inside has enough food and water to last them at least a week."

"They don't really think the storm is going to last that long, do they?" Eva has given up the pretense of her earbuds and has joined the conversation again, though she's definitely staying as far away from Simon as she can get.

"I'm sure they just want to be on the safe side," I soothe. "Depending on how much damage the storm does, it may take us a few days to get back here."

"I don't get this whole thing," Remy comments. "Can't they just portal in to check on the school? Or for that matter, why are we even waiting for boats when they can portal us out? I know student powers are locked down, but surely faculty—"

"They probably weren't thinking about it," I tell him. "We've had a portal block on the island for decades. No one gets around it, not even faculty and staff. Which is probably why they can't portal us out before tomorrow morning—it probably takes that long to bring the block down."

"Really? No one gets around it?" He sounds surprised but also—strangely—not.

"No one," I reiterate. It's the first and most unbreakable rule of Calder Academy. Even my mother takes a boat or a helicopter when she has to leave.

"Seems like a waste of time and effort to me," Remy comments. "I could make it around the world at least twice in the time it takes to get here by boat from the Texas Coast."

"You're that good at portalling?" Eva asks, sounding skeptical. "It usually takes at least a decade for a warlock to—"

"Time wizard," he says with a wink. "Not a warlock."

"Really?" Her eyes go wide as she scoots closer to him. "I've never met one before. What do you—"

She breaks off as a small dagger goes flying by her head and embeds itself in the trunk of a nearby tree.

We all turn to Izzy incredulously, but she just shrugs. "Whoops. It got away from me."

Remy grins in response, but Eva looks pissed. "You're not supposed to have weapons on school grounds, you know!"

"Who's going to stop me?" Izzy asks with the lift of a brow. Then she walks away to retrieve the knife before Eva can answer.

"Can you believe that?" Eva asks Remy and me.

After seeing what she did in class a few hours ago, I absolutely can believe it.

Remy just shrugs as we keep walking. "Don't worry about her, cher," he says. "She's a little feral, but she'll settle down eventually."

As soon as he says it, he shimmies to the right a little—almost like he's expecting the knife that comes flying at him. Either way, he's lucky because all it takes off is a few strands of his shaggy brown hair.

"You know, princess, all you had to do was ask," he calls to Izzy. "If you wanted a lock of my hair for under your pillow that badly, I would have happily given you one."

"Do you really think taunting her is the right way to go here?" I ask as Izzy shows him her very impressive fangs. "She did threaten to cut off a few fingers in English class yesterday."

"Probably not." His wide, larger-than-life grin is completely infectious. "But I like to live dangerously."

"Keep it up and you can die just as dangerously," she snarks as we come to a stop at the admin building's front steps.

"So what's the plan?" I jump in, hoping to distract Izzy enough to keep Remy's fingers—and all the rest of him—in one piece. "Jude and I are taking the menagerie, so I guess you guys just need to divide up the different parts of the admin building, right?"

"Actually, I vote we split up," Simon backs me up as he shoves the instructions into his pocket. "Half of us take the windows while the other half do the food and water. You'll get done with the menagerie quicker that way."

"That's actually a pretty good idea," Mozart agrees, stepping back to take a look at all the huge windows that line the outside of the bottom floors of the admin building. "There's a lot to do—"

"I call windows!" Eva interrupts.

"Me too." Luis throws both of his hands up for emphasis.

I roll my eyes at him in response, but he just grins toothily. "Once a day is enough for anyone. If you had any sense, you'd stay out here, too."

I don't bother to answer him. But then I don't have to, because we both know that's not going to happen. I may be pissed as shit at Jude right now, but I don't actually want him to die at the hands of some pissed-off hydra wannabe. Someone who actually knows what they're doing—and is also a Calder—has to lead the way through the dungeon. I'm pretty sure that's why my mom gave me this assignment.

Either way, there's no way I'm going to send people down there to get hurt while I stay safely up here. Not when I know exactly what's waiting for them down there.

"I'm going into the dungeon," I say. "And Jude's coming with me. That's our side of the plan."

"I'm coming, too," Izzy volunteers. "I want to see this not so petting zoo."

"Me too," Mozart agrees.

Remy steps forward. "I can go or I can stay here—whatever you think will be most helpful."

"Why don't you stay with us?" Eva tells him. "You're so tall, I bet we could get a lot of these windows done in no time."

"I'll do my best," Remy answers with a smiling glance toward Izzy. But the vampire has already turned around, having lost interest in his teasing.

"I think everybody should stay up here. Jude and I can handle this."

I wait for Jude to say something—or at least step forward—but he doesn't say a word. When I glance toward him, I realize that's because I've been doing such a good job not looking at him that I totally missed something really important.

Namely, that he's already gone.

I whirl around just in time to see the main door of the admin building closing behind the big, overly heroic jerk.

Too bad he doesn't have a clue what he's getting himself into.

CHAPTER THIRTY-ONE

LET'S NOT DO THE MONSTER MASH

"**W**here's he going so fast?" Izzy asks. Again, she doesn't sound concerned, just mildly curious.

"To get himself in trouble," I answer as I take off toward the same door Jude disappeared through. I'm vaguely aware of Izzy and Mozart following me at a more sedate pace, but I don't pay a lot of attention to them. I'm too worried about what trouble Jude's going to get himself into before I can reach him.

The fact that one of the others is blasting The Weeknd's "Save Your Tears" from their phone as they get down to work isn't lost on me, either. I'm pretty sure it should be the theme song of our friendship—or lack thereof, considering it feels like I've spent the entire day chasing after the jerk.

What the hell is he even thinking? I know he keeps saying he can handle things, but he doesn't have a clue what he's supposed to handle. I mean, what does the guy actually think he's going to do all alone against a bunch of pissed-off monsters with attitude problems? They hate rain almost as much as ghosts do. I learned that last year...the hard way.

My stomach clenches at the thought of what I'm about to walk into—monster and spirit wise—but I ignore it. Nothing I can do about it at this point besides hope for the best.

Not that the best is ever an option here at Calder Academy. The most we can usually hope for is *not* the worst. Not only can you count on the worst possible thing to happen here at the worst possible moment, but you can also expect that worst thing to be murderous... or at least dangerous as all fuck. On the plus side, when you go into a situation with expectations that low, anything that isn't a total shit show feels like a success story.

I make the turn into the stairwell that leads to the dungeon, and my stomach sinks even more. I wasn't fast enough. Jude has already made his way down the steps into the bowels of the building.

I try to cover up my worry, but Mozart must see it, because she puts a reassuring hand on my shoulder. "Don't worry, Clementine. If he says he's got it, he's got it."

"I'm not worried." But the lie is barely out of my mouth when a new round of thunder booms overhead, shaking the walls and causing the lone lightbulb in the hallway down below—Uncle Carter must have finally replaced it when he chased down the hydra wannabe earlier— to flicker.

Of course, the storm decides to resume right at this very moment.

As if my thoughts conjured it up, a giant screech sounds from down below. For a second, I think the giant snake monster has gotten loose again, but then I hear the clang of a lock followed by the slam of a door and realize it's much, much worse.

Jude has actually gone into the cage with the snake monster.

Oh shit.

I speed up, taking the last of the stairs two at a time as I imagine what that thing's snake fingers could do to him.

Strangle him.

Impale him.

Rip him limb from limb.

On the plus side, the attack from earlier has ensured the ghosts stay gone, but I'm so freaked out about Jude that I barely notice. Instead, I race down the hall, heart pounding and horror twisting inside of me. But by the time I reach the snake monster's unchained pen, Jude is already sliding back out of it, slow and unconcerned. Like he just fed his favorite puppy instead of a wild, bloodthirsty monster.

"Told you he'd be fine," Mozart whispers in my ear as she moves to catch up to me. "Jude's got a way with monsters," she adds as he walks toward the next pen.

"You couldn't possibly have fed him that fast," I tell him as I hustle over. "I didn't even hear a sound from in there. And I know from personal experience it gets very, very loud when it's upset."

Jude gives me a sharp look, one I return with interest until he finally just shrugs. "I didn't even see it when I went in. It must have been sleeping somewhere in the enclosure."

"You want me to believe it was sleeping and you just walked in there, dumped a bunch of that damn sparkly kibble, and it didn't so much as stir?" I know I sound skeptical, but come on. I've been stuck dealing with these damn creatures since sophomore year. They change out pretty regularly—my mom gets extra money from boarding monsters short term—and none of them is easy to deal with. None of them.

But Jude just waltzes in like it's no big deal? Fills up a week's worth of food and water dishes and waltzes back out? It makes no sense.

"I don't know if he stirred or not, Satsuma. I didn't see him. At all."

I narrow my eyes at the nickname and pretend—even to myself— that I'm annoyed he's back to calling me random, citrusy names.

"I guess not. But I don't suggest you try just waltzing in there like that with some of the other monsters, *Eleanor Rigby.*"

"I'm not worried." He nods toward the end of the hall. "Why don't you leave those to me while the three of you deal with the chricklers?"

"You don't really think I'm going to let you do all these pens alone, do you? We'll split up—divide and conquer. And then we can all head into the chrickler enclosure together. It's definitely a job for more than one person. The more the unmerrier."

Jude doesn't look impressed, and I realize it's the first time he's shown anything but his regular poker face in reference to this job. There's something going on with him, and I'm bound and determined to figure it out. I don't have an answer—yet—but if the last few years have taught me anything, it's that whenever something is up with Jude, I end up getting hurt.

No way am I going to let that happen anymore.

"I have a better idea," he suggests. "How about a compromise?"

I laugh, though there's no humor in the sound. "That was my compromise."

"Okay. Then how about a bet?"

"A bet?" I narrow my eyes. "What kind of bet?"

"I thought I was bad about always having to get my way," Izzy comments lazily. "But you two have me beat."

"Jude's only this way with Clementine," Mozart tells her.

I want to ask her what she means by that, but I'm too busy staring Jude down—who's just as busy doing the same to me. Out of eyes that have suddenly gone a myriad of colors. Green and silver, gold and black, all swirled together in the most captivating mix I've ever seen.

I blink to break the spell, then hate myself when the corners of his mouth move in what I'm quickly coming to realize is the closest thing to a smile seventeen-year-old Jude can manage.

"I do the next pen alone—and if I come out unscathed, you let me handle the rest while you three take care of the chricklers."

I turn the bet over in my head, looking for loopholes. As far as I can see, there are none, considering there's no way he's coming out of that cage without at least a few scratches on him. I don't know how he got past the snake thing, but there are two of the creepiest spider monsters I've ever seen in there, and there's no way he can evade them both.

Plus, better to let him get this ridiculous lone ranger routine of his done in there than when he tries to go into some of the other pens...

Still, it doesn't pay to be too easy—or too eager. "And what happens if I have to come save your ass?"

"You won't," he answers, that tiny little smile still playing around the corners of his mouth.

"Of course not," I agree sarcastically. "But let's just say I do have to rescue you. Or, even, that you come out a little banged up. What happens then?"

He shrugs. "Then we do the rest of the pens your way."

"Even the chricklers?"

He grimaces. "Even the damn chricklers."

"Then you've got yourself a deal." I hold my hand out for a shake, then immediately regret it when his palm slides against mine.

Tiny sparks dance along my skin wherever we touch, and I yank my hand back too soon.

Jude pretends he doesn't notice, but that's all it is. Pretense. I can see it in the way his shoulders stiffen and the way he brushes his palm against his jeans a few times, like he's trying to rub the feeling off.

I get it. I'd do the same if I thought it would actually work.

"Okay, then." I nod toward the heavy wooden door that stands between the spider monsters and the rest of us. "Guess you'd better get started before the weather gets worse."

I watch his face closely for some tiny sign of fear, but there's nothing. No tightening of his mouth, no flicker of his eyelashes, not even a deep breath to steady himself. None of the little tells from his childhood. Just pure, confident man.

It makes me want to change my bet—not because I'm afraid of taking on the chricklers alone, obviously, but because I'm terrified about what will happen to him if he goes into some of these enclosures alone.

But it's too late now. He's already unlocking the door and slipping inside.

My stomach clenches as the door closes behind him, and though I'm convinced my poker face is as good as Jude's, Mozart turns to me right away. "He'll be fine."

"You don't know that."

She starts to answer, then breaks off with an alarmed, "What are you planning on doing with that thing *now*?"

I turn around just in time to see Izzy holding on to yet another wicked-looking knife. She doesn't answer Mozart, just walks over to the nearest door and jams the knife into the bottom of the padlock.

"I'm pretty sure that wasn't part of the bet," Mozart tells her warily.

But she just lifts a brow. "I don't remember agreeing to any bet. And if you think I'm just going to stand around out here and wait for Prince Not So Charming to come back in pieces, you're more naive than you look."

She wiggles the knife a little bit, then turns it quickly to the left. The padlock springs open, and so does the door.

"You coming?" she asks, blue eyes wide and not so innocent as she glances over her shoulder at me.

"No way," I answer, but she's already slipping through the door into the enclosure, without so much as a beat of hesitation…or any kind of plan on how to tackle the thing waiting for her inside.

Because, apparently, her instinct for self-preservation is about as strong as Jude's.

I start to follow her, but Mozart steps in front of me. "You sure you want to do that?"

"Obviously not," I answer. "But I can't let her go in alone."

"Fine." She sighs. "We'll go in together—"

She breaks off as a haunting scream comes from the spider beast enclosure.

Finally, she looks as worried as I feel.

"Go check on Jude," I tell her. "I've got Izzy."

She doesn't look convinced—at least until a long, strange chittering sound follows up the scream.

"Go," I urge. Then I pull my elbow from her grasp and dive through the open door, just as another blood-chilling scream fills the air around us.

CHAPTER THIRTY-TWO

SQUID-ZILLA GAMES

I pull the door closed behind me and then blink a few times as my eyes get used to the strange red light that fills the room. The last thing we need is for this thing to escape.

I vaguely remember my mother complaining about having to find special lightbulbs to accommodate this creature, but I didn't pay a lot of attention at the time. But apparently the thing doesn't like regular light, because not only is every bulb in the place red, but the tiny windows near the ceiling are also covered in a strange, red film that gives the whole room an eerie, crimson glow that has the hair on the back of my neck standing straight up.

Izzy doesn't seem the least bit fazed by it, though, as she strides confidently toward the center of the large, barren room.

"Don't you want to know where it is before you expose yourself like that?" I ask, looking around as I follow her deeper into the enclosure. My time with the chricklers has taught me that slow and steady keeps all your limbs and most of your skin attached.

She shrugs. "I don't mind monsters. At least they're honest about who they are and what they want."

"Yeah, but what they want is usually some part of your body. Flesh. Bones. Blood…" I break off as I remember who I'm talking to.

But Izzy just grins, exposing her very long, very sharp fangs. "Hey, don't knock it 'til you've tried it."

"Not really a manticore thing," I answer as I spin around in a circle, trying to figure out where this damn monster is. It's not like there's so much in here for it to hide behind.

There are three large potted trees in the back corner of the enclosure with what looks like scratch marks going all the way to the tops of the trunks. Some of the branches are cracked in half and hanging off the trees, while others are just plain gone—cut or ripped off at the trunks. At least one of the trees must be an apple tree, because the ground around the pots is littered with cores that have been chewed down to the seeds.

The rest of the room is pretty blank—as long as you discount the walls, which are even more scratched up than the tree trunks. There's just a large pallet for what I assume is sleeping, several troughs filled with water and more of the sparkly Z-shaped kibble we feed the monsters, a chained-up cabinet that I'm guessing contains more of its food, and a heavy-duty chain that runs down the center of the room.

I have about one second to register that the chain is probably attached to squidzilla—and start to follow it with my eyes—when a loud, rumbling growl fills the room.

"Where is it?" Izzy demands as we both whirl to the left, where the sound came from.

There's nothing there...except for the huge, heavy chain. Only this part of it isn't on the ground. Instead, it's hanging from the ceiling.

And, it turns out, I was right. It's most definitely attached to the monster. Who is way more terrifying than I imagined from Uncle Carter's description of it when it first came to the menagerie. And also exceptionally pissed off, if the snarls coming from its very large, very sharp-toothed mouth are any indication.

"What the hell is that thing?" Izzy demands, and suddenly she's got a knife in each hand—and the newest edition is even bigger and scarier looking than the first. Before I can process what's happening, she leans forward and presses it into my hand.

"I don't want that!" I yelp, trying to hand it back—partly because I have no idea how to use a knife to defend myself and mostly because whatever that thing plans to do to me is nowhere near as bad as what my mother will do to me if I get caught with a weapon on school grounds. The fact that Izzy's managed to last this long with her knife collection is definitely a testament to who she is rather than Calder Academy's normal policy regarding possession of any kind of weapon on the island.

But Izzy can't take it—she's already holding a third knife. And judging from the way she spins them both around, she definitely knows how to use them.

"*Where* do you keep getting those?" I demand as we continue to back up under the squid thing's watchful black eyes. "I know we search for weapons when you get here."

"Not sure this is the time for that discussion," Izzy answers as she holds the knives up in front of her, like she's just waiting for a chance to impale the beast.

"You know we're here to feed and water it, right? Not kill it?" I lower my knife as I try to figure out what I'm supposed to do with the thing now that it's got my fingerprints all over it. "I'm pretty sure the people who are paying my mother to board it here are going to be really upset if it comes back missing a..."

I trail off as I try to figure out what to call the translucent-skinned thing's appendages.

"Tentacle?" Izzy fills in.

And technically, I suppose she's right. The monster's lower body is made up of close to a hundred tentacle-shaped limbs. Except where most tentacles have some kind of suction cup on them, it has razor blades. Dozens and dozens of razor blades. Which explains the scratches on every available surface in this place.

What the ever-loving hell?

I know the school always needs money, but there has to be a better way to get it than to volunteer to take care of creatures like this.

That awful snake monster got out earlier. What the hell would we do if *this* thing actually slipped its chain and got onto the school grounds?

"I'm going to—" I break off as it skitters, still upside down, across the ceiling straight toward us.

It makes a clicking sound as it moves—the razor blades skipping along the ceiling—and as it gets closer, revulsion turns my stomach. Because it truly is the grossest-looking thing I've ever seen.

To begin with, its top half looks a lot like one of those hairless cats—oversize, pointy ears, wide black eyes, and wrinkly skin. It's even got two small limbs with what look like paws attached to the ends. None of which is bad at all—until you get to the elongated snout and the two-foot-long teeth protruding from its mouth in all directions. Not to mention the fact that the wrinkly skin is not just hairless but also translucent just below it.

And then there are the tentacles. So, so, so many translucent tentacles with greenish yellow blood running just below the surface and—now that it's closer—I can see what I thought were razor blades are actually some kind of knife-edged shells.

All in all, a living nightmare if I've ever seen one.

And it's looking straight at me.

"We need to feed it and get the hell out of here," I tell Izzy as I scoot gingerly toward the food cabinet and try really hard not to notice that it is scooting right along with me, the scraping of its shells over the ceiling like nails down a chalkboard.

"So get busy!" Izzy snarls. "I'll hold it off."

I start to ask her if she's sure, but she's already moved to cover me, knives at the ready. And while I'd tend to doubt nearly anyone else who thought they could handle this thing, there's something in Izzy's eyes that tells me she's more than ready for the challenge. I'm seriously not sure if that thing is bravery or sociopathy, but right now, I don't really care. I just want to do the job we came here to do and then get both of us out of this shithole alive.

I've learned through the years that there are very few people I can trust on this island, but now seems as good a time as any to expand that faith in others. So instead of demanding to be the one to fend off the beast, a task I'm pretty sure I'm unprepared for, I take Izzy at her word and race toward the food cabinet.

The second I turn my back on it, I expect to feel the monster's sharp teeth sinking into my jugular as its razor-tipped talons tear me limb from limb. But, amazingly, I make it to the cabinet completely untouched—though the growls and clicking sounds behind me make me think the same can't be said for Izzy.

A particularly loud squeal of pain has my heart threatening to explode in my chest, but when I glance over my shoulder, it's to find Izzy still standing, her own fangs bared in a snarl. It's all the reassurance I need, at least for now, and I yank open the cabinet doors and pull down two giant bags of food.

With the chricklers, I usually divide up the food into their many troughs, making sure that it's spread out for them all throughout the enclosure. They are notoriously picky about where they eat and who they eat in front of, including each other. But I know very little about this squid thing and care even less. As long as it actually has food out in the open, I don't care if it eats it or not.

Especially since it just wrapped a dozen of its sharp-ass tentacles around Izzy's right arm and is currently trying to wrestle her knife away from her.

"Hey!" I yell to get its attention, then immediately wish I hadn't as it starts click-clacking its way across the ceiling toward me. And while that was what I was hoping it would do, I didn't expect it to drag Izzy along in its wake. Which is exactly what it is currently doing— apparently having a hundred tentacles means it can come after me while holding on to Izzy and still have enough to spare to take on most of the senior class.

Izzy struggles against the monster using what looks like every ounce of her vampire strength to try to hold her ground. But the thing is strong, really strong, and the more she struggles, the deeper its tentacles cut into Izzy's arm.

She's easily just as pissed as the squid thing now, and as it continues to pull her along, she comes out swinging. The creature made her drop the knife in her right hand, but she's still got the one in her left, and she swings it, in a powerful uppercut, straight toward the tentacle holding on to her.

The knife connects, slicing deep into the tentacle but not actually cutting it off. The monster responds with a bellow of rage so loud it makes my ears ring. And then it starts wrapping its tentacles around her, one after another.

They slide around her legs, her hips, her waist, her diaphragm, her chest, her neck, her arms. Nearly every part of her is covered in disgusting tentacles. Nearly every part of her is being cut into by razor-sharp shells.

Izzy doesn't scream or cry, doesn't make so much as a sound. But

I know that it's cutting her, know that she's hurting. I can hear the harshness of her breathing, can see the blood falling onto the ground near her feet.

And that's before it starts to squeeze.

CHAPTER THIRTY-THREE

NAUGHTY AND NOT SO KNIFE

The blood turns from droplets into a stream, and though Izzy still doesn't say anything, I know I have to do something, fast.

I race forward, praying the whole time that the fucking monster will remain preoccupied with Izzy long enough for me to grab—

I duck down as I slide to a stop and grab the knife Izzy dropped. Then I come up swinging, a blade in each hand as I slice through whatever tentacles I can reach. Part of me thinks stabbing might be more effective right now, but I'm terrified of stabbing Izzy, too.

So I swing again, slicing deeper this time. The beast bellows in pained outrage as several tentacles fall to the floor and start flopping around near my feet.

They may be severed, but they're still razor sharp, and I jump over two of them to avoid getting cut. As I do, I take another swing at the thing, but this time it's ready for me.

It unfurls its tentacles in a rush, throwing Izzy at me so hard that I stumble backward, and we both hit the ground. Seconds later, it drops down on top of us, and I scream. I can't help it. Being surrounded— and sucked into—its tentacles just might be the most terrifying thing that's happened to me, which is saying a lot.

Desperate to get both Izzy and myself out of this mess, I grip the knives as tightly as I can and punch out with my right hand. The monster screams as it recoils, and I manage to wiggle a few inches of my body out from under it.

But then it's back, its giant mouth gaping wide open and its razor-sharp teeth on full display as it dives for my head.

Oh, hell no. I'm not about to get bitten by one more thing today. And I'm definitely not getting bitten by teeth that look like *that*.

I kick out, hard, as I grab onto Izzy and try to roll. But she's too busy shoving her fist—complete with gigantic knife—straight into its mouth.

The blade connects with the squid thing's soft palate and sinks deep.

It doesn't kill it—its head is too big for the knife to actually reach its brain—but it does send it spinning away from us, roaring in pain and outrage.

It's the opening we've been looking for, and we bound to our feet, racing for the door. To hell with feeding the thing. At this point, it's on its own.

Izzy makes it to the door first, and she throws it open. But before I can dive through, a bunch of tentacles grab me from behind and yank me back toward the center of the room.

I fly through the air, feeling a little like Spider-Man to this thing's Doc Ock. On the plus side, its tentacles aren't made of titanium, and I've still got one of the knives.

I reach down and try to saw my way through a couple of the tentacles holding me, but the beast is done playing. It wrenches me back and forth, up and down, jarring me to the very core of my being while also making sure I never get the chance to actually do any damage.

That doesn't stop me from trying, though, and I bring the knife down again—this time in a stabbing motion. I know I may hit myself, but right now that seems like the lesser of two evils. Anything does that doesn't involve being eaten alive by an enraged squid monster.

It jerks me away again before the blade can connect, and this time, I'm so off balance that I actually drop the knife. Damn it.

Desperate now, but determined not to die hours before finally getting off this island, I do the only thing I can think of. I duck my head and bite the tentacles holding on to me as hard as I can.

The horror that follows is indescribable.

The tentacle splits in half, and my mouth is suddenly filled with the creature's blood and I don't know what else. I gag on the noxious taste but force myself to keep biting down as it screams and thrashes around me.

I swear, if I ever get out of this nightmare, I'm sterilizing my entire mouth. And every other part of my body as well.

Eventually the tentacle gives way under my teeth, and I spit it out as the fucker continues to knock around the room. I grab onto another tentacle but can't bring myself to bite this one, too, so I try to pry it away from my body.

The monster is in so much pain that it barely seems to notice what I'm doing. At first, I think it's because of the bite, but then I glance down and realize Izzy's sliced off one of its little paw-tipped arms and is currently trying to jam a knife straight through its eye.

The monster ducks and she misses, but she just swings again. And misses again. It reaches down with its non-severed arm and smacks her so hard that she goes flying across the room. She hits the wall hard but bounces right back and starts going for him again.

Before she can reach him, though, Jude races through the open door and straight for the three of us.

"Stay back!" I scream, but he zips straight past Izzy and grabs a handful of tentacles.

It screeches the second Jude touches it. Its tentacles release, and just like that, I'm falling. I brace myself for impact with the stone floor—try to tuck myself up so I hit my shoulder and not my head—but Jude gets there first.

He plucks me out of thin air and grabs onto me, pulling me against his chest as he backs toward the door, his eyes still fastened on the nasty squid thing. But it's not chasing him—or me. Instead, it's tucked itself into the far corner of the room, its tentacles wrapped around itself as it lets out a low moan that is eerily similar to the one I heard coming from the spider creatures' pen.

"Let's get out of here," Jude grinds out as he sweeps Izzy along in front of us.

But she's already fading—moving in the fast way only vampires can—out the door, leaving Jude to follow along behind her.

"You can put me down now," I tell him as soon as Mozart slams the door closed behind us and closes the padlock.

Jude doesn't answer, just glares at me as he strides down the hall.

"Where are we going?" I demand, starting to struggle against him. "We still need to take care of the other monsters."

He still doesn't answer me. And he doesn't stop walking.

I start to yell at him to put me down, to demand an answer for what just happened in that pen. That monster that was out for our blood took one look at Jude and ran from him. It literally shrank into a corner, doing its best to become all but invisible. And I need to know why.

Again, I start to order him to put me down right this instant. But I stop myself, because the truth is I'm trembling so badly that I'm afraid my knees won't support me. So, instead of making him put me down, I press myself against him and hold on for just a little while.

I hold on to the powerful rise and fall of his chest.

I hold on to the strength flowing through his big, muscly body.

And, even though I tell myself not to, I hold on to the warm leather-and-honey scent of him. I even go so far as to turn my head and bury my face, ever so slightly, against his chest.

Later, I'm sure I'll be mortified by my behavior. But for right now, I'll take the comfort.

The thought has me burrowing deeper against him, and that's when it hits me. The shaking I'm feeling isn't coming from me at all. It's coming from Jude.

I pull back so I can look at him, really look at him. And it hits me. Jude isn't angry. He's terrified. Because of me. For me.

"I'm sorry," I whisper, the words coming out before I have a clue I'm going to say them.

"We had a deal," he snaps out, and his voice is so low and rumbly that I barely understand it.

"We had a bet," I correct. "It's not the same thing. But I know Izzy and I made a huge mistake."

Jude starts to snap again—I can see it in the way his jaw works. Feel it in the way his chest tenses against me.

But in the end, he just shakes his head as he bursts out the double doors of the administration building and takes the steps down three at a time.

He doesn't stop until we're on ground level, several yards away from the building. Then, and only then, does he slide me slowly, carefully, to my feet. He holds on to me for a minute to make sure my legs—and everything else—can support me.

Turns out, they can. Barely. I lock my knees, just in case.

Jude watches the whole thing, gorgeous eyes swirling with a million words and even more emotions as he stares down at me.

"You need to trust me, Kumquat," he finally says, and his voice is still all growly. "I won't do anything that deliberately puts you in danger."

"What about yourself?" I shoot back, because nothing Jude does is without risk.

"I was never in any danger. That's what I was trying to tell you."

"This time, maybe." I narrow my eyes at him as the squid monster's reaction to him plays over and over again in my head. "And why is that, exactly? What is it about you that turned that creature from homicidal to terrified in the blink of an eye?"

Again, he starts to say something. And again, he settles for snapping his mouth shut and shaking his head.

"You want me to trust you," I whisper. "But you won't trust me. About *anything*. How exactly do you think that's supposed to work?"

He just stares at me, stonily, and suddenly it's all too much.

Jude's secrets.

The storm.

The fact that I still have the monster's blood in my mouth.

Nausea swamps me, and I stumble backward several steps. Jude reaches out like he wants to help me, but I throw a hand out to stop him. Then I stagger over to the nearest trash can and vomit. A lot.

The only problem is that I've barely eaten all day, which means that all I've got to throw up is a bunch of stomach acid and whatever blood actually managed to make it down my throat.

Just the thought has me dry heaving some more, over and over again, until I'm convinced I've thrown up my stomach lining and maybe even my stomach itself.

I can't even pretend to be sorry, not when the memory of biting that tentacle is forever emblazoned in my brain.

When I finally stand back up, stomach settled but the rest of me absolutely mortified that I just puked in front of a bunch of my classmates *and* Jude, Eva is standing next to me with a bottle of water while Luis rubs my back. I rinse out my mouth several times, then use the rest of it to wash the blood from my face and hands before finally turning around to look at the others.

All of them, except for Eva, Luis, and Jude, are very conspicuously not looking at me. I've never seen so many paranormals so interested in a pile of plywood in my life...

I look around for Izzy and find her leaning against one of the trees, a bottle of water in her hand as well. The only difference between the two of us is she looks hale and healthy and almost completely back to normal because apparently vampires heal a lot faster than manticores, even with their powers locked down. Not that that seems fair right now, considering she's the one who went into that enclosure to begin with.

Still, I'm glad she's all right. I'm in more than enough pain for both of us.

"You okay?" Eva asks, her brown eyes wide and worried as she looks me over from head to toe. "This looks a lot worse than your usual chrickler-related injuries."

It feels a lot worse, too. But there's nothing I can do about that right now. Time is ticking, and we still have to finish up with the menagerie.

The thought makes me nauseous all over again. The last thing I want to do right now is go back in that building.

Still, it has to be done. Jude may be able to handle the other monsters—and I will get an answer as to how that's possible—but the chricklers still need to be taken care of. And I, by far, have the most experience with that.

But when I say as much to Eva, all the people who have been pretending not to pay attention to me puking spring into action.

"The only place you're going is back to the dorms," Luis tells me, looking completely annoyed. "Responsibility is one thing. Self-sabotage is something else entirely."

"I'm okay," I answer.

"I wouldn't exactly say *that, cher*," Remy tells me. And though his voice is relaxed, his eyes are watchful as they slide between Izzy and me. "You look like you're one stiff breeze away from falling headfirst into that trash can."

Considering I feel like I'm barely one tiny gust of wind away from having that happen, I'll count that as a win. I start to say as much, but the looks on everyone's faces convince me that doing so definitely won't help my cause.

"I've got this," Jude tells me.

"But the—"

"We've got this," Mozart repeats just as firmly, her ponytail swaying with each word. "Besides, you wouldn't deprive me of seeing the inside of the chrickler enclosure, would you? It's been a lifelong dream of mine."

"Mine, too," Remy agrees instantly.

I make a face at him. "Tell me what a chrickler is and maybe I'll believe you."

He grins. "Isn't that more reason for me to go find out?"

Even Izzy gets in on the action when she pulls two more knives out of seemingly nowhere, one of which looks like an actual saber.

When I give her a what-the-hell look, she just shrugs. "If the chricklers don't actively try to kill me, I can always use them to make a nice oneiroi kabob instead."

Jude rolls his eyes, but everyone else laughs—including me. But doing so makes my head hurt. Not to mention my stomach. And my side. And my...everything.

Maybe they're right. Maybe I really *should* bow out of this one. That is, if I can walk, which—at this point—I'm honestly not certain that I can.

To test it out, I take a few steps back under everyone's watchful gaze...which isn't embarrassing at all. I start to turn around to block them out and end up slamming straight into a ghost.

CHAPTER THIRTY-FOUR

ROCKED TO MY MANTI-CORE

'm assaulted by sound as it screeches, "Run...run...run." Wild hair, bulging eyes, agony twisted on its sunken face, I'm pretty sure it's the same ghost from earlier in Aunt Claudia's office. But this time it disappears practically as soon as I walk through it, dissolving into what feels like a thousand needles jabbing into every part of me.

I bite my lip as the torment slams through me, and somehow, I manage to hold back the scream of pain welling up inside me. But I can't do anything about my legs—abused, exhausted, and already shaky as hell—as they go out from under me.

I hit the ground, hard, and I'm left quivering on the sidewalk like a little kid who can't keep her shit together, even though it seems to have gone as quickly as it appeared.

I start to push back to my feet, but Jude, Eva, and Luis are all crowded around me, worried looks on their faces. Remy, Simon, and Mozart are a few feet back and look just as concerned—but are still too close, in my opinion.

Only Ember and Izzy are giving me a wide berth. I don't know if that's because they don't care or if they're just afraid of catching whatever is going on with me right now.

Whatever it is that's making them keep their distance, I'm grateful. I just wish the others would take a page from their books. I'm getting damn sick of Jude seeing me as some kind of damsel in distress when that's *not* who I am. And it sure as shit isn't who I want to be.

It's that thought more than any other that has me climbing to my feet. Showing weakness of any kind is dangerous here, even to friends like Luis and Eva. Showing it to everyone else who's standing around— including the guy who has hurt me over and over again through the years?

I need to nip that shit in the bud.

"Sorry, I lost my balance," I tell them once I'm standing under my own power again.

Eva's eyes narrow. "That didn't look like you lost your balance. That looked like—"

She breaks off when I, very deliberately, step on her foot.

"I'm fine," I say again. "Let's just finish up so we can get out of here."

Jude must figure out that that's the only concession I'm willing to give right now, because he doesn't argue with me, just nods before turning and heading back toward the admin building's entrance.

But he's only halfway there when a huge bolt of lightning tears across the dark-gray sky. It illuminates the whole area before slamming into one of the huge purple crape myrtle trees that line the quad. Sparks fly and a strange sizzling sound fills the air for several seconds before a giant branch falls off the tree and slams into the surrounding fence on its way to the ground.

"What kind of storm are we dealing with here?" Mozart demands, eyes wide as she turns to look at us. But the moment the words leave her mouth, a giant flame shoots out right after them.

"Look out!" I yell to Jude, who's directly in the line of fire.

But he's already moving, jumping backward just in time to avoid being flame-roasted by one of his best friends.

"What the fuck?" Simon shouts, looking horrified. "Are you all right, Jude?"

But before Jude can answer, Simon's eyes start glowing a deep, bright gold that has every cell in my body being called to him. His skin is next, the deep brown taking on a glittery, gold glow that emanates in all directions. It takes up more and more space as the rest of him begins to shift.

Eva cries out in alarm, but I'm too busy trying to figure out what's going on inside of me to check what's up with her. Because all of a sudden my entire body feels like it's burning up. Not like Ember, earlier, when she literally caught fire, but like I have a really high fever. One that's melting—and reshaping—my body from the inside out.

"It's okay, Kumquat." Jude's voice is steady as he reaches for me. "You're okay."

I don't feel okay. I feel sick. Really, really sick.

My stomach churns, my breath comes in fast pants that I have no control over, and my skin aches like it's about to split open.

Jude reaches over and calmly rubs my back, but even that small, soothing contact makes the fire inside me worse. I pull back from him just in time to see Simon's legs go out from under him.

No, not his legs. His *tail*.

What the ever-loving hell is going on here?

Seconds later, Simon starts flopping around on the ground, gasping for air. I have one second to register the fact that he can't breathe *because he has gills* and wonder how to help him while an inferno is swallowing me whole before Remy steps up.

"I've got this," he announces, sounding completely unfazed by what's going on. He picks Simon up and seconds later deposits him in the old, broken-down fountain in the middle of the quad. Normally it's empty, but the rain's been so heavy today that it's filled almost to the top with water. Simon sinks under the surface as soon as Remy puts him in it.

Another flash of lightning splits the sky, followed by a loud rumble of thunder that shakes the ground we're standing on. My legs, already aching and rubbery, turn even more unsteady.

I reach out for Jude, and he grabs onto my hand just as Mozart lets loose with another mouthful of flames—right before a giant pair of black-and-silver wings sprouts from her back.

At the same time, Luis ends up on all fours. The hair on his head starts growing seconds before fur starts sprouting up all over the rest of his body. A bunch of rainbow shimmers surround him, and in less than a minute, he's turned into a huge, beautiful black wolf.

I reach for him, and he comes forward, letting me slide my hand along his spine before taking off in a ridiculously fast run around the quad.

"It's okay," Jude tells me, except it's not. The black tattoos on his arms—the ones covered by the hoodie he always wears—are climbing up his neck, onto his jaws and cheeks and forehead. "Everything's okay."

"You—" I start to say, but my voice sounds different. Lower. Almost like a growl instead of a voice.

I try to clear my throat, and when that doesn't work, I press a hand against the hollow of my neck. As I do, my nails prick the delicate skin there, and I look down to realize my fingers have curved and my nails have morphed into razor-sharp talons.

And that's when it finally hits me. I'm not sick at all... *I'm shifting into a manticore.*

CHAPTER THIRTY-FIVE

A MANTICORE DOESN'T CHANGE ITS TAIL

For a moment, everything inside of me goes blank as I try to absorb what's happening.

There's a part of my brain that says I must be mistaken. That no way could this possibly be what shifting feels like—what *magic* feels like. But all around me, people are doing things they shouldn't be able to do. Things the school expressly forbids and stops them from doing.

It's impossible, and yet it's happening right now.

The burning sensation deep inside me gets worse with each second that passes, until I can barely stand to be in my own body.

"It's okay," Jude tells me again. "You're okay."

I don't know how he can be so calm considering he's practically in the same situation I am. Everyone else knows what it feels like to feel their power—they came here when they were freshmen and sophomores *because* of that power.

But Jude's been here since he was a child. Not as long as me, who was born here. But still. My mother agreed to take him on when he was *seven*. And while I know he had experienced his power even at that young age, ten years have passed without him feeling anything.

So, yeah, I'm super impressed that he's handling things as well as he is because I'm freaking out—especially every time I look down at my hands and see paws instead. Or when I glance over my shoulder and see a giant, stinging tail.

Make that a gross, giant, stinging tail. Because, holy shit, is it gross—long and scaly and black with a giant stinger on the end that looks like it can do some serious damage to anyone who gets too close. I don't know whether to be terrified or horrified or a combination of both as it waves back and forth and curls under and over of its own volition.

I try to stop it, but somehow that only makes it worse until the thing is completely out of my control.

Jude jumps back as it slides by him, the stinger coming so close to his face that it nearly takes his eye out.

"Make it stop!" I wail, only it doesn't come out like a wail. It comes out about an octave deeper than my usual voice and sounds a lot like a growl.

"I can't, Kumquat. You've got to figure out what to do."

"You make it sound so easy."

"I know it's not," he soothes. "But it just takes practice. You'll get the hang of it eventually."

Eventually? How long is this lapse supposed to last? Long enough for those things writhing on his skin to cover his entire face? Long enough for me to sting him or anyone else who gets too close? Long enough for the entire school to turn completely magic?

I'm not asking the universe for an exact number here. I just need a ballpark figure so that I can calm my own shit down.

Behind me, Eva screams, and I whirl around just in time to see Jean-Luc fly across the fence, straight at us. His blond hair is streaming through the air behind him, and he's got bloodred fairy wings coming out of his back. Jean-Jacques is right behind him, only his wings are a dark gray.

"Well, that's the last thing you want to see in the middle of a shit show," Jude comments quietly, and I have to admit he's right.

The Jean-Jerks are menaces without their magic. With it…I don't even want to know what kind of destruction these mafia fae can wreak.

As if to prove my point, Jean-Luc flies over to the nearest pecan tree and rips a branch straight off of it. Then he starts pelting us with the green nuts while Jean-Jacques laughs uproariously. Because apparently, even in an emergency, the two of them have the emotional maturity of overtired toddlers.

"What the fuck?" Ember snarls as one of the pecans bounces off her shoulder.

Seconds later, another one hits Izzy right in the face, and she pulls out yet another knife from what is obviously an inexhaustible supply.

But before she can take aim, Mozart—in her full, gorgeous, black dragon form—sends a stream of fire straight at the obnoxious fae.

It singes his translucent, bloodred wings, and he yells, "What the fuck, dragon? I was just having some fun!"

He starts to throw the entire branch at Mozart, but Izzy's knife whirs the air at that exact moment and slices a hole straight through his right wing.

Jean-Luc screams as he drops the branch and goes into a spiral that ends with him slamming into the ground. Another quick blast of fire from Mozart and Jean-Jacques is landing right beside his friend.

Jean-Luc comes up, furious, but one raised eyebrow from Jude— who looks imposing as fuck with the tattoos creeping up his face—and they both decide to head in the other direction. But not before flipping us all off.

I open my mouth to call after them and the scariest roar I've ever heard in my life comes out of it. *Out of me.*

My mom, aunts, and uncles have no trouble talking in their manticore forms, so why do I?

Another attempt, another roar—even as everything, and everyone, around me returns to normal.

The tattoos have slid back down Jude's neck to his chest.

Mozart and Luis have both shifted back into their human forms.

Simon's out of the fountain and back in human form, and Remy is chilling against a tree. Ember looks relieved while Izzy looks a little disappointed. Eva never changed, either, so all four of them look fine to me.

And on the other side of the fence, I can hear the Jean-Jerks cursing and complaining as they walk back toward the dorms.

Apparently, whatever the lightning did to cause that weird power surge has worn off, and everyone has gone back to normal. Even my out-of-control tail is gone.

I close my eyes and breathe a sigh of relief. I really need to read up on how to control that thing before I shift again, because that was *wild*. And not in a good way.

"Everyone solid?" Remy calls as he gets closer.

"Solid's relative, but yeah. We're fine," Mozart tells him.

And, somehow, despite the monsters and the lightning and the power surge, we are.

Except, when I open my eyes again, nothing looks the way it's supposed to.

I can see the individual petals on a flower all the way across the quad. And the spots on the leaves at the very top of the trees. Plus, I can smell the flowers and the trees and about so many other things as well—including Izzy and Mozart and everyone else standing around with me.

I can hear Jude breathing and Izzy tapping her foot against the cracked sidewalk, but I can also hear the soft fall of Remy's footsteps on the grass and the brush of Simon's eyelashes against his cheeks.

Even the air I breathe feels funny, tastes funny—briny and fresh and green and a million other things I can't quite identify.

It's like my senses are all on hyper-alert—which I've heard is a shifter thing. That, alone, isn't alarming. But the fact that the tail and the claws have disappeared while this has stayed behind definitely is.

I must look as weirded out as I feel because suddenly Jude is much closer to me, brows furrowed and mismatched eyes cataloging my face. "Hey, what's going on?" he asks after several seconds.

"I don't know," I answer, except—once again—it comes out as a growl. Unlike the roars of earlier, it's at least understandable, but it's definitely not my regular voice.

Jude's eyes widen as the others crowd around me, looking concerned.

"Everything okay?" Mozart asks, moving closer. Somehow, she looks even more concerned than Jude.

"Pretty sure it's not," I answer in what—again—is very definitely not my normal voice.

And now that she's standing this close, I know she had a turkey sandwich for lunch, while Simon had tuna and Remy had a piece of chocolate cake. I definitely didn't recognize any of that when I was talking to them earlier, but now I can't help but notice it—and a thousand other things about them, too.

"I feel strange," I tell them, proud of how calm I'm managing to be, "like my senses are on overload. I can hear and smell and see everything."

Except the words don't come out sounding calm. They come out like a snarl. Still words, but definitely a snarl.

"Oh, shit," Mozart says, exchanging a long, concerned look with Simon.

"Oh, shit what?" I ask as my heart starts beating double time.

"Does anything else feel weird?" she asks, getting face-to-face with me so she can look in my eyes.

"Umm, my voice?" I say in what should be an obvious tone but ends up sounding like a rumble.

"Her eyes are still manticore," Mozart says, and though she's trying to sound calm, I can hear—and smell—the panic just below her surface.

"Is that bad?" I ask as the same panic starts shooting through me. "Am I going to hurt one of you?"

I start backing up just in case, terrified that my poisonous tail is suddenly going to resurface.

"It's not *us* we're worried about," Luis answers as the three shifters exchange a long look.

"Don't do that," I plead. "Please. Don't talk around what's happening. Just tell me what's going on."

Mozart places a comforting hand on my arm even as she blows out a long breath that has notes of barbeque chips and lime seltzer water. "Don't freak out."

I rear back. "Nothing good ever starts with 'don't freak out'!"

"Don't freak out," she says again, more firmly this time. "But we think you're unmeshed."

CHAPTER THIRTY-SIX

THINGS ARE ABOUT TO GET MESHY

"Unmeshed?" Forget double time, my heart just quadrupled in speed. "I have no idea what that means."

I've never even heard the word before. But whatever it is, it isn't good—at least not judging by the looks on all of their faces. Even Luis looks serious, and he's never serious about anything.

"Normally, when you're a shifter, the two sides of your nature exist together." Mozart makes a kind of braid with her fingers to illustrate. "Being here dampens that for all of us. It brings our human side out a lot more, but the other side is always still there, giving us a little something extra."

"Like how fast the wolves can be?" I ask. "And how strong the dragons are?"

"Exactly like that," Simon agrees. "It's why I can hold my breath underwater for several minutes, even when I'm not in my siren form."

His voice, always musical, sounds downright magical to my ears right now, and I find myself swaying toward him. My whole body physically aches with the need to be closer to him.

Jude rolls his eyes and stops me with an arm around my waist.

"So what do we do?" Jude asks. "How do we get her un-unmeshed?"

"I think the word you're looking for here is meshed," Luis comments dryly.

"I need to fix this," I stress, because it's not just the voice and the senses worrying me. The weird heat in my stomach feels like it's spread to my blood. It's running through my veins and arteries now, making me feel like I'm on fire from the inside out. Or like my skin is going to start melting off me at any second.

None of which is a pleasant feeling.

"Usually shifting again solves the problem," Simon answers.

"But I can't shift! The power surge is over and—"

"We know," Luis soothes, and now he's squeezing my hand. "Just let me think about it for a minute."

As if on cue, lightning flashes right above our heads. Less than a second later, thunder rolls across the sky, so loud I can barely stand it. Agony slams through me, and I clap my hands over my ears until it's done.

But when I pull them away again, my fingers are coated with blood.

"Are you all right?" Jude growls furiously as he turns on the shifters.

"I'm fine," I tell him, but I don't actually know if that's true. My head is killing me, and I'm pretty sure I just popped both my eardrums.

"What the fuck is happening to her?" He glares at Simon, Luis, and Mozart. "And don't hand me that unmeshing shit."

"I'm sorry, but that's what it is," Mozart tells him grimly. "It's actually a really big problem if you can't fix it quickly, because our human bodies aren't built to handle things the same way our animals can. My bones as a dragon are way too heavy for my human body—they would tear straight through my skin every time I tried to move if I was unmeshed."

Well, fuck. Suddenly I'm a lot more concerned about the skin-melting heat I'm experiencing.

"We need to get you to the healer," Eva tells me.

"I'm not sure we can find her. Aunt Claudia is probably somewhere in the middle of all the hurricane prep." Which means she could be anywhere on the island.

"Text her," Jude says grimly.

I do, but I don't get any response.

"Text your mom," he urges.

That's the second to last thing I want to do right now, next to melt into a puddle right here. So I do as he suggests.

But she doesn't answer, either.

The heat is getting worse, and I start yanking at my collar, trying to get some air on my skin.

"What's that about?" Izzy asks, pointing at my shirt, and for once she doesn't sound bored. She sounds concerned, which makes *me* even more concerned.

"I'm burning up," I tell her, waving both hands in front of my face like a fan.

"It's got to be the venom," Remy says quietly.

"The what?" Eva demands, looking even more freaked out than I feel.

"Manticores have venom," he explains. "Calder used to tell me it felt like fire running through her veins."

"That's exactly what it feels like," I tell him.

"That's not good." Eva sounds full-on panicked now.

"That's it. I'm finding the damn healer." Luis takes off running toward the dorms. Seconds later, Mozart does the same, except she's sprinting full-speed toward the cafeteria.

"We should split up, cover more ground," Remy says. "Surely we'll find her."

"Don't just look for the healer," Simon suggests. "Anyone who finds one of the manticores, bring them back here. Maybe one of her aunts or uncles can help. They have to know something."

And just like that, everyone scatters in different directions.

Everyone, that is, except for Jude.

CHAPTER THIRTY-SEVEN

TATT-ME, TATT-YOU

"**Y**ou don't have to wait—" I start.

But he interrupts me. "I'm not going anywhere, Pomelo."

"Pomelo? Seriously?" I try to joke, despite the fact that my entire body is in agony now. "That's the best you've got, Rocky Raccoon?"

"Would you prefer blood orange? Maybe bergamot?" he asks.

"Would you prefer Lucy in the Sky with—" I break off as the pain and heat overwhelm me.

Jude curses softly, then takes my hands. "Look at me, Clementine."

This time when he says my name, it doesn't sound so bad. In fact, it sounds almost tender. So I do as he asks. And even with the pain tearing through me, even with the heat feeling like it's going to melt me from the inside out, I can't help but get lost for a few moments in the intensity of his eyes.

As if on cue, Taylor Swift's "Look What You Made Me Do" finishes and "The Ancient Art of Always Fucking Up" starts streaming from the forgotten phone on the admin building's steps. My breath catches in my throat as my entire body yearns toward Jude as Lewis Capaldi sings about mistakes and breaking your heart over and over again.

At least until he steps back and orders, "Take your shirt off," for the second time today.

I don't take it any better now than I did the first time. "I really don't think my wounds from the monsters matter right now—"

I break off as he suddenly reaches back and grabs his collar before yanking both his shirt and hoodie off in one fell swoop.

My mouth, already dry, turns into Death Valley. Because Jude's strong, muscled, *beautiful* chest is now covered by those same black tattoo things that are all over his back and arms.

Every. Single. Inch.

Covered by looping, swirling, black feathery ropes…it's the sexiest thing I've ever seen. *Jude* is the sexiest thing I've ever seen—between the tattoos and his heavily muscled pecs, his lean stomach and the tiny trail of hair that disappears beneath the waistband of the worn jeans he changed into earlier…

I saw him without a shirt on after he helped Ember. And I know his chest wasn't tattooed then. His back and arms were—and are still—but his chest and stomach weren't. And I know that earlier they started creeping up his neck and face, but they disappeared as soon as everyone's powers got locked back down.

So why didn't they disappear from Jude's chest as well? And should I even care when he looks so damn good?

It makes me wonder just how much of his body is covered in them now…and which parts.

The heat inside me ratchets up another notch, but this time I'm not sure it has anything to do with the venom streaming through me.

"Are you going to take your shirt off or what?" he growls.

I gape at him. "I didn't think you were serious."

"Because I'm known for my sense of humor." He grabs my hands again, and this time he strokes his thumbs over my knuckles. "Do you trust me?" he asks as the wind howls around us, rustling the trees and blowing strands of his black hair into his eyes.

Without thinking, I reach up and brush them away, then immediately wish I hadn't as he traps me in his burning-hot gaze. "Answer me, Clementine. Before it's too late. Do. You. Trust. Me?"

With my heart, no. Not in a million years. But with my life? I lick my too-dry lips, try to think past the inferno raging inside me. "I think so," I finally whisper.

He makes a sad sound in the back of his throat. "I guess that'll have to do."

And then he reaches down and yanks my shirt straight over my head before pulling me tightly against him.

"What are you—?" I gasp out, shocked as much by the fact that we are suddenly skin to skin as I am by the chill of his body against my own.

"Wrap your arms around me," he orders, and now his voice is even more growly than mine.

When I don't immediately move to do as he says, he does it for me—twining his arms and his body around me.

And somehow, even in the middle of all this pain, nothing has ever felt so right.

I take a deep breath, pulling the spicy, honey-and-leather scent of him deep inside me even as instinct has me sliding my arms around his waist.

In response, he pulls me even closer until my cheek rests against his heart.

It's beating nearly as fast as mine.

I breathe him in again, memorizing this moment—memorizing Jude—as the coolness of his skin quenches just a tiny bit of the heat inside me. Because I know whatever he's doing, it's not nearly enough.

But right now, wrapped up tight next to Jude's heart, I can think of a million worse places to die.

"Close your eyes," he whispers as he lowers his head, and his cool breath brushes against my cheek. A shiver that has nothing to do with temperature works its way through me, and embarrassed, I start to pull away.

But Jude is immovable, his body sheltering as much as holding me close.

"Wait." Again, his words brush over my skin. Again, shivers slide down my spine. "Trust me."

And so, just for this one, beautiful, terrible moment, I do.

Minutes pass while Jude holds me, and at first the pain only gets worse. My lungs start to burn, and it grows harder—so much harder—to take a breath.

But Jude doesn't let me go. Instead, he pulls me closer and slowly—so slowly I barely notice it at first—the conflagration inside me starts to ease.

It begins with just a sliver of ice sliding over my shoulders. But then it moves lower, circling my biceps, gliding over my back and ribs to my spine. From there the chill waterfalls into me, seeping through my skin and cascading down my veins and arteries to my heart, my lungs. My brain.

Inch by inch, cell by cell, the agony begins to drain.

And Jude holds me through it all, his strong, powerful body somehow—in some way—saving mine.

When I can finally breathe without total misery, I open my eyes. Then gasp at what I see.

Because Jude's tattoos—those sexy, black, feathered bands—aren't just on his skin anymore. Somehow, they've crept over to mine.

Now they're sliding down my arms, twisting around my waist, swirling in the very air around us. And every place they touch, every brush of them against my body, lightens the heat and the pain a little more.

"I don't understand," I whisper. "What's happening to us?"

But Jude doesn't answer. He just bows his head and holds on to me like his life—not mine—depends on it.

And so I hold him back the same way, my fingers pressing into the lean, resilient muscles of his back as I burrow even more closely against him.

More time passes—seconds, minutes, I can't begin to fathom a guess—as the venom continues to drain from me one slow drop at a time and my wounds continue to heal. And when it's done, when I can finally breathe without bleeding, I whisper, "Thank you."

My hair is falling out of the bun I stuck it in what feels like days ago, and it's Jude's turn to brush it out of my face. As he does, he bends his head so that our eyes—and our mouths—are aligned.

I breathe him in, the cheerful, lemon scent of his breath filling up the barren, empty places inside of me. And for the first time in a very long time, I can believe that Jude really is made of dreams.

Even before he whispers, "Don't you know I could never exist in a world without you in it?"

CHAPTER THIRTY-EIGHT

STOP MESHING WITH ME

His words gut me, and I want to ask him if he means them. And if he does, why is he always running in the opposite direction? Except there's a part of me that's afraid just bringing it up will send him running again. And I don't want this to end. Not yet. Not when he feels so good—so right—pressed against me.

And not when, just for a moment, I can have a dream that doesn't turn into a nightmare.

But too soon Jude's pulling away, his eyes focused on something in the distance.

"What is it?" I ask. And that's when it hits me—not only is the pain from the venom gone, but my senses are back to normal, too.

"Mozart's back and your aunt Claudia's with her."

"How'd she find her so quickly?"

He shrugs as he tosses me my still-sodden shirt. "There's not a lot she can't do when she puts her mind to it."

I can't help shuddering as I shake out my shirt. The last thing I want to do right now is put it back on—it's clammy, bloody, and torn to hell from the damn monster attacks. Just holding it feels gross. But since I also don't want to explain to my aunt why my shirt is off in a gentleman's company, I start to shrug the disgusting thing on anyway.

But Jude must notice my distaste because he pulls it away, then hands me his shirt before yanking his hoodie back over his head.

I take his shirt without argument—partly because it's a much better alternative to my very gross uniform shirt and partly because it smells like him. If he has to let me go, at least it feels a little like he's still got his arms around me. I even duck my head and let the honey-and-leather-and-cardamom scent of him fill my nose as I put it on, then sigh quietly as it slips into place.

Jude turns to me with raised brows. "You okay over there?"

"Okay is a relative term," I answer.

"Fair." He inclines his head. "But it's better than fine."

I grin. "I guess it is at that. Jude—"

I break off as my aunt calls my name.

She and Mozart are full-on running across the quad, and I know it's because she's worried about me.

"I'm okay," I call back, moving to head her off.

She careens to a stop in front of me. "Let me see your eyes!"

"They're okay. I'm okay," I reiterate. "Jude helped me."

"Jude?" She glances toward him, eyes wide. "What did he do?"

I start to explain, but this time he's the one to cut me off. "I didn't really do much. I think she managed to fight it off on her own."

I shoot him a what-the-hell look, but he studiously refuses to meet my gaze. Figuring there must be some reason he doesn't want to tell my aunt what actually happened, I keep my mouth shut. For now.

But at some point, he's going to have to explain all of this to me. And I mean *all*.

"Hmm." My aunt glances back and forth between us with narrowed eyes.

And I get it. Jude and I may not have talked much—or at all—these past few years, but for most of our lives, the two of us and Carolina were inseparable. That means we covered for each other a lot. And as Carolina's mother, she's heard more than her fair share of ridiculous stories and even more ridiculous excuses.

In the end, she doesn't call us on it, though. Instead, she just opens her bright-red medical bag and says, "I still want to check you over, make sure you're okay. I'm sorry it took me so long to get here. You're the third unmeshing we've had today because of that darn power surge. I was dealing with them, and that's why I missed your text." I don't bother to argue about the checkup—unlike my mother, Aunt Claudia rarely forces her will on anyone…unless their health is involved. Then she becomes downright pugilistic.

"There were other unmeshings?" I ask, because I really want to know what causes them.

"Yes." She pulls out her light and checks my eyes. "A dragon and a mermaid. They're okay, but it was touch and go for a few minutes." She taps my chin. "Open up. I want to see your throat."

"I really am all right," I tell her, even as I do what she says.

"We'll see about that." She takes out her stethoscope to listen to my heart.

I turn to share my amusement with Jude, only to find him walking back up the admin building steps. "Where are you going?" I ask.

"To finish up inside." He sounds surprised that I didn't figure it out.

"You should take someone with you. It's dangerous—"

This time he doesn't bother to answer. He just rolls his eyes.

And for a second, I'm not staring at seventeen-year-old Jude at all. I'm staring at fourteen-year-old Jude. Still tall, still beautiful, but a lot leaner and less filled out than now. His face is as somber as ever, but his eyes aren't as guarded. And maybe the biggest tip-off is he's wearing the old chukkas he gave up sophomore year. Not that I go out of my way to notice *what* Jude wears, but it was hard to miss when he traded them in for a pair of Tom Ford Chelsea boots.

"Hey—" I call out, totally confused. But then I blink and fourteen-year-old Jude is gone. And in his place is the guy who just saved my life.

"What's wrong, Clementine?" Aunt Claudia asks intently. "What did you see?"

But I just shake my head—if I tell her, I'll probably end up in the infirmary for the rest of the night. "Nothing. I'm just worried about him."

"Don't be," Aunt Claudia tells me as she looks into my ears, which have magically stopped hurting along with the rest of me. "He'll be fine."

There it is again, my family's pervasive, soul deep belief that Jude can handle the monsters—and he did, at least with the ones I saw. Not to mention the fact that his tattoos just did whatever they did to save me.

Is that it? Do they somehow keep him safe? And if so, how? And what are they exactly?

"You are in remarkably good shape considering everything you've been through," Aunt Claudia announces a few minutes later, after giving me a thorough check. "Mozart said you'd also gone a couple rounds with one of the menagerie monsters, but I see no evidence of that. Jude must have been with you."

I start to tell her he wasn't but then decide there's no point. It will only upset her. Plus, it's obvious no one in my family has any intention of telling me what's really going on with Jude and his powers. Just one more Calder Academy secret, apparently.

I wish I knew more about oneiroi, but Jude is the only one I've ever met. I've tried looking them up several times over the years, including the summer before freshman year when I was falling for him and wanted to know everything I could about him. But none of the information I found about the oneiroi sounded like Jude at all. When the internet failed me, I even went to our spooky, not-so-well-kept library. But the only book I found that mentioned the oneiroi only had a couple pages. Most of the information was super obvious, and again, what wasn't didn't sound like him.

"I do, however, suggest you go back to the dorm, get your dinner, and rest," Aunt Claudia says as she starts packing up her bag. "Shifting burns a lot of calories, and it takes a lot out of you—especially when something goes wrong."

"Is it normal for something to go wrong?" I ask the question that's been bothering me from the beginning. "Or is it just me?"

The thought that maybe my inexperience caused the unmeshing has been gnawing at me. This shift nearly killed me—and a few other students as well, apparently—which only makes it more obvious that Calder Academy has to do something about this mess. They can't just let students leave here to figure this shit out alone. Is there any wonder so many former students die in accidents?

I had Mozart, Luis, and Simon to explain things to me and Jude to help me through it—Serena had no one. And neither did any of the other unlucky ones.

Tears bloom behind my eyes at the thought of Serena going through something like what I just went through. No, she wasn't a shifter, but I'm sure at some point, she knew something was wrong, just like I did. And just like me, she didn't know how to fix it. Only there was no one to help her figure it out. She was all alone.

Rage wells up inside me, but I swallow it down. When this storm is over, when we've made it through, I'm going to talk to my mother again. I'm going to make her listen. Because no one deserves to die the way I almost just did, especially when they're lonely and terrified and broken all to hell.

"Oh, darling, there's nothing wrong with you." Aunt Claudia puts a soft hand on my cheek. "We had all kinds of problems with students when the power surge happened. It messed with the system we use to keep your magic safe and contained. Things went wonky for a lot of the students, not just with unmeshing. A few vampires got stuck in fading mode, a banshee screamed her entire cottage down, and several of the witches spelled themselves invisible. We couldn't even find them to help change them back. Thankfully it's over for now, and we should be off the island before anything like that happens again."

"You don't think we need to worry about tonight?" The last thing I want is to somehow end up unmeshed again. Even knowing Jude can fix me doesn't negate the pain that comes with it.

"I really don't. Uncle Christopher is working on the security system now, making sure it doesn't fail again."

I choose to believe her because I really don't have another choice.

Before I can say anything else, Eva and Luis come running up behind me. "Mozart DM'd us. She said you're okay." Eva turns to Aunt Claudia. "Is she okay?"

My aunt smiles indulgently. "She's fine. But I suggested she get some food." She glances around. "Actually, I suggest all of you get something to eat. You've been working hard, and that little mishap can't have been easy on any of you."

I follow her gaze back toward the admin building and realize that everyone has made it back.

"Go on ahead," Remy calls before continuing to board up a window with Simon. "We'll be done soon!"

Izzy quirks her brows at me before leaning against the building and going back to filing her nails.

When Mozart asks if she's planning on helping, she just shrugs. "I already did my job. This one's all yours."

As if to prove it, she starts sauntering back toward the dorms. Not surprisingly, no one tries to stop her. Not even my aunt.

Instead, she snaps her bag shut and tells me, "All right, then. I'm going to head back over to the gym. We have several students there who still need medical attention after the unfortunate incident."

We watch my aunt walk away, then Eva turns to me and studies my face. "No bullshit," she says. "We left here and I thought you were *dying.* Now there's not a scratch on you. What gives?"

My stomach chooses that moment to rumble loudly. That granola bar is long gone.

Luis makes a face. "Fine, we'll head back to the dorm. But I expect *every detail* on the way. So start talking. Now."

CHAPTER THIRTY-NINE

THIS IS HOW
WE UN-ROLL

I don't know how much I'm supposed to say about what Jude did—or even about the tattoos that he keeps hidden from everyone—so I try to keep it as vague as I can.

Neither Eva nor Luis appreciates that, though, so I try distraction and finally ask, "What do you guys know about oneiroi?"

"Not much." She shoots me a knowing look. "What happened to hating Jude and hoping he'd choke on a kumquat?"

"I—we— It's…" I give up when they both start laughing.

"Yeah, that's what I thought."

"It's been a very weird day," I tell her.

"Oh, please." Luis waves a dismissive hand. "This day left weird in its rearview hours ago."

"True, but you don't even know what else has happened."

His eyes go wide. "There's more?"

"Waaaaaay more," I answer. And then I tell them everything that's happened since Ember burst into flames in the hallway, which feels like days ago.

Their eyes get bigger by the second. But when I get to the root cellar and how one of the Jean-Jerks, and maybe even Jude, literally disappeared once they went inside, Eva loops her arm through mine and starts dragging me toward the other side of the island. "You have to show me this place."

"She has to show *us* this place," Luis corrects.

"Now?" My stomach grumbles in protest. "But I'm starving."

Eva rolls her eyes and fishes in her purse for her emergency pack of M&M's. "Eat these. Because you are definitely taking us there right now. What if the hurricane floods it while we're evacuated?"

"Then I'm pretty sure no one else will be disappearing inside it anytime soon."

"Seriously, Clementine?" she huffs. "I swear, you have no sense of adventure."

"I do, but I've had too much adventure today." But I open the bag of candy and stop protesting. The truth is I've been dying for another look at the place myself. Just to see if I missed something. Because I had to, right? Even fae don't just disappear into thin air—especially when they don't have their powers.

Besides, Eva's right. What if the storm does flood it? It didn't exactly look like it was in the best shape to begin with.

When I say as much, Luis's eyes go wide. "How bad a shape are we talking? Because I haven't had a tetanus shot in a while—"

"You're a wolf," Eva huffs in exasperation. "Can you even get tetanus?"

"I'm a human, too," he says with a sniff. "And humans can definitely get it. By the way, when was *your* last tetanus shot?"

"Worry about your own damn shots and leave mine alone," she shoots back. "For all I know, you could be overdue on rabies, too. You're definitely overdue on distemper."

"I'm pretty sure distemper doesn't mean what you think it does," Luis tells her.

"Yeah, well—"

"Stop!" I tell them both with a laugh. "None of us is getting tetanus from the place! Or rabies or distemper or *tuberculosis*. So chill out or this pack of M&M's and I are going back to the dorm. Alone."

They both grumble a little under their breath, but the bickering finally stops—at least for now. It is their favorite bonding activity, after all.

We walk the rest of the way talking about tomorrow's evacuation. But when we get to the cellar, there's a giant padlock on the door that definitely wasn't there earlier.

"How'd you get in last time?" Eva asks.

"It wasn't here then." I stare at the lock. Did someone really just lock it up because I went in there? And if they did, who was it? Jean-Luc? Or Jude?

Her eyes light up. "The plot thickens." Then she starts searching the ground around the cellar.

"What are you looking for?" Luis starts scanning the ground. "Maybe we can help."

"Hopefully, a key." She keeps searching while I just stare at her incredulously.

"You don't actually think whoever did this went through all the trouble of padlocking the place just to then hide the key in plain sight, do you?" I demand.

"People have a lot less imagination than you might think," she shoots back.

"Especially the Jean-Jerks," Luis concurs.

Less than two minutes of concerted searching later, she lets out a crow of triumph as she bends down and picks up an actual hollowed-out rock. "I told you! No imagination."

"So definitely Jean-Luc and not Jude," Luis comments as she pushes the top of the rock open and pulls out a key.

"Apparently." Eva slides the key into the padlock and lets out another happy exclamation as it pops right open. "Ready?"

I eat the last of the M&M's and shove the wrapper in my front pocket. "As I'll ever be."

The way this day is going, I wouldn't be surprised if a banshee came flying out at us. Or a leviathan. Or, even worse, my mother.

But the cellar is dark and quiet as we carefully make our way down the rickety steps, flashlights on.

"Geez, how deep is this place?" Eva asks when she's halfway to the bottom. "This is a serious amount of really scary steps."

"Deep," I answer, because she's not wrong. "Probably to hide the vegetables from the Texas heat."

"Or kill any intruders who aren't expecting such a big drop," Luis suggests as he starts exploring the cellar. "So where do you think they disappeared to in here? There aren't a lot of places to hide."

"There's *nowhere* to hide," I answer him. "Which is what I was telling you."

"Yeah, but I didn't believe you," Eva joins in. "I figured you missed something, but you really didn't."

"I really didn't," I agree.

But as he and Eva keep searching for someplace, anyplace, they could have disappeared to, I fixate on the tapestry. Because gone is the happy beach scene from earlier today. In its place is a lone man standing on a stormy beach as a huge wave threatens to crash right over him.

"Ooooh, cool rug," Eva says as she follows my gaze. "Depressing, but very cool."

"It didn't look like this earlier," I tell her as I step closer, trying to get a better look at the individual threads. Is this some kind of joke? But why would someone—even one of the Jean-Jerks—go through the trouble of padlocking the place while playing a childish game of bait-and-switch?

When I say as much to Eva and Luis, she just shrugs. "Maybe it's a different tapestry. Someone could have changed it out."

"Maybe," I answer doubtfully. "But somehow I don't think so."

"So what, then?" Now Luis sounds downright intrigued. "You think the tapestry actually changed on its own?"

If it had, it wouldn't even be the second strangest thing that happened to me today.

"I don't know. But I'm going to find out," I finally answer. Then I grab the tapestry and pull it straight off the wall.

"Hell, yeah!" Eva cheers. Then she stops and asks, "What exactly are we doing?"

"What does it look like? I'm taking it with us."

Her brows shoot up. "Don't you think that'll piss off the Jean-Jerks?"

"Do I look like I give a shit about pissing off the Jean-Jerks?"

I lay the tapestry on the floor and start rolling it up. It's heavier than it looks.

Luis stoops down and helps me roll.

Once the tapestry is rolled up, Eva steps closer to the wall it was hanging on and runs her hands over the rocks.

"I was kind of hoping it was hiding a secret passage," she says after a few moments of searching. "But there's nothing."

"I know. It's the strangest thing."

She moves to the next wall and searches it as well. "And you're sure they were in here?"

"I saw Jean-Luc come in with my own eyes. And there were wet footprints all over the floor that led absolutely nowhere that I could see."

She shakes her head. "Weird."

Thunder rumbles across the sky, and Luis sighs in disappointment. "We should probably head back if we don't want to get caught in the next rainband. Especially with that tapestry."

I nod in agreement, then bend down and prepare to heft the huge-ass tapestry into my arms. But the heavy weight of it is gone. Now it's lighter than my backpack.

"Here, let me help," Luis says, grabbing the end closest to him. His eyes widen as he registers the same thing I already have. "Umm, Clementine, are you *way* stronger than I think you are?"

I shake my head.

"Then what—" He looks as mystified as I feel.

"I've got no idea. Maybe whatever magic makes it change images has decided that it likes us."

Eva looks skeptical. "Or it's lulling us into a false sense of security so that it can kill us."

"Trust a witch to blame black magic," Luis teases as we carefully climb the steps out of the cellar.

"It's not pessimism if it's true," she answers with a grin.

"Well, let's hope it's just pessimism this time," I tell her. "For all our sakes."

But we barely get the cellar door closed and locked behind us before a gust of wind slams into us and sends the tapestry flying out of my arms. It hits the ground, edge first, and the impact forces it to partially unroll.

"I'll get it," Luis tells me, bending over to roll it back up. "The mud—" He breaks off. "Holy shit."

"What?" Eva asks, rushing over to him. "What's wrong?"

I'm right behind her, terrified that we've somehow ruined the tapestry.

But what I see is even worse. "Finish unrolling it," I tell Luis as I grab the other end to help.

"Out here?" Luis asks.

I know he's right, know the rain stands the risk of damaging it, but right now I don't care.

There has been one too many creepy things going on since this storm showed up, and I can't take the damn suspense for one second longer.

Eva must feel the same way, because she's already grabbing the roll and walking backward with it so the tapestry unfurls.

And that's when I freak out. Because in just the last couple of minutes, the tapestry has changed *again*.

Gone is the ominous beach scene, and in its place is one giant, dripping, bloodred word.

BEWARE.

CHAPTER FORTY

LIKE A MOM BOSS

"What the hell?" Eva says, her voice rising with each word she speaks. "How is that possible?"

"I told you it changed," I say, but it's not like I'm any calmer.

"Yeah, but I thought you were confused or something. You've had kind of a rough day. But this—" She stares down at the tapestry. "This is really creepy."

"Really creepy," Luis echoes.

They're not wrong. I know what I saw earlier, and I know the scene was different, but there was a part of me that thought there had to be an explanation. But this... There's no explanation for this. At least, no explanation that doesn't freak me the fuck out. Especially when I think about all the ghosts that keep telling me to run.

What is happening on this island? And what does it have to do with me?

"Do you think that's about the storm?" Eva asks, her voice still a full octave above normal.

"I don't know, but I'm not about to wait around and find out." Luis starts rolling the tapestry back up as fast as he can. "The way this day has been going, that could be a warning about anything from the apocalypse to a giant T-Rex bursting out of the woods over there. And I know how these things go. The gay best friend always dies first in horror movies."

"Not always," Eva tells him. "Sometimes it's the spunky sidekick."

Luis shoots her a dirty look. "Yeah, well, I'm the spunky sidekick, too. And I say we get the fuck away from here, fast."

"No argument from me," I tell him.

"Me, either," Eva agrees. "But are you sure we want to bring that thing with us?"

"I want to know what else it's going to say. Don't you?" I have to shout to be heard over the wind, which has picked up significantly in the last couple of minutes.

"Umm, definitely," Luis says as he finishes rolling up the tapestry and swings it over his shoulder. "Now let's get out of here, shall we?"

We take off running back toward the dorms. The rain is coming down so fast and hard that the ground is waterlogged, making every step a misery as we slog through mud and wet, loose sand.

It's slow going, made worse by the giant gusts of wind that keep hitting us head-on. More than once, Luis almost loses his grip on the tapestry. Somehow, we keep going, though, and finally make it back to the sidewalk that leads from the academic buildings to the dorms.

That's when we start booking it—or try to. But our muddy shoes slip and slide on the slick path. As a particularly terrifying bolt of lightning splits the sky, I start to wonder if we'll ever make it back.

Finally, finally, we get through the fence and make a beeline for the main dorm. We're almost there when a flash of pink catches my eye, and I stop dead in my tracks. I attempt to wipe the rain from my eyes and trace the streak of pink roaming through the downpour.

It's her again—the pregnant woman in the rose nightdress, pacing in front of the dorm.

Her hair is unbound now, and the wind has blown it so that it's covering her face. But there's something about the way she walks and carries herself—even in the middle of this storm—that seems familiar to me.

Even stranger, I know she's a ghost, but she looks lifelike. Yes, she's a translucent, milky gray. But unlike other ghosts, her hair is a deep, dark brown, and the flowers on her nightgown are a bright, vivid magenta.

I don't know why she looks so different than the other spirits or why she acts so peculiar. Instead of interacting with the others—or trying to interact with me—she just wanders back and forth. She doesn't even appear to notice I exist, while I can't help but notice her.

Lightning booms across the sky yet again, and Eva wraps a hand around my upper arm. "Why are you stopping?" she shouts. "Come on!"

"Sorry!" I lay on the speed, and we burst through the main door of the dorm like our lives depend on it. And maybe they do, considering the door has barely closed behind us when the sky opens up with a lightning show like nothing I've ever seen before.

We collapse the second we're inside. Luis drops the tapestry and stretches out, spread-eagled on the ground. Eva leans back against the wall, breath bellowing in and out. And I just lean over, bracing my hands on my knees, as I try desperately to catch my breath.

But we can't lay around the dorm common room forever—I'm wet and freezing. Eva picks up the tapestry, and we head toward the table to get our dinners. But I've only gone a few steps when my mother's voice rings out behind me, followed by the *clip, clip, clip* of her shoes against the worn tile.

"Clementine! Are you all right?" she asks.

Eva and Luis take one look at her and hightail it across the room with the tapestry while I step in front of them to block her view.

"I'm fine," I tell her, forcing myself to straighten up even though I still can barely breathe. "We were just trying to outrun the lightning."

Her eyes are intense as she catalogs me from head to toe.

"Your aunt told me there was a problem earlier. Is everything okay now?"

A problem seems like an understatement, but since I don't want her to chain me to her side for the next twelve hours, I just shrug. "It wasn't that big of a deal. I'm okay."

"You're sure?" Her eyes search mine.

"Oh, yeah. I freaked out a little in the middle of the unmeshed thing, but I'm good now. Really."

"All right, then. Grab your dinner and get back to your room. We've instituted an eight o'clock curfew tonight, and the staff will be patrolling to ensure everyone stays safely where they belong."

I nod.

"And take a hot shower, will you, please? The last thing you need is to get sick right now."

It's such a motherly thing to say that, at first, I'm convinced I heard her wrong. But she definitely still looks worried.

"I really am fine, Mom," I tell her.

"You always are," she says, blowing out a long breath. "Claudia reminded me this afternoon that I can be too harsh on you sometimes, and I'm sorry about that. I know we don't agree on much right now, but I do love you, Clementine. Very much."

"I know you do, Mom." Tears burn at the backs of my eyes. I beat them back for what feels like the millionth time today. Because we do have our disagreements. And I do think she's wrong about a lot of things, especially how she runs this place. Not to mention, I'm still furious with her about what happened to Serena. But… "I love you, too, Mom."

She nods, her throat working in a way I've never seen before. "Okay. Get going before your friends get tired of waiting for you. I'll see you in the morning."

"Okay." Impulsively, I lean forward and give her a quick peck on the cheek. "Make sure you get some rest, too."

"I'll rest when I get every one of my students and faculty to safety. Until then, I've got work to do."

As if to underscore the point, the walkie-talkie she's got fastened to her waistband starts to crackle. "To your room," she tells me with a stern look before walking away, putting the radio at her ear.

"What was that all about?" Luis asks, eyes wide as I join him and Eva next to a large pile of folded towels.

"I think she was worried about the whole unmeshing thing," I answer as Eva hands me a towel. "I think she wanted to check on me. I told her everything was fine."

"I'd rather not get a massive punishment for our little magic carpet–snatching adventure, so good call," Eva tells me. "Now, I'm starving, so do you guys mind if we grab dinner and head out?"

"Already ahead of you," Luis says. "I've got stuff back at the cottage, so I'll see you guys later. But call me if that thing does anything else, will you?"

"Absolutely," I promise.

Luis heads out with a little wave while Eva and I grab the tapestry, our box dinners, an umbrella, and a couple of ponchos from the table set up near the door before signing out. Then we head toward the center mall that runs through the entire dorm area and leads directly to our cottages. But we've only made it about halfway when we look up to find Jean-Claude walking down the sidewalk straight toward us.

CHAPTER FORTY-ONE

RUG RAGE

"**W**hat should we do?" Eva hisses at me.

"Not a lot we can do," I say, even as I avoid making eye contact with him. No need to rile the jerk up, and maybe if we don't pay any attention to him, he won't pay any attention to us...or the not-so-subtle tapestry we're carrying.

The wind is bad enough that we're all having to hunch forward against it, and I think maybe we'll actually have a chance to get through this without attracting his attention.

It almost works, too. But just as we're about to pass him, Jean-Claude steps in front of me.

"Where did you get that?" he demands, and when I look up at him, he looks pissed off but also totally freaked out. Then again, that could just be the rain—it's frizzed out his green curls to the point that he looks like he's wearing a whole chia pet on his head under his poncho.

My stomach drops a little—so much for the hope that he wouldn't recognize the tapestry.

Not to mention any small thought I might have had about them not all being involved in whatever goes on in that root cellar just went right out the window.

But what exactly is going on?

The minute Jude told me to stay away, I was suspicious. But when we found the padlock, I was certain I'd stumbled on something I shouldn't have. Now, looking at the fear in Jean-Claude's eyes, I'm more convinced than ever that something not okay has been happening in that root cellar.

But what? And what does Jude have to do with it? He's not exactly the joining type and never has been. So what is he doing with the Jean-Jerks of all people, when he's never given any indication that he has anything but contempt for them?

It doesn't make sense.

Then again, neither does a tapestry that changes at will, so we're all dealing with a brave new world here.

When I don't immediately answer him, Eva jumps in. "This?" she asks, acting surprised. "Clementine's mom asked us to retrieve it from her office. Apparently, it's been hanging there for as long as Calder Academy's been around. She didn't want to leave it, in case the hurricane is as bad as they think it will be."

His eyes narrow suspiciously as they dart back and forth between us. "You're telling me you got that from the headmaster's office?"

"We did." I back Eva up. "It's my mom's favorite."

"Oh, yeah?" He leans forward, but I'm not sure if he's trying to be menacing or just brace against the wind. "What's on it?"

At the moment? I have absolutely no idea. It could be anything. But since that's exactly what I don't want to tell him, I do the only thing I can think of. I make something up.

"A manticore. Like a lot of manticores." Eva looks at me like I'm very confused, but I keep bumbling around, trying to sell my absolutely ridiculous story. "Like a family portrait type rug thing that's totally an heirloom."

"A family portrait *rug*?" he repeats. "That has a bunch of manticores on it?"

"Absolutely," I tell him. And somehow, I even manage to keep a straight face.

"You know, I've been in your mom's office a bunch of times. I've never seen anything like that in there."

"Well, it's not like she keeps it out for public display," I bluster. "Obviously. It's personal."

"Oh, really? It's personal?" Now he really does sound menacing, even before he takes a step forward. "Let me see it."

"Excuse me?" I act a lot more offended than I feel. "No!"

"What do you mean no?" He looks like he's never heard the word before, which to be fair, maybe he hasn't. The fae mafia tend to get whatever they want, whenever they want it.

"I mean, which part of 'personal' do you not understand? I'm not going to show you my family's personal, private heirloom," I snap. "And if you've got a problem with that, then it's too damn bad."

This time, I'm the one who advances on him. "Now get out of my way. I'm sick and tired of being in this rain."

He backs up a couple of steps, but he doesn't clear the way. And when I move to go around him, he moves with me, blocking my path. And while a part of me wants nothing more than to kick him in the balls, I also know that if I don't play this right, the incoming storm will be the least of my problems.

At the same time, there is no way I can let him see this tapestry. Jean-Claude has already proven he has no trouble beating up girls— the asshole has given me more than a few bruises through the years. No way am I about to let him do the same to Eva.

"I'll get out of your way as soon as you let me look at that manticore rug of yours," he tells me, arms crossed and snide look on his face.

"I already told you that's not going to happen. And I have no idea what makes you think you have the right to order me to do anything, especially with something that is obviously school property."

This time when I step forward, I knock him in the shoulder with my own. And then I keep going, keep moving forward until he has no choice but to step back or push back. Thankfully, he's not nearly as brave alone as he is when the other Jean-Jerks are around, and he steps back. At first, it's just a couple of steps, but then it's several, and now I know I've won—whether he's willing to acknowledge it or not.

And while I can see him psyching himself up to push me back— literally and figuratively—for once, the storm comes to our rescue. Lightning shoots through the sky, slamming into a tree that's much too close to us for comfort as thunder shakes the ground beneath our feet.

Seconds later, an ominous crack sounds, and a huge branch comes crashing down.

I throw myself at Eva, knocking her out of the way just in time to keep the heavy branch from falling on her.

She's okay—we all are—but in the middle of being knocked sideways by me, Eva loses her grip on the tapestry.

It flies through the air before crashing to the ground and unrolling, right at Jean-Claude's feet.

CHAPTER FORTY-TWO

A SINGLE RUG IS WORTH
A THOUSAND WORDS

Eva and I exchange a look as Jean-Claude bends down to get a closer look at it through the streaming rain.

"Run!" I whisper to Eva as I prepare to fight Jean-Claude for the tapestry.

Common sense says I should let it go, but there's something really odd and magical about the damn wall-hanging. The Jean-Jerks are the last people on the entire island that I want to be in charge of something with that much power. Every instinct I have is screaming at me to make sure I hold on to it.

"I'm not leaving you alone with him," Eva snarls. And then we both move closer, looking for a way to yank the tapestry back from him.

But as I bend down to get it, I realize it's changed again. Gone is the warning from earlier and in its place is *a family of manticores, sitting around a table smoking cigars and playing poker.*

Holy. Shit.

It heard me. It actually heard what I was saying and changed to help me out.

What kind of magic carpet *is* this thing?

Jean-Claude snarls when he gets his first good look at the tapestry. "Seriously? This is your family heirloom?"

"Hey, that sounded very judgmental," Eva scolds him as she crouches down to help me roll the tapestry up. "Everyone's family has their own special thing. Just because yours might not enjoy playing poker—"

She breaks off as another explosion of lightning splits the sky. "We should get out of here," I say uneasily. "Before we all end up crushed under a falling tree."

As if to back me up, the trees that line the path creak ominously.

Jean-Claude shoots the waving branches a worried look before backing up. "This isn't over."

"I kind of feel like it is," I tell him as I pick the rug up and sling it over my shoulder. Once again, it weighs almost nothing, and we start back down the path to our cottage.

This time, he's too busy booking it in the opposite direction to even think about stopping us.

"What the hell?" Eva says, shouting to be heard above the storm. "We almost got mugged for an old, enchanted tapestry."

"Actually, I think we almost got mugged for something a lot more complicated than that," I tell her. I still can't believe the thing can listen to what goes on around it—and can change accordingly. "I just wish I knew what this thing actually was. What I do know is that something isn't right."

"Well, I don't like the sound of that," she shouts over the howl of the wind. Then she nearly gets knocked over as she picks my umbrella up from where I dropped it and tries to hand it to me.

But the storm has gotten worse in the time we've been standing here, and a gust of wind slams into us, knocking me back several feet.

"I know we just hid this from your mom, but Jean-Claude's attitude changed my mind. Now I'm wondering if we need to call in reinforcements. What do you think?"

"I have no idea," I answer as we start walking. The wind and rain are coming so furiously now that we're almost bent in half as we force our way through it. "I agree that something's weird about it, but I don't have a clue what it is."

"What about talking to Jude about it? If he was in the cellar, he obviously knows something about what's going on."

"Yeah, but that just means he could be involved," I shout to be heard over the storm. "It's not like he's told me anything about it."

"Have you asked him?" When I remain silent, she gives me a look. "How can you know what he knows or doesn't know—or what he's doing or not doing—if you don't talk to him?"

It's not bad advice. It really isn't. But still, I instinctively start to say no. Then I think about the look on Jean-Claude's face and reconsider. Maybe I need to manticore up and talk to Jude about this damn tapestry. Maybe he can help.

Or maybe he'll tell me something that sets my teeth on edge.

Either way, though, it might be time I actually ask.

"Maybe," I agree as we finally get to the covered picnic area in the center of the mall. It's left over from resort days, and while the tables aren't in the best shape, it provides a little bit of shelter from the elements, and right now I'll definitely take it. "If I can ever pin him down for longer than a few seconds."

"Text him," she suggests.

I seize up. "Oh, I don't think—"

She rolls her eyes and yanks my phone out of my back pocket. "Obviously, your relationship—whatever it is—is going through some kind of shift. He *saved* you today. *Twice.* Plus, I saw the way he looked at you when he carried you out of the dungeon. It won't bother him *at all* if you text him."

"I don't care if it bothers him," I tell her. "I care if…"

"If what?" she asks impatiently.

"I don't want to look…"

"What?" she demands when I trail off again.

"Needy, I guess. I mean, he kissed me again today and then rejected me again. What about that says, 'I'll be there for you when you need me'?"

"Oh, I don't know. How about when he saved you from dying unmeshed?" she asks archly. "Or when he saved you yet again from the grossest monster in existence? The guy obviously has no problem being there when you need him." She holds my phone out to me. "Besides, it's not needy to try to get information from the one guy who seems to have a clue about what's going on. Text the boy already. Ask him your question."

She's right. I'm totally not the kind of girl to stand around dithering about what a guy is going to think of something she does. And the awkwardness between me and Jude isn't about to change me into that, either. So I fire off a quick couple of texts in a row, refusing to let myself think about if he's going to answer or not.

Me: Are you done at the menagerie?

Me: Something weird is going on, and I was hoping I could talk to you about it

Me: Something even weirder than what's already happened, I mean

When he doesn't immediately answer, I shove my phone back into my pocket and start walking again.

"He's probably still shelling out snacks for the monsters," Eva tells me.

It's my turn to roll my eyes as we leave the relative safety of the covered patio and turn the corner and start down the path that leads to our cottage. "I know. It's *fine.*"

"I *know* it's fine. I was just saying—"

She breaks off as the door of the first cottage on the path flies open, and a lean, muscled arm drags her inside.

CHAPTER FORTY-THREE

HEY JUDE

She screams, then goes silent. I race after her, heart pounding and tapestry knocking against my shoulder, only to come face-to-face with a grinning Mozart.

"Welcome to Ember's and my humble abode," she says with a flourish of her hand.

"We've been watching for you," Simon adds as he shuts the door behind us.

"Seriously?" Eva shrieks. "You couldn't have just DM'd us?"

"Where's the fun in that? Besides, how am I supposed to keep my old skills sharp if I never get to practice them?"

"Considering your old skills involved charming the pants off people and then divesting them of their property, I don't particularly care if you get to practice them or not," I shoot back. "Although you're doing fine—at least in the former department."

"I knew there was a reason I liked you," he tells me as he ushers us deeper into the cottage, where—it turns out—Remy, Izzy, and Ember are already sitting around, talking while Luke Combs's "Fast Car" plays over the speaker. "You've got that take-no-bullshit attitude that's hard to resist."

"I don't know about that. Some people have no trouble resisting me at all."

"You might be surprised," he says, then gestures to the coffee table where there are several bags of chips set up, along with some sodas and sparkling waters. "Help yourself."

"Storm Party, obviously!" Eva answers, shimmying her way over to the coffee table. "I *love* this song."

"It's a remake of an old Tracy Chapman song," Remy tells her. "If you like this, you should hear the original."

"Really?" She looks intrigued as she reaches for a chip. "You should play it next!"

"Are we really just doing this? Having a party when we should be packing?" I know I sound as bewildered as I feel.

"Packing shmacking." Simon waves a hand, and those moonlit-ocean eyes of his are glowing again in that way that makes me majorly uncomfortable. "Throw a uniform and a couple pairs of jeans in a duffel bag and you're done. It's not like we're going to be gone that long."

"Unless the whole school blows away," Izzy interjects dryly.

He shrugs. "So pack a lot of underwear and socks. You'll be fine."

Part of me is tempted to stay, even though I know I shouldn't be. The storm is set to get worse anytime now, and the last thing I want is to be stuck in someone else's cottage. At the same time, though, this looks like a lot more fun than moping around my room for the next several hours. Plus, Jude will probably text one of them while I'm here, and I can at least be sure he's okay—

"Jude just finished at the menagerie and is on his way," Mozart says as she hands me a towel. "So why don't you put that thing— whatever it is—in the corner—and dry off? I put some sweats and tees on my bed for you and Eva. Grab something to drink while you wait for him."

"I didn't come here looking for Jude!" I tell her, and I don't need a mirror to know my cheeks are turning bright red.

"You didn't come here at all," Remy soothes. "We dragged you in."

Oh. Right. "I should go—"

Mozart steers me toward her bedroom. "Go get changed, Kumquat."

"What did you just call me?" I demand, eyes narrowed.

"Oh, sorry." She holds her hands up in a whoops gesture. "I didn't realize old Sergeant Pepper was the only one who can call you that. My mistake."

My cheeks go from pink to flaming in a second, and I duck my head to try to hide my embarrassment. Now I want nothing more than to flee, but I'll look even worse—even weaker—if I run away. So fuck it. Just fuck it.

I close the door behind me, then dry off and quickly change. Mozart's even taller than I am—and a little more curvy—so I have to roll the sweats up a little so I don't trip on them. But they're dry and warm and feel pretty damn luxurious after the nasty, wet clothes I've been wearing for way too long. I don't even mind that they're Calder Academy red.

I flop down next to Remy, who snags the bag of spicy dill pickle chips and hands them to me with a waggle of his brows.

"How'd you know these are my favorite?" I ask. Then, before he can even answer, I do it for him. "Carolina."

He smiles, and this time it's only a little bit sad. "When you're locked in a cell together for several years, you tend to talk about everything. Including what flavor chips you and your favorite cousin like."

"Apparently." Sadness squeezes my stomach at the thought of Carolina telling him a bunch of stories about us to make the time in prison pass faster, but I try not to give in to it right now. I've got more than enough painful emotions roiling around inside me.

"Hey, why *did* your cousin get sent to the Aethereum anyway?" Izzy asks. "Normally, fourteen is way too young for that kind of prison."

"Hey, now," Remy answers, acting offended even though I can tell he's just trying to deflect the question—and the attention—away from me. Which I appreciate. A lot. "I was there my whole life."

"Exactly," Izzy agrees, batting her big blue eyes at him in mock innocence. "And look how you turned out."

"Very well, if I do say so myself," he shoots back with a grin.

She shakes her head. "You're impossible."

"Aww, you know I've grown on you."

"Like a wart, maybe," she growls back.

"Everyone's gotta start somewhere." He gives her what I'm pretty sure is his most charming grin. "In fact—"

He breaks off as a knife goes flying by his head and embeds itself in the wall directly behind us.

Eva, who is just walking out of the bedroom after changing, lets out a small scream while the rest of us jump a little. But Remy takes it in stride, blowing Izzy a kiss as he pulls the knife from the wall.

She snarls in response, but I notice she doesn't send another knife his way. And he doesn't give her back the one she already threw.

I take a sip of La Croix to steady my churning stomach, expecting the conversation to move on now that the excitement is over. But it turns out everyone is still watching me, waiting for me to answer Izzy's question.

So I do, though even I don't know why. Except, in some strange way, it feels good to talk about it when my family never does. "I don't have any idea what Carolina did. Everything was fine when I went to bed that night, but when I woke up the next morning, I had a bunch of missed calls and a couple of text messages from her. But it was too late. She was already gone, and no one would tell me why."

"What did the messages say?" Ember asks. It's the first time she's spoken to me since I got here.

"She told me to take care of Jude, that he was going to need it." I smile sadly, because we all know how that ended up. "And to trust that there would always be enough time. Except there wasn't. Hers ran out."

Remy makes a small, unconscious sound at that, and when I turn to him, it's to find that his hands are clenched so tightly that his knuckles have turned white. And I know he's blaming himself.

I reach over and place a hand over his. I don't say anything because I don't have the words yet, don't know if I'll ever have the words. But I know that no matter how much I want to blame him, it's not really his fault Carolina is dead.

My mother is the one who sent her away from the island when nothing she possibly could have done at fourteen would have warranted that. But she did it anyway, and now Carolina is dead.

My mother and I had the worst fight we've ever had the morning I woke up and discovered Carolina was gone, that she had sent her away. I begged her to bring her back, begged her to change her mind. Told her she was handing Carolina a death sentence.

My mother didn't agree, said she was doing what she had to to keep the people she cared about safe and that this situation wasn't any of my business—something she made sure I understood before she let me leave. And when it got bad, really bad, for a minute, I thought she was going to send me to the prison right along with my cousin. But instead, she just gave me my first month's worth of chrickler detentions, among other things.

And nothing has ever been the same since.

Not between my mother and me.

Not between Carolina and me, obviously.

And not between Jude and me, either, because that was the day he decided we no longer had anything to say to each other. Even though I've never stopped having things to say to him. And I don't think I ever will.

The pain of it all comes crashing back to me, and for a second, I want nothing more than to get out of here as fast as I can. But that will just make me look like a coward—the one thing I can't afford to be, even in front of these people who appear to want to be friends.

But appearances tend to be deceiving, especially the ones that look good. The ones that make everyone around feel normal, if only for a little while. So I stay where I am, even force myself to eat a few of the dill pickle chips Remy handed me. No one needs to know they taste like sawdust in my mouth.

Before I can think of anything else to say, Orville Peck's "Dead of Night" comes on. Because of course it does.

"Turn it up," Ember tells Mozart.

She complies, and the macabre and melancholy beat fills the room and my senses.

Whenever I hear this song, all I can think of is Jude. Maybe that's why I'm not the least bit surprised when the door flies open and he walks in, looking as dark and mysterious as the song itself.

CHAPTER FORTY-FOUR

I COULD TOTALLY
TAP-ESTRY THAT

The first thing I notice is that he just came from feeding and preparing no fewer than six monster enclosures, and there's not a scratch on him—not even from the chricklers.

The second is that he doesn't look happy at all.

As soon as the door closes behind him, his eyes meet mine from across the room, and for one second, I get a glimpse of pure, pissed-off misery. I start to ask him what's wrong, but before I can get the words out, the emotional shutters come down, locking me, and everyone else in the room, out.

Not that anyone else seems to notice. Then again, this is how he always looks to them.

"How'd it go?" Mozart asks as she hands him a bottle of water.

Jude shrugs. "Fine. But I can't stay. I have—" He breaks off, swallowing back whatever he was going to say.

Mozart, Simon, and Ember exchange a look, but they don't say anything as the song reaches the chorus—and neither does anybody else.

I wait for him to say more, but he doesn't. He just leans back against the wall and drinks the water down in two long swallows. And he doesn't look at me once.

A little spurt of hurt starts deep inside of me, but I beat it back.

Because, despite everything, this isn't about me. It's about something being wrong with him. And I can't help wondering if he's not looking at me because he's afraid I'll figure that out.

When he's done, Jude tosses the bottle toward the small recycling can in the corner of the kitchenette without so much as glancing its way. Seconds later, it flies straight in, not even brushing against the rim.

"Show-off," Simon mutters with a roll of his eyes.

But Jude's attention has already been snagged by the rolled-up tapestry in the corner.

"What is that?" he demands hoarsely.

And because I want answers from him, I do something I haven't done with anyone else. I tell him the truth about the tapestry. And watch him closely for his reaction.

"Just something I found in that old cellar on the other side of the island. It's what I was texting you about." I watch him carefully, wanting to see his reaction. Does he know what the tapestry can do? And if so, is that why he was so adamant that I stay away from there?

I didn't think it was possible, but somehow his face goes even more blank—but in a very obviously disturbed way.

"It's really cool," Eva starts. "It does this thing where it—"

She breaks off when I shoot her a look.

"Where it does what?" Ember's dark eyes are intrigued as she glances back and forth between Jude and me.

Eva looks at me helplessly.

"It's just a picture of the island the way it used to be, when it was still a resort," I tell her. "No big deal."

I'm pretty sure Jude's eye twitches when I say the last part. Which has my own eyes narrowing as I try to figure out why he's so upset. Is it that I took the tapestry? Or that Eva and I might know its secret? And what's the big deal if we do? Why does this tapestry matter so much to the Jean-Jerks? And—apparently—to Jude as well?

"I should probably get going—" I start.

At the exact same time, Simon comments, "You know what this get-together could really use?" he asks, climbing to his feet.

"A backup generator?" Mozart answers wryly as the lights start to flicker.

I freeze, heart beating wildly as I wait to see if my manticore is going to rear its head again. It doesn't—and, as far as I can tell, nothing happens for anybody else, either. Maybe Aunt Claudia is right and Uncle Christopher really did manage to get things fixed for the time being.

I'd like to say I'm disappointed, but after what happened to me earlier, I'm actually really relieved—at least for now.

"*I* was going to say a game of Never Have I Ever," Simon tells her, and now his entire body is glowing in a way that makes it impossible for me to look away from him. Remy's right. This whole siren thing *is* a trip. "But I suppose your answer works, too."

"Give me a break," Ember snorts. "We're locked in a school in the middle of the fucking Gulf of Mexico. A better game would be 'Maybe I did something bad once a long time ago.'"

I laugh despite myself, because Ember may be a tough nut to crack, but when she's right, she's right.

"All right, then. How about Truth or Dare? But I am not kissing Jude again." Simon mock shudders. "He tastes like peppermint."

"No, he—" I break off as I realize what I'm about to give away.

Thankfully everyone else is too busy laughing at the you-should-be-so-lucky look Jude is currently giving Simon to notice my faux pas. Well, everyone but Remy, who is watching me thoughtfully.

Desperate to get him to focus on something other than my ridiculous slipup, I blurt out the first idea that comes to mind. "We could play Two Truths and a Lie," I suggest.

"Hey, now," Simon says with a wide grin. "That's what I'm talking about!"

"How's that supposed to work when most of us barely know each other?" Izzy asks in a voice that says she's more than fine with things staying that way.

"That's the fun part! It'll make the guessing extra interesting," Eva tells her, and she sounds surprisingly into what *was* a suggestion made out of desperation. "And it's not like we have so much else to do tonight."

"What if we don't want to know more about each other?" Ember growls. But when Eva's face falls, she quickly backtracks. "Ignore me. I probably need to eat something."

Mozart picks up a bag of chips and tosses it at her face. She catches it, then flips her roommate off before opening it and shoving a handful in her mouth.

"Okay, then," Simon asks, grabbing another drink, "who's going first?"

No one volunteers, which doesn't actually surprise me. It's one thing to listen to other people's secrets—it's another thing to tell your own. I half expect Mr. I-Can't-Stay to leave now, but Jude doesn't move.

Instead, he just watches and waits—though I'm not sure for what. I'm pretty sure it's not the game we're playing.

As the wind howls by the cottage, rattling the windows and shaking the chairs on the front porch, we all kind of stare at each other questioningly before Eva finally says, "I'll go."

She does, however, take a long, slow sip of her soda before actually starting. "First one—I was born in Puerto Rico, and when I finally graduate from here, I want to go back there to live. Second, I'm terrified of heights. And third, I have no idea what element I draw my power from."

None of what she says surprises me—and I know immediately that her being afraid of heights is the lie. Just last week she was hanging out on the roof of the cottage, weaving twinkle lights around the gutters to "give the place a little pop of fun."

And I'm not the least bit surprised about the fact that she doesn't know what element is hers—she'd barely had a chance to explore her powers before she got sent to Calder Academy. She was sent here because she was trying to do the most basic, elemental spell a witch can do—light a candle using magic. Unfortunately, the spell went terribly, terribly wrong, and she ended up burning down her entire apartment complex. Several people died, and a lot more were injured. Eva's been terrified of fire ever since.

"I say the element thing is the lie," Simon guesses. "I'm sure witches can just feel whatever element they have an affinity for."

"Says the mermaid who spends as much time as possible in the water," Ember teases.

"Siren," he answers emphatically. "Not the same."

"You have a tail, gills, and live in the water," she shoots back.

"Sounds the same to me."

He doesn't say anything else, but he does keep looking at her. At first, I think it's because he's annoyed, but then I actually glance at his face.

And I can't help thinking how good Simon looks, eyes dark and brown skin awash with light. Also, he smells really, really delicious. I lean forward to try to catch more of his scent and realize that somehow, it's all of my favorite things. Vanilla, cardamom, honey, lemon, all rolled together in a way that makes me want to scoot even closer to him. And this time when he says, "I'm a siren," it feels like the words somehow seep through my very pores.

I take a deep breath, pull his scent deeper inside me, and—

"Knock it off," Jude growls, and suddenly he's not across the room anymore. He's crouched down beside me, his hand on my shoulder as he gently pulls me back until I'm once again sitting up straight.

I start to get offended, thinking he's telling me to stop when I'm not actually doing anything. But when he leans closer, I get a whiff of his own warm honey-and-spice scent and I realize Simon's is just a poor imitation.

I take a deep breath before I can stop myself, and suddenly Jude is right there, inside me. Filling up all the places that have stood vacant, dormant, for the last three years. Then he lifts his face to mine, and I fall straight into his kaleidoscope eyes. And keep falling and falling and falling.

"And that, my friends," Simon tells us with a little click of his tongue in the corner of his mouth, "is the difference between a mermaid and a siren—even one whose powers are locked down."

The words remind me where I am, and I jerk my gaze from Jude's. Only to see everyone else in the room slowly blinking as if awakening from a trance. I glance at Simon, who wiggles his brows at me, and it finally occurs to me what happened. Ember was messing with him, and he responded by showing her exactly what a siren can do.

Even before Ember says, "You are such a jerk!" and throws a chip at him.

He catches it with a grin. "Hey, I was just providing an educational demonstration," he tells her before popping the chip in his mouth.

"I think you should have to go next. Punishment for that little 'educational demonstration.'" I use my fingers to make quotes around the words.

He shrugs. "Sure. But first Eva has to tell us what was the lie. The element thing, right?"

"Actually, it was the heights. Being high up doesn't scare me at all."

"So you like to fly?" Ember asks, suddenly looking very interested in the conversation.

"I've never been. I didn't really know a lot of shifters in my old life, before I came here."

"I'll take you," Ember offers. "When we graduate. If you want, I mean."

Eva lights up. "I'd love that."

"Then we'll do it." Ember looks as close to happy as I've ever seen her. But the moment she realizes we're looking at her, the normal scowl comes back in force. "Who's next?"

"I've been to forty-seven countries. I'm actually seventy-eight years old. And I've never killed anyone." Izzy yawns as she runs a hand through her long, red hair, her expression clearly saying she doesn't care if we manage to guess her lie or not.

"Umm, that was…" Simon looks flummoxed, like he has no idea what to say. And I don't blame him. That was a lot to take in…and trying to figure out which one of those things is the lie is mind-bending.

I glance at Jude, to see what he thinks, but I don't think he even heard her. He's sitting next to me, but he's completely focused on the tapestry in the corner, eyes narrowed and foot tapping the way he always does when he's trying to figure something out.

"I'm going to go with the forty-seven countries thing," Mozart says as she leans over to hand me a bottle of Topo Chico.

I lift a brow at her, but she just grins and whispers, "You're looking a little thirsty."

My whole face burns with embarrassment—I know she's not talking about the sparkling water—and I drag my gaze away from Jude.

"Is she right?" Eva asks curiously. "How many countries have you actually been to?"

"They're all lies," Remy says as he kicks his feet out and leans back on his elbows.

"All?" Eva squeaks, and I know she's thinking about Izzy's last lie. "That's not how the game—"

"Please," Izzy says with a roll of her eyes. "I just met you people. You don't actually think I'm going to tell you anything about myself, do you?"

"But you kind of just did," I say because one of the things this game always proves to me is that a person's lies tell as much as their truths do. And Izzy isn't the only person at this school to kill someone—accidentally or on purpose. Her knife use alone makes that truth not surprising at all.

But what is surprising—and makes me wonder—is the fact that she lied about it. The only question now is were these lies just throwaways or did she pick them because she wished they were the truth?

An awkward silence ensues—one where I remember that, despite what Izzy and I went through together, I really don't know her. I don't know any of the people in this room, except Eva...and maybe Jude.

Oh, I used to know him. But now? The way he keeps looking at that tapestry and then glancing out the window like he wants to be anywhere but here makes me wonder how much I've missed in the last three years.

We all kind of stare at each other for a moment, trying to figure out what to say or do next. And then Simon must decide, fuck it, because he jumps in with a, "Looks like it's my turn."

He gives us a choice between *I've crashed two dozen ships, I like to hunt for sunken treasure,* and *I write unrequited love poetry*—all of which sound totally believable to me.

But Ember just laughs. "You're a siren. No way is your love unrequited."

I wait for him to make a comment about his obvious crush on her, but he just shakes his head no instead.

"I think—" Mozart starts, but Ember interrupts him.

"Really? Who in this school can't you get if you put your mind to it? Especially considering that little demonstration you just treated us to." She's clearly not ready to let this go, and part of me wants to ask her how she can be so dense. Especially since Simon is looking at her steadily while Jude and Mozart look anywhere but.

Because I'm obviously not the only one who knows what he's so clearly trying to tell her. And she, just as clearly, isn't getting it. I just can't figure out if that's because she's clueless or willfully ignorant.

Mozart clears her throat, but Ember ignores her, clearly waiting for an answer that Simon is not going to verbally give her. So Mozart clears her throat again. And again. And—

"Are you trying to hack up a fur ball over there or what? You're a dragon, not a damn werewolf!" she demands, finally wrenching her gaze away from the siren.

"I was trying to take my turn," she answers, eyes narrowed in annoyance.

She throws up her hands. "Well, then, what are you waiting for? Go!"

Mozart thinks for a second—whether about her statements or about biting her hand off, I can't tell—but then she says, "I'm a dragon. I've been on the island three years. And...I'm a vegetarian."

For several seconds, dead silence meets her proclamations. And then we all burst out laughing at the exact same time.

"Hey, what's so funny?" she asks, sounding bewildered.

"You—" Simon starts but then ends up laughing so hard that he can't finish the statement.

"I what?" The bewilderment has turned to insult.

"We just can't decide," I tell her, swallowing down the laughter still bubbling inside of me, "if you are terrible at this game or an absolute genius."

Mozart preens at that. "A genius, obviously."

"I'm going to go with vegetarian as the lie," Ember says dryly. "Considering you had three turkey sandwiches for lunch."

"So I'm an open book." Mozart shrugs. "Nothing wrong with that."

"Nothing at all," I agree, but I'm still grinning, and so is everyone else.

The game moves on to Remy and me, but nothing earth-shattering comes from either of us—probably because we have the same problem. We've never had the chance to do much of anything because we've spent our entire lives locked up.

But then it's Jude's turn. And I can't help holding my breath as I wonder what he's *finally* going to share.

CHAPTER FORTY-FIVE

FOUR JEAN-JERKS
AND A LIE

For some reason, Jude looks completely nonplussed that it's his turn, even though it's no different from when it was anybody else's. But before he can say anything, a knock sounds at the door.

"Who do you think *that* is?" Simon asks. "Everyone we like is in this room already."

Ember snorts. "And some we don't."

I try not to take it personally that she's looking straight at me when she says that, but I'm pretty sure she means it personally, so...

"Be nice!" Simon admonishes with a shake of his head.

"Probably a teacher, checking to make sure we're where we're supposed to be," Mozart says as she gets up to answer the knock. "Looks like this party's over."

Izzy looks at Jude. "Saved by the knock?" she asks, brows raised.

He gives a little you-said-it-not-me shrug, then jumps to his feet when Mozart steps back to reveal all four Jean-Jerks at the door.

"Can I help you?" Mozart asks, brows raised so high they almost touch her hairline.

"I know the manticore is in here," Jean-Luc snarls. "We want to talk to her."

If possible, Mozart's brows go even higher. "Careful who you talk to like that, fae." Her tone stays mild, but there's a subtle shift in her body that says she's not looking for trouble, but she's more than capable of handling it if they want to bring it.

"Careful who you hang out with, dragon," Jean-Claude taunts. "You might wake up with fleas."

"Pretty sure that's not how that saying goes," Simon comments as he moves to stand behind Mozart.

"Dragons don't get fleas," Mozart tells him with a smile that shows an inordinate amount of teeth. "Maybe you should go find a few trolls to ply with your brilliant witticisms."

"Get the manticore," Jean-Luc orders in a voice I've heard too many times not to be wary of. "Now."

Jude has moved so that his big body is blocking mine from view, but the last thing I want is for him or anyone else here to get into an altercation with the Jean-Jerks to protect me.

Eva shakes her head at me, but I ignore her as I stand up so they can see me. "I'm right here."

Jude snarls at me under his breath as he moves to once again position himself between the Jean-Jerks and me.

"Where is it?" Jean-Jacques demands.

And since I don't like his tone or his inquiry, I play dumb. "Where is what?"

But that must only piss the Jean-Jerks off more, because all of a sudden Jean-Luc snarls and shoves Mozart out of the way so he can plow, uninvited, into her cottage.

Which sets off every other person in the room.

"Don't you fucking touch her," Simon growls in a voice I've never heard from the playful, easygoing siren before.

Meanwhile Jude is across the room before Jean-Luc can even step one more foot into the cottage.

Ember and Remy are right behind the two of them, and even Eva has her fists clenched as she moves to stand next to me.

Izzy is the only one who stays where she is, but she's running her tongue over her fangs in what I've learned is a sign of her irritation. Knives have also materialized in each hand.

As for Mozart, well, she looks like she's about to turn the Jean-Jerks into fae flambé for her next meal.

As I move around them to get to the Jean-Jerks—I don't want any of them getting hurt because of me—I suddenly have a glimpse of what my mother is trying to prevent with the magic lockdown. Because something tells me if Mozart had access to her dragon right now, the faes would already be flame-broiled.

Because these people who I've just been eating chips with, who've been playing games and teasing each other, suddenly look a lot more like the troubled teenagers who landed themselves at Calder Academy to begin with. Dark, dangerous, and more than ready to do whatever needs to be done—they're more than just scary.

They're downright terrifying.

"Get the fuck out of my house," Ember tells Jean-Luc. Her tone is low, even, and somehow much scarier because of it. "Now."

His eyes meet mine and narrow to slits. "I don't know what you're trying to pull, Calder, but you need to rethink it—before we make you."

"Get. The fuck. Out," Mozart says, echoing Ember. Only she adds the same shove to Jean-Luc's chest that he gave to her.

Which pisses him off enough that he comes out swinging. He aims for her face with his balled-up fist, and I throw myself forward to stop him. I've been hit by him enough to know what it feels like, and I sure as hell don't want it to happen to Mozart for trying to protect me.

But I'm about two steps too far away to reach him in time.

Jude isn't, though. His hand darts out in front of Mozart's face at the last second.

Jean-Luc's fist slams into Jude's palm, and he curls his fingers around it in response. Then he starts to squeeze.

It only takes a second or two for the fury to drain from Jean-Luc's face and pain to take its place. It takes even less time for that pain to turn to fear as Jude continues to squeeze.

"Come on, man. We just want the tapestry," Jean-Luc gasps as he struggles against Jude's grasp. "Give it to us and we'll leave."

But Jude barely seems to notice—his struggle or his words. He just keeps squeezing, even as Jean-Luc's knees buckle and he hits the ground, hard.

"Come on, man. That's enough. Fucking let him go." Jean-Jacques steps forward.

When Jude doesn't even bother to look at him, Jean-Jacques throws himself at him, fists raised. At the same time, Jean-Claude and Jean-Paul move in from the sides and try to grab him.

But none of them lands so much as a finger on Jude.

Simon grabs Jean-Jacques and sends him spinning across the room.

Mozart lands a very solid kick to Jean-Claude's balls.

And I stick a foot out just far enough to trip Jean-Paul and send him flying. I don't mean for him to end up careening into Remy, but when the time wizard lays him out with a well-placed elbow to the throat, I can't say that I'm particularly sorry, either.

The Jean-Jerks spring up—way angrier than they were to begin with. Not that that's exactly a surprise.

They've spent their whole lives getting everything they want. They capitalize on their reputations, their money, their power, and the fear that comes with it. They *do* whatever they want. And when someone tells them "no," which doesn't happen very often, they use whatever means necessary to turn that "no" into a "yes."

Which is why I've had more than a few fists to my face and other body parts over the last three years...but it's better than just lying down and letting them walk all over me.

"We're not leaving here without that tapestry," Jean-Luc snarls. And this time, when he takes a swing, he's now wearing brass knuckles on both his hands.

Jude dodges the first punch, but it turns out he wasn't Jean-Luc's real target. Instead, he whirls around at the last second and throws a second punch straight at me.

I stumble back in an effort to dodge, but I know I'm not fast enough. There's no way I'll actually avoid the hit.

But then Jude moves faster than I ever imagined he could, sliding in front of me at the last second and blocking me with his body. Jean-Luc's fist connects solidly with Jude's ribs.

And I swear I hear a bone crack.

CHAPTER FORTY-SIX

PARTY-ING IS SUCH SWEET SORROW

Jude doesn't move. In fact, I'm not sure he even breathes. Though, to be fair, I don't think anyone else does, either. Even Jean-Luc, who seems as shocked as the rest of us that he actually managed to connect with Jude.

"What the—" Mozart starts, then freezes as Ms. Aguilar's familiar trill suddenly fills the air around us.

"Yoo-hoo, Ember and Mozart! You really shouldn't have your front door open in the middle of this storm." A chartreuse umbrella pops through the open front door, followed closely by my English teacher in a matching coat.

"The rain will dama—" She breaks off mid-word, her bright-blue eyes going wide as she looks from Jude to Jean-Luc to me to Jean-Claude to Ember. "Oh my! What exactly is going on in here?"

"They were just leaving, Ms. Aguilar," Mozart starts.

"Who particularly are you referring to?" she asks.

Jean-Claude gives his friends a cocky I've-got-this smile as he shakes out his hair and turns around to—I have no doubt—harass Ms. Aguilar yet again. Only this time she's not all alone in front of her classroom. Because Mr. Danson, anger management instructor and hard-ass extraordinaire, walks in the door right behind her. And he looks as annoyed as she does bewildered.

"You want to tell me what the hell's going on in here?" he barks as he, too, looks us over one by one.

"We were just—" Mozart starts, but he cuts her off.

"Having a storm party," he fills in, his gruff, deep minotaur voice filling the room even though he hasn't raised it at all. "Despite the fact that all of you are supposed to be in your rooms right now."

"Technically, I'm—" Ember starts.

"Don't push it, Collins. This may be your room, but that's not exactly to your benefit right now." He turns his eyes to the Jean-Jerks, two of whom are slowly sidling toward the corner where I dumped the tapestry earlier.

"Don't think I don't know that you're here to cause trouble," he rumbles. "Now get out."

"We're just here for the party," Jean-Paul tries.

"Yeah, well, party's over." Danson's eyebrows come together to make a very angry-looking caterpillar across his forehead as he jerks his head toward the door. "Move it."

"Of course." Jean-Claude takes over, trying what I know he thinks is a charming smile. Too bad he just ends up looking like a total jerk. "We just need to get—"

"Let me put it to you this way. I don't know exactly what's going on in here, but I know it's not good. Which means I'm not leaving this room without the four of you. And since I'm leaving right now..." He cocks his head to the side. "I'm sure you can see where I'm going with this, right?"

"Yeah." Jean-Claude mutters something beneath his breath that I don't quite catch. Apparently, Mr. Danson does, though, because his eyes narrow dangerously—right before he crosses the room in a single bound and picks Jean-Claude up by the back of his T-shirt.

"Now means now," he says as he frog-marches Jean-Claude out of the room—directly behind the other three Jean-Jerks, all of whom are now racing for the door. Apparently, Danson is one of the only people on the island they can't buy, harass, or intimidate into doing what they want.

I have to say, it makes me like him more.

"Everyone else needs to leave, too," Ms. Aguilar says in a singsongy voice that I know she thinks is stern. "You've already missed curfew, and I'm supposed to write you up. But if you head back to your rooms now, I'll pretend this didn't happen."

She turns and heads for the cottage's small front porch, but not before she waves at me and whispers, "Hi, Clementine! Hi, Jude!"

I smile back—she's so ridiculous that it's impossible not to—and a quick glance at Jude out of the corner of my eye tells me he does, too. Or at least he gives her the tiny uptick at the corners of his mouth that's the closest he gets to smiling.

I go to grab the tapestry from the corner, but Eva's already got it. She shoots a meaningful look toward Jude—her way of telling me to stay and talk to him—before making a big deal of how tired she is and how she's taking the tapestry back to our dorm.

Remy, Izzy, and Simon file out right behind her, then head off in different directions—Remy and Izzy to their cottages at the back of the senior section, and Simon straight across the center mall to his cottage.

Which leaves Jude and me staring at each other in silence—right up until Ms. Aguilar sticks her head back in the room and says, "Let's go, you two. There will be plenty of time for you to stand around and stare at each other in the warehouse tomorrow."

Embarrassment shoots through me at her words, and I all but dive for the door. Jude follows at a more sedate pace, while Mozart calls, "Don't do anything I wouldn't do!" after us.

Ms. Aguilar gives a nod of satisfaction, then turns away as I grab my poncho and head down the front steps. But I don't even make it to the bottom stair before Jude rests a hand on my shoulder.

"Can I talk to you?" he asks, voice raised to be heard over the storm.

My heart starts pounding even as I freeze. "Of course!" I raise my voice as well as I wait for him to say something—anything—about what happened between us just a couple of hours ago.

But when I turn back toward him, his face is grim, and I can feel the fragile bubble of hope inside me burst. Even before he says, "I need you to give me that tapestry."

I'm half expecting the words, and still they hit me harder than I expect—and harder than I want them to. But just because I'm reeling doesn't mean I need to make it easy for him. Not when he's done nothing to make any of this easy for me.

There are a million things I want to say to him right now, a million things I want to ask him, but as the wind whips around us, I start with the most basic. "Why?"

"What do you mean why?" He looks shocked by the question. "If you hold on to it, Jean-Luc and his crew are just going to keep coming for you. It paints a damn target on your back."

"What do you care? It's my back."

His eyes go dark and swirly in that way they do when he's really upset. Which is fine by me—it means he's finally catching up.

"Look, Orangelo, this is no time to be stubborn. You need to let me have the tapestry."

"And you need to tell me what's going on, Penny Lane. Because your interest in that tapestry has to do with a lot more than keeping me off the Jean-Jerks's radar."

"The Jean who?"

"The Jean-Jerks," I snarl. "It's what I call them."

He does smile then, his lips curving up into what would be a grimace on most people but what is definitely a smile for Jude. "Nice alliteration," he says.

"Not-so-nice subject change," I counter. "You know, you could stop playing games and just tell me what's really going on here."

"Do you think that's what I'm doing? Playing games?" His face is as intense as the words themselves.

"I don't know what to think!" I shoot back. "Because you won't talk to me. About anything!"

"It's not that easy!"

"Sure it is." I'm not backing down this time to make him more comfortable, not easing off because I'm as worried about upsetting him as I am about the answers he has locked up. "You just take a deep breath, open your mouth, and let the words come out."

He opens his mouth, then closes it. Shoves a frustrated hand through his hair, then opens his mouth again. And closes it again.

"Is it really that hard to be honest with me?" I ask after several seconds go by.

"Is it really that hard to trust me?" he counters.

Yes! I want to shout at him. Especially when I feel like I'm one betrayal away from shattering all over again.

But telling him that will only build the walls between us even higher. And it will just keep us at this impasse we seem to have reached, where neither of us is willing to give the other an inch.

So even though there's a huge part of me that wants nothing more than to hurl a bunch of painful words at him so I can build that wall to protect myself, I bite them back. And extend a tiny, little olive branch instead.

"I know there's something weird about the tapestry."

CHAPTER FORTY-SEVEN

I'M NOT IN THE JUDE FOR THIS

If possible, Jude's face grows even more shuttered. "I don't know what you mean."

"Seriously? That's how you want to play this?" I demand, moving closer so that I'm in his face. Or as close to in his face as I can get when I'm ten inches shorter than he is.

"I'm not playing at all," he growls back. "I'm trying to protect you. Why can't you see that?"

"Has it ever occurred to you that maybe I don't want you to protect me? Maybe I want you to trust me, too."

"I don't trust myself, Kumquat. It has nothing to do with you."

His words hang in the hot, steamy air between us. Part of me thinks that's the saddest thing I've ever heard, and part of me is just spinning them around in my head over and over again, trying to figure out if this is just another excuse. Just another lie.

But Jude doesn't lie, not really. He omits. He clams up. He disappears when you need him most, but he doesn't actually lie. So what does it mean that he doesn't trust himself? And more importantly, why?

"Is this what you want, then?" I ask, and for once I don't bother to hide my bewilderment or my pain. "To just keep pushing me away until I don't come back? To destroy everything—not just what we used to be but everything we could be as well?"

The mask slips, and for a second I can see the torment underneath. I can see the pain and the indecision and a whole lot of self-loathing that I never knew existed in him. It calls to the pain inside me, has my whole body pulling toward him with a need to comfort even as he tears me apart.

"I just don't want to hurt you," he tells me in a voice gone hoarse with agony.

"You're doing nothing *but* hurting me," I counter as the storm continues to rage around us. "You've done nothing but hurt me for three long years. How can telling me the truth be any harder, or any worse, than what we've already gone through?"

Jude's whole being seems to recoil at my words.

But then he's reaching for me.

Pulling me into his big, warm, powerful body.

Holding me so tightly and so carefully that I can barely breathe from all the emotions welling up inside of me.

"It feels like I've spent my whole life trying not to hurt you," he whispers against my ear.

The words go through me like one of Izzy's knives, slicing what's left of my defenses to ribbons and tearing me wide open. "It feels like we've spent the past few years unintentionally hurting each other," I whisper back. "Maybe it's time we try something new."

He doesn't answer right away—at least not with words. Instead, his lips graze my temple slowly, gently, before sliding oh-so-carefully down. He presses kisses to the curve of my cheekbone, along the line of my jaw, to the sensitive spot just behind my ear.

And just like that, he has me. All of me. The lover and the fighter. The good girl and the rebel. The skeptic and the woman so desperate to believe that she's standing in the rain and literally begging a boy— begging *the* boy—to let her help him carry his burdens.

My arms wrap around him of their own volition.

My fingers clutch at the damp, rough fabric of his sweatshirt.

My body melts into his, and I hold him as tightly as I can. So tightly that maybe, just maybe, I can keep him from shattering, too...if he lets me.

Lightning flashes across the sky, and still I hold him.

Thunder shakes the ground, and still I hold him.

Rain pours from the sky like a waterfall gone wild, and still I hold him.

And I can't help thinking that I want to hold him like this forever.

But then he lets go. He pulls away. He takes several steps back and tells me, "I can't," in a voice gone gravelly with sorrow.

"Can't what?" I whisper, though I already know what he's going to say.

"I can't tell you what's going on. And I can't be with you—not the way you want us to be together. It's not safe."

"You don't know that."

"I do know that," he answers with an intensity so strong his eyes glow. "I knew it three years ago, when I kissed you. And I knew it this afternoon, in the forest. I just couldn't stop myself. I ruined everything three years ago. I can't let that happen again."

My heart speeds up at his words, but in a very bad way as I think of everything that happened three years ago. As I think of Carolina. "What did you ruin, Jude?"

But he just shakes his head as he steps off the porch and into the rain. "You need to give me that tapestry, Clementine."

I shake my head even as his words about what happened in ninth grade continue to reverberate through me. Is he just talking about us? Or is he talking about something more ominous?

But before I can ask, he shoves a frustrated hand through his rain-soaked hair and growls, "I don't want to fight, Clementine."

"You never want to fight," I tell him as I walk straight into the wet. "That's the problem, Jude. I just hope one day you find something or someone worth fighting *for*. Maybe, if you're lucky, it will be yourself."

And then I turn and walk away, praying with every step I take that he'll follow me. That just once he'll fight for me *and* for us.

CHAPTER FORTY-EIGHT

DON'T GHOST THERE

B ut he doesn't, and all my worst fears come true in an instant.
I fought as hard as I could. Tore myself open—laid myself bare—
and none of it mattered.

I'm still walking home through the pouring rain...alone.

Only now it's worse—so much worse—than it was before. Because
now I can't stop thinking about what Jude said about ruining everything
three years ago. Can't stop wondering if somehow, he was referring to
so much more than just us. If somehow, maybe, he was also referring
to what happened to Carolina.

I've always thought it was so strange that the night Jude kissed me,
the night I went to bed thinking that, for once, everything was right
with my world, is also the night everything fell apart.

I woke up the next morning happier than I could ever remember
being only to find Carolina gone.

I had the hugest fight of my life with my mother over it, and we
both said things we can never take back. Things I'm still not sure I
want to take back.

Then I turned to Jude for comfort and he turned me away, just cut
me off completely, like the kiss—and the seven years of friendship that
came before it—didn't exist.

And now, here he is, doing the same thing again...and telling me it's all linked together.

Is he right? Are our kiss and Carolina's disappearance somehow tied together, after all? Was it not just my traumatized, fourteen-year-old brain putting them together? Or maybe it's just my traumatized seventeen-year-old brain doing the same thing right now.

It's been a hell of a day. I've lost Serena, and in some ways, it feels like I've lost Jude all over again.

At this point, I honestly don't have a clue what's real and what's just my tortured imagination. All I know is that I'm going to figure this out. No matter how much Jude obfuscates, no matter how much my mother lies, I'm going to find out the truth. About everything.

Just...not tonight. Tonight, I'm tired and broken and sad. Really, really sad. So I'm going to take a shower, climb into bed, and try to sleep for a few hours before we have to evacuate.

Normally, I'd be excited about the evacuation—not the storm part, obviously, but the chance to finally, finally, get off this damn island. But between Serena and all these new questions I suddenly have, now seems like the absolute worst time for it to happen. How am I supposed to get any answers if we're locked in a warehouse somewhere?

Then again, this is Calder Academy. Whenever you think things are as bad as they're going to get, look out. Because they can always get worse.

The wind picks up, snarling and circling me like a wild beast, but I bend forward against it and keep going. I was so upset I ended up leaving my poncho on Mozart and Ember's porch, but there's no way I'm going back for it now. Instead, I hunch lower into the T-shirt Mozart gave me and walk as fast as I can while the wind continues to push against me.

Lightning cracks the sky in half, but at this point I'm so used to it I don't pay much attention to it—or the thunder that comes after it. And when it happens again, seconds later, I don't even bother to look.

But then it happens again and then again, and I realize two things simultaneously. One, the lightning is getting much, much closer to me. And two, despite that fact, there's been absolutely no thunder.

Shit.

I whirl around at the next flash, only to realize my instincts were right. The last few flashes haven't been lightning at all.

Dread pools in my stomach as a huge guy in a prison uniform appears right next to me. He lumbers forward, a haunted look on his face as he reaches for me.

I jump out of the way, but when he turns to catch me, I realize the left half of his face is covered with a giant tattoo that reads *You Should Run*.

Is that his actual tattoo or another warning?

Before I can figure out the answer, he disappears.

And if it is a warning, what the actual hell? It's the second one I've gotten in less than twelve hours, which is a little bizarre considering it feels like I've done nothing *but* run for those same twelve hours.

Too bad there's nowhere for me to go.

I take a deep breath, but I barely have a second to try to figure things out before there's another blink of light on the path. It's to my left this time, and I turn just in time to see a woman—half human, half feral animal—flicker onto the path.

There's blood dripping from her fangs, and I have one second to wonder if she died unmeshed—a terrifying thought considering what happened to me earlier—before she lunges for me.

I stumble backward, screaming. She disappears, and another flicker—a little boy of around seven this time, with mismatched eyes and spiky black hair—takes her place. He clutches a worn, brown teddy bear in his arms as he sobs.

"Jude?" I whisper, because—with the exception of the green T-Rex pajamas—he looks just like him at that age.

But that's impossible. Jude is alive—I just saw him. I just fought with him. This boy has to be a ghost, right?

Still, when he walks right up to me and lifts his hands like he wants to be picked up, I'm startled enough to drop down to one knee. "Are you okay?" The words come out before I can stop them.

"I need Daddy," he tells me, eyes wide. "I had a bad dream."

"Oh, baby." Even though I know he can't hear me, the words come out before I can stop them. "Where *is* your daddy?"

"I *need* Daddy," he repeats urgently, his little fingers patting my cheek. And that's when I realize—just like the toddler in the dungeon—he can hear me. More, he can *feel* me. "Go get him, please!"

"I'm sorry. I don't know who your daddy is," I whisper, and he starts to cry. I pull him to me, and a strong electric shock runs through me as he buries his face in my neck. It's not as bad as it usually is, though, so I do my best to ignore the pain.

"What's your name?" I ask him as I slowly rock him.

But he doesn't answer. He just shakes his head and says, "You have to find Daddy! He'll keep the monsters away."

I start to ask him what he means, but he disappears as suddenly as he came.

There's a hitch in my throat now, a weight on my chest that wasn't there before, though I don't know why. That doesn't stop me from feeling awful that I couldn't help him.

As I turn down the last path that leads to my cottage, I'm half walking, half running. The wind and rain continue to pummel me, and I'm determined to get inside before the storm gets worse—or another flicker appears.

But I've barely taken more than a few steps toward my dorm when a Calder Academy student appears out of thin air. I don't recognize her at all, so I blink a few times to clear the rain out of my eyes. Once I do, I realize the reason I don't recognize her is that she's not a student at all. Or at least not a current student. She's a ghost.

Like the spirit I saw earlier in the floral nightgown, her skin is the translucent gray I'm used to seeing. But also like that woman—and the little boy I saw just a few moments ago—her clothes are in color. And so is her shaggy brown hair, which throws me off completely.

She's wearing the very same red plaid Calder Academy skirt I've got hanging in my closet right now, as well as the same black polo shirt. But she's got a large, black beanie on her head, mirrored oval sunglasses perched on her face, and an oversize plaid shirt wrapped around her waist. Not to mention the dozen or so rope bracelets that adorn both her wrists.

Also, she's got a wide smile on her face, which definitely isn't the usual for the Calder Academy I'm used to, as she half walks, half skips straight toward me like she doesn't have a care in the world.

Considering this is all unfolding in the middle of a storm, as rain she can't see pours down on her and wind she can't feel whips through her hair, it feels extra weird.

Especially since there's something familiar about her face and about the way she walks that lulls me into a false sense of security. Instead of backing up, I stay right where I am, watching her even as a bunch of flickers appear around her.

Men, women, and children flick all around her as she walks—here and then gone, from one moment to the next.

As they get closer, I finally turn to look at them. And that's when the girl strikes. Her eyes sink into her head, blood drips in rivers down her face, and her mouth opens in a silent, jagged scream as she morphs from the nineties student I've been staring at into the hideous ghoul from earlier in Aunt Claudia's office. As she does, she throws herself straight toward me, and I end up falling backward onto my butt as I try desperately—and futilely—to avoid her.

One bony hand latches onto my forearm, electric shocks surging through me the moment it connects. Every nerve in my body lights up in the worst way, and images pour through my mind like icy raindrops— there for a moment and then swept away in the floodwaters of emotion that threaten to drown me a little more with each second that passes.

Calder-blue eyes.

A newborn baby, crying.

Tentative hands.

A rocking chair.

A grave.

Fear.

Grief.

And pain.

So much pain it swamps me. I try to fight through it, but it's impossible, even before she lowers her distorted face to mine. "Look!" she rasps, even as she pins me in place. "I need you to see."

"I'm trying," I gasp out, yanking desperately against her grip.

But she holds on tight as more visions flood my mind. This time they're all of Carolina. My beautiful, lost cousin.

Carolina, in my mother's office. Carolina, looking into a pen in the dungeon. Carolina, in the old root cellar. Carolina, in chains.

My roiling emotions collide like comets, sending sparks of agony showering through me as everything goes dim.

I gulp for breath as I struggle to stay conscious. I've never passed out around the ghosts—or the flickers—before, but something tells me doing so right now is a very, very bad idea.

I keep struggling, keep trying to free my arm as the shock waves burn deeper and deeper. Except she's not letting go, and things around me have gone from dim to dark.

But I have one more struggle in me, and I do the only thing I can think of. I grab onto her shoulder with my other hand and pull my arm back as hard as I can.

Electricity slams through me as my hand slips right through her. I scream as I go down, face-first. Her hand finally—finally—slips off my wrist as she disappears. And thankfully, so do all the other flickers as well, vanishing as quickly as they came.

I'm left on the soaking wet ground, huddled in a ball and trying to drag a much-needed breath in my lungs as the rain continues to pummel me.

"Clementine!" All of a sudden, Ms. Aguilar is crouched down next to me, her ridiculous yellow-green umbrella shielding me from the storm. "What happened? Are you all right?"

I push to a sitting position, my body still trying to assimilate to the sudden lack of gut-wrenching pain. "I'm okay," I tell her after a moment, but even as I say the words, I'm not sure they're true. Because that was terrifying.

My mind is still racing, my heart beating way too fast. And my whole body is shaking—whether from fear or because I just had a shit-ton of electricity pumped through it, I don't know.

Part of me wants to check for burns, because I can't imagine feeling all that and not having some physical sign of it.

I blow out a long breath and try to get my shit together. But it's hard because I am really, really freaked out right now.

The ghosts have *never* been like this before, so something has to have changed. I just need to figure out what. Because I'm not a fan of the flickering, and I'm damn sure not a fan of having thousands of volts of electricity pumped through my body.

But the only thing I can think of that's different is the storm. Could it be the lightning that comes with it that changes the ghosts into flickers? That *might* account for that sudden, awful influx of electricity I felt when she touched me.

But there've been storms on the island before. None as big as this, true, but they've had a bunch of lightning and thunder, and this has *never* happened.

So what's so different this time? And how can I fix it before I end up electrocuted for real next time?

"You don't look fine," she says, pulling on my arm in an attempt to help me up.

But pixies aren't exactly known for their strength, so I push to my feet under my own power. If my legs still feel a little wobbly under me, she doesn't need to know. No one does.

Besides, how could they not be shaky? That was a hell of a lot of electricity that just poured through me.

"I thought we told you to get to your room," Danson growls, and I realize for the first time that he's standing behind me.

"Sorry," I tell him. "I'm on my way."

"We'll walk you," he says, and I don't know if that's because he doesn't trust me or because I look as bad as I feel. No one wants the headmaster's daughter to drop dead on their watch, after all...

Or maybe it's because he doesn't trust the Jean-Jerks not to come looking for me again. To be fair, neither do I.

Whatever the reason is, he and Ms. Aguilar walk me to my cottage, and she holds her umbrella over my head the whole time. I'm already soaking wet from the first half of my walk, but it's still a nice gesture, one I thank her for when we finally get to our cottage.

"Don't be silly!" she exclaims with a wave of her free hand. "I can't let my fellow poetry lover catch a cold, now, can I?"

"Get inside," Danson orders gruffly.

I nod, but when I turn to do as he says, he stops me with a giant hand on my shoulder. "You really shouldn't be out here alone again tonight."

I don't know if he means for the words to sound ominous, but they definitely do. I want to put it down to the fact that he uses his very serious voice, but the truth is it's more than that. He looks like he's expecting trouble. Even before he turns to Ms. Aguilar and says, "Let's go, Poppy. Something tells me, storm or no storm, these kids are going to make sure we have a long, long night."

CHAPTER FORTY-NINE

DOOM-ATORY

I watch them go until the dark of the storm obscures them from view. They make a ridiculous pair—Danson, so huge and serious and tough alongside Aguilar, so tiny and happy and a complete pushover. But, somehow, I get how they're friends.

After they disappear, I finally head inside. Eva unrolled the tapestry on our living room floor, but it hasn't changed since the last time I saw it—it's still filled with manticores playing poker.

Still, I crouch down next to it and just watch it for a while, looking for...I don't know what. Some clue as to why it changes, maybe. Or a hint of what it's going to do next.

Eventually, though, exhaustion weighs me down, and I make my way back to the bedroom Eva and I share. She's got *Heartstopper* playing on the TV, but when I head in to tell her everything that just happened, she's already asleep, a chocolate chip cookie still in her hand.

I slip the cookie from her surprisingly tight grip and grab a blanket from the foot of my bed to cover her. Then I head into the bathroom for a shower so I can clean my newest wounds and try to get myself in some kind of state of mind to sleep.

But the second the hot water hits me, I start crying. It's not completely unexpected—for as long as I can remember, the shower is the only place I let myself break down. The only place I let myself be vulnerable.

Still, tonight, I was kind of hoping for just a quick scrub and hair wash. I'm exhausted—physically and emotionally.

But that doesn't seem to matter as everything that's happened today wells up inside me.

It all hits me at once, and I don't even try to stop the flood of tears that rolls out of me.

I cry for Serena, who died alone and probably terrified.

For Jude, who is more broken and tortured than even I knew.

For the flickers that seem hell-bent on torturing me—and for the little boy just looking for his father.

For the terror and the pain of being unmeshed...and the beauty of being held by Jude, even for a little while.

I cry for all of those reasons and for a bunch more I can't even think about right now, like my broken relationship with my mom and how much I miss Carolina.

And when the tears run dry, I stand under the water until it runs cold and let it wash away the agony and the grief.

Only then do I turn the water off and focus on what I have to do to be ready for tomorrow.

I put my hair up in a towel and dry off before slipping into my favorite pair of rainbow polka-dot pajamas. Then I head into the kitchen and make myself a cup of my favorite barley tea. Jude's always loved the stuff, and he got me hooked on it when we were ten or eleven.

I've been drinking it ever since—partly because I like the taste and partly because, in some small way, it makes me feel close to him... though I would have died before admitting that before today.

I spend the next few minutes drinking tea, packing my backpack for the evacuation, texting Luis, who is having trouble sleeping, and studiously avoiding thinking any more about the shit that happened today. Once I have my uniform, a few outfits, and my toiletries packed, I dry my hair, set my alarm, and then—finally—turn out the lights and crawl into bed.

Surprisingly, or maybe not after the day I've had, sleep claims me easily.

But sometime in the middle of the night, I wake up with my heart beating fast and a scream trapped in my dry throat. Mouth open, eyes wide, I scream and scream and scream, but nothing comes out.

Snakes.

So many snakes.

So many, many snakes.

Slithering all over me.

In my bed. In my hair. In my *mouth*.

I can feel one wrapped around my neck, and I reach up to claw it off, another scream rattling in my throat.

But there's nothing there, just the collar of my pajamas and my own sleep-warm skin.

This time, I swallow back the scream and take a deep breath as I reach for the reading light next to my bed.

It was just a nightmare, I tell myself. *Just a bad dream. They're just figments of your imagination. They can't actually hurt you.*

I switch on the light so I can prove to myself that everything's okay. Then I freak out because sitting in the middle of my bright-orange bedspread is a large, coiled, black snake. And it's staring straight at me.

For a second, I just blink at it, convinced that I'm still trapped in the nightmare. But then it moves, its head swaying back and forth as its forked, black tongue darts out to smell the air. To smell me.

I leap out of bed and across the room so fast that my feet barely have the chance to touch the floor.

What do I do, what do I do, what do I do?

When I was twelve, I was bitten by a rattlesnake on the far side of the island. While Jude and Carolina got me to Aunt Claudia within half an hour, it was still a very unpleasant experience, and snakes have pretty much been one of my worst nightmares since then.

For a second, I think about waking Eva up to deal with it—she doesn't like snakes, but she isn't terrified of them the way I am—but that seems like really, really bad roommate karma.

I can do this.

I can do this.

The snake starts to creep across my comforter, and the scream that I swallowed back earlier escapes.

I slap a hand over my mouth to stifle the sound, and it must work because Eva only grumbles a little, swipes at her face, then rolls over and starts snoring all over again.

The snake is still sliding across my comforter, but it's getting closer to the edge. Which means if I don't do something soon, I'm going to spend the rest of the night searching for the damn thing in all the nooks and crannies of this room. And if I don't find it, I'm pretty sure I won't be getting any more sleep tonight. Or, you know, ever.

I take a deep breath, count to three, and then go. I dive for my bed, grab the edges of my comforter, and wrap the snake up in it. Then I run through the cottage, open the front door, and throw the snake—and the comforter—out into the pouring rain.

Which is totally fine because there's no way I'd be able to sleep with that bedspread ever again.

I slam the door and lock it—because that's going to keep a wandering snake at bay—then lean back against it as I try to catch my breath. Except for yesterday when I was trying to outrun the snake monster, I don't think I've ever run that fast in my life.

When I can finally breathe again, I grab a glass of water from the kitchen and sneak back into the bedroom. I try to decide if there's any way I can get back in my bed tonight without changing the sheets.

Logic says it was just one snake, just one big, ugly snake, and that there's no way another one is lurking under my bed or between my sheets. But logic and phobias don't normally go hand in hand, and after sipping the water and catching my breath, I decide if I have any chance of catching a couple more hours sleep, the sheets have to go.

It takes about ten minutes to remake my bed and thoroughly—I mean, thoroughly—check my blankets and under the bed. But I'm finally satisfied that there will be no more surprises and crawl back in between the sheets and reach to turn off the light.

But just as I'm about to flip the switch, Eva makes a strange gasping noise.

I turn to check on her and watch in horror as she goes up in flames.

CHAPTER FIFTY

SCORCHED SORROW

For one long, horrible second, I don't believe my eyes.

For two even longer seconds, I think that maybe she's a phoenix, like Ember, and just never knew it.

But somewhere about four seconds in, I realize this is nothing like what happened to Ember.

Eva is on *fire*.

She reaches for me, and I jump up, screaming, as I look for something to smother the flames with. Because I'm a total jerk, I just sent my comforter flying into the rain, so I rip my sheet off my bed and throw it over her in a desperate attempt to stop her from burning. And then I swat at her much like Jude did to Ember, but the fire just keeps on raging. Even worse, Eva is screaming now, too, and it's the most horrific sound I've ever heard.

"You're going to be okay," I tell her as I grab the glass of water I just got and throw it on her before reaching for my bottom sheet, too. But even as I slap it down on top of her, I know it isn't going to work.

"Eva, you're going to be okay!" I yell as I grab my phone and dial the emergency dorm director for help.

Then I pull my extra blanket from the basket at the end of my bed and thrust it outside to get wet.

It only takes a couple of seconds for the rain to soak it, but even that's too long. Because the fire is spreading, climbing up the walls and curtains to the ceiling. I throw the soaking-wet blanket on her anyway, but she's not sitting up anymore, and she's not moving. What's left of her is just lying, still, in the center of the bed as flames engulf the entire room while the phone I'm holding goes straight to voicemail.

I stare at Eva in shock as the fire spreads across the floor, its greedy fingers eating up the cheerful rug we'd picked out together as soon as we found out we were going to be roommates this year. There's a part of me that knows I need to get out, that knows it's dangerous for me to be in this room any longer.

But I can't just leave Eva here to burn. Even if she's gone, I can't just walk away and let her—

"Clementine!" A voice makes its way through the roar of the fire and the creaking of the wood as it's slowly burning away. "Clementine!"

"Jude?" I scream back as the owner of the voice registers in my mind.

"Where are you?"

I start to answer—maybe he can help me get Eva out of here—but the smoke sends me into a coughing fit that nearly brings me to my knees.

"Clementine, goddamn it, where are you?" Jude roars as the front door of the cottage slams open.

And that's when I know I can't stay here any longer. I can't let Jude risk his life coming into this room, not when the entire cottage is about to go up in flames.

I turn back to look at Eva—one last look—at the girl who just a few hours ago was telling me that everything was going to be okay.

And then I run.

CHAPTER FIFTY-ONE

SET FIRE TO THE PAIN

"Clementine!" Jude yells my name from what sounds like the living room.

"I'm here!" I scream back as best I can as I race down the hall toward him.

We slam into each other in front of the bathroom doorway, and he grabs me, yanking me into his arms and burying his face in my hair. "I thought you were dead," he tells me, his whole body shuddering against mine. "I thought you were *dead*."

"Eva—" I start, but my voice breaks.

"Where is she?" he demands. But then his eyes go toward our room and the flames licking the door and out into the hallway, and he figures it out.

"I'm sorry," he says. "I'm so sorry."

And then he's picking me up and racing out the front door into the torrential storm that only seems to have gotten stronger in the last few minutes. All the rain only makes what happened in there seem so much worse—there's tons of water everywhere, and I still couldn't save Eva.

"Are you okay?" Jude is still shouting to be heard above the roar of the storm. "Are you hurt anywhere?"

I don't have a clue what I'm supposed to say to that, so I just stare at him, eyes wide and wild.

When I don't answer him, Jude runs his hands over me from head to toe, looking for injuries. When he doesn't find any, except for a few minor burns on my hands, he yells, "Stay here!"

And then he darts back into the cottage.

"She's gone!" I yell back, ignoring his order and running up the stairs after him. If I thought there was any chance that Eva was still alive, I'd never have left her there. But she was dead. I know she was, and having Jude risk his life to try to save someone who is already gone—

But before I can even pull open the cottage's screen door, he's back, grim-faced and covered in soot. He's also carrying the damn tapestry. Only now the manticores are gone and in their place are the words YOU'RE RUNNING OUT OF TIME in huge, bold black letters.

No shit. The warning's a little late, if you ask me.

"She's gone," he confirms, like I don't already know that.

"Did you go back in for Eva or that damn rug?" I demand as anger wells up inside me.

"Both," he answers, because he's Jude and he doesn't lie. Ever.

And just like that, the anger drains away, drowning in the grief and confusion slamming through me like a tsunami.

"I don't know what happened!" I tell him as lightning streaks across the sky and rain—fucking buckets of rain—pours down on top of us. "She was fine. I was awake. I saw her. I swear she was fine! And then, just like that, she was on fire. I don't know how it happened."

"She just burst into flames?" Jude asks. "Like Ember?"

"Exactly like Ember, only *not*. I could see right away—" My voice breaks, but I clear my throat. Force myself to keep talking. "I could see right away that it wasn't the same."

"Because she was really burning," he supplies.

"Yes. I swear, I tried to put the fire out. I used everything I had to try to—" I'm shouting to be heard above the continuous roll of thunder above us, and my voice breaks again. "I tried to put *her* out, but I couldn't. Nothing I did worked. No matter what I did, I couldn't save her."

"It's not your fault," Jude tells me, face grim.

"It feels like my fault," I answer. "I tried to call for help in the middle of it all, but Michaels didn't answer and then...then it was too late. It just happened so fast."

"Michaels didn't answer?" He looks surprised, and I get it. Michaels is the dorm director, and he *always* answers.

"No one did. I don't know if the storm..." I trail off, suddenly too exhausted to say any more.

"We need to call him again," Jude says, pulling me over to the front porch of one of the other cottages to get us out of the rain. "And we should probably call your mom, too."

"I know. I was about to—" I break off as my cottage shudders violently before starting to collapse in on itself. Flames lick along the caving-in roof, but it's only a matter of a couple minutes before the downpour takes care of it, extinguishing the flames just as the roof falls in completely.

"Eva's in there," I whisper, my whole body shaky as I stare at the rubble that was once my home.

"We'll get her out," Jude promises as he wraps his arms around my waist from behind so I can lean back against his chest for support. "But there's nothing that can hurt her in there anymore."

Knowing that doesn't make it any easier to just leave what's left of Eva there. Alone. In the dark and the storm.

But Jude's right. There are things that need to be done right now. "I'll call my mom. You call Michaels."

He nods as he pulls out his phone and starts dialing while I do the same.

But the moment I hit the green phone icon, the call drops.

I try again, but it happens a second time. And a third time. And a fourth time.

"I'm not getting through," Jude says, shoving a hand through his hair in obvious frustration.

"It's got to be the storm, right?" I tell him. "It's blocking out the cell signal."

"Gotta be," he agrees. "We're going to have to go to Michaels's place."

"I know." I glance back at the cottage, at Eva. I don't know why, but leaving her alone seems so wrong.

Jude sees the look. "I can go by myself. You can stay here." The *with Eva* part goes unsaid but not unmeant.

"No. I need to tell him what happened. He's going to have to try to get in touch with her family." I'm not sure her parents will care, but they deserve to know what happened to their daughter. Not that I actually know the answer to that. I just know what I saw.

Jude nods, and we head toward the main dorm. Since it houses the underclassmen, the dorm supervisor's apartment is always on the first floor.

"It's strange that Danson and Aguilar haven't come," I tell him. "I thought they were patrolling all night."

"Me, too," he answers, sounding more concerned than confused.

I start to ask what he's thinking, but before I can get the words out, an explosion rocks the air around us and sends us flying off our feet.

CHAPTER FIFTY-TWO

HARD-CORE COTTAGE GORE

I go sailing through the ragged, bleached-out railing of the cottage we're in front of—Caspian's cottage—and land, face-first, on his bright-red Calder Academy welcome mat. Seconds later, Jude lands half on me and half in a hole he created in the porch.

"What the fuck was that?" he demands as he braces his arms on either side of me and pulls himself out of the hole like it's the easiest thing in the world. I suppose when you have biceps like tree trunks, it is.

"I don't know." My ears are ringing, and there isn't a part of my body that doesn't hurt right now. Still, I grab onto the hand Jude offers and look around as he pulls me up. "It sounded like something exploded, but—"

I break off mid-sentence as I see what has, indeed, exploded. The cottage on whose front porch Jude and I were just taking shelter. "Oh my God!" I yell as I knock on Caspian's door, hard, before I begin running/hobbling down the steps. "There were people in there! Jude, there were people in there."

Two mermaids to be exact—Belinda and Bianca. I've had classes with both of them through the years. We've been lab partners and on the same teams in P.E. and...

"Where are they?" I demand as I get my first good look at their cottage—or should I say what's left of their cottage, because the place is decimated. The explosion leveled it. "They have to be here. They have to be here somewhere. They have to be—"

I start desperately scouting around, looking for any sign of the two mermaids.

Please don't let them be dead. Please don't let them be dead. Please don't let—

Suddenly, I hear Jude yelling from beside another cottage, two doors down from Belinda's and Bianca's. But I can't hear what he's saying over the insanity of the storm.

I make my way over to him, going as fast as the pain in my side will let me. Above us, the thunder is so loud it sounds like it's getting ready to rip the sky apart while lightning strikes shake the ground every few seconds.

If these are just the outer rainbands of the hurricane, what on earth is the center of the storm going to be like? Either way, we have absolutely no business being out in the middle of this. But it's not like we have a choice. My cottage just burned down—I don't let myself think about why it burned down—and another cottage just exploded.

Something awful is happening here, but I don't know what. I just know that it doesn't feel like there's anywhere safe for us to go.

Plus, two girls are missing and we have to find them.

When I finally make it to Jude, he's on his knees, leaning over a Black girl in short pink pajamas who's lying on the ground, her arm bent at an unnatural angle.

Belinda.

"Is she okay?" I yell as I drop to the ground on the other side of her.

But the second I do, I realize, no. She isn't okay.

Her beautiful face is scraped up, and her sightless eyes are staring blankly into the distance.

"How did she—" My throat seizes up, and I can't get the word out. I just can't. There's been too much death here tonight, too much devastation and destruction.

"She hit her head," Jude says in a monotone voice. "It's still bleeding."

I glance at him, sharply, because he doesn't sound any more okay than I feel. But he keeps his face averted, refusing to look me in the eye.

Figuring he must need a minute, I reach over and close Belinda's eyes before pushing to my feet. Then I jog over to the orange comforter I tossed into the rain earlier and pick it up. After checking to make sure the snake is long gone, I drape it over the girl who was my lab partner sophomore year.

Then I say, "We need to find Bianca." Dread fills me even as I say the words. I'm terrified we're going to find her the same way we found Belinda, and I don't think I can take it. First Serena, then Eva, then Belinda.

I can't handle any more.

Not that I have a choice. I'm going to *have* to handle it, because wherever she is and whatever has happened to her, Bianca *has* to be found.

"What's going on?" I whisper to him. "Why is this happening?"

Jude doesn't answer as he climbs to his feet beside me. He's still refusing to look at me, too. I wonder if it's because he knew Belinda, too, or if he's as sick of death as I am.

But when we turn around, we're no longer the only people around. Students are pouring out of their cottages—and out of the underclassmen dorm—onto the center mall that runs through the whole housing area.

The rain is still pounding, thunder and lightning still devastating the sky, but terrified students are coming out in droves anyway.

Which can only mean one thing.

Eva and Belinda aren't the only ones.

CHAPTER FIFTY-THREE

NIGHTMARE ON MY STREET: PART ?

My stomach churns at the thought that more people are *dying*, and I swallow down the sudden fear that's dragging me into an abyss of horror. Because if all of these students are outside, and none of the adults who are currently in charge of us are anywhere to be found, something really bad is happening.

Or, more likely, has already happened.

"What do you think is going on?" I whisper to Jude.

He must not hear me above the chaos of the storm, because he doesn't answer.

I turn to look at him, but his face is stoic even as the rain slaps against him again and again.

"Jude." I raise my voice this time to make sure he can hear me, but he still doesn't answer as he stares, blindly, into the storm.

"Jude!" I yell his name now. "We've got to help them."

He nods, but he doesn't move. Just keeps peering into the dark.

I don't know if that means he's in shock or if he's just as overwhelmed as I feel. Either way, I can't leave him like this. Can't leave any of them like this—not when so many people obviously need help.

I grab his shoulders and shake him until his multicolored eyes meet mine and snap back into focus. "We have to help them," I say again.

"I'm trying," he answers, which makes no sense considering he's just standing there.

But now that I have his attention, I'm not going to ask what he means. Instead, I say, "I think we need to find our friends. They can go get help while we look for Bianca."

I studiously avoid mentioning the fact that our friends might not have made it through whatever this is. Eva didn't. And neither did Belinda.

I can tell by the clench of his jaw that the same nightmarish thoughts are running through Jude's head.

I pull out my phone again and try to text Luis. But—just like earlier with Michaels and my mom—it doesn't go through. I try to keep the panic at bay, but it's hard when I think about Eva.

"Where do you—" Jude starts but breaks off when a scream splits the night, followed by a series of several more.

I whirl around, heart in my throat, just in time to watch a girl run out of her cabin and melt not twenty feet from me. Like actually dissolve right in front of me.

"Oh my God!" I scream and take off down the ramp toward her while Jude simply vaults over the railing.

But he's only gone a couple of steps before he snarls, "Fuck!" and turns back toward me, holding a hand out to stop me in my tracks. His voice is hoarse when he says, "Don't come this way."

At first, I can't figure out what he means. But he's standing under one of the old hurricane lamps that line the center mall, and I watch in horror as the rain washes blood off his shoes.

A scream wedges in my throat, and it takes every ounce of self-control I have to swallow it down.

"Whose is that?" I ask when I finally succeed.

Jude shakes his head, and for a second, he looks as defeated as I feel.

"We need to find them," I tell him. "We need to—"

"We already have," Mozart says as she and Simon come up on Jude's left. "It belongs to one of the freshman girls. A fairy."

"What happened to her?" I ask.

Mozart just shakes her head.

"The same thing that's happening to a bunch of people in the dorm," Izzy tells me as she and Remy come toward us, making sure to skirt the ever-growing puddles of blood-tinged water pooling on the sidewalk. "They wake up all freaked out and then—"

She breaks off as more screams split the air.

My stomach plummets as I glance toward the cries just in time to see one of the senior banshees walking on the roof of her cottage. Her eyes are closed, and it seems like she's still asleep as she walks closer to the edge.

"No!" I scream as I run toward her, waving my arms. "Wake up!" Izzy races ahead of me, but even the vampire can't get to her before she dives straight off the roof of her cottage. A sickening crack fills the air as she lands right on the top of her head.

"We have to stop this," Ember whispers, eyes wide with horror as she comes up behind me. "We have to..."

She trails off, as lost as the rest of us are right now.

Across the center mall from her, a sophomore dragon is crawling along the ground, pulling himself forward one slow inch at a time.

Jude gets to him before I can and crouches down beside him, looking devastated.

At first, I don't know why, but as I get close, I realize that half the boy's face is missing and his jugular is torn. He's hemorrhaging blood all over the path, and it doesn't take much more than a freshman health class to know that if we don't stop the bleeding, he'll be dead in three minutes, maybe less.

I drop to my knees beside him and press my hands to his wound, but Izzy—who is right behind me—says, "That's not going to be enough, Clementine. He's already bled out too much."

"We have to try," I tell her. "I can't just leave him like this."

"No one's asking you to." She squats down next to me. "Move over a little bit."

"If I move, I'll—"

She gives up waiting and just flat-out shoves me out of the way. Then she leans down and licks the wound several times.

My stomach revolts, and I turn away. I know vampires' saliva has special coagulating properties that our power lockdown doesn't take from them, but it's one thing to know that and another to see it in action. Still, I'm grateful she wants to help the boy, so I force myself to look anywhere but at them until she's done.

When Izzy finally lifts her head, I whirl back around and do my best to ignore the fact that she has blood dripping down her chin. "Did you stop the bleeding? Is he going to be okay?"

She says something, but there's so much going on around us right now—screaming and crying and yelling and fighting—that I can't hear her even though she's only a few inches away from me.

I glance at the boy, and he's still alive, which is saying a lot considering the shape he was in. But his eyes are at half mast, and his breathing is so shallow that it's hard to believe he's not going to die any second.

"We need to get him to your aunt," Jude says as he starts to pick him up.

"We've got him," Remy answers, and there's a seriousness to his usually amused tone that I've only heard when he's talking about Carolina. "You stay here, see who else you can help."

At first, I think Jude is going to argue, but then he nods grimly and hands the boy over to Remy, who takes off running toward the faculty quarters with Izzy right behind him.

"We need to find my family members," I say as I watch them go. "And anyone else who can help."

"We can do that," Ember volunteers.

"Yeah, we'll split up. See who we can find," Mozart agrees while Simon nods.

As they take off running, I turn to Jude. "We still need to find Bianca. She could still be alive."

"She's not," he answers.

I'm really scared that he's right, but still, we can't assume. "You don't know that—"

"I do. I found her on our way over here." He points to a broken-down bench in the shape of a giant pink sea anemone that's been here since resort days. "She's right there."

There's one of the old-fashioned standing hurricane lamps not far from the bench, and now that I know where to look, even through the rain, I can see her legs sticking out from behind the bench, both bent at weird, unnatural angles.

Sorrow floods through me as I think about the year we spent in group therapy together. She used to talk about how she wanted to move to Greece one day. She'd tell me stories about the Mediterranean and how beautiful it is and how amazing the people there are. She even memorized Greek recipes so that she could make them when she got out of here.

It seemed like she had a really nice life planned there, and it guts me that she'll never get to see the sun sparkle off the water like in the pictures she showed me.

Because she's gone, just like Eva and Serena and Belinda and who knows how many others at this point.

It's heartbreaking and terrifying, and I would give anything to wake up in my warm bed—even with a snake on top of me—and realize that this is all just a bad dream. That none of it is true. That everything in my life, in all our lives, hasn't gone completely sideways.

But as I look at Jude's face, I realize that's just a fantasy. This *is* real. It's happening right now, right this instant, to all of us. And it's going to *keep* happening if we don't figure out what's going on.

"We have to stop this," I tell Jude.

He nods grimly, the sharp planes of his face gone craggy with a pain I don't understand. "I will," he tells me, and it sounds like a vow.

"You? How can you—" I break off when I hear someone calling my name from behind us. I turn to find Luis staggering toward me, his shirt soaked with blood.

CHAPTER FIFTY-FOUR

ALL THROUGH THE NIGHT-MARES

*N*ot Luis, too. Please, please, please, not Luis.

I sprint toward him, slipping and sliding on the slick, broken sidewalk. Jude passes me, catching my best friend just as he stumbles and starts to fall.

"What's wrong with him?" I demand as Jude lowers him to the ground.

"I'm okay," Luis says, but his eyes are glazed with pain, and he's trembling despite the heat. "I just need a minute to…" He trails off in a coughing fit.

"We need to get his shirt off." Jude's face is bleak as he crouches down next to me. "See what we're dealing with here."

I nod, but the moment I try to ease Luis's shirt over his head, he gasps in pain.

"I'm sorry," I whisper as I try to pull his good arm through its armhole.

"It's okay," he bites out. But he's gray and sweating, and he's clearly anything but okay.

Before I can figure out what to do, Jude steps forward and grabs the neckline of Luis's shirt.

"What are you—" Luis gasps out, right before Jude rips the shirt in half with one quick yank of his hands.

I blink at him, shocked, for a second, but he just gives an impatient nod toward my best friend.

And he's right. Now is far from the time to marvel at just how easy that was for Jude. So I turn back to Luis. And try not to gasp at the gaping wound that covers his side, stretching from right under his armpit to his waist.

"Who did this to you?" I ask as I use his torn, sodden shirt to wipe away as much of the blood as I can. Thankfully, his shifter metabolism has already started to clot the wound, so it's a lot easier than it normally would be.

As long as it's not a life-threatening wound like the dragon we were just trying to help, most shifters can heal themselves pretty quickly. That ability is slowed down a little bit by the power dampening on the island but not completely decimated as it's part of their normal body chemistry as opposed to their magic. The same goes for the coagulating properties in Izzy's saliva and Simon's ability to seduce anyone with a pulse.

"A wolf." Luis's voice is grumpy as he answers my question.

"Who?" I demand. No one should be able to shift right now, not while the power lock is still in place.

"Not a student," he answers, trying—and failing—to sit up. "An actual wolf."

What the hell? I shoot a baffled glance toward Jude, but he doesn't look anywhere near as confused as I feel. Instead, he looks... devastated.

"We don't have wolves on the island, Luis."

"Tell that to the giant gray one that sliced me open," he answers. Then he yelps, "Fuck, Clementine! Could you be a little more sadistic?"

I ignore him as I continue to wipe his wound clean as gently as I can. "We need to get him to Aunt Claudia, too," I say to Jude. "He's going to need stitches."

"I'm okay," Luis gasps. "I just need to shift and I'll be much better."

"Yeah, well, that's not exactly an option at the moment, in case you've forgotten."

"Just get me out of this rain and I'll be fine." This time he actually makes it to a sitting position—though he curses quite a bit as he does it. On the plus side, the wound already looks much better than it did when he collapsed.

"You should probably lay back down for a few more minutes," I suggest.

"In this mess?" He shoots a disparaging look at the rain- and blood-soaked ground. "No, thank you."

And just like that, I breathe a sigh of relief. If Luis is back to his normal, snarky self, then I'm pretty sure he's going to be just fine—unlike a lot of the people we've seen in the last hour.

At least the screaming has stopped.

I look around, trying to figure out what's happening. I've been so worried about Luis that I stopped paying attention to everything else.

Right now, the students are all milling around in the rain, looking traumatized but not hysterical anymore. Some of them are obviously injured while others look fine, but no one appears to be actively bleeding or fighting.

"It's over," I say to Jude as I stand up.

He doesn't answer, and when I turn to him, it's to find him staring into the distance again.

Jaw clenched, face blank, eyes far away. But this time his hands are out in front of him, like he's reaching for something.

For one horrible second, I'm terrified that he's suffering the same thing so many of the other students suffered. That he's about to burst into flames or have his jugular ripped out or any of the other awful things that have happened tonight.

"Jude!" I call his name, but he doesn't answer.

I put a hand on his shoulder and shake him like I did earlier, but there's still no response.

"Jude!" Panic sets in, and I start shouting. "Damn it, Jude! Answer me!"

Still nothing.

"Hey, help me up," Luis tells me uneasily. When I turn back to him, I realize he's watching Jude, too. And he looks just as concerned as I feel.

Reaching down, I grab Luis's hand and pull him up before turning back to Jude and shaking him much harder than I did the first time.

But this time he doesn't just look out of it. He looks like he's in some kind of a trance, completely out of reach. I can't begin to imagine what's happening to him right now, but judging from what everyone else has gone through, I know it must be horrible.

Fear claws at my throat, has my heart beating wildly and my hands shaking as I grab onto Jude's arms in a desperate attempt to anchor him.

"Help me!" I tell Luis as I frantically try to pull Jude back from wherever he's gone, tugging him onto the porch of a nearby cottage.

Luis nods, but he doesn't look like he has any better ideas. Though he does say, "You know what was weird about that wolf that attacked me?"

I shoot him an incredulous look—I can't believe he thinks now is the time I want to talk about that. "The fact that there was a wolf on the island at all?"

"Well, yeah. And also, the fact that I used to have nightmares about him when I was a kid."

I'm barely listening, too busy trying to get through to Jude, so it takes a few seconds for Luis's words to hit me. When they do, I remember waking up with the snake on my bed—my worst nightmare. I also remember Eva telling me that burning alive, like Ember did in the hallway, was her worst fear.

I turn to Luis, eyes wide. "Nightmares?" I whisper. "You think these are all people's nightmares coming to life?"

"I don't know what to think," he answers me with a solemn shake of his head. "But I don't have a better explanation, right now. Do you?"

No.

I want to. I really, really want to. But I don't.

Luis's idea seems far-fetched, but Jude *is* an oneiroi, a dream daimon. And all I can think about right now is him standing, just like this, a few minutes ago and telling me that he *was* trying to help people.

I didn't understand it then—hell, I don't understand it now—but somehow, I'm not surprised at all when I turn back to Jude and see that the black tattoos are back to slithering around on his body. And like yesterday, they're not content to stay on his back and arms anymore.

They're climbing up his neck to his jaw, his cheeks, even his forehead.

I glance down at his hands, which I'm currently holding in mine, and realize the black things are there, too. Dozens—maybe hundreds—of the serpentine, feathery black ropes are crawling all over him.

The realization has fear turning to absolute terror inside of me. I must not be the only one, because Luis says, "I'm going to go try to find help."

I'm too busy freaking out over Jude to answer. Instead, I grab his shoulders again, and this time I shake him over and over and over again. When that doesn't work, when he continues to stare sightlessly past me, I do the only thing I can think of.

I slap him across the face. Not hard, but—hopefully—enough to get his attention.

Jude's body recoils from the slap, his eyes jerking to mine. I barely stifle a scream as I see the black things there, too. Crawling through the whites of his eyes, but also spinning themselves around and around in the depths of his multicolored irises.

They look beautiful and macabre and absolutely terrifying, all at the same time.

"Jude!" I gasp out. "Are you okay?"

He doesn't answer, and that's when I realize he isn't looking at me. Not really. He's still lost somewhere deep inside himself. Whether by choice or because of the tattoos currently covering his body, I don't know.

What I do know is that I can't leave him like this. Not when I can't tell if he's okay. Not when I can't tell if he's in control of the black feathery things or if *they* are in control of *him*.

I've been so angry at him for so long, but the idea of losing him turns me inside out. I've lost so many people. I can't lose Jude, too. I just can't.

So I do the only thing I can do. I let the anger go as I step closer, going up on tiptoes so I can reach him better. Then I cup his cheeks in my hands and whisper, "I'm here, Jude. I'm right here. Please don't do this. Please, please come back to me."

CHAPTER FIFTY-FIVE

KISS AND BREAK UP

Jude doesn't answer.

He doesn't move. He doesn't blink. I'm not sure he even breathes.

He just stares straight ahead, with eyes that reflect a myriad of horrors that I can't see and don't know how to free him from.

His nightmares? I wonder as I stroke his wet hair back from his face. *Or all of ours?*

If it's the latter, I can't even imagine what he's going through.

I've always wondered what it's like to be an oneiroi. When we were little, I used to ask him if he remembered from his time before Calder Academy what it felt like to have access to people's dreams and their nightmares. He never wanted to talk about it back then, and now I can see why.

This is awful. Beyond awful.

"Jude, please," I whisper, leaning in even closer to him, until the chill of his body bleeds into the heat of mine.

"Please," I plead again as the wild, unsteady beat of his heart has my own stuttering in my chest.

"Please," I say one more time as if it's a secret I've kept for years—even from myself—wells up inside of me.

It scorches the inside of my throat, batters against the walls I've kept in place for so long. But what do those walls matter if Jude gets lost in this abyss? I've already lost too many people—Carolina and Serena and now Eva. I'm not going to lose Jude, too—not if there's anything I can do to save him.

And so I take a deep breath and say the only words I have left to reach him. The only words that actually matter. "I love you, Jude. I love you, and I need you, and I can't lose you, not like this. I *won't* lose you."

He jerks back then, gasping as his whole body convulses like a wave of red-hot electricity is suddenly flowing through him.

"Jude?" Fear shakes my resolve. "Jude! What—"

"Don't," he tells me in a voice gone gravelly from I can't even imagine what.

"Don't what?" I ask, confused.

He blinks, and the black feathery things slowly slither out of his eyes until—finally—I'm looking at Jude again, the real Jude, and he is looking at me. "Don't love me."

The words hit me like a brick—like a million bricks—falling back into place as the wall I've worked so hard to tear down reconstructs between us. I reel under the pain of it, under the hurt of being pushed away by Jude yet again.

But I don't back off, don't run away like so much of me wants to. Partly because where would I go anyway? And partly because I refuse to give up so easily—not this time. Because Jude is worth it, and so am I.

"Too late," I tell him with a cockiness I'm far from feeling. "It's already happened. Besides, when have I ever listened to you?"

"For once, you *need* to listen," he says hoarsely.

"Maybe I need to do something else." I push back up on my tiptoes, as high as I can go this time. And then, as the rain and wind crash against us, I sink into him. Melt into him. And press my mouth to his.

At first Jude doesn't move—not his lips, not his arms, not even his body. He just stands there like a statue.

I pull back, mortified. Traumatized. Hurt—so hurt—because I thought I mattered to him. I thought we mattered. And instead, I've made a fool of myself again.

"I'm sorry," I mumble as I pray for one of the bolts of lightning to smite me. "I don't know why I—"

And that's when he strikes.

Jude reaches out and grabs my waist. I have one moment to wonder what's happening and then he's yanking me forward, his mouth slamming down on mine.

My brain short-circuits for one second, two, as he... There's no word for what he does to me.

Devours me?

Consumes me?

Turns my world upside down with the need that pours off him in wild, storm-tossed waves that slam into me—that pull me under—in the best, most indescribable way?

Heat streaks through me, and my whole body—my whole soul—fades into him. I wrap my arms around his waist. Pull him closer. Take every piece of him that I can get—every tiny little molecule that he's willing to give me.

And still, it's not enough. Still, I want more of him. Need more of him.

I press closer until I can feel the shuddering of his breath and the wild, rampaging beat of his heart against my own.

Somewhere in the back of my head, there's a voice telling me that this isn't the time or the place for this, but I don't care. I can't care.

Because finally, finally, finally, this is Jude. And me. And for this one, so not perfect but somehow absolutely perfect moment, that's all that matters.

He nips at my lip, and I open for him, offering him all the broken, battered, so not perfect pieces of me. Giving him everything that I have, everything that I am, and—

He wrenches himself away.

I whimper, clutching at him with greedy, desperate hands, but he's already backing away. His cheeks are ruddy, his rain-slicked hair tousled from my fingers, and the black, feathery ropes fill the air around us.

He's right here, right in front of me. But I can see it in his face. In his blown-out pupils. Jude is already gone in all the ways that matter.

"You can't love me, Kumquat," he tells me in a voice so deep and violent I barely recognize it. "No one can."

"That's not true," I whisper from lips still swollen and stinging from his kiss. "*I* love you."

He shakes his head. "If you knew—"

"But I don't know." I reach for him, but he backs away again. "Because you've never told me. If you want me to back off, if you want me to leave you alone, tell me whatever secret it is that has you locking yourself away from me. Tell me why you keep running away."

He gestures to the air around us, to the swirling, black plumes that fill the air. And then he throws his arms out, and right in front of me, he pulls them back onto his body. One after the other after the other.

They disappear in moments, but he doesn't stop there. He keeps his arms where they are, his fingers curling into fists as he grasps at the air over and over again. And keeps pulling more and more of the ropes through the air and onto his skin.

Not just the ones around us, but from everywhere. I turn to watch them float like black mist out of the students still milling on the center mall, one after the other. Then they glide through the rain-drenched air straight toward Jude, swirling themselves into tighter and tighter ropes until they finally reach Jude and slither straight onto his skin.

"I'm not just an oneiroi," he tells me jaggedly. "I'm the Prince of Nightmares. And this"—he gestures to the broken, battered students all around us—"is all my fault."

CHAPTER FIFTY-SIX

HAPPILY NEVER AFTER

Shock reverberates through me at his words.

I know there are royal families for each kind of paranormal—along with whole, elaborate courts for each as well. Just like I know that the reinstatement of the Gargoyle Court has swept through the paranormal world like a cyclone, shaking everyone up with its new queen. We're isolated here at Calder Academy, but not so isolated that something like that doesn't show up on our radar. Especially since my cousin, Carolina, died trying to help the new Gargoyle Queen in a war against the Vampire King.

But the *Prince of Nightmares*? *The Nightmare Court*? Those are things only whispered about in the scary stories kids tell each other—or by adults, late at night, after they're sure the kids have gone to bed.

The Nightmare Court—and its ruler—is so feared that no one wants to attract their attention. Yet Jude, apparently the *Prince of Nightmares*—has been here at Calder Academy all along.

How is that possible? And why?

But he's still watching me with eyes gone prismatic with pain. I know I have to say something, know I have to answer him. But I don't have a clue how to respond right now.

So, in the end, I say the only thing that I know is true. "I don't understand."

"What's there to understand?" he asks with a pained laugh. "Haven't you ever wondered why you never had nightmares after I got to the island? Why no one has? It's because I harvest them."

"Harvest?"

"I still have my magic, Clementine. All of it."

"What do you mean?" I demand as I cross to stand next to him. "The school locks down everyone's powers."

"Not mine," he says quietly. "The island's power blocking has never worked on me—I don't know why. It's just how it's always been."

His quiet explanation shakes me to my core, has me reevaluating everything my mother and aunts and uncles have ever said to me about student magic and how they control it on the island.

"I don't understand," I finally say. "How is that possible?"

"I don't know," he answers with a baffled shrug. "When I got here, no one ever mentioned anything to me about locking my powers down, and no one ever did anything to dampen them. I didn't even know it was school policy until you and Carolina mentioned it weeks later."

I'm still reeling, so I let that go—as well as the question about why he didn't tell me any of this sooner. We have bigger things to worry about right now. Though I am curious about one thing. "That's a lot of magic that you carry around with you. How did you keep anyone from noticing?"

"I use it, every night. Too exhaust my power and keep it in check—keep it from hurting anyone—I harvest nightmares from everyone on the island. I store them—"

"On your skin," I whisper, part fascinated and part horrified. "All those twisty black things. They're nightmares."

He nods.

"But there aren't enough. I mean, there are a lot," I tell him, especially now that they're all over his face. "But not enough to be every nightmare you've harvested from every person on the island for the last decade or so. Right?"

"After I harvest them, I funnel them into something else and that takes care of them."

I want to ask him what he funnels them into—and how exactly they are taken of—but right now, that seems like the least of our problems.

So I settle for something more pertinent.

"So, after you harvested them, they accidentally got loose somehow?" I look at the devastation all around us. "That's what did this?"

"Not accidentally," he answers. "This time I deliberately set them free."

"Deliberately?" I'm so shocked I can't even be angry. Because I know Jude—I know how conscientious he usually is about everything—well, everything except our relationship. This isn't like him. At all. "Why would you—"

I break off because, suddenly, it all becomes clear. "For me. The unmeshing. You set them free to save my life."

"I couldn't let you die," he answers, throat working and eyes glazed with something that looks suspiciously like tears. "Not if there was anything I could do to stop it. Even this." Now he's the one looking around, a deep-seated horror on his face.

"Did you know?" I whisper, heart lodged in my throat. Because I think I would rather have died than know that saving me meant all these people—meant Eva—would suffer and die the way they did.

"That this would happen?" He shakes his head. "I used the same magic that I use to pull nightmares from people to pull the poison from you. But I was so careful. I worked so hard to pull them all back. I was afraid one might have slipped away, but I never imagined this many could have."

"That's why you were so upset," I say, putting things together now. "When you showed up at Mozart and Ember's earlier. You were afraid you had let a nightmare escape. Why didn't you ask for help then?"

"Because no one can help me with this. No one can fix the mistakes I make—not these kinds of mistakes."

"You don't know that—"

"I do know it!" His voice raises but ends in a whisper. "I do."

"The only way you could know is if this happened before—" I break off as the truth dawns on me. "Is that why you were sent to the island? You were only seven!"

"That's not what I'm talking about." His face closes up like it always used to when I asked about what got him sent to Calder Academy to begin with, so I don't poke at it. There's more than enough here to unpack as it is.

"Then when?" I ask. "Because I've been here with you the whole time, and nothing like this has ever happened before."

"The night I first kissed you."

"What?" I whisper.

"I lost control." He swallows. "I lost myself in you and I..."

And just like that, it becomes clear. Everything does. Carolina leaving has always been my worst nightmare—way worse than some ugly snake—and after Jude and I kissed... I trail off because the thought is too horrible to fully comprehend.

"That's why you ghosted me. Not because you don't care about me, but because—"

"I love you, Kumquat. I've loved you for years. But I can't be with you. Not when there's a chance that something like this might happen again."

"You love me?" I repeat the words, like I've never heard them before. To be honest, I haven't. Not the way he means them.

"You really have to ask me that?" He laughs, but there's no humor in the sound. "I love you so much that I had to cut you out of my life completely because I knew I wasn't strong enough to be around you and not want you."

"You love me." I say the words again, blankly. Because I'm pretty sure my brain has reached its capacity for revelations for the day. The week. The month. Possibly even the year.

"I love you," he says for the third time tonight, reaching out and running a finger over the tiny indentation in my chin the way he used to.

The small, familiar gesture brings tears to my eyes—I didn't know how much I'd missed it until right now.

"I love everything about you," he whispers sadly. "The way you always do the right thing. The way you always care about other people, even when they don't deserve it—especially here. The way you take a little coffee with your milk instead of the other way around and the way you never, ever, ever give up. Even on me."

Tears threaten, but I hold them back with sheer willpower and a whole lot of blinking.

"But that's why I have to do it," he whispers. "I have to give up on us, because you never will. Unleashing nightmares, destroying people's lives... I lose control when I'm with you, and I can't—I won't—let it happen again."

I know he's right. I do. Our happiness isn't more important than other people's lives. But that doesn't make it hurt any less. Suddenly I can't hold the tears back, no matter how hard I try.

They blur my eyes, turn Jude—and the whole world around me—fuzzy, until it looks like I'm seeing three of everything.

There's a part of me that can't help marveling that this is what it feels like—what it looks like—to cry when you're not in the shower. But the rest of me can't stop sobbing long enough to really process this. Not when the pieces of my already broken heart have crumbled into so many shattered dreams.

CHAPTER FIFTY-SEVEN

THREE STRIKES AND YOU'RE DEAD

"Kumquat." Jude's voice breaks as he skates a thumb over my cheekbone and wipes away my tears. "I can't walk away from you when you look like this."

I want to beg him not to walk away at all. But I can't. Not when I can still hear Eva scream and see her remains every time I close my eyes. Not when I can't help but think of the years Carolina spent in a prison cell for no reason. And not when I can feel the weight of everything that's happened tonight—the weight of everything that's gone so horribly wrong—pressing on my shoulders.

And so I do what feels like the impossible. I stop crying. I wipe my eyes. And I tell him, "It's okay. Just go. I'll be fine."

If possible, he looks even sadder. "Don't you mean okay?"

I know what Jude's asking, and the answer is no. I don't mean okay. I mean fine. Because right now I'm as fucked up and emotional as it gets. But so is he. So yeah, "I do. I'm okay."

He doesn't say anything else then. Just nods and slowly starts to back away.

"Clementine!" My cousin's voice tears through the pain between us. "Oh my God, there you are! We've been looking for you everywhere! We're moving up the time for the portal."

I force myself to take my eyes off of Jude to look at him. It's the hardest thing I've ever done. Because I know, deep in my soul, that when I turn back, he'll be gone.

"Who's we?" I ask when he gets closer, even though I already know.

He rolls his eyes, but I'm too busy trying to figure out why he looks so strange even though I'm not crying anymore. All I can say is, if this is what crying outside of the shower does to you, I am even less of a fan than I thought I was.

I blink a few times, rub my eyes, blink a few more. Then look back at Caspian again.

Only nothing has changed. In fact, it's gotten clearer. He's gotten clearer.

All three of him.

"Are you okay?" I ask again, trying not to panic.

"I'm fine." This time the middle Caspian—the one decked out in Calder red and who looks like I expect him to—eyes me strangely. "Are you?"

"I don't—" I pull my gaze off of all three of him and look around... which turns out to be a big mistake.

I'm already unsteady after everything that happened with Jude, and what I'm seeing now is only making me shakier. Because it's not just Caspian that I'm seeing three of. It's everyone.

More, it's *everything*.

CHAPTER FIFTY-EIGHT

CRASH AND LEARN

blink again.

Nothing changes.

Rub my eyes really hard.

Still nothing.

I blink again, and when that doesn't work, either, I do the only thing I can think of. I freak the fuck out.

My heart rate goes wild.

I forget how to breathe.

And my head—actually, my entire body—feels like it's going to explode.

Because the whole world isn't just in triplicate—which would be bad enough. No, the world I'm seeing, the world spread out right in front of me, appears to be the past, the present, and the future.

All at the exact same time.

The Caspian in front of me, talking to me, is the eighteen-year-old cousin I'm used to, dressed head to toe in Calder Academy red pajamas. But the Caspian next to him is the little boy with the perennially skinned knees who I used to build tree houses with. And the Caspian next to him is a forty-year-old man in a three-piece suit, who, unnervingly, happens to be missing a hand.

What. The. Hell. Is. Happening?

"Clementine?" Caspian sounds concerned, but I'm too busy trying to figure out what's going on—while also keeping my brain from imploding—to answer him.

Frantic, confused, and more than a little horrified, I turn back to the center mall, where some of the teachers have finally reached the horde of traumatized students spinning around themselves and each other. I search the sidewalks for Jude—he shouldn't be hard to find considering how tall and broad he is—but everything's such a mess that I can't find him.

Honestly, I can't find anyone. Because the center mall doesn't look like the center mall anymore. Or at least not a singular version of it.

Because it's rainy, windy, and filled with broken sidewalks...and even more broken students.

But when I blink, it's also sunny and filled with smiling paranormals walking down a sidewalk edged in beautiful flowers. Some have shifted—there are wolves and leopards and even a couple of dragons flying overhead—but there are also witches in old-fashioned bathing suits and vampires strolling along under huge, black umbrellas.

And then there are a bunch of other people again. I don't recognize any of them, and the fact that they're dressed in regular clothes instead of uniforms makes me wonder where they're from. Especially since the sidewalk they're walking on isn't broken. And they don't look scared. And it isn't raining.

WHAT THE HELL IS GOING ON?

I press a hand to my galloping heart, try to suck a breath into my too-tight lungs. And I guess I succeed because the world isn't going dark around me. Which is a shame, because right now, I kind of wish it would.

"Your mom wants me to bring you to her," one of the Caspians says, eyeing me uneasily. "She's down at the beach, overseeing the portal. She says we're leaving early."

Considering what's happening here, I can absolutely believe she wants to get out as fast as we possibly can. But that doesn't exactly solve the problem I'm having.

I close my eyes and force myself to calm down—which isn't exactly easy. I take another breath, promise myself that whatever happens when I open my eyes, it's going to be okay, and exhale the breath out slowly.

Then, I open my eyes to a world that is still completely upside down. I ignore it for a moment, refusing to look at anything or anyone but eighteen-year-old Caspian. And I ask, "But what about—"

Words fail me, and I lift my hand up in an all-encompassing gesture, too overwhelmed by everything that's just happened to even try to find the right words to talk about Eva. And Bianca. And all the many, many others.

Thankfully, though, Caspian understands. "We've been making plans for the last half an hour on how to deal with everything. The dorm is a mess—" His voice breaks, but he clears his throat and tries again. "We've got rosters, and we'll be checking off every student who goes through the portal so we can make sure that we've found...all the others. We won't leave anyone behind, Clementine, I swear."

"Eva—" This time it's my voice that breaks, and Caspian looks like he wants to cry with me. The other two versions—past and future—are doing their own things, with future Caspian scrolling through his phone and little Caspian bouncing a tiny rubber ball.

"We'll get her body," he promises me after clearing his throat. "We'll get everyone. But I need to get you to your mom before she completely freaks out."

I nod, because I know he's right. No matter how difficult my relationship with my mother is—and it is exceptionally difficult—I'm just as relieved to know that she's alive, that the nightmares didn't get her.

"Jude?" I ask, my voice breaking once more because just the sound of his name has pain swamping me all over again. I can't believe it has to end like this. Not after ten years. Not after everything we've gone through. And not after he finally told me what I've wanted to hear for so long.

He loves me. Jude loves me. But instead of being with me, he's walking away—for good this time. And I'm left standing here, broken and brokenhearted, in a world that makes absolutely no sense anymore.

"My dad just found him." Caspian sounds grim. "He told me Jude must have lost control of a lot of nightmares."

"You know?" I gasp. Terror moves through me as we start to walk down the cottage steps. Because now that my mom and Uncle Christopher know that Jude lost the nightmares, I don't know what they're going to do. But whatever it is, it's not going to be good. And there's a part of me that can't help thinking the Aethereum might have something to do with it.

"I don't really get what's happening," Caspian admits. "But I know my dad isn't letting him out of his sight until we can get to the warehouse and figure it out."

I don't say anything to that, partly because I don't know what to say and partly because I barely make it down one step before I trip over nothing. My brain is completely freaking out right now, trying to process the multiple images in front of me. Except it's not actually three cottages this time because, in what I think is the future, there is no cottage. And no steps. So, it's actually two cottages and a bench surrounded by several small potted trees.

And I keep thinking I'm about to crash into one of the trees.

I throw a hand out to try to grab the railing that I know is there but also can't see. Thankfully, my palm connects, and I force myself to go down the stairs that my brain doesn't quite believe are there anymore as I finally say, "Jude told me."

"He told you?" Now Caspian sounds incredulous. "Did he say why he did this? What did he think he was going to gain? Was he—"

"Stop!" I know I sound harsh, but I can't take a bunch of condemnation being heaped on Jude right now. "Just stop for a—"

I break off as I trip over a huge crack in the sidewalk that I didn't know was there. I catch myself and blink several times, trying to focus on seeing only the present. But it's not as easy as it sounds.

I take a couple more steps, then jump to the side to avoid a bench— only to walk straight into a bike someone has abandoned in the middle of the center mall. I end up tripping over it and nearly fall flat on my face.

Caspian somehow manages to catch me, but he shoots me a very concerned look. "You okay, Clementine?"

I have nothing to say to that, so I turn around, trying to keep myself focused solely on the present. The inner tubes in the middle of the mall aren't real. And neither are all the rose bushes. Only the cracks are real.

I step over a big one and start to congratulate myself for not falling on my ass, and then run directly into a dragon shifter.

She whirls around. "What the hell is your problem?" the present version of her says.

"Sorry!" Caspian steps in, pulling me away. "She hit her head pretty hard."

"I didn't hit my head," I tell him. He's got a firm grip on my shoulders now and keeps it that way as he steers me down the walkway.

"Well, you're acting like it," he says. "Just try to keep it together a little longer, will you please?"

"I'm trying!" I tell him. "It's harder than it looks."

I don't know how to explain it—except everything keeps changing. Every time I move or blink or look someplace new, I have to try and figure out where I am all over again. And if I'm focusing on the past, the present, or the future.

If they lined up in the same order every time, it would be easier. But sometimes the future is first. Sometimes the present is last. And sometimes the past is in the middle, which really fucks me up because I keep thinking present day is always in the middle—which is exactly how I ran into that damn dragon.

"What's going on?" Caspian asks, looking half concerned and half bewildered. "Seriously, are you all right?"

"I'm fine," I grind out as I keep walking—and try not to dwell on how the word makes me feel. Now that I'm off the porch, I have more than enough to contend with in the open. Things have gotten exponentially harder because walking down the center mall with people existing in different realms of time is a lot like how I imagine bumper cars would be. Or a real-life game of *Frogger*.

I dodge to the left to avoid a Calder Academy student before realizing they're not actually there before immediately diving to my right to avoid a woman in a short, yellow sundress and cat-eye sunglasses.

She gives a startled yelp and drops the drink she's holding. The fruity concoction—it looks like a piña colada—goes flying everywhere.

What just happened? Did she actually feel me even though we're separated by decades? How could that— My thoughts are interrupted just as something cold and sweet-smelling smacks me in the face.

Huh. Not a piña colada after all. A mai tai.

I'm so shocked by the revelation that this past woman and I can feel, see, and even spill things on each other that I totally miss the pink anemone bench in front of me. I crash into it so hard that I tumble to the ground as pain shoots up my foot.

"Clementine!" Caspian yells, half exasperated and half concerned. "What are you—" He breaks off when he sees what is directly in front of me. Bianca's broken body, crumpled and bloody, beneath the bench.

I saw her earlier from a distance, but this—this is awful. Especially because a very lost-looking past version of her hovers right beside her, turning a transparent gray as the color slowly, methodically, leaches from her.

Like her roommate, her arms and legs are bent at an unnatural angle and her eyes are vacant, staring sightlessly into the distance. A huge puddle of blood has pooled beneath her head, protected from the rain by the big, plaster bench she's stretched beneath.

"I'm sorry," I whisper, hysteria becoming a crushing weight on my chest.

Because I did this. I. Did. This.

Oh, Jude blames himself, but I'm the one who was unmeshed. I'm the one he set the nightmares loose for. I'm the one he saved.

The guilt is overwhelming, and so is the sorrow.

"I'm sorry," I whisper again. "I'm so, so sorry."

"We have to go," Caspian urges from somewhere up ahead of me.

"Go," I tell him as I reach out and close Bianca's eyes. "I'll catch up."

"I can't leave you!" he says. "Aunt Camilla will kill me. Plus, no one is allowed to stay on the island."

The irony is rich.

He gestures to the teachers herding kids down the sidewalk toward the beach that is usually completely off-limits.

But as I sit here at her feet, all I can focus on is the girl whose death I caused.

"We need—" He breaks off as someone crouches beside me.

"Hey, Clementine." I look up at the familiar voice, only to find three versions of Simon crouching down next to me. "You knew her?" he asks sympathetically.

"I've been here my whole life," I answer. "I know everybody."

He nods and reaches out a gentle hand to hold mine. "I'm sorry," he says in that quiet way he has.

"You're not the one who should be sorry." I am. I did this.

My stomach revolts for the second time today, and I find myself puking what's left of my favorite dill pickle chips into one of the potted plants behind the bench as lightning splits the sky above us.

"Go!" I tell Simon and Caspian, waving them away as my body continues to go through the motions of vomiting long after my stomach is empty of bile or anything else.

When the nausea finally passes, I rest my head on the cold, wet pot for a few seconds and try to catch my breath—and my will to go on—back.

The former is a lot easier to find than the latter.

"Can I help you up?" Simon asks, and it's the first time I realize that he's still here—and so is Caspian. They didn't leave me.

I want to say no, want to tell them to just go on without me. I was never supposed to step foot off of this island anyway. But it's becoming more and more obvious that neither one of them has any plans to head anywhere without me.

So I nod, and Simon wraps a surprisingly strong arm around my shoulders and helps me to my feet.

"We can't leave her like this," I tell him and Caspian.

"They're coming for her," my cousin answers. "I promise, Clementine."

As if on cue, two of the staff warlocks head toward us, a large black bag in their hands—at least I think there are two, since I can see six of them.

I step aside so they can get to her, and Simon—who still has his arm around my shoulders—begins to guide me down the path.

Normally, I'd tell him that I've got this, but the contact helps me focus on present Simon, while past and future Simon—both of whom are dressed in Calder Academy uniforms just to make things extra complicated—hover nearby.

Add in the fact that, for once, I'm not reacting to his siren pheromones and this seems like the path of least resistance. Also, since he's steering us, I don't have to work so hard to try to figure out what's real and what's not.

More lightning splits the sky above us, followed instantly by a rumble of thunder that shakes the very ground beneath our feet. At the same time, the wind picks up so fast and hard that Simon and I stumble and nearly fall.

Sheer strength of will—his, not mine—keeps us upright as the eerie wail of the hurricane siren splits the night. It's just my mother, calling us all down to the beach, but the low, discordant blast of it blends with the shriek of the wind, turning the sinister into the apocalyptic. Caspian must think so, too, because he speeds up until he's as close to jogging as he can get considering the headwind he's pushing against.

"What are you doing back here anyway?" I shout so Simon can hear me above the storm. "Caspian said they're holding everyone on the beach."

"Jude," he answers simply. "They've got him locked down, but he wanted to make sure you made it to the portal."

I don't know what to say to that as a fresh wave of pain flows through me. It's just one more layer to add to what's already inside me.

"Careful!" Simon pulls me to the right, steering me around something on the ground.

No, not just something.

The tapestry. The fucking tapestry.

Only now the warning about time is gone. In its place is nothing but a bunch of squiggly, fuzzy lines in every color imaginable.

CHAPTER FIFTY-NINE

HAIL, HAIL, THE GANG'S ALL HERE

It looks like the technical difficulties fuzz on old-fashioned TV screens that you see in TV shows and movies.

I stare at it for a few seconds, trying to decide if I want to pick it up or just leave it here to get blown away by the hurricane. Maybe it's ridiculous, but I can't help blaming it for its half-assed messages. Telling us to beware isn't the same as giving us any kind of warnings about the horrors that were coming. Especially because I can still see Eva's face as she read the warning that didn't help save her.

And yet Jude wanted it enough to fight with me about it. And someone cared about it enough to lock that damn shed up tight—Jude or one of the Jean-Jerks, I don't know.

"What's wrong?" Simon shouts, following my gaze to the wet, muddy tapestry.

And fuck it. Just fuck it.

I crouch down and roll the damn thing up. Despite the rain that's drenched it for the last hour, it's still light and easy to maneuver as I stand back up and hold it out to Simon.

"Can you get this to Jude?"

"To Jude?" His eyes go wide with realization. "This is what you two were fighting over earlier."

It's not a question, but I nod anyway. Because it all seems so foolish now.

All the arguments.

All the secrets.

All the wasted time when the tapestry got one thing right—we are so completely out of time.

"I'll make sure he gets it," Simon tells me, his face more serious than I've ever seen it.

"You guys, come on!" Caspian yells as a full-blown lightning storm fills the sky. "We have to go *now*!"

Seconds later, hail starts falling onto anything and everything. It's not big hail, thankfully, just dime size, but it still hurts like hell when it slams into us.

Caspian takes off running, with Simon and me right behind him. But the hail just makes things more complicated for me as I try to avoid...everyone.

I dodge a man in a bathing suit carrying a kayak—*a kayak*—only to end up running straight through a future Calder Academy student on a bicycle. Pain assaults me, electric shocks racing through my body from head to toe.

I stagger a little but manage to keep going as I fight through the agony.

"Clementine?" Simon calls, looking both confused and concerned as the hail continues to pummel us.

Up ahead, Caspian screams as he brushes up against a giant strolling along the center mall with a fishing pole the size of a large tree branch slung over his shoulder.

"What's wrong?" Poor Simon looks completely bewildered now as my cousin stumbles to a stop.

"What is that?" Caspian wildly flails his arms.

"Do you feel something?" I ask.

But before he can answer, one of the other students starts shouting and spinning around in circles. I can see that she's walked right through a group of future Calder Academy students, but she can't, and she is completely freaking out.

As are a number of the other students surrounding us, screaming and scratching at themselves and looking completely possessed to everyone around them as they lash out at nothing.

Or, at least, what looks to be nothing to everybody else. To me, it looks like somehow—some way—they're suddenly feeling, but not seeing, the people from the past and future that surround us.

But *I* can see them, and everyone who is freaking out is doing so because they've just brushed against or walked through or gotten too close to someone who was either exactly where they were in the past— or who will be, one day in the future.

It's the wildest thing I could ever have imagined, and to see it happen right in front of me is even wilder. Plus, it's made a million times worse by the fact that the island's ghosts have decided to join in the melee. They're shuddering and complaining about the rain, but they're here in all their nondescript grayness, nonetheless. Probably because every ghost I've ever met has a terrible case of FOMO. They all know something strange is going on here, and they don't want to miss out on whatever it is, even if it means braving the worst storm to ever hit the island.

But their presence makes a complicated situation infinitely more complicated, though—at least for me. Because not only can I see decrepit old Finnegan as he waves to me, I can see past Finnegan as well. I can't help but stare at the guy in a peacoat and work boots who is floating along behind him, a wide smile on his very handsome face.

This is what Finnegan looked like when he was young?

As if he can read my thoughts, young Finnegan shoots me a wink and a thumbs-up.

And, just like that, I give up on even trying to figure out what is going on in this shit show that has become my life.

Caspian hasn't, though, considering he looks straight at me and demands, "What is happening here, Clementine?" as he shudders nonstop.

I reach out and grab his hand, pulling him several feet forward— and away from the young girl with ponytails and a teddy bear that he was literally standing halfway through.

I don't have time to explain it, so I just say, "Get right behind me and follow in my footsteps *exactly.*"

"Umm, why?" Simon asks.

"Because she can see ghosts!" Caspian tells him.

Simon's eyes go wide. "Seriously?"

But I'm too shocked to answer him. "You knew? But I never—"

"Carolina told me!" he says, rain streaming down his face. "She wanted to make sure I could watch out for you if she wasn't around."

His words hit like body blows, and I nearly go down.

It's too much. It's all just too much.

Too much grief.

Too much pain.

Too much struggle only to lose again and again and again.

It never stops, and I don't want to do it anymore.

I can't do it anymore.

I'm so tired. So hurt. So broken beyond repair.

I just want it all to stop.

But then I look at Caspian, and I can't help thinking that he's kept my secret all these years. That, in his own way, he's protected me all along, and I didn't have a clue.

I take a deep breath and do my best to fight off the sorrow that presses down on me with the weight of the whole ocean. Because I can't give up. I can't let anything happen to him—or to Simon, or to anyone on this path with us. I have to get them through the tangle of time that stands between them and the beach.

Them and the portal.

So I shove the grief and the horror back down to a place I don't have to think about right now. And then I run straight for the fence that surrounds the whole island and normally cuts the students off from the beach and the docks.

As I run, I dodge ghosts and flickers, past and present and future, and pain. So much pain. But I just keep shoving it back down and keep going because students and teachers alike are following the path I'm cutting now.

Only the retrieval crew stays behind, packing up student remains so they don't get left behind, either.

The hail gets bigger and harder the closer we get to the beach, but there's no time and no place to take shelter anyway. So I duck my head, throw my hands up to shield myself as best I can, and keep going while Caspian and the others follow right behind me.

Past the main dorm, through the dense copse of trees that stands between the students and the fence, and finally—finally—through the brand-new opening in the fence to the beach beyond.

And then I run some more. I don't stop—none of us do—until I make it to the loose sand right before the ocean meets the beach.

We've been running so hard for so long that my breath is whistling in and out like a freight train. I bend over, hands braced on thighs, and try to bring it back under control as I stare out at the roiling ocean.

It's the most beautiful thing I've ever seen, but also the most perilous. Because the surf is churning in the storm, causing giant waves to continuously hit the shore. They kick up detritus and carry it up the beach in seawater that's gone black and foamy. The roar of the sea is deafening, overwhelming, and I can't help wondering—even with the portal—how we're going to get everyone through this.

Each wave that rolls in is bigger than the last, and it's only a matter of time before a tsunami comes crashing down and floods this whole part of the island.

I look around for Jude, for our friends, for my mother, but between the storm and the hundreds of people from all different times milling around, it's an utter disaster out here. I can't see shit.

At least not until my mother starts shouting my name through a megaphone.

I follow the sound through the crowd—and even manage to get past the Jean-Jerks unscathed—until I finally see my always impeccable mother drenched in rain, hair plastered to her head, and blood, which I'm pretty sure isn't hers, streaked across her face. Next to her is a younger past version—all bright and shiny in a pair of pinstripe pants and a white button-up, with a backpack slung over her shoulder—and a future version, stooped with age, an afghan thrown over her shoulders.

For a second, I can only stare at these two versions of my mother that I don't even recognize. But then something else catches my eye, and I turn to see my uncle Christopher standing next to her. Next to him is Jude, looking as broken—as defeated—as I feel.

I stumble toward them, calling his name as I go. But the storm is too loud and he can't hear me—none of them can. At least not until I'm standing right in front of them.

"Clementine!" My mother looks dizzy with relief as she pulls me into her arms. "Oh my God. I was so worried that the nightmares had…"

She trails off as I hug her back, and though I'm relieved she's okay, I've only got eyes for Jude, who is staring back at me like I'm the only lifeline he's got.

"There she is!" I hear Uncle Christopher growl at him. "She's fine. Now it's time for you to keep your end of the bargain, Jude. Let's go."

At first, Jude doesn't seem to hear him. He just keeps staring at me with haunted, kaleidoscope eyes.

"Clementine," he whispers, and for the first time ever, I don't mind that he's used my real name. How can I when he makes it sound like I'm the most important thing—the only thing—in his world?

Even knowing what he told me, even knowing what we've somehow done, I can't stop myself from reaching for him. From needing him.

He closes his eyes as my fingers brush against his hand, his face alive with an agony that slices me to the bone.

"Jude," I whisper, clutching at him because I can feel him slip away. Even before he pulls his hand from mine.

And this time, when he looks at me, his face is completely blank.

"Jude," I say again.

But he doesn't respond. He doesn't say a word. Instead, he takes three steps back and just disappears.

CHAPTER SIXTY

ANY PORTAL
IN A STORM

I scream his name as I dive after him, but my mother grabs me around the waist as all three versions of Uncle Christopher quickly follow Jude into the portal.

"Let me go!" I tell her as I struggle against her.

But my mother has manticore strength, and she uses every bit of it to hold me tight as she orders, "Calm down, Clementine! You'll see him soon enough."

"He'll be at the warehouse?"

"Honestly, where else would he be?" She eyes me impatiently.

"I don't know," I answer slowly. "I just thought, people are..."

I trail off because I don't want to say it. I'm not sure I even can say it.

"Dead?" My mother doesn't shy away from the truth. "Not saying it doesn't make it not true, Clementine. Just like not saying it doesn't make it not Jude's fault. There will be consequences for this—severe consequences. But did you really think I would banish him for one mistake? This school doesn't work like that, and you should know that. Besides, there's nowhere else for him *to* go. *We* are the last resort."

The words *the Aethereum* dance on the edge of my tongue—it's where I've been terrified they would send him from the moment he told me what happened, just like they sent Carolina—but if my mother hasn't thought of it, I'm certainly not going to bring it up right now.

Or ever.

"Now, can you please help me with this?" She thrusts her tablet with its waterproof cover at me. "Christopher was marking people off as we send them through the portal, but now you can do that. And let's move, shall we? The sooner we get everyone through, the sooner we can go through, too."

I take the tablet from my mother, and as I do, there's a strange flicker—half beside her, half on top of her—and then I'm staring at a younger woman who looks a lot like her, but also doesn't.

At first, I think it's just her past self, but that doesn't make any sense. Because her past self is on her other side, right next to her future self. There can't be four versions of my mother, can there?

Except, when I look closer, I realize the flicker is the same woman that's been haunting me—same brown hair, same floral nightdress, same pregnant belly.

I try to ignore her as she stares straight at me with big blue eyes the same color as my mother's—and mine. That's when I realize that she's in color. Like full, actual color. Not just her nightdress now, but all of her. Dark brown hair, soft blush lips, freckled ivory skin, nightdress in varying shades of pink.

She reaches for me, her long, skeletal hand flying for my wrist as, instinctively, I flinch away. She cries out then, a long, low wail that turns into a scream just as she morphs into the wild-haired, desperate sunken creature that's been haunting me since this storm began.

Her fingers wrap around my wrist in an iron grip, and the moment they start to squeeze, pain radiates through me. Sharp, visceral, overwhelming.

Visions engulf me, slamming into me like wild, storm-tossed waves against the shore, before dragging me down into an abyss.

A man—a fae with the same orange eyes as Jean-Luc.

My mother, grabbing onto a wrist stacked with multicolored friendship bands.

Carolina, struggling to free her wrist as tears pour down her face.

My mother looks so angry, Carolina so scared.

Fear swells inside of me, blends with the wild confusion whipping through my mind. But for the first time since these visions began, the fear is nearly drowned by rage.

"Clementine!" My mother's voice—sharp and impatient—cuts through the fear. "Will you please pull yourself together and help me?"

I blink, and the creature vanishes like mist, though the emotions it invoked take longer to fade.

"Clementine! Are you listening?" my mother demands.

"Yes!" I wave the tablet as I force myself to pay attention to what's happening right in front of me in the real, corporeal present. "What do I need to do?"

"I just went through the whole thing," she tells me. "Were you not listening at all?"

I duck my head and mumble, "Sorry."

She gestures to the tablet. "We've got the students divided alphabetically into groups of twenty. Each group is with a teacher that will accompany them through the portal. We mark each student off as they enter the portal, and your aunt Carmen marks them off as soon as they get to the warehouse on the other side of the portal. We are not taking any chances with leaving even one student behind, so you have to do this right. Do I make myself clear?"

"Yeah, of course." I stare down at the list on the tablet in front of me. Juniors with last names *A* through *C*.

"We've already got the freshmen and sophomores over, so let's get the juniors and seniors over now. Then we can finally get out of this hellish storm."

As if to reinforce her words, the wind chooses that moment to let loose with a long, low, animalistic yowl. It slams into me with the force of a wrecking ball, almost knocking me off my feet.

My mother steadies me, and her face is even more grim, though I didn't know that was possible. "Let's get this done," she tells me.

"Why did we choose to do the portal out here?" I ask, shouting to be heard over the roar of the wind and the sea.

"The security witches said this was our best bet to build a portal this complex that would allow us to transfer several students at the same time," my mother answers with an annoyed wave of her hand. "Something about the meeting of three powerful elements being much stronger than two not-so-powerful ones."

I can't help glancing back at the ocean. Yeah, there's definitely power there. Too much power, at the moment, if you ask me.

We start the first group through, and I mark each of them off as they step into the portal. "Are all portals like that?" I ask my mom as the sky shimmers and vibrates above us. I can't actually see any defined walls for the portal, but there's definitely something there because everything kicked up by the wind keeps slamming into something as it flies through the sky.

"Secure ones are," she answers. "We have a very specific protocol in place in order to keep these students safe and their powers locked down. That shimmer you see is part of it."

I'm not sure what about this screams safety to her, but I don't say anything else as we start on students with the last names *D* through *F*. Then again, how else could we safely evacuate people in the middle of all this? There's no way any traditional modes of transportation would get through this mess.

So, as the storm rages around us, I concentrate on doing my job as quickly and efficiently as I can—as does my mom. We're all the way up to the junior class *T*s through *Z*s when another bout of lightning fills the sky.

Again, there's that weird shimmer in the sky that doesn't seem quite right to me. I blink and rub a hand across my soaking-wet eyes and look again. And scream as I watch dozens of students suddenly fall through the air.

"Clementine!" My mother turns to me wild-eyed. "What's wrong with you?"

"What do you mean what's wrong?" I point at the disaster unfolding in front of me. "Can't you see?"

"See what?" she asks.

I blink and the scene disappears as quickly as it came. "I don't understand," I whisper. "I saw—"

"What?" my mother demands. "What did you see?"

"I don't know. There were students falling through the sky. It didn't make any sense to me."

She studies me for a few seconds, her eyes moving over every inch of my face as if she's looking for something. I don't know what. And then she turns and walks several feet to Ms. Picadilly and Mr. Abdullah—the two most powerful witches on campus—who, I now realize, have been casting the portal this whole time.

"Is everything okay?" she asks them. "Any problems holding the portal?"

"No," Ms. Picadilly shouts to be heard over the storm. "Everything's perfect. It's going like clockwork."

"Abe?" my mother asks, turning to Mr. Abdullah. "What do you think?"

"I think it's fine, Camilla," he says. "Why? Do you think something's wrong?"

She ignores the question. "There are no fluctuations? The lightning isn't bothering it?"

Now he just looks baffled. "No. Why?"

She shakes her head. "No reason."

"We've got this, Camilla. I've done it a thousand times before, and this feels just like every other time."

She studies him—and Ms. Picadilly—for a moment, her gaze shifting back and forth between them. Then she seems to make a decision. "Okay, then. Keep up the good work."

She hustles back to the opening of the portal. "Let's get this done, Clementine."

"Of course." I'm still shocked that she took what I said seriously when I don't even know if she should have. What I saw only lasted for a split second before it vanished. Unlike everything—and everyone—else around here, all of which are sticking around in triplicate.

She calls for the first group of seniors—in reverse alphabetical order this time—and I start checking them off just as another gust of wind rips across the beach. Seconds later, lightning flashes while thunder rumbles at the exact same second.

"Get in there," my mom orders Izzy, who has been patiently waiting her turn. "Now."

Izzy shoots her a very unimpressed look, but she does what my mom asks, disappearing into the portal just as giant, cantaloupe-size hail starts falling from the sky.

One slams into the ground inches from my feet, and I jump back, horrified.

All around us students start yelling and running for cover. But there is no cover out here. The dorm is too far away, and there's nothing else. We're sitting ducks.

"Mom, we have to—"

I break off as another huge hailstone slams down right in front of my mom, so close that it catches the toe of her boot.

She jumps back with a startled scream.

"Are you hurt?" I ask, bending to check her foot.

"Get in the portal," she tells me urgently.

"What?"

"Get in the portal, Clementine." She raises the megaphone to her lips. "Everyone, get in the portal, now!"

Pandemonium ensues as everyone left on the beach stampedes for the portal all at once—except for Ms. Picadilly and Mr. Abdullah, who stay exactly where they are so they can hold the portal open.

"Go, go, go," my mom shouts, rushing students in three and four at a time.

Behind us someone screams, and I turn to see one of the senior witches on the ground, her head cracked open and blood slowly leaking out.

"Come on," my mother yells into the microphone as Ms. Picadilly and Mr. Abdullah widen the opening of the portal. "Everyone in!"

She turns to me. "Get in there, Clementine!"

"I'm waiting for you!"

She doesn't bother to answer me. Instead, she just puts a hand on the center of my back and shoves me into the portal as hard as she can.

I'm not expecting it, and I fall forward just enough that the portal grabs me.

And then I'm falling, falling, falling.

CHAPTER SIXTY-ONE

IN GRAVE AND PORTAL DANGER

I've never been in a portal before—they've been blocked on the island my whole life—so I don't know what it's supposed to feel like when you're in one.

But this feels weird. Really, really weird. As if my whole body is being stretched out like one of those rubber pop tube toys. It's like with each second that passes I'm getting longer, narrower, *flatter*... And then suddenly I'm not. The stretching stops in an instant, and then I boing back together, my body going from elongated to normal in the blink of an eye.

I take a deep breath and try to adjust to the feeling of being normal again. Then wonder why I bothered when abruptly the walls of the portal start to close in on me. I throw my hands out to try to stop them, but it just keeps pressing and pressing and *pressing* in on me until I can feel myself getting smaller. Feel myself compressing down, getting shorter and flatter with the contraction of the portal.

At first, I'm just a little alarmed as I wait for it to spring back like the first time. But it doesn't. It just keeps squeezing inch by inch until it's like a piano sitting in the middle of my chest.

I know there are a lot of people in this portal with me—I can hear them banging around, knocking into its weird, elastic walls. Some are even screaming, though I have no idea where they get the oxygen for that. Is this normal? And if it is, who would travel like this? I know it's supposed to be faster and safer than a boat, but right now I'd rather take my chances with the storm-tossed Gulf of Mexico.

But I can't even lift my head to look around, to try to find someone else going through this same thing. All I can do is lie here, suspended, and try not to freak the fuck out while the portal does its best to crush me to death.

It's not easy.

All of a sudden, the weight on my chest gets heavier, and it goes from hard to breathe to impossible. Instinct takes over, and I start to claw fruitlessly for air. But everything hurts and things start to go fuzzy, until there are just a few small points of light in the distance.

The fuzziness gets worse as darkness takes over inside my head, and I start to float away on a sea of—

The compression stops as abruptly as it started, and I free-fall several feet in an instant.

Instinct has me throwing my arms out again as I suck breath after breath into my starving lungs. The fuzziness fades, and I'm alert again...just in time for a terrible ripping sound to echo through the air around me.

Suddenly the screams get worse. More terrified and definitely more desperate. And then I'm falling again.

Only this time it's not in a vacuum. It's through fierce winds and rain and *lightning*, straight into the raging, roiling ocean.

I hit the water hard and go down, down, down into the sea. There's one moment where I wonder if this is just part of the portal, part of the magic. But then a big fish—a really big fish—swims by, and it sinks in. I'm not in the portal anymore. I'm in the freaking Gulf of Mexico.

At night.

In the middle of a hurricane.

With sharks.

And I'm sinking fast.

Everything I've ever read about getting pulled under in the ocean always says to find the light and swim up. But from where I'm at, there is no light. Just fathomless darkness in all directions.

I tell myself the monsters I've faced at Calder Academy in the last day or two are way worse than anything in the ocean. All of which sounds well and good until something brushes against my leg in the water, and I finally give in. I freak the fuck out.

I start flailing and thrashing—the absolute worst thing I can do, but terror is a desperate, clawing animal within me, and all I can think is, *Get out, get out, get out.*

Plus I've been underwater for at least a minute now—maybe more—and my lungs are burning.

So I do something that feels so wrong but may be my only chance of survival. I read somewhere that as long as you have air in your lungs, your body will try to float. So I roll myself around until I'm lying prone in the water—or at least, I think I am. And then I force myself to relax every muscle that I can.

It takes a few terrible, nerve-racking, desperately important seconds, but then I break the surface and take a deep breath, inhaling almost as much salt water as air, before I am dragged under again.

But that's all I need. I spin around and start swimming without any hint that I'm going the right way. Panic tries to set in again, but I beat it back.

Seconds later, the water changes—somehow it grows even choppier and harder to move through. I take that as a sign that I'm getting closer to the surface, especially since what's beyond the water, directly above me, seems a little lighter. Like maybe, just maybe, I'm getting closer to shore. My head breaks through the surface of the water again, and this time when I try to take another deep breath, I slap my hand over my mouth as a makeshift filter. It works, kind of, and I actually manage to get more oxygen than water this time around.

I do that a couple more times before I feel up to looking around and trying to get my bearings. If I'm lucky, I'll be close to the island, and I can swim to shore.

The irony of wanting to get back on the island, now that I'm finally off, is not lost on me, but I figure, at this point, it's any island in a storm. Literally. I'll worry about getting off again if I manage to live through the next ten minutes.

But bobbing around in an angry, storm-tossed ocean isn't exactly the best vantage point, and I can't see the island. I can't see anything but the next wave set to crash over me. And then the next one. And then the next one after that.

Every wave takes more energy from me, and every struggle to stay on the surface leaves me more and more exhausted. But I manage to keep from going under again. With no idea of which way I'm going, only knowing that I have to do something, I wait for the next wave to roll into me. Waves move toward shore—or at least, I think they do. It's not like I've had much experience with them, despite growing up on an island. But maybe, if I go with the wave instead of fighting it, it will take me closer to the island.

Closer to safety.

The wind is wild now, and it's got the ocean whipped into a frenzy, so it doesn't take long before another wave comes through and I get to test my half-baked theory.

I can see it building, see it growing taller and taller. So I take a deep breath and tell myself that when it rolls over me, I shouldn't fight it. Instead, I should relax and just let it take me.

It's the hardest thing I've ever done. Harder than losing Jude. Harder even than losing Carolina—to the prison and then to death. It's definitely harder than accepting that I might die out here, without ever seeing anything but the walls on this island.

I think I've always known that, though. It's why I've fought for control for as long as I can remember. Control over my choices, control over my body, control over my magic. Control over anything and everything in a world designed to wrest that control from me at every opportunity.

I've lost more battles than I've won—a lot more. But no matter how bad things have gotten, I've never stopped fighting. Never stopped trying to hold on to some manner of control over my own life.

So now, to have to give that up? To have to give myself over to this storm, to this wave, to this endless, roiling ocean that doesn't give a damn about my life or my choices, is the hardest thing I've ever had to do.

But I know if I don't, it will be all over anyway. Because I've already lost any chance I had of controlling anything that matters. All that's left is accepting it...and then seeing what happens.

The wave is bigger now, so big I can't even see the top of it. Fear is a nightmare running rampant inside of me, but I ignore it. And then, as the wave finally crashes through me, I stop fighting, take a deep breath, and I give myself over to whatever comes next.

CHAPTER SIXTY-TWO

WHERE THERE'S A WILL THERE'S A WAVE

I t turns out what comes next is nothing good.

The wave takes me down, spins me around, tosses me back and forth under the water so that I lose track, once again, of which way is up. But I force myself to wait for a few seconds, force myself not to use up all my energy fighting something that can't be fought.

No one is more surprised than I am when it works. Instead of continuing to pull me down, the current pushes me back up as the wave rises and swells. My head breaks the surface, and I suck a giant gulp of air into my lungs before the wave rolls forward and takes me under once more.

Again, I fight every instinct I have and let the water take me.

Again, it drags me under and then lifts me up on another cresting wave.

This happens several times, and each time I come up the wave is a little bigger and takes me a little higher—until finally I can see something besides the roiling ocean and the pounding rain.

Far ahead of me—so far that I can't be sure it isn't a mirage considering my eyes are burning from the salt water and I'm still seeing everything in triplicate—I can see lights.

Bright lights and a lot of them, like the flood lamps that line the wall that surrounds the island.

I blink and rub my eyes several times to try to clear them. But that just makes the burning—and the cloudy vision—worse. So in the end I have to give up on confirming anything and just trust that what I'm seeing is real.

Yet another thing I'm really not good at.

But the storm is getting worse and the waves more violent. Lightning splits the sky above me followed by thunder so loud that not even the roll of the ocean can mask it.

The next current that grabs me is completely dominating. It drags me under, deeper and deeper, until my lungs ache and I begin to think that this might be the time it doesn't bring me back up.

So I start to swim up, determined to get to shore now that I know it's there and that I'm going in the right direction.

The ocean showed me what I needed it to. It gave me the course for my escape route. The rest is up to me.

And so I push myself to the limits—and then past them—as I swim harder than I've ever swum before.

After what feels like an eternity, I finally break through the ever-growing wall of water. I expect to be on the surface, but when I look down, I realize I'm actually several yards above the ocean's surface—in the crest of a wave that's growing higher and higher with each second that passes.

I only have a moment to notice there are other students with me in the wake of the wave and think that this is going to hurt all of us before it crashes back down, taking me with it.

I slam back into the surface of the water—all that work swimming, for nothing—and get rolled, hard. I turn over and over again, completely out of control as the ocean tosses me around like spindrift.

I finally stop rolling after what feels like hours but is probably less than a minute. I start to kick out, to try to move toward the lights I can see in the distance. But another current grabs me and starts pulling me down, down, down.

Panic sets in as it drags me steadily lower, and though I try to shut it out, try to think logically, it's almost impossible. Because this time feels different.

This time it feels like I'm not going to find my way back up.

I start to struggle, start to claw at the water dragging me steadily downward. But the current has me in its grip, and it's not letting go. Not this time.

The realization comes to me slowly, the understanding that I'm going to die out here and there's nothing I can do about it.

Grief slams into me hard—along with the knowledge that I'll never see Jude again.

I'll never get to see his eyes swirl wildly with all the emotions he refuses to acknowledge.

I'll never get to smell his warm honey-and-cardamom scent as it wraps around me like a hug.

And I'll never again get to feel his heart beat against my cheek or hear his low, gravelly voice tell me that he loves me.

Losing that—losing him for a third and final time—hurts as much as losing everything else put together.

It's at that moment that I realize that my love for Jude is infinite.

It's as deep as the ocean, as powerful as this hurricane, as endless as the sky that stretches above me even now. It's every dream I've never had, every monster I've ever slain, and it's...forever. That's what it is. Forever. No matter what.

And admitting that, even to myself—even alone in the middle of this raging sea that seems hell-bent on killing me—brings me an incredible sense of tranquility.

An incredible sense of right.

Another wave crashes over me, and I'm going down now, sinking farther and farther under the water. Surprisingly, it isn't so bad. In fact, now that I'm not fighting it, it almost feels kind of...nice.

There's no pain anymore.

No hunger for air.

No struggle to somehow best a world that doesn't give a shit whether I live or die.

Instead, there's an insidious kind of peacefulness to this, an odd, syrupy lassitude that slides through my veins. That quiets my brain and my frantic heart. That makes it almost easy to slip lower and lower and—

All of a sudden, something grabs my wrist and yanks on me, hard.

CHAPTER SIXTY-THREE

HOW DO I LOVE THEE?
LET ME COUNT THE WAVES

At first, I think it's some kind of shark or something, but there's no pain in the hold, no teeth slicing into my skin. Just determination, as whatever it is pulls me up, up, up.

I break the surface several seconds later and immediately start coughing as I try to drag air into my starved and waterlogged lungs.

Dawn has broken across the sky, and though it's still gray and dim inside the storm, I can see my rescuer for the first time.

And somehow, someway, it's Jude. But that's impossible he already went through the portal. He should be at the warehouse in Huntsville.

At first, I think I'm hallucinating, that I've blacked out and am about to die and he's a figment of my oxygen-starved imagination. But then Jude spins me around and drags me against him, my back to his chest. He joins his hands just below my bra line and starts jabbing them into me over and over again.

It hurts way more than drowning did. As does the copious amount of seawater that immediately comes rushing up my trachea.

I start coughing as I vomit it all into the sea.

I've barely finished, barely had a chance to take a breath, when Simon surfaces right in front of me. There's three of him—big surprise—but they all look so different that it's easy for me to figure out which one is present Simon, even before he grins at Jude and says, "Looks like you beat me to her."

"I was motivated," Jude answers.

But Simon is already casting an uneasy glance at the ever-worsening weather. "We need to get to shore, fast."

I can feel Jude's nod against the back of my head even before he growls, "Grab onto me, Kumquat."

I start to protest, but he just shoots me a *don't push me* look, and for once, I decide to heed the warning as I wrap my arms around his shoulders.

And then we strike off for shore, with Simon right beside us in case we need him.

The wind is fiercer now, the waves growing bigger, pounding harder. We get rolled more than once, and more than once Jude has to claw his way back to the surface with me on his back.

But he does it every time, his huge, powerful arms eating up the distance between where we are and the shore despite this storm that seems determined to stop us.

I know that's not true, know the storm is just an inanimate thing that cares about nothing—it just exists. But it doesn't feel like that right now. It feels malevolent, like the heart of it is determined to get to shore and take all of us down as it goes.

But that doesn't matter because we're almost there. The lights on the fence are so close now that it seems like I could almost reach out and touch them. Jude must feel it, too, because somehow his kicks get longer, his strokes more measured until finally—*finally*—we're washing up on shore.

The second we get sand beneath us, I start to roll off of him, so grateful to have land beneath me again that I don't care about the rain or the wind or the lightning tearing the sky in two. I just want to lie on the sand for a moment.

But Jude obviously doesn't feel the same way, because he's up again in seconds. He runs up the beach with me still on his back and doesn't stop until he gets us completely clear of whatever wave might roll in, no matter how high it goes.

Only then does he help me off his shoulders before collapsing beside me on the beach.

My throat is raw from salt water, my eyes feel like they've been scoured with sandpaper, and my lungs burn with each breath that I take. As soon as I find the energy to actually move—I roll over to look at Jude, who is currently stretched out on his back, bent arm over his eyes to shield them from the rain that continues to pour down upon us.

"What are you doing here?" I demand. My raw throat burns in protest, but I don't pay any attention to it. I need answers. "You went through the portal a long time ago. You were safe at the warehouse in Huntsville."

He doesn't answer, just shakes his head back and forth as he continues to suck air in at an alarming rate.

I know I should wait until he catches his breath, know I should give him a couple of minutes to recover, but that will also give him a chance to put his armor back in place. And no. Just no. I am beyond tired of omissions and evasions and half answers that don't tell me anything.

So, even though every muscle in my body is screaming at me, even though I'm still shaking from exertion and shock, I force myself to sit up and push his arm away from his face so I can see his beautiful eyes. I expect them to be shuttered, distant, as they so often are. Instead, they're burning hot and more than a little wild as he sits up to meet me.

But he still doesn't answer, just looks at me in a way that has every nerve ending in my body going on high alert in all the best ways. Still, I need answers. "I'm serious, Jude. Why are you here? You were safe and—"

"The portal broke," he answers abruptly. "And your mom came through on the other side. The second I saw her there without you, I knew you hadn't made it through, so..." He trails off with a shrug.

"So you what? Just dove into a breaking portal?" I ask incredulously.

The corners of his lips twitch in his almost Jude smile as he reaches forward and rubs a finger over the small dimple in my chin. "I already told you, Satsuma. I'm not okay living in a world without you in it."

I let the ridiculous citrus name go and focus on the rest of what he has to say. It's hard not to when my entire body lights up from the inside, an inexplicable warmth moving through every part of me. But still, I need more.

"What about the nightmares?" I ask. "You said we could never be together. You said you loved me, but—" My voice breaks as the tranquility I felt in the ocean slips away in the face of all the pain of our last encounter.

Jude grows solemn. "I don't know what we're going to do. Or how the fuck I'm going to learn better control over these nightmares." His jaw tightens. "I just know that when I thought you were..."

This time it's his voice that breaks. He clears his throat, tries again. "When I thought you were dead, I..." And again, his tight throat won't let the words pass.

So I fill them in for him, a strange confidence flooding me that's been missing from our relationship—and everything else I do—for far too long. "You realized how foolish it is to try to run away."

Jude gives me a look. "I'm not so sure I would say foolish—"

"Maybe not, but I would," I tell him.

He ignores me and continues. "More like futile. I spent three years staying away from you. I don't think I have it in me to try to do that again."

"Jude." I reach for him just as a chorus of screams rings through the air.

CHAPTER SIXTY-FOUR

TIME TO MANTICORE UP

I whirl around just in time to see another huge wave crash down on the beach. It carries a bunch of students with it, only a few of whom manage to actually crawl up the beach before the wave drags the others back out to shore.

"Shit!" Jude takes off running back toward the water, and I'm right behind him—or as behind him as I can be when my exhausted body threatens to collapse with every step I take.

But people are dying, drowning just like I was, and I have to at least try to save them. Especially since Luis and the others might be out there.

Simon, thankfully, is already on it as he pulls a waterlogged Ember out of the sea. Each of the three versions of him is carrying a different version of her, all of whom he drops at our feet as he yells, "Take care of her!" before turning and racing back into the ocean.

"I lost Mozart!" Ember gasps before rolling over and coughing up a bunch of seawater.

"It's okay," I tell her even as my stomach drops. "She'll be okay, right, Jude?"

But he looks as grim-faced as Ember does. "She can't swim," he tells me.

"What? How—"

I break off as Ember grabs onto Jude's hand. "She was with me when the portal broke, but I lost her when we fell. I couldn't hold on to her. I couldn't—" She breaks off on a sob. "You have to find her, Jude!"

But he's already gone, running straight into the ocean after Simon.

Terror clutches me, and I think about running after him. But I know if I do, he'll just have to save me again. I'm better off helping here.

I wrap an arm around Ember and move her out of the reach of the waves that keep coming farther and farther up the beach.

Once I get her settled out of range, she brushes me off to go help the others.

Please let Luis be okay.

Please let Jude be okay.

Please let Mozart be okay.

The words are a desperate mantra in my head as I run to the first person I see—a banshee I had P.E. with our freshman year. I don't remember much about her, except she was really great at dodgeball.

But right now, present her is lying face down in the sand, while past version wrings her hands just beyond the reach of the waves.

"Alina!" I call her name as I drop to my knees beside her, but she doesn't respond.

I roll her over and try again. "Alina!"

Still nothing.

The rain is coming down in sheets, the wind whipping along the beach, making it impossible to see if she's unconscious or—

I don't even let myself think it—any more than I let myself think about there not being a future version of her hovering around—as I press a hand to her chest to see if she's breathing. Several seconds pass and nothing happens, and horror fills me.

I call Alina's name as I lean down and try to hear if there are any breath sounds at all coming from her, but the storm is too loud. Even if she was breathing, I wouldn't be able to hear her.

My brain is telling me she's dead, but I can't leave her without at least trying to save her, so I start CPR as I desperately try to remember the health class I had to take sophomore year.

I recall the teacher saying we're not supposed to do mouth-to-mouth anymore, just chest compressions—so I start with those. But I remember the textbook explaining that there were a few exceptions, and though I can't swear by it, I'm pretty sure drowning was one of those exceptions.

But I don't remember for sure, and I really don't want to mess this up.

I look around for help, but there's no one to ask. Everyone I see is either unconscious, dead, or trying to crawl their way up the beach. I really am on my own here.

Fuck it. I bend down and blow two breaths into her mouth. Maybe I can save her, maybe I can't. But right now, she's already gone. At least this gives her a chance.

I do a series of chest compressions, followed by two more breaths and more chest compressions. This time, water spews out of her mouth, which I take as a good sign and keep going.

Seconds later, Alina's eyes fly open, and she comes up swinging, even as loud, hard coughs rack her slight form.

I fall back onto my butt just in time to dodge a fist. "It's okay!" I shout at her as a particularly virulent gust of wind howls by us. "You're okay."

She freezes mid-punch, her eyes wide as she registers that I was actually helping her. Then she rolls onto her knees and starts bringing up a ton of water.

And just like that, a future version of her appears in front of me.

That more than anything else convinces me that she's okay, so I don't stick around. Instead, I stumble to my feet and move onto the next person—a male wolf I haven't met before. He's relatively new to the school, and he looks like an asshole, so I've always given him a wide berth.

But since he's currently crawling up the beach and puking water everywhere, I race over to see if he's okay. His subsequent growl—which is echoed by his past and future selves—has me backing up just as quickly. Apparently, he's just fine.

I help a few more people—a leopard who is alive but too weak to crawl up the beach and a witch who was definitely not okay until I did CPR on her as well—before another major wave slams into the sand.

I run back up the beach to avoid getting caught in the undertow, but it grabs me anyway and starts pulling me backward. I fight my way through it, escaping just in time to see present Izzy staggering up the beach, her arm wrapped around an unconscious Remy's chest. Their past and future selves hover nearby.

I run over to them and start to help her with Remy. But she just gives me an oh-please look and drags him several more feet before dumping him on the sand. "Is he breathing? Does he need CPR?" I ask.

"He's fine," she answers with a roll of her eyes. "He kept fighting me, so I knocked him out."

I don't know what to say to that, so I just nod. Then, even though I know it's a ridiculous question, I can't help asking, "Did you see..."

"Jude?" She shakes her head. "Honestly, I couldn't see shit out there. It's a damn miracle Remy found me. And by found me, I mean glommed on to me and thought he could help. As if." She rolls her eyes.

"If you're okay, I'm going to go see if anyone needs help," I tell her.

Izzy waves a hand as she drops down onto the ground next to Remy's still-unconscious form. "Go. I've got this."

I spend the next I don't know how long staggering up and down the beach, helping people and trying to find Luis. But I have absolutely no luck. I remember Jude saying my mom somehow made it to the other side of the portal in Huntsville, despite being the last one into it, and I keep praying that that's where my best friend is as well.

He may not be any safer there than he has been for the last three years here at Calder Academy, but at least he'll be alive. And right now, that's all I can ask for.

It's all any of us can ask for.

Please let Luis be okay.

Please let Jude be okay.

Please let Mozart be okay.

I start my mantra again, just as I trip over someone in the sand. I crouch down to see if I can help and realize it's Mr. Abdullah, one of the witches who built the portal. One look and I know he's dead. As is Ms. Picadilly.

A sob catches in my throat, but I swallow it down. I don't even know them very well, so it makes no sense for me to be so upset.

Except they were only trying to help. They stayed on that portal as long as they could and—

This is awful. This is really, really awful.

I run a hand over my eyes to wipe away the tears and the rain just as another wave pounds into the shore, bringing with it a ton more people.

I run to the first person I see. Because of the rain, I can't see much more than a body at first. But as I get closer, things become a little clearer, and I can't help gasping when I see her distinctive, bright-yellow hair.

It's Ms. Aguilar, and she doesn't look good. Neither does her future self, who is currently sitting on the sand hugging her knees to her chest—and getting fainter with each second that passes.

She's all banged up, her formerly hot-pink sweatsuit ripped and soaked with blood from a wound I can't currently see.

I call her name, but she's totally nonresponsive—whether because she's passed out or because she's dead, I can't tell. All I know is that I'm not going to leave her like this.

I grab her shoulder and roll her over, then almost wish I hadn't. Because her skin is gray, her normal sparkle long gone. On the plus side, she's still breathing, albeit shallowly. On the not-so-plus side, I can now see where the blood is coming from—a nasty-looking wound on the side of her head.

Panic fills me—I can do rudimentary CPR on a bunch of healthy people who stopped breathing due to drowning. But a head wound is way beyond anything I know about.

Still, I have to try. A quick glance out at the ocean tells me another wave is building—and this one looks even bigger than the last. Which means the first thing I need to do is get both of us out of the strike zone. With the last of my energy, I get her at least halfway up the beach. Then I drop to my knees beside her and start gently shaking her as I call her name. She doesn't answer—big surprise—but I don't know what else to do at this point.

I look around for help, but before I can find anyone, a loud sizzling sound fills the air around us. I glance up, expecting lightning to slam down on the beach any second. But instead, a very loud popping noise fills the air followed by...nothing.

Well, nothing except the continued roar of the storm.

I look around, trying to figure out what the hell just happened. And that's when I notice that the lights on the top of the huge wall that blocks the beach from the rest of the school—the lights that I know were on just a little while ago because I used them to guide myself toward shore—are no longer lit. And, as I look more closely, I realize that several of the huge lightbulbs look like they've literally been blown apart.

I tell myself it's not a big deal, that it's just the lightning or something. But it's hard to believe that when I look down and realize that the hands holding on to Ms. Aguilar's shoulder—my hands—are suddenly paws.

CHAPTER SIXTY-FIVE

I'M TOTALLY
SHIFT FACED

Not now.
Please not now.

I can't deal with everything that's happening with this storm and also deal with having my magic back, too.

Apparently, though, my manticore is here, whether I want her to be or not. I watch my nails as they transform from the short, stubby ones I painted cyanide green with Eva and Luis two nights ago—God, it seems so much longer than that—to the long, sharp, skinny claws of a lion. Claws that are also, somehow, still green. My whole body feels strange now, too, like it's not my own. And when I glance behind me, it's to see that yes, my scary-ass black tail is back, as well.

Because what this shit show of a day really needed was for a bunch of messed-up paranormals who've never been taught to use their powers to get them back right in the middle of a giant hurricane.

And yes, I know exactly how ironic it is that I've spent my whole life wanting to have access to my manticore. But right now, I'm terrified and angry. I don't know how to use this body I'm stuck in, and it's all my mother's fault.

Just the thought of being unmeshed again leaves me feeling helpless, as is the thought that I won't be able to help anyone with these claws—and while they are retractable, I sure as hell don't know how to do that yet.

If my manticore would go away right now—preferably without leaving me unmeshed—that would be just fine with me.

I glance back at the fence, wondering if this is just another glitch, but the lightbulbs look indubitably dead. I watch in horror as one of the vampires grabs a fae standing nearby and starts to feed.

Not far from them, a couple of leopard shifters circle around a witch named Olivia that I know from therapy, while—behind them— two wolves start sparring with each other in what I'm pretty sure is a dominance fight.

Because what this day needed was one more thing to make it even more screwed up.

Must be nice that my mom is safe in Huntsville while all of the students she never believed should have a chance to slowly learn how to handle their magic responsibly now have it back all at once.

And are definitely not using it responsibly.

I have no idea where to start, but I take off running toward Olivia in full panic mode. I can't just leave the poor girl at the mercy of two pissed-off leopards—especially since, right now, I can only see two of her, the little girl she used to be and the teenager she is now. I don't know if the fact that I can't see her future means she doesn't have one if I don't intervene—like Alina—but I'm not about to risk it.

"Hey!" I yell, the deepness of my manticore voice messing with my head as I race to get between the witch and the leopards. "Stop for a—"

I break off as Olivia obviously casts some kind of spell, because all of a sudden, the leopards go hurtling through the air. The present versions of them land several feet from her, while the past and future stay where they were.

I skid to a stop. Because Olivia didn't just send the leopards flying with that spell. She actually blew herself up as well.

Horror wells up inside of me as I career to a stop a few feet from her body. She's crumpled on the ground on her side, and at first, I think maybe there's a chance of saving her. But when I bend down and roll her onto her back, half of her face is missing—and so is a lot of the head that was beneath it. Something that only gets worse as the rain continues to pound down on all of us.

I freak out at the sight of what used to be Olivia, and I stumble backward as tears prick my eyes. Nausea churns in my stomach, and every nerve in my body is screaming at me to run. To flee. To put as much distance between me and her and this beach as I can possibly get.

Because when I look back at her still, broken body a second time, it's not Olivia that I'm seeing at all. It's Serena. And it feels like my heart is breaking all over again.

I start to back up, start to look for an escape route, but there isn't one, not really. I'm trapped on this island, just like everyone else, and there is no escape until this storm decides to finally let up.

But I can't spiral. Ms. Aguilar still needs help. I turn to head back to her only to find the two large cats have returned. And have apparently decided that I'm the next best snack to Olivia.

They stalk toward me, and though I back up as fast as I can in an effort to escape, I know it's already too late. Because it's not just their present selves stalking toward me. It's their future forms as well.

This whole past, present, and future thing is completely disconcerting, not to mention awful now that I know that it really does show me the future.

I've dealt with angry shifters before, but never in their animal forms, so I hold out my hands in an effort to placate them *and* ward them off.

"Look, we can just go our separate ways—" I tell them, then break off as I back right into one of their other selves—past or future, I can't tell. All I do know is that it hurts in the same way it hurts when I run into a flicker. It's like, all of a sudden, I can feel all of the cells that make up my insides vibrating against each other. Burning heat and needle-sharp pain spread through me until I can barely breathe, barely think.

Desperation has me jerking forward away from—I glance behind me—an old man with an eye patch, to be exact.

While the pain immediately ceases, I instantaneously create another problem. Because the leopards don't know that their past and future selves are here at all. So, when I jerk forward, they obviously take it as an act of aggression.

And respond accordingly.

One of the leopards leaps at me, mouth wide open and teeth on full display as he goes for my jugular. I duck, but because manticore Clementine is several inches taller than regular Clementine, the leopard ends up crashing straight into my face.

With its teeth.

White-hot pain slides through me as his razor-sharp teeth connect with my cheek and forehead. Desperately afraid that he's going to bite my head off, I bring my hands up between us and push. Hard.

The moment I shove him away, the leopard screams bloody murder. A quick glance at his chest as he hits the ground tells me why. My painted lions' nails have made long, deep furrows in his chest.

I know I should probably kick him when he's down, but that's not really my thing. So I start to retreat up the beach, praying they take the hint and stay away. But it's only a matter of seconds before the leopard I injured is back on his feet, roaring in pain and fury. He lunges again, only this time the other leopard jumps with him.

Suddenly, I've got two furious cats coming at me and absolutely no idea about how to deal with either of them.

Again, I hold my hands up to ward them off. My claws are fully extended, partly for defense and partly because I have no idea how to retract them. I prepare to swipe at the first cat, but my unwieldy tail—the one I have absolutely no control over—decides to get in on the action, too.

It comes straight over my shoulder as the first leopard connects with my paws and stings him right in the eye.

He screams at the first contact and tries to twist in midair to get away. But apparently that's not how manticore tails work, because the barbs have sunk in tight and he is well and truly stuck.

He starts to thrash around, determined to get my tail out of his eye. I can't blame him. I would really like my tail to be anywhere else on this planet beside in his eye, too. But then the second cat connects with my paws.

Only he's ready for me this time, his powerful jaw and teeth closing around one of my paws.

It's my turn to scream as pain rockets through me, and I lose all thought of trying not to hurt him. All I can think about is finding a way to end the agony.

He's got a good grip on me, and trying to struggle just drives his teeth deeper.

Terrified I'm about to lose my hand, I do the only thing I can think of in this situation. I flex my fingers, stretching them out as far as I can, and go for the soft palate at the back of his mouth with my claws.

He screeches once I connect, but he doesn't disengage. So I go all in, digging my nails into the velum as hard as I can before raking my fingers across the top of his mouth and straight down the back of his throat.

His eyes go wide, and he gags as blood immediately begins flowing out of his mouth. His jaws unlock instantly, and he drops my paw, but not before the fur is completely coated in his blood.

In the meantime, the other leopard is still thrashing back and forth, making the damage to its eye a little worse with each desperate yank of his head.

As ready to have my tail back as he is to have his face back, I take a deep breath and try to concentrate on my tail. It's hard because, unlike my paws, I have no corresponding body part that matches with it. So, while I control my paws like I control my hands—minus the opposable thumbs, of course—I have no idea what I'm supposed to do to make my tail work.

Still, we're in a catch-22 here, one that is only getting bloodier and more dangerous as time goes on. So I've got to figure it out.

I picture my tail, and I concentrate on what it feels like as it moves itself back and forth, then do my best to try to move it consciously. First to the right, then to the left. To the right, to the left.

Nothing happens at first, or at least nothing beyond what my tail seems to be doing all on its own. But somewhere around the seventh or eighth try, it moves to the right, which is the direction I tell it to. To be fair, I don't know if it's a coincidence or if I actually managed to do it, so I try again.

As soon as I think left, my tail moves in that direction, too. Then back to the right again.

Okay, so I'm getting this. Now I try to think about the barbs on my tail as well, each one individually.

That's a lot harder, partly because I haven't spent enough time looking at my tail to know where each barb is. And partly because the pain from my hand—my paw—is really distracting.

I try to compartmentalize, to forget about the pain and focus only on what I need to do to retract the barbs.

Focus on the barbs.

So I do, starting with the ones closest to the end of the tail. *Release. Release, release, release.*

They don't budge.

I take another deep breath and focus. And slowly, one by one, I manage to get the barbs to release.

The second the last one slides free, and we separate with a squelch that turns my stomach as he goes flying backward.

I spin around prepared to fight them both if I have to—only to realize that they're several feet below me. Because somewhere in the middle of all this mess, my wings started to work.

Now I'm *flying*.

CHAPTER SIXTY-SIX

GETTING AN
EYE-FUL

I give myself one moment to freak out—because being up here is way better than being on the ground with those leopards.

I can tell that I'm wobbling around up here like a toddler who's just found her feet, partly due to lack of experience and partly because of the high winds. But I just need to figure out how to use my wings before I go careening into something—or someone—else.

Below me, the leopards are circling and jumping for me, trying to catch my feet or tail or any other part of me they can get. And since I'm currently not flying much higher than they can jump, the idea that they'll soon succeed isn't a far-fetched one.

I concentrate on flapping both of my wings at the same time so that I can fly in a straight line. As I do, I can't help noticing that being up here gives me a hell of a vantage point. Also, a terrifying one because I can see the ocean in triplicate, too. A sunny, beautiful day from the past. The nightmarish storm of the present. And a starry night from the future.

It messes with my brain, makes my eyes hurt and my head ache as I try to only see the present. And anyone who can fly or swim—dragons, mermaids, sirens, firebirds—are making a break for it. I watch in horror as they fly and swim straight into the storm only to be buffeted back, again and again. They crash into the ocean, slam into the land, get pulled under the water and don't come back up.

Those who can recover do and try again. While those who can't...
I don't let myself think about that right now.

For the first time, I start to wonder about this storm. All along I've
been thinking it was just a normal hurricane—a bad one—but being
back here watching the way it's currently refusing to let anyone out
makes me wonder if there's something else at work here besides just
Mother Nature. Especially when I think about how the portal my very
conscientious mother made sure was the strongest and best quality
possible broke before we could finish evacuating.

Alarm bells sound deep inside me.

But before I can think any more about it, a giant gust of wind
comes howling along the beach and slams straight into me. It sends
me careening backward, tumbling ass over teakettle, through the
sky.

Just as I start to go down, well within range of the leopards, three
giant gold-and-red birds come flying toward us. I have one second to
register that there's actually only one bird—that the other two are past
and future incarnations—before it attacks the leopard's face with its
claws.

The bird is Ember's phoenix form, and she's come to help me.

I land—or, more accurately, fall—to the ground beside the leopard
whose throat I clawed earlier. He's still bleeding, but he's on his feet.
Then the leopard is flying through the air. He lands several yards away
and comes bounding back toward us, but Jude steps in front of me,
looking more fierce than I've ever seen him.

A black dragon—Mozart, I assume—swoops in and snags the
leopard mid-run in her talons. She carries the leopard all the way to
the surf and dumps him in before flying back toward the rest of us.

In the meantime, the other leopard leaps at Jude in a rage. I freak
out and step in front of him—there's no way I'm letting Jude die for
me.

I swing my uninjured claw and catch him in his underbelly as my
tail comes back around and stings him in the neck. This time, I feel
something strange as it happens, something red-hot coursing through
my whole body before magnifying in my tail.

My venom, I realize with a little bit of horror. It's the same warmth that I felt when I was unmeshed, only a lot more manageable. And as my tail cools down as quickly as it heated up, I realize it's because I've emptied my venom into the leopard.

And just like that, the leopard falls to the ground, convulsing.

CHAPTER SIXTY-SEVEN

DÉJÀ YOU

I'm freaking out. I didn't mean to kill him. I didn't want to kill him. Jude sees the panic work its way across my face. So he bends down and puts two fingers on the leopard's neck.

"He still has a pulse," Jude announces. "You just stunned him. He'll be fine once he comes to."

"Kind of wish he was dead," Ember mumbles.

"Let's at least get him away from the waves," Mozart offers, taking one of his arms. Jude takes the other, and they start to drag his rag doll of a body up the beach.

As they do, a wolf crests the ridge by the admin building, running straight toward us. My fight-or-flight mode immediately kicks in, and I raise my paws in defense. At first I'm completely freaked out, but when he comes into view and his silver eyes meet mine, I realize this isn't just some random wolf.

It's Luis. And he's okay. Roughed up, but okay.

For the first time since I washed up on the beach, fear gives way to relief, because Luis is alive. He made it through the portal and the ocean, and he's right here, in front of me.

He runs straight toward me, shifting and wrapping me in a hug. I try my hardest to keep my tail exactly where it is so I don't hurt Luis more than he already is.

"How did you get out of the water?" he asks when he finally lets me go.

"Jude found me." I do my best to keep from blushing. "How about you?"

He lifts a brow. "I'm a wolf, baby. I doggy paddled my ass back to the beach."

"That's got to be one hell of a doggy paddle," I tell him with a huge grin.

"We should probably hurry this reunion up," a British accent calls as Remy and Izzy come into view. Looks like Remy has recovered from his brush with Izzy's control issues.

She points to the beach where the leopard Mozart dropped in the ocean has emerged looking like a drowned rat. And he looks pissed.

But right behind him is past, present, and future Simon. He's got legs, but water is streaming off him in sparkly waves, and his eyes are glowing a deep, rich gold. It's mesmerizing.

The leopard by Jude's feet stirs as his waterlogged counterpart realizes fresh meat is right behind him.

"Go!" Simon yells at us as he locks the leopard in his hypnotic gaze.

"The dorm," Jude declares, and everyone takes off running against the buffeting winds.

It takes longer than it should—running in a hurricane when you're flat-out exhausted sucks—but eventually we stumble into the middle of the dorm's common room. Or at least, what I think is the dorm's common room. Because, from what I'm looking at, it looks like at one point this place was decked out in ornate plaster starfish and glass sea urchins. While in the future, it's become an arcade, complete with air hockey tables and very high-tech game machines.

One by one, everyone comes bursting in through the doors, drenched and panting for breath. Even Simon, who has miraculously caught up with us. He skids to a stop and slams the doors closed with the force of his whole body.

Everyone has shifted back to their human form, which leaves me the only one not to have done it. It's not that I don't want to transform. I just don't know how. I'm petrified to end up unmeshed all over again.

Ember figures out what the problem is before anyone else, because all three versions of her pull me aside.

"You're overthinking it. You just need to imagine being in your human form and it'll work."

"That's it?" I ask, highly skeptical.

She snorts. "Well, don't imagine you're Zendaya and expect it to happen. But if you picture yourself, it should be a pretty easy transformation."

I'm not sure I buy it, but I figure what's one more near-death experience for the day?

"Don't think about what happened earlier," Ember advises as I start to close my eyes. "Just picture your human form and will it to happen."

I do exactly what Ember tells me. I close my eyes, picture myself in my human form, and try to manifest it.

Except...nothing happens.

Ember rolls her eyes and barks, "Concentrate. You have to really believe it's going to happen or it won't."

I spend several seconds thinking specifically about my dark-brown hair, which I'm pretty sure looks like a rat's nest at this point, courtesy of the monster attack, rain, and seawater.

Then I move on to thinking about my blue eyes and their surprisingly long lashes. And the freckles on my nose. And the small dimple in my chin—

All of a sudden, a bunch of sparks start to go off inside my body. They start at my feet and work their way all the way up to my chest and neck and head. Moments later, I'm back to regular human Clementine.

"See? Told ya it was easy." Ember looks me over from head to toe, then holds out her hand. "Give me your hand." She nods to the one the leopard tried to gnaw off.

"What?" I ask, mystified.

It looks better than it did in paw form, but I think that's because something about the magic in the shift helps heal wounds.

Warily, I do as she asks.

"What you did with those asshole cats earlier," she says as she holds my hand up to right below her face, "it was pretty badass."

And then she bats her eyes several times until a number of tears run down her cheek and onto my hand. "I don't do this very often, but..." She shrugs.

At first I have no idea what she means, but then a weird tingling starts in my hand. At first it's only where her tears touched, but then it's all the way to the bone. Instinctively, I pull it back only to watch in astonishment as my skin—and the sinew below it—knits back together without so much as a scratch.

As soon as I'm healed, Ember drops my hand before wiping her damp cheek a little self-consciously.

"I don't understand," I tell her, still a little shell-shocked at what just happened.

"Phoenix tears can heal a lot of things," she answers with a little quirk of her brows. "They can't bring people back from the dead, and they can't completely reverse mortal injuries, but they do a pretty good job on everything else."

"Thank you."

She turns and heads back to the others, all of whom are standing around trading war stories.

Everybody but Jude and Remy, that is. I start to ask where they went, but before I can, the door to the supply closet bursts open and the two of them pile out, their arms filled with whatever Calder Academy uniforms they could get their hands on.

Hoodies, T-shirts, sweats, athletic shorts, socks—all in a variety of sizes and all in bright cardinal red and black. "Well, at least the rescuers will be able to spot us," Luis comments as Remy tosses him a red T-shirt and shorts.

"True story," Simon laughs, clapping him on the back.

Jude hands out clothes to everyone else before walking up to me with a black T-shirt and a pair of red shorts. "There are sweats, too, if you want them."

"These are good, thanks."

I wait for him to say more, but he doesn't. Instead, he just kind of stands there and watches me. I start to get annoyed, but then I realize I haven't said anything to him, either. Not because I don't want to, but because I have absolutely no idea where to start unraveling the jumble of words and emotions spinning around inside me right now.

Maybe it's the same for Jude.

So instead of reaching for sarcasm like I usually do, I just take the clothes and start to walk away. Hopefully one of us will figure out the right thing to say sometime soon.

But I've barely gone a step when Jude's hand closes lightly over my elbow. The second his fingers brush my skin, my heart speeds up and my head goes a little dizzy. Which is stupid. This is Jude, just Jude. Only...not.

I force myself to calm down—to take a breath—as I turn back to face him.

He looks the way he always does—eyes serious, full lips pressed into a straight line, face blank. Except then everything softens—he softens—and I feel the tight ball inside me, made up of too much emotion and too much loss in too short a time, start to slowly unwind.

Even before the corners of his lips quirk up in that teeny tiny curve that's as close to a smile as Jude gets and he says, "Whatever happens, I've got you, Kumquat."

I lift a brow and give him a small smile of my own. And answer, "I think you mean, I've got you, Sergeant Pepper."

And then I turn and walk away before I grab him and kiss him the way I've been wanting to since we were fourteen years old.

CHAPTER SIXTY-EIGHT

IT TAKES TWO
TO TAPESTRY

Luis is waiting for me outside the bathroom when I'm done changing. It's the first chance I've had to talk to him since all hell broke loose. I throw my arms around his neck and hold on tight. When I step back, I can't stop looking at Luis. His past form is about four years old, completely precocious, and absolutely adorable. No wonder he got away with so much shit...until he didn't.

"I don't think I recognize you dry," he teases.

"I'm trying out a new look," I say with a huge grin, pretending to flip my hair.

"It's almost like you're trying to impress someone." Luis bats his eyes at me—and then at Jude.

"Oh my God, you're terrible!" I say with mock annoyance.

But then his smile fades. "You okay?"

I know he's talking about Eva now and everything that's happened since then, so I shake my head. "Not really, no."

"Yeah, me neither." He pulls me in for another hug, this one even longer than the first. "I can't believe this is happening."

"I just wish I knew how to get the hell out of it," I tell him as we grab one of the buckets of snacks from the admin tables and make our way back to the others.

As we do, the winds outside get even faster. I can see it in the way the trees are blowing back and forth, hear it in the sudden uptick of their branches knocking against the windows in the halls.

Only about a third of the windows were boarded up before Jude's nightmares got loose. Is this really the best building to hole up in during the worst part of the hurricane?

At the same time, at least the unboarded windows are letting in as much light as the storm allows. Plus, we've got medical and storm supplies, dry clothes, snacks…plus a host of student rooms to ransack for supplies if we end up needing to.

Not to mention the fact that we're already here, which trumps a lot of the downsides in my opinion.

I grab a pack of peanut butter crackers from the top before handing the bucket to Simon.

"We just have to wait it out, right?" Mozart says from where she's sitting cross-legged on one of the room's worn-out sofas. "I mean, the storm can't last forever, can it?"

Izzy grabs a granola bar and tosses it to Remy, who's currently sitting on the floor, his back against the wall. "Can you portal us out?" she asks.

"What does she mean?" I've never given portals much thought before—why should I when they've been blocked on the island my whole life? Plus, I'm not particularly eager to get back in one, if I'm being honest.

"It means Remy's got the portal mojo," Izzy says as she twirls a dagger between her fingers. "His portals are legendary…at least in his own mind," she finishes.

"Damned by faint praise." Remy's voice is rueful as he turns back to the group. "But to answer the question, I've already tried. Several times. Even though the portal block is still down, the storm must be stopping me because I can't get out."

"Is that normal?" I ask. "You not being able to use your powers in a storm?"

His New Orleans accent is heavier than usual when he answers, "To be fair, *cher,* I'm not sure I know what normal is. I have spent most of my life in prison."

"Oh, right. Sorry." I can't believe I'd forgotten that.

"No worries." He shrugs. "Just one more thing you and I have in common."

I'm not expecting the hurt that truth brings.

"Why are you asking about his powers?" Luis's silver eyes are intent as they study me. "What does it matter if they can't help us now?"

"It probably doesn't matter," I admit. "I just keep thinking that there's something strange about this storm."

"Thank God!" Simon exclaims. "I'm not the only one."

I jerk my gaze to his. "You think it's strange, too?"

He shakes his head. "Before I came here, I spent my whole life in the Atlantic. I've been through more hurricanes than I can count—category one all the way up to category five. I've never seen anything like this before. Never."

"What do you mean?" Jude asks. He's half sitting, half leaning on one of the tables, his long legs stretched out in front of him.

He's been silent up until now, not because he isn't listening, but because he is.

"What's so different about it?" he continues.

"The portal breaking the way it did. All the mermaids, selkies, and sirens getting their asses kicked when they tried to make a break for it after getting their power back. And now Remy not being able to get us out of here?" Simon shrugs. "I don't know, man. Maybe I'm imagining things, but it's like the storm is working overtime to either trap us or kill us."

"Why either or?" Luis remarks dryly. "Can't it be both?"

"Right?" I agree. "When I was on the beach, I kept thinking that the storm was doing it on purpose, too. And I know"—I hold a hand up to ward off any objections or explanations about the indifference of the natural world—"that nature isn't out to get us. But this doesn't feel indifferent. It feels…"

"Malicious," Mozart finishes for me. Future Mozart looks impressed as she looks at both of us over the top of the book she's reading.

"Exactly," I tell her. "Then add in all the other weird stuff that's been happening around here and I can't help thinking something else is going on. And we're missing it because we're blinded by—"

"A bunch of fifteen- to twenty-foot waves that keep trying to kill us?" Izzy comments, her voice dry.

"Pretty much," I agree.

"What other weird stuff?" Ember speaks up for the first time. She's been stretched out on the floor, eyes closed and hands behind her head. I thought she was sleeping, but apparently, she's just been soaking in the conversation.

I don't answer right away. Not because I don't think I should tell everyone what's going on—hell, Caspian literally just dumped it on Simon—but because I don't know how to explain it.

"I can see...things," I say after a moment.

Luis's eyes widen because he knows how I feel about telling people about the ghosts. But this isn't just about ghosts anymore. Everything tells me it's about something much bigger than that, and if we're going to figure out what it is and save ourselves, we're going to need to figure out what it is.

I nod to Luis to let him know I appreciate his concern—but that I know what I'm doing. Then I turn to Jude, and he's watching me steadily, his mystical eyes dark but supportive. And when he glances down at the empty spot next to him on the table, I accept the invitation and walk over to sit next to him.

I don't know what's going through his head, don't know where we go after what happened at the cottages and then on the beach.

But Jude says he's got me, and for now, that's enough. While I'm ready to face whatever's coming in the next few hours, I can't do it alone.

"What kind of things are we talking about here?" Remy asks, and suddenly he seems very, very interested in listening to me.

I don't say anything until I'm settled next to Jude, his hand resting on my lower back to send support that I didn't know I needed.

"I know this sounds strange, but I've always been able to see ghosts. The island's power blocking never shut it down the way it did my manticore abilities." I give a little shrug to let them know it's as confusing to me as it probably is to them.

"Ghosts?" Mozart repeats, her eyes going huge. "Seriously? Like scary ghosts or normal ghosts or something in between?"

I think about the wild-eyed ghost who has taken to popping up when I least expect her and say, "Both."

"That's badass," Ember comments, and for once she actually looks interested in what comes next.

"It's something," I tell her. "Not sure badass is the right word. Especially since I've been seeing more than just ghosts ever since last night."

Luis's eyes go even wider at that revelation, and Jude stiffens against me. But before either of them can ask what I mean, Remy's brows go up. "What exactly does that mean?" he queries, and his eyes are more than curious. They're watchful.

How do I explain to him that right now I can see three of him and everyone else in this room, except for Jude. Oh, and I can also see where the old hotel concierge desk used to be—as well as the old guy who worked it.

"I know this sounds bizarre," I start. "But I'm pretty sure I can see the past *and* the future as well as the present."

A long silence greets my revelation, one filled with confused what-the-fuck looks and nonverbal exchanges among our group. Jude and Luis both look worried as hell. Izzy turns to stare at Remy, but he's too busy studying me to notice.

"So you can see what's going to happen?" Ember looks like she's suddenly regretting the tears she shared with me. "Because, if so, I've got to say you really should have warned us about that portal breaking."

"It's not like that," I answer. "I can't tell what's going to happen in the future. I can just see static pieces of it."

"What is it like?" Mozart asks. She doesn't look concerned so much as fascinated. "Can you see something from the past or the future right now?"

"I can."

"Like what?" Luis leans forward, obviously intrigued.

Instead of telling him that future Luis looks exactly like present Luis, right down to the clothing—which concerns me greatly, considering everything that happened on the beach—I say, "There's a little girl over near the snack table. She's wearing a frilly dress and playing with a yo-yo."

Everyone turns to look—everyone except Remy, that is.

"Where?"

"She's on the side with the boxes. And there's an old guy sitting on the couch next to Mozart. He's reading the *New York Times* from

Monday, February 7, 2061. That's why you keep rubbing your arm."

Mozart's eyes go wide, but all she says is, "I keep rubbing my arm because it feels like something's crawling on it."

"You do it every time he turns the page on the newspaper."

"Holy shit!" She jumps off the couch and whirls around to face it, like that's going to show her something. "There's really someone sitting there?"

"Not at the moment, but apparently there will be in a little under forty years."

"Weird. Very, very weird." She settles back on the couch a lot more gingerly than before. "But why can I feel him when I can't see him?"

"I don't know. But I noticed people were acting weird last night after the nightmare attack."

"I can't imagine why..." Izzy mutters. I choose to ignore the quip.

"Especially when they were waiting to go into the portal. They were acting like Mozart. They would trip over nothing, swat at a nonexistent pest, itch at something bugging them, but I could see exactly what was provoking the reaction, so..."

"Yeah, but how can you tell they're not just ghosts?" Luis asks as Ember gets to her feet. "You've always been able to see details about them."

"A ghost from 2061?" Simon sounds skeptical.

"I don't know, maybe. She sees a lot of weird stuff on the regular," Luis tells him before turning back to me. "How *can* you tell?"

"I don't know how to explain it," I answer. "I just know. When I look at a place, I can see it in the past and future and the people that belong in those eras. It's like a movie playing in front of me. Whereas ghosts have a weird kind of mist that they trail, and they tend to be aware of me in a way these people aren't."

"What about the little girl?" Ember asks abruptly. "Is she from the past or the future?"

I glance back over at the girl and can't help smiling as she tosses her yo-yo in the air over and over again. "I think the past—she's wearing her hair in those big Shirley Temple curls that were popular a long time ago."

I watch as Ember crosses the room to the spot where I told her the little girl was. And while she's got the general area, she's about four feet too far to the left.

"I don't feel anything," she calls once she comes to a stop.

I sigh as I tell her, "Move to your right."

She looks even more skeptical, but she does as I say. "Still don't feel anything."

"Keep going," I answer.

She takes another step, and it's obvious that she thinks I'm full of shit.

"Take another two steps to the right."

"Seriously?" she demands.

"What do you want me to say?" I throw my hands up in exasperation. "The kid is where the kid is. I can't change that to make you believe me."

"Whatever." She rolls her eyes and takes another two small steps, which still leaves her several inches from the young girl.

I know Ember's about to call me on it. But just as she opens her mouth to say something, the little girl throws her yo-yo straight at Ember's shins.

CHAPTER SIXTY-NINE

YUZU COULD DO WORSE

The second the yo-yo touches her, Ember grabs her shin and jumps about three feet. Seeing the skeptical, normally too-cool-for-school phoenix freak out is extra amusing.

Everyone else rears back as she loses it, even before she books it back across the room to the rest of us.

"Okay, so maybe Clementine knows what she's talking about after all." She shudders violently. "What did that kid hit me with anyway?"

"A yo-yo," I answer as I struggle not to laugh.

She still looks more than a little freaked out when she settles back down on the ground.

"So you can see things that previously happened or that will happen in whatever place you happen to be in," Simon recaps as he ticks off the point on his finger. "Which you've never been able to do before." He moves to the second finger. "And at the same time you became able to see these things, the rest of us became able to feel them."

"Pretty much," I agree.

"It's like the two different time periods or dimensions or whatever are brushing against each other," Mozart says in awe.

"I have no idea if they're brushing against each other or not. I just know that what Simon described is happening."

"Okay. And—"

She breaks off when Jude holds up a hand. "Is that it?" he asks me.

"Isn't that enough, man?" Simon exclaims incredulously. "Your girl is seeing things that aren't actually there—"

"Oh, I'm not his girl—" I start but then stop abruptly when Luis, Ember, and Mozart all make half-choking, half-laughing noises, all of which I'm pretty sure are sounds of disagreement. Luis throws his hands in what is definitely an I-just-call-'em-like-I-see-'em gesture. Remy and Simon are studiously avoiding my eyes, while Izzy is rolling hers so hard, I'm a little insulted.

I glance at Jude out of the corner of my eye, only to find that ridiculously small smile of his playing around the corners of his lips. "Careful or you'll break my heart, Yuzu."

"What the fuck is a yuzu?" Luis asks blankly.

Jude and I answer at the same time.

"A citrus fruit," we say.

This makes everyone laugh even harder. And my cheeks go red with utter mortification.

"It kind of tastes like a grapefruit," Jude answers, which only makes it worse. I give him a disbelieving look.

"What do you do? Just sit around researching fruit?" Simon heckles.

He shrugs. "Maybe I just know a lot about fruit."

"Maybe you just know a lot about messing with me," I shoot back.

For the first time in maybe ever, the corners of his mouth curve up into what can only be described as a half smile. "Maybe I do."

I just stare at him, speechless, mind completely blank. Partly because his smile turns his whole face from gorgeous to *I can't even describe the glory* and partly because I haven't seen this version of Jude—the one who looks at me with warmth in his eyes while he teases me—for a long time.

All I can do is stare at him with a little lopsided smile.

"Now that we've got that out of the way," Simon continues, breaking the awkward silence, "maybe we can find out when you started seeing the past and the future all at once."

I snap out of my trance. "The past and future thing happened about the same time the tapestry broke."

All amusement drains from Jude's face in an instant. "What do you mean it broke? Like it started to unravel?"

"No, I mean it went all wonky, almost like static on a TV screen. Just a whole bunch of dots with no picture in it at all. It was really weird."

"Where's the tapestry now?" he asks, and he's already up and heading for the door. "Is it where we left it?"

"I think it's lost," I tell him. "Since it seemed like such a huge deal to you, I gave it to Simon, since I was supposed to go across the portal with my mom. But then the portal broke and—"

"It's in the ocean?" Jude's face is blank again, but there's a look about him that makes me think this is even worse than I imagined. Even before he repeats, "The *tapestry* is in the *ocean*?"

"I assume so, since Simon was in the portal when it broke." I turn to look at Simon, but he's jogging away. "Hey! Where are you going?" I call after him.

He doesn't answer, just waves a quick hand in acknowledgment as Jude takes off after him, darting up the main stairs of the dorm.

Only a couple of minutes pass before Simon and Jude are back.

"I stashed it in a closet upstairs after Caspian took you up to the portal," Simon tells me sheepishly. "I don't know what kept me from bringing it with me—"

"Common sense, maybe?" Ember comments.

"Pretty much, yeah." The smile he shoots her lights up his whole face, but she doesn't seem to notice. "Well, that and a bad feeling that I couldn't shake."

"Maybe you're seeing the future now, too," Izzy suggests dryly.

I walk over to where Jude has put the tapestry down and is currently unrolling it. Part of me has been hoping that it will be back to normal, that whatever weird thing made it go awry last night has somehow resolved itself.

But I can tell before it's halfway unrolled that that's not the case. It looks as strange and eerie as it did last night—maybe more so now that we're out of the rain.

"So I'm not trying to sound ignorant," Mozart says as she gets up and comes over to look at the tapestry. "But what is it?"

"It's a textile," Simon answers. "A weaving of—"

"Seriously?" she cuts him off. "I know what a tapestry is. I'm asking what *this* tapestry is, since it's obviously special or the Jean-

Jerks wouldn't have come looking for it and Clementine wouldn't have been able to break time or whatever the hell she did."

"I didn't do anything!" I object. "I wasn't even near the tapestry when it happened. I just know that things went off-kilter for me, and then when I picked it up, it was messed up, too."

Mozart turns to look at Jude. "I saw how freaked out you got when Clementine had the tapestry. So what is it? Why did it bother you so much that she had it?"

Jude stares at her for several seconds, jaw working and face going expressionless like it does when he doesn't want to talk about something. I see the moment he gives up on prevaricating and decides to just tell the truth.

"It's a dream tapestry," he finally tells us reluctantly. "Or, I guess in this case, it's a nightmare tapestry."

"A what?" Simon asks as he takes a big step back away from it.

Not that I blame him—after everything that happened in the middle of the night, it's taking every ounce of courage I've got to stand my ground as well.

"A dream tapestry—it's woven with people's dreams."

"Dreams?" Remy asks, moving closer to get a better look. "Or nightmares?"

Jude lets out a long slow breath before saying, "I *am* the Prince of Nightmares. So you do the math."

It's the second time I've heard those words, but they still feel like a punch to my stomach. A quick glance around tells me they feel like that to everyone else, too—well, everyone but Izzy, who hasn't bothered to look up from her nails or her knife.

But before I can ask Jude for a better explanation, a massive crack of thunder rattles the whole dorm—right before we hear the sound of the outer door crashing open.

CHAPTER SEVENTY

TIME SLIP AND SLIDE

"What the hell was that?" Luis exclaims as he leaps to his feet. I head toward the hallway that leads to the outer door to investigate, but I barely make it across the room before Ms. Aguilar, Danson, and—I'm guessing—what's left of the student body pour into the room.

There are only sixty or so students in total, which makes me a little sick when I think about how many students were still on the beach when the portal broke. Just about the entire senior class—which is well over a hundred students—and there are juniors here, too, so who knows how many of them were caught in the portal and spat back out when it broke. Not to mention a handful of teachers.

Maybe some of them, like my mom, got sucked through the portal to the other side and are currently warm and dry and not the least bit concerned about hurricanes or nightmares or any of the things I'm currently freaking out about.

But I know that has to account for only a small number of the missing. The rest drowned in the waves or died in the nightmare attack or, worse, at the hands of their peers once we all got our powers back.

It's a terrible thought, one that has tears welling in my eyes and sorrow clogging my throat.

I force myself to breathe through the pain and the horror.

There's time later to deal with everything that's happened. Right now, we just have to make it through the next twenty-four hours or so, until the storm hopefully dissipates.

"Oh, Clementine!" Ms. Aguilar trills as she catches sight of me.

I'm glad to see she's okay. I've been worried about her since I pulled her out of the surf on the beach—but she's definitely looking a little worse for wear. The rain has washed away a lot of the blood from her head injury, revealing the gaping cut on her forehead. Plus, her normally sparkly clothes are ripped and covered with mud, and one of her brightly colored wings is half torn off her back.

"There you are, Calder!" Danson growls as he barrels into the room. He's looking better than she is, but barely. The minotaur doesn't have any visible wounds, but one of his horns is hanging by a thread next to his cheek, and somewhere along the way he lost his shirt. "We could have used your help out there."

"To be fair, I could have used yours, sir. I ended up in a fight for my life with a bunch of leopards."

As if on cue, one of those leopards—now in human form—lets out a loud growl.

"Cut it out," Danson snaps. "We're not doing this territorial shit anymore, got it?"

The leopard doesn't answer, so I take it as a yes.

So does Danson, who says, "Good," then proceeds to bark out orders like he's a captain in the Minotaur Court guard.

He sends me to raid the store closet for more clothes to hand out to everyone as Ms. Aguilar checks them in on a bunch of loose-leaf paper my very strict mother would never approve of.

Once that's done, he puts Luis and me on snack distribution duty while Jude and the others are put in charge of towel and blanket distribution. Thankfully the kitchen witches had conjured up a lot of snacks back when we were running around trying to secure the school from the storm.

Not that our efforts seem to be doing much good right now as I've never felt more insecure. Especially since Luis and I are currently walking around the common room handing out pretzels and Cheez-Its to a bunch of paranormals who look like they want to kill us.

And by us, I mean me.

Which I understand. They're looking for someone to blame for the mess, and I'm the only one in the room with Calder in their name.

If I was them, I'd blame me, too.

I'm seeing most of them in triplicate, so their extra heap of enmity doesn't make the job easier. Something needs to give with that damn tapestry of Jude's, because I really can't keep doing this.

I yelp as a flicker appears right in front of me, and I walk through it before I can stop myself. I jump back as soon as it registers, but not before burning pain explodes through me.

For a second, it's like I can feel every single individual molecule inside me and they're all slamming against each other and against the inside of my skin all at the same time. It hurts even worse than I remember.

My eyes meet the flicker's, and I gasp, because for once I recognize this flicker. Not just because I've seen him before, but because it's *Luis*, only now there's a huge, gaping wound right in the center of his chest.

CHAPTER SEVENTY-ONE

LET'S NOT DO THE TIME WARP AGAIN

"Clementine—" he gasps as he reaches for me. I'm so shocked, so shattered, that I don't even jump back to avoid the contact. Instead, I move forward, tears I'm barely aware of crying pouring down my face as I reach for him, too.

"Clementine! Are you all right?" The perfectly healthy Luis standing next to me looks totally freaked out as he grabs my arm. "What's going on?"

Pain ricochets through me the second I connect with flicker Luis, but it's nothing compared to the emotional devastation rampaging through me.

Not Luis.

Not Luis.

Please, please, please, not Luis, too.

I can't take it. I can't—

A sob tears from my throat, and even though I know it's impossible, I try to grab him, try to hold on to him, try to help him. But when I do, my hand goes straight through the bleeding, oozing hole in the center of his chest, and he collapses.

I start to catch him, but he falls straight through me, and that's when I scream. I scream and scream and scream as my legs go out from under me and I hit the ground, hard.

Not Luis.

Not Luis.

Please not Luis.

He's writhing on the ground now, his body convulsing right in front of me, and I try to get to him. Try to fix him. But this time when I touch him, he blinks out as quickly as he came.

Real Luis grabs onto me, tries to pull me up. But I can't even look at him, because every time I do I see him on the ground in front of me, dying.

"Damn it, Clementine!" he yells, sounding as freaked out as I feel. "You've got to tell me what's happening here. You have to—"

He breaks off as Remy skids to a stop in front of us.

"Hey," he says, crouching down in front of me.

I try to answer him, but all that comes out is another sob. And I know it hasn't happened yet, I know Luis is alive and healthy and whole right beside me, but I can't get the picture of him, bleeding and broken, out of my head.

It blends with the last image I have of Eva, the last image I have of Serena, the last image I have of Carolina, and I can't breathe. I can't think. I can't do anything but sit here and cry.

"I don't want to do this anymore," I babble to Remy as he takes my shoulders in his hands. "I can't do this. I don't want to do this. I can't—"

"Clementine." Remy's voice is firm but composed as he calls my name, but I'm too far gone to listen. So he does it again, and this time he grabs my chin between his thumb and his index finger when he does, tilting my face up until I have no choice but to look him in his calm, dark eyes.

"The past is set, but the future can change," he tells me, his tone low and urgent.

"I don't—I can't—"

"Listen to me," he repeats, and there's a look in his dark eyes I can't help but respond to. "The past is set, but the future can change. Nothing that hasn't happened yet is set in stone."

"You don't know," I tell him, my voice breaking on the last word. "You don't—"

"I do," he says. "I swear I do."

And this time when I meet his eyes, I see it in there—the knowledge and the understanding of exactly what I'm going through.

"How?" I whisper, the word raw and broken in my too-tight throat.

And even though I know the answer, even though I can see it as clearly as I can see Luis and Jude and Mozart standing right behind him with worried looks on their faces, I still need him to say it.

Remy must see that I need it, too, because present Remy leans forward and very quietly answers, "Because I can see the future, too."

CHAPTER SEVENTY-TWO

DON'T JEAN-JERK ME AROUND

Even knowing what Remy was going to say—seeing it in his eyes—I don't believe him at first. Still, I let him help me to my feet.

Ms. Aguilar is bearing down on me with a determined smile, and I just can't take her bizarre brand of cheer right now. So I wipe a hand across my face to dry my tear-wet cheeks and announce, "I'm fine now," to the entire room—most of whom have been watching me freak out.

Now that I've calmed down, I'm so pissed off at myself. I've spent all these years hiding any weakness, and then I end up completely losing my shit in front of the biggest dicks in the school.

Plus, Luis is looking at me like he thinks there's something very, very wrong with me. I'm sure he'll eventually want some kind of explanation about what just happened. Yet I don't think it's a good idea to tell him that seeing him dying is what set me off.

Still, he doesn't protest when I turn on my heel and make a beeline away from Ms. Aguilar as fast as my feet can carry me.

No one does.

They just speed up right along with me.

We're about halfway to the area we've claimed as ours when the Jean-Jerks step directly into our path—because the assholes have never seen a vulnerability they didn't want to exploit.

"Never a good straitjacket around when you need one, huh, Clementine?" Jean-Paul starts with a smirk. "Does your mommy know—"

Jude doesn't even wait for him to finish before shoving him out of the way. Then he puts himself between me and the Jean-Jerks as we move around them without so much as a word.

"Hey!" Jean-Luc snarls, leaping in front of us while Jean-Claude and Jean-Jacques flank him on either side. "You don't fucking put your hands on him, Jude."

They're all in full fae mode now—eyes sparkling, skin shimmering, wings standing at attention, and I know it's only a matter of time before they do something way more obnoxious—and way more dangerous— than making snarky comments about me. Everything about them says they're spoiling for a fight.

"Maybe you should muzzle him, then," he shoots back.

"Are you threatening me?" Jean-Paul asks as he slides over to stand next to Jean-Luc.

Jude tilts his head to the side, like he's thinking about it.

But before he can answer, Jean-Luc calls, "Did you hear that, Poppy?" His gaze cuts over to Ms. Aguilar, who looks incredibly nervous as she gingerly approaches the group of us. "One of your students is threatening my boy here. He feels unsafe. Don't you, Jean-Paul?"

"Very unsafe."

"Come on, let's go." I slip my hand through Jude's arm and try to tug him away. But he's not willing to be moved.

I glance at Luis, Remy, and Mozart for help, only to realize they're looking about as immovable as Jude. In fact, judging from the expression on Mozart's face, I'm pretty sure she's contemplating flame-broiling all four of them.

To head that off, I step directly in front of her. I know I've made the right decision when she huffs out, "Party pooper."

Part of me wants to let her at them. After all, it's not like the Jean-Jerks don't deserve it. And it's not like they'll be missed by anyone here, besides each other. But there's been enough death and maiming here today. I don't really think there needs to be any more.

Plus, I've had enough beatdowns from the Jean-Jerks to know they don't play fair. The last thing I want is for any more people that I care about to be hurt—either in an unfair fight now or in a very unfair fight with the even more dangerous fae mafia later.

"Oh, I'm sure it was just a misunderstanding, Jean-Lúc," Ms. Aguilar says. "Right, Jude?"

Jude doesn't answer.

"Clementine, why don't you and your friends head back to your area? And I'll have Mr. Danson escort Jean-Luc and his friends back to theirs."

Danson is walking toward us, his face as dark and stormy as the sky outside.

My friends don't seem in any hurry to follow Ms. Aguilar's directions—with or without Danson to enforce them. But once the Jean-Jerks eventually move toward the opposite side of the common room, Jude and Luis finally let me tug them along.

But when we get back to the others, the first thing Izzy says to me is, "Forget their fingers. One day very soon I'm going to cut out those assholes' tongues."

"Why not today?" Mozart asks as she flops back down on the sofa.

Jude grabs a bottle of water out of our allotted stash and cracks the top before handing it to me.

"Thanks," I say, relieved that he hasn't asked me any questions. But that relief is short-lived when our eyes meet and I realize he may not be asking any questions, but he's definitely searching for answers.

Everyone is.

I know I owe them an explanation, but the truth is out of the question, and I have no idea what else to tell them.

Before I can say anything, though, Remy jumps to my rescue. "Sometimes when you see the future, you see shit you don't like. It's happened to me dozens of times. But I think we should focus on fixing that damn tapestry instead of whatever Clementine saw." I've never been as grateful to another person in my life as I am to Remy at that moment.

But his rescue doesn't stop Jude and Luis both from giving me looks that promise a reckoning later.

It also doesn't mean the group doesn't have questions—only now, they're aimed at Remy instead of me. Thank God.

"You mentioned before that you were a time wizard," Simon says.

"But I thought they were really rare."

"I think they are." He shoots him a rueful look, and when he answers, his Cajun accent is thicker than usual. "Though, to be fair, I've been in prison nearly all of my life. I have no idea what's actually rare and what's not."

I don't know what to say to that, and judging from the looks on their faces, I don't think anyone else does, either. I think being stuck on this island for my whole life is bad, but I can't imagine what Remy's been through. Born into the worst, most notorious prison in the paranormal world, only to finally escape and end up here.

"Fair enough," Mozart finally says. "But just so you know, they are very rare. And yet we seem to have two in our friend group alone. Does anyone else find that weird?"

"I'm not a time wizard," I tell them. "I don't know what's going on with me at the moment, but I am definitely not a witch of any kind. I'm a manticore—you've all seen it."

"There's no law that says you can't be both," Izzy says.

"Yeah, well, it makes no sense."

"Except for the fact that you can see a whole lot of things you shouldn't be able to," Simon tells me quietly.

I don't know what to say to that, because he's not wrong. But I also don't want to talk about it anymore, not when everything they say just gets me more freaked out.

Remy must sense it because he crouches down to look at the tapestry and does the most obvious subject change in the history of subject changes. "So tell me how this thing works, Jude. You wove it with people's nightmares?"

CHAPTER SEVENTY-THREE

INSOMNIA IS A WITCH

At first, I don't think Jude is going to answer. But then he sighs and says, "My father wove it a long time ago. I came to Calder Academy with it ten years ago."

"And you've been using it to play in people's nightmares ever since?" Simon asks.

"That's not exactly how I would describe it, no."

"So how *would* you describe it?" Remy asks.

"He uses it to give people nightmares," Mozart answers with a shrug. "How complicated could that be?"

"I haven't used it to give *anybody* nightmares," Jude snaps. "Why don't all of you think back? When's the last time—before last night—that you actually *had* a nightmare?"

I start to argue, but then I do what he suggests. The last time I had an actual nightmare, before the snake last night, was probably *ten years ago.* How could I have never noticed that before?

How could none of us have noticed it before?

Then again, people don't think about being sick when they're healthy—maybe it's the same thing with this. It's easy to forget nightmares exist if you aren't actually having any.

"So you're funneling our nightmares away from us *before* we have them?" I ask, trying to understand how he does it.

He blows out a long breath. "Something like that, yeah."

"Now that I think about it like that, that's totally badass," Mozart says. "I've actually really enjoyed my three years without nightmares, so...thanks, Jude."

I can tell her words matter to him, can see the way his shoulders and his jaw relax just a little bit when he realizes that he's not under attack. We're really just trying to understand.

"When you take the nightmares, where do they go?" Ember asks, and for once she doesn't sound pissed off at the world. Just curious.

"Forget *where* you put them," Mozart interjects. "I want to know how you can do this when your powers are locked down. None of this should even be possible."

"They can't lock my powers down."

"Seriously?" Ember asks, eyes all but bugging out of her head. "You have your magic?"

"And you didn't say anything to us?" Mozart looks as surprised by that as she does by the fact that he still has his power.

"I didn't know what to say," he answers, exasperated. "It's a huge deal to everyone here and it seemed like a real dick move to brag about it."

She thinks about it for a second—everyone does—and then Simon shrugs. "To be fair, you pull a lot of dick moves, so you can understand our confusion."

Jude rolls his eyes at that while the others laugh, and apparently, the crisis has been averted.

"While all of this is fascinating," Izzy suddenly comments in a voice that says it's anything but, "none of it is getting us any closer to figuring out why the tapestry is broken."

The ghosts must be over whatever drama is happening on the beach because they've started to appear, milling around me, looking for attention. I try to ignore them, but it's getting harder and harder to pretend I don't notice them.

"Plus, none of this explains why the Jean-Jerks want the tapestry," I say.

"Or why Clementine is suddenly seeing past, present, and future," Luis adds.

"None of this makes any sense." Jude sounds adamant. "The tapestry doesn't have anything to do with that stuff. It's just where I filter the nightmares, so they can go back into the Firmament, before slowly filtering back into the world again."

"But there has to be something you're missing," Simon tells him, sounding as frustrated as Jude looks. "Talk us through the process. Maybe we can find the answer if you break it down for us."

"It's not that complicated," Jude answers. "Every night, I filter the nightmares away from people and onto my skin, where I store them."

As if to underscore what he's saying—or maybe because they just know he's talking about them—the nightmares around his neck begin to wriggle up past the crewneck collar of his shirt to his neck.

Jude ignores them.

"From there, you funnel them straight into the tapestry?" Remy asks, though he looks as distracted as I feel. He keeps scanning the room like he's waiting for something, while I can't help noticing the telltale sparkle that points to the fact that a bunch of flickers have joined the ghosts inside.

"Not exactly," Jude answers. "Nightmares can't go directly into the tapestry—"

"What do you mean?" Simon asks him incredulously. "What's the point of having a dream tapestry, then?"

"Why can't they go directly in?" Mozart asks him.

"It seems like an illogical design—" Ember starts.

"He was seven!" I say loudly enough to be heard over all of them. "When he got here. He was seven, and he had nobody to really teach him. So maybe if you have problems with the way the tapestry works, you should take it up with the person who actually designed it!"

My voice is definitely loud enough to command attention in the group, considering they all turn toward me as one—notably Mozart with raised brows and Ember with a self-satisfied little smile dancing around the corners of her lips.

Unfortunately, my raised voice has also attracted the attention of the ghosts and flickers in the room, none of whom look particularly happy about my outburst.

CHAPTER SEVENTY-FOUR

TAKE ME OFF
THE SHIFT LIST

"The person who designed it is dead," Jude says quietly, his voice completely devoid of emotion.

"Then why can't you change it?" Luis asks him with a nonchalant shrug. "I mean, what's the point of being a prince if you can't do exactly what you want?"

Izzy lets out a harsh laugh at that, but when we turn to look at her, she just shrugs and goes back to spinning a jewel-encrusted dagger over her knuckles now that she's done with her talon-like nails.

"If you don't put the nightmares directly into the tapestry, what do you do with them? Just walk around wearing them all?" Remy nods to the black, feathery rope that's in the middle of slowly and stealthily sliding up Jude's cheek.

I watch it, fascinated, until Jude rubs his hand across his jaw and it slips back under his shirt. How does he lose control of them when they respond to him so readily?

"There are way too many for that. I store them up, then—when there are enough of them—they are generated into monsters. It's those monsters that get filtered into the tapestry." He pauses and shakes his head. "Those monsters under the bed aren't bullshit. They're just nightmares taking on a corporeal form."

His words go off like a bomb inside of me as I realize what he's saying.

"Are you telling me that the monsters in the menagerie—the snake thing and squidzilla and the chricklers—are all there because of you?"

My voice raises on the last part, but I can't help it. I've spent the last several years of my life being tortured by these things, and I am so not impressed.

Now it makes sense why they don't attack him. He's their creator. I shudder at the thought.

And apparently I'm not the only one. "Hold up there, Dr. Frankenstein," Luis tells him. "You're over here making monsters that regularly try to kill the girl you've been tortured over for the last three years, and it's never occurred to you that the system might need a revamp?"

"Luis!" I give him a what-the-fuck look.

"What?" He throws up an aggrieved hand. "Come at me if you want, Clementine, but I'm just calling it like I see it. He hasn't been helping you in that damn dungeon for the last three years. And he sure as hell hasn't been the one patching you up all the fucking time. So, yeah, I'm more than a little pissed off on your behalf."

At first, Jude doesn't say anything, but when he turns to me, I can see the regret in his eyes. His jaw tightens as the guilt and pain take over.

"I'm sorry," he finally whispers.

And I realize what Luis doesn't—that Jude didn't leave me alone, at least not the way my best friend thinks he did. On a lot of the days I was down there feeding the chricklers, he was down there, too, just before me.

Because I can't help but remember the glimpse of a shadow racing by in the dark or a black hoodie disappearing around a corner. I thought it was my mind playing tricks on me or a ghost but all along it was Jude. I wasn't alone.

No wonder there were days when the chricklers still had full food and water bowls. Really, Jude had taken care of it, so I wouldn't have to—and so I would only get a bite or two instead of my usual dozen or so. And I never had a clue.

I'm getting a whole new look at the last three years, and I'm finding out they're nothing like I thought they were. Something unlocks within me, and another chain keeping me from trusting Jude slowly slides away.

"It's okay," I whisper back. "I understand."

"That makes one of us," Luis says with a snort.

I shoot him a knock-it-off look. He crosses his arms over his chest and rolls his eyes in response.

But then I remember the red streak we saw rush by us yesterday before the ghosts descended on us.

"Was that you in the dungeon yesterday?" I whisper.

"No, I—" Jude starts, concern painted on his face, but Simon interrupts him.

"So how do you make the monsters? Like, is there a formula or..."

"I don't know," Jude says. "I don't make them."

"What do you mean, you don't make them?" Ember asks. "Who the fuck would you trust to whip up shit that goes bump in the night?"

"Again, I was seven when I first got here," he reminds her. "Would you trust a seven-year-old making those monsters? So Clementine's mom took on the job, and she's been doing it ever since."

I thought I was beyond being shocked, thought everything that's happened in the last twenty-four hours had already rendered me unshockable. But it turns out I was wrong, because there's a part of me that can't process what he just said.

My mother makes monsters out of Jude's nightmares?

My mother creates those nasty, terrible things in the dungeon using magic from the guy she knows I've hated for the last three years and then sends me down there to clean up after them?

Because wow. There's diabolical, and then there's just completely fucked up. My mother definitely falls into the latter category, especially when I add in all the lies she had to tell me through the years to keep the whole system going. She doesn't *board* monsters short term for money for the school. She houses them until Jude can put them back in the tapestry, where they apparently dissolve back into nightmares.

My mind boggles, the pieces of this very complex puzzle swirling around in my head, and I have no idea how they fit together.

I cut the thought off as another question occurs to me. One that has nothing to do with my mother, because I'm definitely not ready to deal with her part in this mess yet. I know I'll have to eventually, because there has to be more to the story of Carolina being sent away than Jude knows. After all, my mom's not really the type to be motivated by nightmares—hers or mine. But not yet.

"If the nightmares are condensed into monsters for the sole purpose of putting them back into the tapestry, why do those monsters stay in the dungeon for so long?" I ask Jude. "Some of them are there for months."

"Because the tapestry only accepts them four times a year," Jude answers grimly. "We have to wait for when magic is at its most powerful to put them back into the tapestry."

"The solstices?" Luis guesses.

Jude nods. "And the equinoxes."

I can tell by the look on Remy's face that he's already come to the same realization I have.

"Tonight's the equinox," he says slowly.

And Jude looks even more grim than he did a few seconds ago.

CHAPTER SEVENTY-FIVE

OH NO
BAN-SHE DIDN'T

No wonder he was freaking out about me taking the tapestry yesterday—and about it being broken now. He needs it for tonight or those monsters are going to have to wait around for another three months.

"So what do we do?" Ember asks, looking back and forth between Jude, the tapestry, and me.

"We fix it. What else can we do?" Simon shoves a frustrated hand through his hair.

"And you think fixing the tapestry will also fix Clementine?" Luis taps a nervous finger on his knee. "She can't go through another incident like that again."

I shoot him a grateful smile.

He returns my smile, but he's still got that look in his eyes—that eventually we are going to be talking about what happened.

The thought makes my stomach ache, so I hold on to what Remy told me. That the past is set, but the future isn't. I don't know what I have to do to make sure Luis doesn't end up like that flicker, but somehow, I'm going to find out.

"If Clementine is right and the tapestry is talking to her because her new power is related to it, then it stands to reason that fixing the tapestry should also fix whatever's going on with her," Remy says.

"But if it isn't…"

"What do you mean if it isn't?" I sit forward, alarmed now. "I absolutely cannot go through the rest of my life seeing everyone and everything in triplicate. I just can't!"

Jude takes my hand and strokes a soothing thumb over my knuckles. "We'll figure it out," he tells me with such confidence that I almost believe him.

Of course, the fact that he looks as stressed as I feel doesn't help with that.

Luis leans down next to the tapestry, and as if to prove he means business, he tugs on a couple loose threads at the corner of the tapestry. Instead of unraveling that little section, the tapestry lights up. It goes into some kind of defense mode, and all four of its edges roll under so that no one can get to any of its end threads.

"Did anyone else see that?" Luis asks. "Or is the stress making me hallucinate?"

"Oh, we saw it," Simon tells him.

"Because this wasn't hard enough," Mozart deadpans.

"There has to be some way to—" I crouch down next to the tapestry so I can get a better look at it.

I'm cut off as an argument breaks out on the other side of the room. I turn just in time to see a dragon in human form go tumbling across the front half of the common room.

He hits the wall hard, and it takes him a moment to recover. But then he's running full tilt toward the vampire that hit him. As he runs, he stays in human form except for the huge pair of greenish yellow wings he sprouts out of his back.

When he's about five feet away from the vampire, he grabs her and takes to the air, climbing all the way to the top of the room's thirty-foot ceiling before dropping her.

Amazingly, she lands on her feet, then launches herself into the air after him. She can't fly, but she can jump pretty damn high, and she almost manages to grab his foot.

But he kicks out at the last second and hits her square in the face. This time when she falls back to earth, it's more of a crash. She lands on her side and goes skidding across the worn-out tile, only to come to a stop at Danson's feet.

He blows a whistle, and when the dragon ignores him, he bellows up at him, "Land, now!"

But the dragon is suddenly the least of his problems, because a pack of four wolf shifters in their human forms takes advantage of the momentary distraction and surrounds a small group of banshees.

"Oh, shit," Jude murmurs next to me.

"They wouldn't," I tell him.

"Fuck, yeah, they would," Izzy says, as if there's no doubt in her mind about what's going to happen.

Danson's got his hands full, so I look around for Ms. Aguilar, only to find her mediating some kind of disagreement between a siren and a witch.

I want to yell at her that we're about to have a major problem, but it's not worth it. Because no matter how strangely endearing Ms. Aguilar is, her discipline is no match for an obstinate kindergartener, let alone a bunch of pissed-off paranormals.

So instead, I take off running toward them just as the wolves advance. If I can get there soon enough, maybe I can stop this from turning into an absolute, unsalvageable shit show.

Jude passes me about halfway across the room and all but throws himself between the wolves and the banshees. But it's already too late, because the second one of the wolves makes a grab for one of the banshees, she lets loose with a scream that is one of the most horrifying things I've ever heard.

In the first couple of seconds, she brings the entire room to a halt. The next few seconds she has all of us—even the fighting vampire and dragon—covering our ears and dropping to the ground. Several seconds after that, the wolves start howling right along with her as their delicate eardrums burst from the extremely high-pitched scream. And finally, about thirty seconds after the banshee starts to wail, the windows explode into a million shards of glass.

And that's when all hell really does break loose.

CHAPTER SEVENTY-SIX

SPOILING FOR A FRIGHT

As the windows crack one after the other, the storm rushes inside and the banshee finally stops wailing. But her screams—or the sudden lack thereof—are the least of our problems as the wind and rain tear through the room.

Ms. Aguilar calls for everyone to take cover and then dives behind the closest piece of furniture she can find—a TV cart with an empty center console that gives us a perfect view of her cowering behind it.

At the same time, Danson starts shouting for all the witches to assemble in the center of the room—I'm guessing because he wants them to do some kind of spell to fix the windows. But only three witches show up. Which means either the ocean got them or their nightmares did.

For a second, Eva's face flashes in front of me, but I blink it away—blink her away. There will be time later for me to mourn. Right now, I just have to get through this.

Fights break out even as glass flies across the common room, shards turned into projectiles by the vicious, violent wind.

Fae against dragons.

Dragons against vampires.

Vampires against sirens.

Sirens against leopards.

The list goes on and on.

"What do we do?" Luis shouts, and I realize with a shock that he's right behind Jude and me.

Everyone is, except Izzy, who's sitting on the couch with her AirPods in. At first I think she's just taking herself out of the equation, but then I notice the rolled-up tapestry at her feet and realize she's standing guard.

I glance behind me at the others—at Mozart, whose eyes have already gone dragon. At Simon, who is glowing all over. At Luis, who is watching everything with a familiar canine tilt of his head. At Remy and Ember and Jude, all of whom look braced and ready for whatever fight comes their way—and I realize, for the first time in my life, I'm actually part of a pack.

It's a slightly strange, mismatched pack, but it's still a pack. And they're all mine.

Despite the nightmare we've all found ourselves in, a profound gratitude fills me. As does an overwhelming need to keep these people safe against all odds.

"What do you want to do?" Remy shouts to be heard over the brutal cacophony that surrounds us.

"Stop them from killing each other and, more importantly, Danson and Aguilar?" I answer, though it's more of a question.

Ember snorts. "Good luck with that."

But even as she says it, she slides her foot out and trips a senior fae who is currently chasing after a junior mermaid with what is clearly nefarious intent.

He goes flying, careening headfirst into one of the tables. He comes up fighting mad, eyes doing that weird sparkly thing they do when fae are up to no good. But he barely takes a step before Luis plows a fist into his face and takes care of it.

I hear the crunch of bone against bone, and then the fae pitches forward in a dead faint.

He hits the ground with a thud, but we're already moving on.

"One down. One million to go," Mozart says as her wings and her talons come out.

"I'm going to go get Ms. Aguilar," I tell them because she's still behind the TV cart, only now past, present, and future versions of

Jean-Claude and Jean-Paul are all fucking with her, per usual.

"I'm with you," Jude says, voice gone extra deep with rage.

"We'll try to help Danson," Luis volunteers with a questioning look at Remy, who nods.

"We'll figure out where to take everyone," Ember says as she dodges a vampire who currently has his fangs sunk deep into a leopard's jugular. "Because this place isn't safe anymore."

A gust of rain-laced wind chooses this moment to tear through the broken windows. It's fast—like a couple hundred miles an hour fast—and it sends glass shards flying through the air like missiles from all directions.

We manage to dodge the four or five that come our way, but some of the others aren't so lucky. A howl goes up at one end of the room as a long shard slices right through one of the wolf's clothes and imbeds itself in her abdomen.

I turn to look, only to realize a siren wasn't so lucky. A shard of glass whipped right by her neck, slicing open her jugular.

All around us, the same scene is playing out—if not from the window glass firing at people at hurricane speeds, then from the other paranormals turning on each other.

It's way worse than the beach, way worse than I ever imagined it could be.

We have to do something. We can't just let them all kill each other.

"Get to Danson!" I shout to Luis and Remy.

Jude and I take off toward Ms. Aguilar, who is currently rolling herself into a ball as Jean-Paul leans over her. I don't know what he's saying to her, but judging from the way she's crying, it's not okay.

Jude grabs Jean-Paul by the shoulder and swings him around, slamming him face-first into the TV cart.

Jean-Paul lets out a screech as his face cracks the screen, but Jude just pulls him back and does it again.

In response, Jean-Claude launches himself at Jude's back. I move to intercept him, but Jude's already whirling around, eyes fierce and tattoos giving off a strange, mesmerizing glow as they slide down his hands and up his throat.

"Stop!" a familiar voice yells from the center of the room. "Stop this right now!"

I turn to see my grandparents racing back and forth from one end of the room to the other. Several times, Grandpa stops to try to help someone, but he can't. His hands go right through whoever he's trying to save, and it's obvious he's getting more and more worked up.

I turn back to Jude because the last thing I want to do is leave him if he needs me. But both Jean-Jerks are now face down on the floor, and he's helping Ms. Aguilar to her feet.

"I'll be right back," I tell him before racing to my dead grandparents.

But halfway there, I notice something else. Something absolutely terrifying. Jean-Luc and Jean-Jacques are in full fae form as they creep toward Izzy—and that damn tapestry.

CHAPTER SEVENTY-SEVEN

FEEL THE RUG BURN

"Jude!" I scream to be heard over all the fighting and confusion surrounding us.

He turns around instantly, raised brows following my pointed finger.

His face goes dark as soon as he realizes what's happening, and then we're both running straight for Izzy, yelling her name.

But she's got her head down and her eyes closed. Could she possibly be...sleeping? She's facing away from us and doesn't turn around when we shout her name. I will her to turn around, will myself to go faster, but it's too late. The Jean-Jerks are already on her.

Jean-Luc walks up to the back of the couch and grabs her by the hair, twisting it around his fist before yanking her head back to rest against his shoulder.

Then he flicks one of her AirPods onto the ground before leaning down and whispering God only knows what obscenities into her ear.

In the meantime, Jean-Jacques moves around to the front of the couch and grabs the tapestry. As soon as he's got it in his hands, he does a little victory dance, right in front of all of us.

What the hell is it with these guys and that damn tapestry?

I pray that's all they want, pray that they take the tapestry and go. We can track them down later. I just don't want them to hurt her. I've learned the hard way just how petty and vengeful they are, and Izzy has already made them look like fools more than once. If they decide now is the time they want payback, things are about to get ugly. Quick.

As Jude and I close in, Jean-Luc pulls a knife out of his hoodie and runs the hilt of it up Izzy's arm. She doesn't so much as flinch, even when he flips the knife over and scrapes the blade against her skin.

I can't say the same as I shudder when I recognize it as one of the blades she stabbed into Jean-Luc's desk yesterday. Looks like petty and vengeful is definitely on the current agenda.

Considering the chaos around us and that Danson is distracted, I can definitely see why this is the perfect moment to strike.

I put on a final burst of speed, but Jude still gets to them a second before I do.

"Let her go, asshole," he snarls as he jumps the couch so he can look Jean-Luc and Izzy in the eye.

Jean-Luc has already moved the knife to Izzy's throat by the time I race around the couch. "I have to admit, I've always been curious," he says as he presses the blade into Izzy's skin just enough to draw one perfect drop of blood. "Do vampires bleed as much as other paranormals or do they have the same coagulant in their blood that they do in their saliva?" He presses a little deeper. "Don't you think now seems like a perfect time to find out?"

"Seriously?" Izzy tells him. "Where do you get your lines? Creepers 'R' Us?" And then she yawns. She *actually* yawns while a dangerous jackass with an axe to grind has a knife to her throat.

"Fuck you!" Jean-Luc snarls as he yanks her roughly over the back of the couch. As he does, the knife digs even more deeply into her throat, and blood starts to run freely from the cut.

"Don't hurt her!" I yell, hands out in front of me in an effort to prove that I'm not a threat.

"You don't get to tell me what to do, Clementine," he says in a sing-songy voice that makes the hair on the back of my neck stand up. Because all of a sudden, he doesn't sound sane.

"Fine, I'll tell you what to do," Izzy says in a bored, monotone voice. "Let me go or you'll be sorry." But then her gaze shifts to mine, and there's an impishness there that I don't understand. At least not until she continues, "That's my line, right? Or should I beg the big, bad man not to hurt me?" She makes her voice small and childlike as she says the last part and even flutters her eyes for effect. "Please, please, I'm so scared."

Jude shoots me a what-the-fuck look.

The others, all of whom came running, stop a few feet behind Jean-Luc, knowing it's not the best idea to get closer.

"Shut up!" Jean-Luc growls, his face twisted in rage as his gaze shifts to Jean-Jacques. "Did you check it? Is that the tapestry?"

Jean-Jacques nods. "This is it."

"Good. Get it out of here." His grip tightens on the knife, and suddenly a lot more blood slides down Izzy's throat.

Alarm shoots through me even before he continues. "I'm going to take care of this and then I'll be right behind—"

And that's when Izzy strikes.

CHAPTER SEVENTY-EIGHT

HERE TODAY, JEAN TOMORROW

She reaches up and grabs the thumb holding the knife and bends it straight back until a loud cracking sound fills the air.

Jean-Luc's corresponding scream is high-pitched and childish as he jerks back and immediately drops the knife. Which Izzy catches in midair, spins around in her hand, and then plunges directly into the center of his chest.

She twists it—several times—before pulling it out.

Jean-Luc is dead before he hits the floor.

Izzy doesn't even bother to step out of the way. Just kicks him once he falls, then brings the knife to her mouth and licks the blade from hilt to tip.

When she's done, she looks up to find all of us staring at her, eyes wide and mouths agape. But she just shrugs and says, "What? Everyone else got a snack."

I have no idea what I'm supposed to say to that. I don't think anyone else does, either.

Except for Remy, who steps forward to press gentle fingers to Izzy's throat. "It doesn't look too bad, but we should probably bandage it up."

"Oh, please." She rolls her eyes. "I got worse than this from dear old Dad on nights he was actually pleased with me."

She leaves the rest unsaid, but considering she just killed a person and is completely unfazed, I figure it wasn't good.

Jude turns to Jean-Jacques, who is currently staring down at Jean-Luc's body in shock, and yanks the tapestry out of his hands. "Get out of here," he snarls.

Jean-Jacques nods as he stumbles backward, but before he can actually move away, Jean-Paul flies straight toward us, with Jean-Claude right behind him. Their wings are working double time, and their faces are twisted in rage as Jean-Paul screams, "You fucking bitch!" at Izzy.

Her brows go up and a dangerous smile plays around her lips, one that hints that Jean-Jacques might be the only Jean-Jerk left alive. *If* he's lucky. Which is why, when her hand tightens on the hilt of the knife, I all but throw myself in front of her.

"You guys need to go—"

Jean-Jacques kicks me in the head, hard, and I reel back, seeing stars. Jude bounds forward and snatches the fae out of the air and plows a huge fist straight into the middle of his face. That's all it takes for Jean-Jacques to go out.

Moments later, Jude does the same to Jean-Paul before dumping both unconscious fae next to Jean-Luc's body. Then he turns to Jean-Claude, both brows raised—which is all it takes to have the other fae stumbling over his own feet to get away.

Once he's gone, the rest of us take a moment to let everything that just happened sink in.

I know it was justified—or as justified as killing ever could be.

But Jean-Luc is dead. And Izzy killed him like it was the easiest thing in the world.

I don't know how to deal with that even though I'm surrounded by so much death. All I can do is look at the singular past version of Jean-Luc standing over his still-bleeding present body, somehow, a smug look still on his face.

"Are you okay?" Jude asks, voice low and urgent as he searches my face.

"Yeah, of course," I tell him, because I am even though my head is now throbbing.

He doesn't look convinced, and neither does Remy, who comes up right behind him.

"You need to open up," Jude tells me in a voice so gentle I barely recognize it.

"Wow, you really do have all the best lines."

"She's coherent enough to give you shit," Remy says dryly. "I figure that's got to be a good sign."

"For someone else, maybe. But she could give me shit in her sleep."

But Jude must decide I really am okay after all because he lets it drop.

It's still chaos. The wind and rain whipping through the room ensure that. Despite Danson getting the room under partial control, the low growls and dominance challenges continue.

There are several unconscious—and worse—bodies scattered around the room that my friends and I *aren't* responsible for.

I ignore my churning stomach, swallow down the bile attempting to crawl back up my esophagus, and try to figure out where we're supposed to go from here.

Danson is currently climbing on top of a table in the middle of the room, a bullhorn in his hands—which I'm hoping means he has a plan, because I am fresh out of ideas.

Ms. Aguilar is right below him, as she shushes students and tries to get them to pay attention. None of them pay any attention to her at all, but they do at least quiet down when Danson calls for attention through the megaphone.

"First of all, I want to start by saying that what just happened here can never happen again." He pauses for effect and takes his time looking from group to group. "If you believe nothing else that I tell you today, believe this. This storm is going to get worse before it gets better."

His words ring through the room, and though some people scoff, the majority of students quickly grow serious. "The eye of the hurricane hasn't even reached us yet, which means that whatever rainbands come through next are going to be worse than what we're already experiencing. They will have harder rains, faster winds, and more than likely worse lightning and thunder."

As if to underscore his words, lightning flashes across the sky at the same time a huge gust of wind rips from one end of the room to the other. It topples chairs, sends several students in its path careening into walls and each other, and nearly overturns the table Danson is standing on.

He manages to jump down just before it goes sliding wildly across the room, but the wind catches him and he nearly goes with it.

"What are we going to do?" Ember asks uneasily. "We can't stay in a building with its windows blown out if things are going to get as bad as he says they are."

If it really is a category five, half this island is going to get leveled. And we're stuck here, a bunch of sitting ducks with nowhere to go and nothing to do but to kill each other.

The thought chills me to the bone as I try to figure out where we can go that will be safe. The dungeon in the admin building would be the logical choice...if the place wasn't filled with nightmare monsters waiting for fresh prey.

The old dance hall has a lower level, too, but no one has been in there in years—not since my mom closed it up after students kept getting caught doing "illicit activities" there.

Other than that, our choices are limited. Maybe the gym, because it's got no windows or exposed doors. But that also means we'll all be sitting around in the dark. The library has huge book stacks that can be pushed to cover up windows from the inside. Not sure if that will actually do any good against one-hundred-and-fifty-mile-an-hour winds, but it's a nice thought.

Danson finally gets his bearings and manages to command everyone's attention.

"We can't stay here," he says. "Not with the broken windows and its proximity to the ocean. We'll be safer inland. Leaving here won't be easy—it was rough a couple of hours ago, and conditions have only declined since then. But staying here will only get more and more dangerous, and the storm is getting worse with every passing minute."

"Forget anger management teacher," Simon says with a roll of his eyes. "This guy should be a motivational speaker."

"To be fair, I'm feeling very motivated right now," Mozart tells him with a grimace.

"Aren't we all?" Remy asks dryly.

"So Ms. Aguilar and I have decided that we're going to move

all of you to the gym," Danson continues. "It has close proximity to the cafeteria so we can get food moved over right away, plus it has no windows and is surrounded by other buildings to help block the wind. But to get there, we're going to need every single one of you to cooperate."

Again, he pauses, and this time he makes a point of looking the room's biggest troublemakers directly in the eyes. "We need help picking up your remaining personal belongings, supplies, and whatever food we have left so we can take them with us. Meet us by the front doors in five minutes."

He takes a second to clear his throat before reiterating, "We're leaving here in five minutes, so there will be *absolutely* no fighting with one another. We need to get to the gym before the storm gets any worse, and we have no time for any more hostility. Do I make myself clear?"

When no one answers, he narrows his eyes and asks again, "Do I make myself clear?"

A few people grumble out answers that sound affirmative, and I guess that's good enough for Danson because he doesn't ask a third time. Instead, he reminds us that we've got five minutes to get our shit together and get to the door, and then he dismisses us.

I lost my backpack and phone in the portal, so I don't have anything but the misappropriated clothes on my back. But I do grab a duffel bag and stuff it full of extra hoodies for all of us while Jude and Remy do the same with snacks and water bottles.

Five minutes pass in what feels like five seconds, and suddenly it's time to go.

"I've got a really shitty feeling about this," Jude mutters as we line up with everyone else.

"To be fair, it's not like there's a whole hell of a lot to have a good feeling about right now," Simon tells him.

"Right?" Ember blows out a long breath. "We're stuck on an island with a bunch of assholes who try to kill each other at the slightest provocation. A category-five storm is bearing down on us, and we're completely cut off from any form of communication—no weather reports, no internet, no phones, no lights."

"Sounds like any old, regular camping trip to me," Remy deadpans.

"If by camping trip you mean the Hunger Games, with Mother Nature as one of the participants," I tell him, "then yes, this is absolutely like camping."

The others laugh, but only for a second, because Danson weaves his way through the double line of students to the main door. "We're heading straight for the fence and from there to the north side of the gym. Don't stop for any reason. Don't turn back for any reason. And do not, under any circumstances, get in a fight for any reason. Got it?"

But whether we're ready or not doesn't matter anymore, because just like that, Danson opens the door, and we all pour outside, two at a time.

Somehow, it's even worse than I ever imagined.

CHAPTER SEVENTY-NINE

KNOW WHEN TO PICK YOUR FRIGHT

Rain slaps me in the face. Whole sheets drench my clothes and my hair, making it impossible for me to think, especially when paired with winds that make every step total agony.

The temperature has dropped, so the sticky heat is gone. But the cold rain just makes it a million times more uncomfortable, which I didn't think was possible.

All around me, people are gasping and swearing and fighting to keep going against winds that seem determined to knock us off our feet. I think about shifting into my manticore, just because it gives me more body mass, but now doesn't seem like the time to complicate the situation.

So instead, I just hunch my shoulders and bend forward as I hope for the best.

Beside me, Ember—who is much shorter and slighter than I am— keeps getting pummeled by the wind. And while phoenixes have a lot of really cool things about them, physical strength isn't one of them. So, for every two steps she takes, the wind sends her back until it feels like she's walking in place.

"Stay behind me!" I shout, stepping forward to block the wind from her present version as much as possible, while her past and future continue to be blown to hell and back.

Jude adjusts himself as I do, and for the first time, I realize he's been using his big body to do the exact same thing for me.

"Thank you!" I shout to be heard above the roaring wind and ocean. Ridiculously, my heart pitter-patters just a little bit as I wait for a response from him. But in the end, Jude doesn't say anything. He just casts a long, unwavering look over his shoulder that somehow has the power to make me hot and cold and fluttery and steady all at the same time.

And just like that, another piece of the proverbial wall I'm trying so desperately to keep between us crumbles.

Except for that moment on the beach, we've had no time to talk since everything went haywire. And though jumping through a crumbling portal to save someone is about as serious as it gets—I have no idea what that means for our friendship or anything else.

But right now all that matters is getting somewhere safe before the next level of hell hits.

We finally make it to the fence, and as we're waiting our turn to file through, Jude turns and stares at me with a look so intense I start to think reading minds is another one of his powers. Then he leans in so close that I can feel the heat of his breath against my ear and says, "I've got a bad feeling about this. Keep your eyes out for the Jean-Jerks."

I can't help laughing because he's taken to calling them by my nickname, too, but also, I agree with him. "You think they're going to do something gross, too?" I ask.

"I think they're going to do something reprehensible," he shoots back. And I can't argue with him. That's pretty much the definition of the three of them.

The next five minutes pass uneventfully. Though I stay vigilant, there's no sign of the three fae, thankfully, and it isn't long before it's our turn to go through the fence. But we've barely made it a hundred yards from the gate when I hear a familiar noise.

My ears perk up as chills work their way through my body. Because there's only one thing on Earth that I know of that makes that particular noise.

I turn to look around, only to find that Jude and Luis are doing the same thing. When our eyes meet, Luis grabs my arm and says, "I knew this was a bad idea."

"You hear it, too?" I ask, the chill inside me getting worse as the sound gets louder. "Oh, shit."

"Oh, shit is right," he answers.

"What's wrong?" For the first time since she killed Jean-Luc, Izzy actually sounds interested. "What's hap—"

She breaks off in the middle of a word, her eyes going wide. Which...fuck.

And even though I tell myself it can't be, that we need to stay the course, I can't resist turning around to look at what she's seeing.

Then really, really wish I hadn't as hundreds of pissed-off chricklers come racing down the path straight at the whole group of us.

"What do we do?" Luis hisses as the rain continues to pour down on us.

"Freeze," I tell him, because all our options are bad at the moment, but of all the bad ones, that is definitely the best one.

"Seriously? You want us to let them catch up?" he hisses.

"What I want is to give the rest of the students a chance to make it to the gym," I answer. "So, yeah, I want to let them catch up."

He rolls his eyes. "Picking the self-sacrificing best friend was so not the way to go," he grumbles. But he moves to position himself directly in the middle of the center walkway.

The others are catching on to what's happening now, too, and it only takes about thirty seconds for us to make a kind of blockade with our bodies. I really hope Danson appreciates the help this time, because if he gives me a hard time about not following him to the gym, I might break my own rules about my tail and deliberately sting him.

"What now?" Simon asks as he moves to my right.

"We wait," Jude tells him grimly. "And something tells me it won't be very long."

CHAPTER EIGHTY

WAY TOO HOT TO HANDLE

He's right. It's not. Because, less than a minute later, Ember asks, "What are those things?" She sounds more curious than afraid, which is proof that she's never had to deal with the evil little monsters before.

"Chricklers," I answer, my heart dropping to my toes as what looks like an entire army of the assholes scampers up the walkway toward us.

"Chricklers?" Mozart repeats. "Those tiny, fluffy little creatures are what you keep complaining about?"

"They're evil," Luis tells her flatly as he starts to back up, a horrified look on his face.

"Don't move!" I bark at him, and he freezes instantly.

"No way! They're adorable." Mozart crouches down so they can get to her more easily.

"They're the devil incarnate," Luis corrects her, though he's obviously heeded my warning about not to move seriously because he's talking out of only the corner of his mouth. "They each weigh less than five pounds each, and the wind hasn't been able to move even one of them off course. What do you call that if not a direct line to Hell?"

"But what should we do here? Should we run or…" Simon asks as he starts backing away slowly.

"No! Whatever you do, don't run!" I tell him. "They respond to movement."

"Like a T-Rex," Luis adds.

The others laugh, but he's not wrong. It's why feeding them and cleaning their cage is always so hard.

"Can't you just portal us all out of here?" Izzy asks Remy. "Get us to the gym and away from those things? Or better yet, portal us the fuck off this island."

He shakes his head, looking grim. "I've tried several times. The portal block has supposedly been lifted, but every time I try to open one to somewhere off the island, it doesn't work. The door slams in my face."

Izzy rolls her eyes. "Remind me why I keep you around again?"

But when she starts to shift her weight, I warn her, "Don't move!"

"So what? We just have to stand here, hope the wind doesn't blow us away, and hope they don't notice us breathing?" Ember asks incredulously. "Or does that not count as movement?"

"Oh, it counts," I tell her.

"Fuck that." She starts to turn, but I reach out and grab her wrist to hold her in place.

"Stop!" I hiss.

"How bad can they possibly be?" Remy asks, eyes wide, but at least he has the good sense not to move.

"Give me a break. You aren't bad at all, are you?" As they get closer, Mozart coos to the chricklers the same way she would a puppy or a baby. Something I'm pretty sure she's going to regret very quickly considering she's got the little black-and-white ones with the floppy ears—which look precious but make a really big bite. "You're just misunderstood. That's all. Just misunderstood and completely adorable."

She's right about one thing. All chricklers are adorable—and every color of the rainbow. Some have big paws and fluffy ears. Others have long tails and the sweetest, biggest googly eyes you've ever seen. And still others have long, sparkly whiskers and the softest, most glittery fur imaginable. Not to mention they all have the absolute cutest faces in existence.

But they are also total and complete devil spawn. Every single one of them.

"I've got this," Jude tells us as he moves in front of Mozart. "You guys go ahead."

"Are you sure?" I ask doubtfully. "There's a lot of them."

"They're fine. They're just baby nightmares," he says with a roll of his eyes. "And I already told you, the monsters don't hurt me."

Logically, I know that's true. I saw for myself when the nasty squidzilla ran the moment he walked in the room. So maybe he's right. Maybe we just leave the chricklers to Jude.

"I guess we could head to the dance hall while you deal with these," I tell him as I loosen my death grip on Ember's wrist.

"Yeah, why don't you—" He breaks off as the first chrickler reaches him. It scurries straight up his leg and sinks its very large, very sharp, very pointy teeth directly into his biceps.

"What the fuck!" he growls, shaking it off and sending it flying right about the time a bunch of its siblings swarm the still-cooing Mozart. And bite every single piece of her they can manage.

"Ouch!" she yelps, jumping to her feet, trying to swing them off. But they've got a piece of her now—several pieces of her—and they're in no hurry to let go.

Jude tries to pull them off of her, and they respond by turning around and biting him, too. Several times.

He looks shocked but honestly more insulted by their betrayal.

"Get them off!" Mozart screams, whirling in a circle and flinging her arms up and down like she's trying to take flight.

A whole group of the hot-pink chricklers have definitely caught sight of Ember now, too.

"Shit, shit, shit!" she exclaims, and as the first one leaps at her, she shifts into her phoenix and takes off. But two of the chricklers aren't willing to let her go so easily and leap after her, each managing to grab onto her bird feet.

As they chomp down, the phoenix screams and tries to fly higher in an effort to make them let go. But the violent wind sends her slamming back to earth, right in the middle of another pile of chricklers.

She shifts back just as the rest of us rush forward to help her. But that alerts the chricklers to our presence, too, and the ones racing toward her switch course, their oversize paws eating up the short distance between them and the rest of us.

"Oh God," Simon whimpers out of the corner of his mouth. "They've found me."

An all-black chrickler is on his foot, several orange-and-white ones are on his back, and an industrious silver one is perched on his neck, way too close to his jugular for my liking.

This time it's Izzy who joins the fray, yanking the chrickler off his neck and throwing it as far away as her vampire strength lets her—which is, admittedly, far. But it's also the last thing she does—before she's swarmed, and unlike Simon, she doesn't stay still when it happens.

Instead, she lets out a very un-Izzy-like shriek and uses her preternatural speed to yank them off herself and hurl them into the wind—which only pisses them off more. More are biting and scratching her until even her vampire speed isn't enough to keep up with them.

Remy tries to come to her rescue, darting forward and tearing away several of the little beasts who are caught in Izzy's hair. But they don't go without a fight as they turn to snap at Remy.

Mozart is fighting her own battle as she lets loose a stream of flames meant to keep them at bay.

It's dragon fire, so it takes the rain at least a minute to tamp it down. Miraculously, they've lost interest in us for a moment as they watch the blaze—before jumping straight into the fire, one after the other, only to emerge seconds later at least five times bigger than when they went in.

"What the hell, Clementine!" Luis snarls. "You didn't tell us they evolve like fucking Pokémon."

"Sorry, but it's not like I've ever set them on fire before!" I shout back.

At that moment, one of the now Great Dane–size chricklers—a blue one—turns to face me, its giant fangs dripping a noxious combination of blood and spit.

And fuck this. We are way too outnumbered to do anything but, "Run!" I yell.

So we do, all of us taking off in the direction of the old dance hall. But, impossibly, the wind and the rain have gotten worse, so that every step feels like we're slogging through quicksand.

One of the largest ones—who now happens to be the size of a

Great Pyrenees—jumps straight at me. I juke to the left, but the wind is too strong, and it slows me down. The thing lands on me and goes straight for my jugular.

Jude, who is running right beside me, grabs onto it and tears it off right before it sinks its teeth—each one now the size of a large pizza slice—into my neck.

Jude manages to fight it off—and slam the thing into the nearest tree.

But something about the attack—maybe being in such close proximity to a bunch of condensed nightmares—activates his tattoos, and they start glowing in the dim gray of the storm.

The second they start moving, the chrickler attached to his back lets go with a yip. When it lands on the ground, its whole body is shaking like it's just been zapped by electricity.

Jude looks as surprised as I feel, but now that the monster isn't in the way, I watch the tattoos swirl restlessly on his back, up his neck, and up and down his arms through the tears in his hoodie. It looks like they're trying to get free, trying to help him fend off the attack.

Jude suppresses them with a quick clench of his jaw and touch of his hand against his exposed skin so that the glow fades as quickly as it came.

But the second the glow fades, the chricklers are on him again. Dozens of them swarming him at the same time.

"Go!" he yells to us as they start dragging him to the ground.

He breaks off as even more pile on, smothering him beneath their sheer weight and numbers.

I watch in horror as Jude falls to the ground.

His tattoos start to move and glow again, but there are so many chricklers on him at this point that the outer layer can't see or feel the tattoos and keep burrowing, and the inner layer are screaming in fear as they try to get away. They are in a total frenzy.

Simon, Mozart, Remy, and I rush over to him—or do the best we can to rush when we're dragging our own chrickler accessories along with us.

"Can you charm them or something?" Mozart asks Simon as we work together to try to tug a couple of the vile beasts off of Jude.

"I've already tried," he tells her, and he sounds as panicked as I feel. "They aren't really sentient, though, just nightmares in an organic form."

"So what do we do?" Mozart sounds near tears.

But no matter how hard we try to pry them off Jude, nothing works. I look around for something to do, some idea I haven't tried yet, but before I can find anything, Izzy stabs her knife into one of the chricklers trying to bite her leg.

The second the blade enters the monster, it hisses—then instantly condenses into one of the dark, wispy nightmares that Jude wears on his body.

Now that she's figured out she can kill the chricklers by stabbing them, she's in her element. With a knife in each hand, she starts hacking away. Seconds later, a dozen nightmare ribbons are spinning through the air.

I watch in astonishment as the wind catches them. "Give me a knife!" I yell to Izzy, but she's having too much fun taking on the next layer of chricklers attached to Jude to listen.

So Remy takes things into his own hands and reaches up the back of Izzy's shirt to get a knife—and almost loses a hand for his effort.

"The fuck?" she asks him as she turns to look at him, wide-eyed. And somehow, she still manages to kill two purple polka-dotted chricklers—one after the other even though she's facing in the other direction.

"We need knives!" he tells her urgently.

"Why do you always have to take the fun out of everything?" she pouts. But then she pulls a giant knife out of her pant leg and hands it to him.

One of these days she is going to tell me where she gets them. Because there is no way that any person carries this many knives on her person. No way. I swear, this one is almost as big as she is.

Remy turns around and starts hacking away at the chricklers, too, wielding the knife like a scythe.

"What about the rest of us?" Mozart calls desperately.

Izzy rolls her eyes and pulls out the tiniest dagger I've ever seen. She lobs it at Mozart and says, "Knock yourself out."

"Seriously?" Mozart looks totally offended.

"Yeah, well, next time think before you fire."

I lean over and try to pull a chrickler off Jude—apparently, I'm not blade-worthy—and get a pair of teeth in my hand for my trouble. But, on the plus side, I can actually see part of Jude's leg, so I feel like we're getting close.

Izzy must feel the same way, because she gets a little too enthusiastic and cuts a massive swathe through a bunch of chricklers—and, also, Mozart's forearm.

"Ow!" Mozart shrieks, dropping her knife. "You're as big a menace as the chricklers."

"Please," Izzy scoffs. "This is me with the child locks on."

"That's what I'm afraid of." Mozart doesn't look impressed.

Since she's currently bleeding and can no longer use it, I pick up her knife. I've never stabbed anything before, and if you'd asked me ten minutes ago, I would have told you I'd be quite happy living the rest of my life without ever stabbing anyone or anything.

Refusing to give myself a chance to think too much, I plunge my knife into the nearest chrickler. Then nearly recoil, not because it's gross, but because it isn't.

It's the strangest feeling. The monster is nowhere near as solid as I'd expect it to be. It feels almost…empty. There's no resistance once the knife slides in, and the moment it's buried to the hilt, this chrickler does exactly what the others did. It condenses into a black plume and blows away in the wind.

I take aim at a second one, then freak out because a whole new horde of chricklers is racing up the path toward us. And they all look loaded for paranormal.

Simon, who has been behind us with Remy, Ember, and Luis trying to keep the other chricklers off us so we can help Jude, groans. "Damn, Clementine. We can't fight them all."

"I know," I answer grimly as I brace myself for what may very well be a bloodbath.

When all of a sudden, a loud shriek fills the air—followed by the sound of teeth clattering to the ground.

"Oh, fuck no," Luis says, voice dripping in horror.

But he and I aren't the only ones to hear the battle cry of that hydra snake monster thing we had to fight in the dungeon. The chricklers hear it, too, and their heads come up in alarm.

Ears pricked, eyes straining through the rain, they freeze for several seconds. Then with howls of terror, they abandon the fight and scatter in all directions, leaving the eight of us to stare after them.

"So, dance hall, anyone?" Luis asks.

The rest of us don't have to be asked twice. We take off running straight for the run-down old building.

CHAPTER EIGHTY-ONE

NO REST FOR THE SCARY

We fight the wind as we haul ass toward safety. Every once in a while, we run across a rogue chrickler, but Izzy's got popping them down to a science, and we make it to the dance hall with almost no more injuries.

We skid to a stop at the door, ready to pile inside. But a giant padlock and chain hang from the door handles, clattering in the wind. I look nervously behind me to make sure no more chricklers have found us.

"What do we do now?" Ember asks, desperation in her voice.

"Allow me," Mozart says as she steps up to the door and breathes a precise stream of dragon fire directly at the lock. Granted, she melts the door handles and a small chunk of the door right along with it, but who are we to complain? It works.

We race inside just as a group of chricklers round the corner and set their sights on us. "Move it!" Jude yells as he sweeps the door shut and throws the lock just in time. Seconds later, we hear the *bang, bang, bang* of chricklers slamming into the door and bouncing off.

"Let's not do that again," Simon comments as we all take a second to catch our breaths. When we can breathe again, Luis and Remy grab a couple of old chairs from a stack in the corner and barricade the door, just in case, and then we all move deeper into the dance hall.

The whole place is dim and quiet, except for the whoosh of the wind outside. There's no electricity, but there are enough small windows so that the place isn't completely dark as we amble to the middle of the dance floor, finally able to breathe—though we are all drenched, bleeding, and exhausted.

As we walk, we kick up dust in our wake—it's been a long time since anyone has been in here. It creates an eerie haze in the low, natural light, but it's a million times better than being out there with the monsters in the hurricane.

And that is not a sentence I ever imagined thinking.

"If those are the baby nightmares, what the fuck do the grown-up ones look like?" Simon asks as he sinks to the ground, resting his back against the old-time stage at the front of the dance floor.

"Like Hell itself," Luis tells him.

I start to explain in more detail, then stop myself because Luis really did give the perfect description.

"You know what this group really needs?" Remy says as he, too, slides to the ground.

"To get the fuck off this island?" Mozart answers, sprawling out on the floor.

"Well, yeah. That," Remy agrees with a laugh. "But we also need a healer."

"I'll put that on the wish list," I tell him dryly as I reach a hand out to help Jude sit down. I really hope his self-sacrifice out there doesn't end up killing him.

Just the thought has my lungs aching and my heart beating violently in my chest. But when I turn to look at him, the cuts on his face are already healing.

The scratches on his arms—which I know were really bad because I saw them just a minute ago—are already gone, and the ones on his chest are fading right before my eyes.

"How?" I gasp, shocked at the fact that he has almost no damage on his body even though I saw those bastards bite and claw the hell out of him.

When he doesn't answer, I look around at the others, then glance down at myself. But nope, all of our wounds are still very much present. And I know Jude healed fast in Aunt Claudia's office, but that was only after I mixed up an elixir for him. This is happening in real time, and it's the most astonishing thing I've ever seen.

"I don't suppose there are any medical supplies in here, are there?" Jude asks, brushing my hair out of my eyes. The chrickler attack finally did in the bun I've been wearing since yesterday afternoon.

"There are some in my backpack," Ember tells him. "I picked them up from the basket when we were at the dorm. Give me a few minutes, though, because there's no way I can get them for you right now." She is lying face down, arms outstretched, cheek splayed on the cold hardwood floor, completely spent.

"I'll take care of it," Jude tells her before turning to me. "You should sit down."

"You're not wrong," I tell him.

I'm about ten seconds from the adrenaline wearing off and I'm not sure what's going to happen then.

Ironically, Jude's the one who helps me sit down before picking up Ember's pack. "Do you mind if I go through it?" he asks her.

"Mind? If you can find me the damn ibuprofen, I'll have your babies."

The rest of us laugh at that, but I realize Simon doesn't.

Jude gets the supplies out and starts by hand-delivering ibuprofen to everyone in the room—except Izzy, because she's healing almost as quickly as he is.

Vampires, man. And apparently Nightmare princes.

Then he makes the rounds, cleaning wounds and patching us up as best he can. He starts with me.

I suck in a breath as he uses an alcohol wipe to clean a particularly deep chrickler bite. On the plus side, he's at least gentle about it. He *does* have practice.

When the burning finally stops, I ask the question that's been bugging me since we stepped through the door. "How are you healed so fast? You were in the worst shape out of all of us."

He nods to acknowledge the question but takes his time answering it as he continues to doctor the bite. After a minute or so, though, he answers, "I've been wondering the same thing—I've never been bitten by one of the monsters before, so healing this quickly is a new experience for me. But I think it's because nightmares can't hurt me."

"No offense, man, but I beg to differ," Simon tells him. "I saw you get your ass *kicked*."

"That's not what I mean. I mean, they can momentarily cause me pain—bite me, scratch me, whatever—but nothing else they did to me stuck. But the rest of you look like you've been trapped in a cage with a hungry bear, so the difference has to be that..."

"You're the Prince of Nightmares," I finish for him when he trails off.

He shrugs.

Jude finishes cleaning my last wound, then moves on to Ember and the others.

The ibuprofen kicks in about ten minutes later, and I push myself up to help.

It must be kicking in for the others because they're moving around, too. Mozart even heads over to the old, out-of-tune piano at the edge of the stage and starts playing "It's the End of the World as We Know It" from R.E.M. And holy shit, I think it's at least as good as the original—and that's on a decrepit old piano. I can only imagine what it would sound like on a decent instrument.

Apparently, she got her name for a reason.

Also, I can't think of a more perfect song to sum up the shit show of the last twenty-four hours.

Not to mention the even bigger shit show I have a feeling is still to come. So good on her.

As if to underscore my feelings, an ear-piercing screeching—louder even than the thunder, the wind, or the other distant roar—sounds from just outside the dance hall.

CHAPTER EIGHTY-TWO

TWO TRUTHS AND A LOVE

"What the hell is that?" Mozart demands as she stops mid song. When it comes again, I kind of wish she'd just keep playing because I'm pretty sure I know exactly what's making that noise.

"Squidzilla," Izzy says so that I don't have to. "That thing sounded just like that when it was trying to kill us yesterday."

"So that means all the monsters are out?" Luis asks flatly. "Because that's three now."

"I don't know about all—" I break off as a different scream fills the air, higher and more eerie than the first one.

"Pretty sure that answers your question," Remy tells him dryly.

"But how? I've been down there a hundred times with you. The cages aren't electric. Maybe one lock failed. But all of them?" Luis shakes his head. "No way that happened."

"The waves haven't hit hard enough to have fucked things up in the admin building. If they had, this whole area would be flooded," Mozart comments. "So what did it?"

"I think you mean who," I answer.

I can't help remembering Jean-Luc's face yesterday in Brit Lit, after that snake monster thing attacked. He was really excited, gleeful even. At the time I couldn't figure out what had him in such a good mood, but now that I know Jude wasn't the mysterious visitor in the dungeon yesterday, all of this is starting to add up.

"The Jean-Jerks." Luis beats me to it. We've been best friends for a long time, and he can obviously read my face.

I tell them about yesterday and finish with, "It's the kind of petty bullshit thing they would do." I look over at Jude, who looks absolutely guilt ridden. Because the mafia rule tends to be if you fuck with them, they go after the people you care most about. Jude shut them down in class, and I nearly got my ass kicked by the grossest snake monster imaginable.

"Kill our friend and I'll let loose a plague of monsters on everyone?" Remy sounds skeptical.

"I'd do it if someone pissed me off enough," Izzy tells him.

As one, we all turn to stare at her in horror. But Mozart is the only one brave enough to ask, "Really?"

Izzy draws it out for a second, then laughs and says, "No. But I one hundred percent believe those assholes did it."

"For what purpose?" Ember's been listening to the whole conversation, but this is the first time she actually has something to say.

"Revenge?" I suggest.

"To watch the world burn?" Simon contributes.

"For the tapestry."

It's Jude's first time speaking as well, but he says it with such certainty that we all listen to him.

"Think about it," he continues. "For some reason that makes absolutely no sense to any of us, those assholes want the tapestry. They've tried to get it twice already, would even kill for it, and have failed both times. And the second time, one of them ended up dead."

I studiously avoid looking straight at Izzy when he says that, but it doesn't seem to faze her.

"They're running out of time and options, so what better way to get one more shot at the tapestry than to distract us?" Jude concludes.

"With nightmare monsters?" Mozart asks incredulously. "You really think they're willing to take that risk?"

"I think they were *dying* to take that risk," he tells her.

"Because at the end of the day, they're reckless assholes," I say, ticking the points off on my fingers. "They do want revenge, they're dark fae, and they are absolutely the kind of jerks who mess stuff up just to watch it burn."

"Pretty much," Jude agrees.

"Well, this is a problem." Luis stands up and crosses the high-polish parquet floor to look out one of the windows. The administration didn't bother to board them up for the hurricane, probably because no one uses this place anymore and they didn't think anyone would be riding out the storm in here.

"I don't actually think it is a problem," Izzy comments from where she's kicked back on her elbows with her legs stretched out in front of her.

"Of course *you* don't," Mozart snorts as she exchanges an amused look with Simon.

A smile plays around Izzy's lips, but all she says is, "I'm serious. We have the tapestry, which means our problem is exactly the same as it's always been—figure out how to fix the tapestry so Jude can do his little nightmare magic trick and send the monsters back to where they belong. Whether they're in the dungeon or wandering the campus doesn't matter, especially not until we figure out how to fix the damn rug."

"You're right," I tell her.

"I know I'm right." She shrugs. "But once we do figure it out, I get to kill three more Jean-Fuckheads. We'll consider it a bonus for a job well done, once we take care of the monsters."

I have absolutely no idea what to say to that—especially since I kind of think she's kidding, but I also kind of don't.

"So does anybody have any ideas?" I look at Jude, since it's his tapestry. But he just looks back with a solemn shake of his head.

"I say we take a break," Ember suggests, reaching for her pack. "I'm hungry, and I'm tired, and I'll think a lot better if I can take care of both of those situations. Can we just take half an hour of downtime before we try to figure out how to solve this mess once and for all?"

The others agree, so we do as she suggests. Between us we've got about a dozen granola bars, several packets of trail mix, and a bunch of peanut butter crackers.

It's not optimal, but it's way better than nothing.

After I eat a packet of trail mix and drink some water—thankfully the dance hall has a working bathroom and bar faucets—I get up and wander around the elaborately decorated ballroom as Mozart continues the piano. This time it's Olivia Rodrigo's "hope ur ok," and I can't help but think of Carolina.

When we were kids, she and I loved to come in here—with its bold, floral fabric walls and gorgeous wood floor with inlaid stars, it was a little girl's paradise. Especially a little girl like Carolina, who loved to turn on the chandeliers with their bright lights and missing crystals and dance across the floor to the large stage that takes up one whole end of the room. Most days, she didn't even need music. She just danced.

Some days she'd climb on up to that stage and give a speech or recite a monologue or pretend she was accepting an Academy Award while I clapped enthusiastically from the upstairs balcony.

I turn to look at the stage, and I swear I can almost see her on it. That's the real reason I haven't been here in three years—not because I got too busy to come visit this beautiful place, but because every time I do, it just makes me miss Carolina more.

If I have to see ghosts, why can't I, just once, see her?

I shake my head to ward off the newest wave of sadness rolling through me and catch Jude wandering up the ornate, art deco stairs to the balcony. He sits in one of the gold velvet chairs, eyes pensive and far away, so I decide to join him.

I don't know what I'm going to say to him, and I definitely don't have a clue what he might say to me. I do know that we haven't had a chance to talk, really talk, since he fished me out of the ocean this morning. And I really want to hear what he has to say.

He seemed pretty clear in those moments—*I'm not okay living in a world without you in it* is simply a certain level of...something. But this is Jude, and this wouldn't be the first time he's given me pretty words only to yank them back when I need them most. Before I start letting myself think about him...us, I need to make sure this isn't all in my head.

Even knowing what I want—what I need—the climb up those stairs is one of the hardest things I've ever done. My hands are trembling by the time I make it to the top, and my knees are so wobbly that I'm surprised they manage to hold me up—even before Mozart switches to playing Coldplay's "The Scientist" and my already shaky stomach falls to my toes.

My feet forget how to walk.

My lungs forget how to breathe.

And my heart—my poor, battered heart—forgets how *not* to break.

The phantoms of our broken past litter the space between us, and now that I'm here—now that *we're* here—I can't force myself to cross the divide. Not again. Not one more time.

Not when I've been hurt so many, many times before.

Jude's gaze collides with mine from across the room, and a sob wells in my throat. Though I try my best to hold it back—to swallow it down—it escapes.

His eyes widen at the sound, and humiliation burns through me. All these years I've worked so hard to hide my pain—to focus on the fury—that its escape now feels like one more betrayal in a wild, raging ocean of them. Only this time, there's no one to blame but myself.

I turn to flee back downstairs, where the only monsters I have to fight are the ones with teeth and claws. But I only make it to the second step before Jude is there, pulling me into his arms. Holding me against his heart. Whispering fast and frantic words against my ear.

"I'm sorry," he tells me over and over again. "I'm so sorry. I never meant to hurt you. I only ever wanted to keep you safe."

"It's not your job to keep me safe." All the years of pent-up fear and confusion explode in an instant. "It's your job to be my safe place—they're not the same thing."

"I know," he whispers, pulling back just enough to look in my eyes. Just enough to run his finger over the tiny dent in my chin in that sweet and serious way he has that breaks my heart every fucking time. "I've finally figured that out."

"Then why—" My voice breaks like my resolve, and I sink into him before I can stop myself.

Despite everything, he feels good and safe and right. So right. I breathe deep, wrap myself in the scent of warm honey and confidence. Then burrow closer as I wait for what feels like an eternity for him to speak.

When he does—when he pulls away and strokes a hand down my cheeks—he says the absolute last thing in the world I would ever expect him to say.

"I hate brussels sprouts."

At first, I'm convinced I've heard him wrong. Convinced that too many chrickler bites and monster fights have done some serious damage. "I'm sorry?" I shake my head. "What did you say?"

The corners of his mouth turn up in that tiny smile that is only a smile if you're Jude, and though I'm confused as fuck, my heart starts beating overtime anyway.

He holds up a finger. "I hate brussels sprouts."

What the—

He holds up a second finger, and his eyes never leave mine. "I love you."

Everything inside me freezes at his words—and at the realization of what it is he's doing.

He's finishing what we started last night before our world turned upside down. His very own Jude Abernathy-Lee version of Two Truths and a Lie.

I'm afraid to move, afraid to breathe, afraid to hope, as I wait for whatever comes next.

He holds up a third and final finger. And this time I have to strain to hear as he whispers, "I got sent here when I was seven because I killed my father."

CHAPTER EIGHTY-THREE

A SHOULDER
TO DIE ON

H is words demolish me.

They shatter me.

They tear me open and break down the last remnants of every last wall I've ever tried to put between us.

Because Jude actually really likes brussels sprouts—Caspian used to tease him about it when we were younger.

And also because I can still see that little boy getting off the boat on that long-ago day. Eyes shuttered, face closed up, shoulders hunched as if bracing for a blow with every breath he took.

"Oh, Jude." The words are torn from me. "I'm sorry. I'm so, so sorry."

He shakes his head, his throat working as he tries to keep himself together. "He was teaching me how to channel nightmares, how to pull them into myself, and how to farm them out so I could keep people safe."

He blows out a breath, then runs a frustrated hand through his hair. "Nightmares get a bad rap. Everyone's afraid of them, and nobody wants to have one. But when you do them right—they're not so bad. People go through a lot of shit, you know? Nightmares help them figure it out, help them *work* it out before all that shit impacts their real lives."

"I've never thought of it like that before."

He laughs at that, but there's no humor in it. "No one ever does. But it's only when I don't do my job—when I fuck up—that really bad shit happens."

There's torment in his eyes, in his voice, in the way he holds his body like one more blow might break him.

"You let a nightmare escape the day your father died?" I ask, gently resting a hand on his biceps.

He nods. "We'd spent the whole day practicing, and I was certain that I had it. Certain that I was good enough to do it on my own. So, late that night, I tried, and all I could think about was how proud he would be when he found out. Except I let one get by me and—"

He breaks off, shaking his head.

"You were seven," I tell him. "Seven-year-olds mess up."

"He died screaming," he answers flatly. "I couldn't stop it. I couldn't save him. All I could do was watch it happen. It was…"

"A nightmare," I fill in for him.

"Yeah." He presses his lips together, and for a second, I think he's going to leave it at that. But then he continues, "My mother tried to get past it. She really did. But she could never look at me the same way after that night. By the end, she couldn't look at me at all—but that's okay. I couldn't look at myself, either. That's when she sent me here."

"You were just a child," I whisper as horror snakes through me.

"A child with unimaginable power he couldn't control," he corrects. "Isn't that what this school is for?"

"Honestly, I don't know what this school is for anymore. But I do know that what happened when you were seven…it wasn't your fault."

"I *killed* my father. It doesn't get any more my fault than that. Just like with Carolina. I still don't—"

"What?" I ask, because whatever it is he's holding back, I want out in the open. We've had enough secrets festering between us, and all they've done is hurt us both. If we're ever going to be together, we need to get the last of them into the light.

"I don't even understand how it happened, how I let it get away. I spent the next seven years making sure it would *never* happen again," he whispers. "When I got here, they couldn't take my powers away, so I spent all night, every night, learning to control the nightmares.

Learning to control that power. Making sure I never lost control and hurt someone again. And it worked. For seven years, it worked, and I started to believe that maybe, just maybe, things would be okay. That maybe, just maybe, I could trust myself again. And then...

"I kissed you, and I lost control, and Carolina..." His voice goes out, and he takes a deep breath before trying again. "It was your worst nightmare that she'd be sent to the Aethereum. She was always getting into trouble, always breaking some rule or another and getting detention because of it. We were ten when they started threatening to send her away, but no one ever believed they would actually do it. Except for you."

"That's because I know my mother better than anybody else."

"I know you do." He smiles sadly. "It's why there was a part of you that was always so afraid of it happening. But it wouldn't have if I hadn't made your worst nightmare come true. But I did, and I ruined everything."

It still hurts to hear him say it.

I haven't been able to get it out of my head since he told me last night, and part of me wants to scream at the unfairness of it. Wants to rail at the bizarre circumstances that put all of us together at the exact spot and the exact moment in time to set all of these things in motion.

If Jude wasn't the Prince of Nightmares.

If Carolina wasn't so wild.

If I didn't have the fear of losing her.

If my mother wasn't such a hard, unyielding woman.

If my family—if this school—actually did their jobs and taught the students how to control their powers.

So many what-ifs. So much waste. Because if any one of those things weren't true, maybe Carolina would still be alive. Maybe she'd be here with us right now.

Maybe everything would be okay.

But they are true. Every single one of them.

Yet, out of that whole list, the only one that couldn't have been changed is *who Jude is*.

He *is* the Prince of Nightmares. Blaming him for that is as nonsensical and unfair as blaming rain for being wet.

So I do the only thing I can do, the only thing that's right. I bury the pain, at least for now, and focus on the love instead.

I step forward, cup his face in my hands so that he can't look away. Can't look anywhere but in my eyes so that he knows that I'm telling him the truth now. So that he knows I mean every word I'm saying. "I love you."

He just shakes his head. "You can't."

"But I do." I look him straight in the eye. "I know who you are. I know what you did. Just like I know that you've beaten yourself up about it every day. Just like I know you'll be beating yourself up for many years to come. But here's the thing. And I need you to listen to me. I need you to believe me." I take a deep breath, let it out slowly. And tell him what I know is true. "It's not your fault."

"Clementine, no." He tries to step away, tries to back away from the truth, but I hold him fast.

"It's not your fault," I tell him again. "It wasn't your fault when you were seven and just beginning to understand what your power is. It wasn't your fault when you were fourteen and you had a momentary slip. And last night wasn't your fault, either. You were seven years old when you were put in an untenable situation, at a school that promised to protect you and instead left you to fend for yourself. It isn't your fault, Jude."

He doesn't blink. He doesn't breathe. He doesn't even move. He just stands there staring at me, his face carved in stone until fear tightens my stomach and makes me wonder if I've made everything worse.

But then it happens. I watch, breath held and heart in my throat, as his eyes—his mystical, magical, marvelous eyes—start to change, and for the first time in a long time, maybe ever, he lets his walls down. I can finally see all the way to the depths of his beautiful, broken soul.

And what I see there nearly brings me to my knees. Because Jude loves me. He really, really loves me. I can see it. More, I can feel it. And nothing in my whole fucked-up life has ever felt so good.

"I love you," he says, and this time he doesn't need a game to get the words out.

"I know," I answer.

And then I go up on tiptoe so I can press my mouth to his.

CHAPTER EIGHTY-FOUR

I'VE BEEN TOTALLY THREADING THIS

The second our lips connect, everything stops.

My heart.

Our world.

Even time itself.

Everything grinds to a halt, until there is nothing but Jude, nothing but me, nothing but us and this moment that's been a lifetime—an eternity—in the making.

Need.

Friendship.

Pain.

Absolution.

Reassurance.

Fear.

Love.

It's all there.

In the slide of his hands over my skin.

In the gentle caress of his fingers against my cheek, my shoulder, the nape of my neck.

In the give and take of his mouth against my own.

Every moment before this and every moment that will come after this somehow meld together, and I can see them all.

Sweet and sexy.

Fun and terrifying.

Easy and more difficult than anything I've ever imagined.

They're all right there, a million points of light spread out before me, so close I can almost touch them. And Jude is in every single one.

For the first time in my life, I understand why the Ancient Greeks saw life as a thread to be spun and, eventually, cut. Because that's what I see in this moment when Jude and I are broken open and laid bare. Thousands of multicolored threads connecting us to the world, to our friends, to each other. Thousands of multicolored threads woven together to—

"Oh my God!" I pull back as it suddenly comes to me.

"Clementine?" Jude looks freaked out as he lets me go. "What's wrong? Did I hurt—"

"Nothing! Nothing's wrong! I know what to do!"

I don't waste time explaining it to him. Instead, I grab his hand and pull him down the stairs to where our friends are.

They're lying around or still dozing. But around them I can see the men and women of the past, dressed in suits and beautiful dresses, as well as other people in clothes the likes of which I've never seen before. They're obviously people from the future. Only now, they're not separated by space *or* time. They're together, mingling and talking, dancing and laughing and whirling around the room. The past and the future combined into one beautiful tapestry of life.

One couple—a man from the future and a woman from the past— get a little overenthusiastic and crash into a table that isn't there in the present. Ember, who is lying in that spot, screams and leaps up from where she was napping.

"Did you hear that?" she asks.

"Hear what?" Mozart starts looking around.

"That! People are laughing! Can't you—" And that's when I realize she can feel them. Not just as a nebulous brush against her arm or a shiver down her spine. At this moment, she can actually hear and feel the people from the past and the future who are gathered around her.

"It's nothing to worry about," Remy tells her soothingly, and I realize he can see them, too. That he's always been able to see them.

"The monsters—" she starts.

"Not the monsters," Remy says, sharing a conspiratorial smile with me. "The future."

"And the past," I add.

"The fuck?" she asks.

"There's a party going on right now, and it's getting a little rambunctious."

Ember makes a face. "We have to figure out how to fix this shit soon, because it's really freaking me out."

"One problem at a time," Luis tells her. "And I say the monsters are a little more important right now."

"That's because you can't hear a bunch of people talking about their favorite song."

"Actually, I can," he tells her. "I've just been ignoring it—and the horrible swing music—for the last hour."

"That's not swing music," Izzy comments, rolling over onto her side. "That's 1950s rock and roll."

Luis gives her a look. "I don't know what kind of rock and roll you listen to, girl, but Elvis is definitely not in this building."

I'm particularly fascinated by their argument because I'm hearing the Beatles. To be fair, what else would be playing while kissing Jude?

"Is that what happened upstairs?" Jude asks, looking fascinated. "You heard all this?"

"No. I mean, yes, but it's been here all along. I saw something else, and it gave me an idea to fix the tapestry so we can trap the monsters."

"Oh, yeah?" Remy asks. "How?"

Suddenly everyone looks a lot more interested than freaked out as they wait for my answer. "We've got to unravel the tapestry."

"I'm sorry, what?" Simon asks. "You want to unravel the only thing we have that can actually stop the monsters?"

"I do. Because it's the only way to fix it."

And just like that, the enthusiasm is gone.

"That's a pretty big move," Mozart tells me. "If you're wrong, we're completely fucked."

"To be fair, we're completely fucked already," Izzy says. "In case you haven't noticed..."

She's right. We are. The wind is rattling the windows continuously, and lightning flashes across the sky every couple of seconds. All of which means it's only a matter of time before buildings start getting damaged. The only thing I want less right now than to be out in the elements is to be out there with a bunch of nightmare monsters.

"If we unravel the tapestry and we can't put it back together, I'll never be able to channel another nightmare again," Jude tells me. "I'll have nowhere to put them and no way to upload them back into the ether."

"You can't channel them now anyway, not with the tapestry broken." I put my hand on his arm and watch as the nightmares start spinning around from the contact. "But that tapestry is made of nightmares, right?"

"Yeah, of course."

"And you can control nightmares, right?"

"Yes..."

"Then you can unravel the tapestry."

He looks completely horrified. "Why would I do that?"

"If each thread is a different nightmare, once it's unraveled, then you'll have all the different threads separated and can weave them back together any way you want."

I can see the second my plan starts making sense to Jude, because, instinctively, he starts to back away. "I can't do that. There's no way I can control that many nightmares at the same time. What if I lose one?"

"What if you don't?" I shoot back.

"Seriously?" he demands. "After everything that just happened?"

"You won't be alone this time, Jude." I close the distance between us so I can wrap an arm around his waist. "We'll all be there to help make sure none of the nightmares go anywhere."

"And how exactly do you think we can do that?" Luis asks.

I shrug. "In the last two days, we've fought off squidzilla, an angry snake monster, and a bunch of mutant chricklers—all of which are made from a ton of nightmares. How hard could a few more nightmares be?"

Jude still doesn't look impressed, but Simon is definitely coming around. "You know, she's got a point, Jude."

"Do you have any idea how many threads make up a tapestry?" Ember says. "It has to be thousands. So how is he going to store them all? I mean, he's big, but I'm pretty sure they won't all fit on his body."

"Good point," I say. "But there has to be a way."

"How do you store them now?" Luis asks.

"In jars," Jude tells him reluctantly.

"Jars?" I repeat as things start to become clear to me.

"Yeah, jars," he answers, looking even more wary.

"Like canning jars?"

"Canning jars?" Mozart says. "There's no way—"

"Yes," Jude finally admits with a sigh. "I store them in canning jars."

"That's what you were doing at the root cellar yesterday. Channeling nightmares into the jars there." I shake my head. "How did I never think of that..."

"To be fair, most people don't see a jar of jelly and think, *Oh, that's my worst nightmare*," Luis says dryly.

"So we need to go to the cellar," I tell them. "You can pull the tapestry apart as slowly as you want and store the nightmares in the jars there. Then, when you're ready to weave them back into the tapestry, you can pull them out the same way. You'll be in total control."

Jude doesn't immediately jump at my suggestion, but I can tell he's thinking about it.

Even as Ember asks, "What happens if you're wrong?"

I don't like to think about that, because if I'm wrong, we're fucked. But we're also fucked right now, like Izzy said. Plus, I don't know if it's the being able to see the past and the future thing I've got going on or what, but I have a really, really strong feeling that I'm right.

"Then we come up with a new plan," I tell her after a second. "But unless anyone else has a better plan right now, I think this is the one we go with. Does anyone else have a different idea?"

I look around, but none of them volunteers anything. So then I turn to Jude and say, "I know this sucks. But I promise, whatever happens, you're not in it alone. I'll be there, and so will everyone else. I swear, we'll figure it out."

"Okay." He nods.

"Okay?" I repeat, because I really didn't think it would be that easy.

"You said you've got me, right?" His eyes search mine.

"I've definitely got you."

"All right, then," Jude says, sounding anything but enthusiastic. "Let's go unravel some nightmares."

"You sound like a damn psychologist." Simon snorts. "Maybe we should all start calling you Dr. Abernathy-Lee. You can tell us what our dreams mean."

"Or I can make sure that the first nightmare I accidentally let slip is directed straight at you."

"That doesn't sound like much of an accident," Simon protests.

Jude smiles thinly in response. "Exactly." Then he turns to me and says, "You ready to do this thing?"

CHAPTER EIGHTY-FIVE

DESPERATE TIMES CALL FOR DESPERATE PORTALS

"Hey," Izzy says as we all migrate unenthusiastically toward the door. The root cellar may be the place to be, but between the hurricane and the monsters, getting there is going to be rough. "Do we really want to go out there?"

"Want? No," Luis tells her. "Need to? Kind of. Because I'm pretty sure the Prince of Darkness over there isn't going to be able to do what he needs to in here."

Izzy flashes her teeth at him in a smile that's definitely more of a threat than a gesture of goodwill before turning back to Remy. "I think you should try the portal thing one more time."

He rolls his eyes. "I already told you, I've tried like *five* times. I can't get us off this damn island."

"We're not trying to get off the island anymore. We just need to get to the root cellar. Surely, you can do *that* much." She makes it sound like a dare and an insult all rolled into one.

"It's not about what I can do," he answers, looking insulted. "It's about the portal block."

"Which was lifted to create that shit show of a portal that got us stranded here to begin with. We already decided there's something weird about this storm, that it's trying to keep us on the island. So, again, stop being a baby about a little failure and get us into that root cellar."

"I wouldn't call it a failure." Remy lifts a brow. "And what do I get when I actually get us there?"

"Not attacked by monsters?" Jude suggests dryly.

"Pretty much a win-win, in my opinion," I add.

Remy doesn't look impressed...at least not until Izzy flashes her fangs at him in a very different look than she gave Luis. "How about I bite you?"

"Not sure how exactly *that's* a prize," Simon murmurs.

"Spoken by someone who's never been bitten by a vampire," she counters with a smile that is anything but sweet.

"*I've* never been bitten," Remy tells her.

Izzy lifts a brow. "Do this for me and we'll see if we can fix that."

Thirty seconds later, Remy has us all inside the root cellar in the pitch black. And, can I just say, it was a much smoother ride than that portal Mr. Abdullah and Ms. Picadilly created.

When I say as much to him, Izzy says, "Told you he's got the portal mojo." She sounds almost proud, a fact that definitely doesn't seem to slip by Remy. All of a sudden, a massive crack of thunder booms overhead, and I jump. The storm sounds a million times worse out here, the doors rattling like they're about to come off their hinges. I remind myself that it's actually safer for us to be underground right now, but it's hard to believe it.

I pull one of the emergency flashlights out of my back pocket, but just as I go to turn it on, a ghostly face appears in front of me. It's the woman from yesterday, the pregnant one in the pink nightgown. But instead of calmly walking with a hand on her pregnant belly the way she was earlier, she looks bedraggled and in pain.

Her hair is sweaty and plastered to her face. Her pink nightgown is wet and bloody, and her face is contorted with fear.

"My baby!" she calls, and her hand is trembling as she reaches for me. "My baby!"

I have one second to register that she must be in labor, but as I do, another ghost appears suddenly right next to her.

It's the terrifying one from Aunt Claudia's office. Her eyes are wild, her hair limp, and she's covered in blood. And when she screams, it's not to ask for help. Instead, it's the epitome of agony—low and long and desperate, so desperate. Her eyes are darting all around, just like they were in the infirmary, like she's seeing past, present, and future all at once and it's torturing her.

"What the hell!" Luis says, sounding totally freaked out. And that's when I realize he can hear her, too.

"Who is that?" Mozart asks, sounding desperate. "How can we help her?"

"Hey. It's okay," I say soothingly, reaching for the ghosts even knowing it's going to hurt. But they're both so terrified, so in pain, that I have to at least try to do something. But before I can figure out what that something is, a third ghost joins them—the brown-haired girl in the Calder uniform and nineties beanie and sunglasses. She doesn't look as scared as the others, just resigned. And sad. So sad. It's such a marked contrast to the girl I saw on the center mall that it breaks my heart.

"It's going to be okay," I say again as I reach out to them.

"*What's* going to be okay?" Ember asks.

I don't answer, because the moment my hands touch the three ghosts, they merge into one. The moment they do, the physical pain inside me ceases. And for the first time, I realize I've been seeing the same woman in three different time periods.

And that's when it comes together. She has always wanted me to see. And for the first time, I actually understand.

She lost her life and her baby all in one moment. And I was that baby.

Shock reverberates through me, has my knees shaking and my heart pounding out of my chest. All this time, all these years, and I never knew. I never knew.

I blink, and the ghost has faded into the background while her tiny infant, with its shriveled fingers and cheeks ruddy from crying, is handed to a young woman. The baby—it's so hard to imagine that it's me, but deep down I know it is—wraps a tiny hand around a finger tipped with a bloodred nail. My stomach plummets as a whole new shock vibrates through me. That hand belongs to my mother. No, not my mother. To the woman who raised me. Camilla.

But then her hand closes around mine, and she lifts me to her chest and presses soft kisses against my head even as tears run like rivers down her cheeks. And she whispers, "No matter what, I'll keep you safe here."

And just like that, the picture—the flicker—fades away.

So much pain. So much love. So many lies and broken promises.

"Who's crying?" Mozart sounds even more concerned than she did a few moments ago. "She sounds devastated."

Luis, Simon, and Remy all take out flashlights, and as they move them toward the sound, I realize it's me.

The ghosts are gone, and I'm the one crying, my newly mended heart breaking wide open all over again.

Mozart gasps and rushes toward me, but Jude puts himself between us. His hands are tender on my shoulders, his dark eyes solemn as they search my face. "What do you need?" he asks. "What can I do?"

"Let's just finish this. I need it to be over."

I still have questions that need answers, and breaking down won't get me what I need. I'll have time enough to think this through later. Right now, we just need to make the nightmare stop.

"I've got you," he says and takes my hand. "Let's get this done."

I look around the room, a blatant ploy to avoid everyone else's worried eyes, then freeze as I notice that something is very, very wrong.

All of the jars that had been neatly lined up on the shelves are now knocked over. Some are still on the shelves turned on their sides, while others are lying on the ground, and still others are smashed into pieces. The one thing they all have in common, though, is that they're all open, their lids scattered haphazardly around the room.

"Gotta say, Jude, you're not much of a housekeeper," Simon teases, his voice strained despite his attempt at normalcy.

But Jude doesn't even notice. He's too busy looking at all the damage.

"This wasn't him," I say, and it's my turn to squeeze his hand in support. "When I was here yesterday, they were all neatly lined up on the shelves."

"Do you think the storm did it?" Mozart asks, but her voice is doubtful.

"I think the Jean-Jerks did it," I answer as a combination of anger and horror courses through me. "I saw Jean-Luc snooping around out here yesterday."

I don't bother to go into the whole disappearance thing—it's not important right now. What is important is Jude and what this means to him—*for* him.

"Hey," I say, trying to gauge Jude's state of mind. "Are you—"

"No," he growls in a voice I've never heard before. "I'm nowhere near okay."

But instead of saying more, he strides to the last shelf. On the top shelf is one lone jar. Not only is it the only one still standing, but it also still has its lid on it.

I start to ask what it is, but before I can, Jude grabs the top of it and tips it forward.

As he does, the ceiling pops open, and a full staircase slowly descends.

"What the hell is that?" Luis exclaims, sounding excited and disgusted at the same time. And I get it.

Luis, Eva, and I checked every nook and cranny of this place, but we never thought to check the ceiling. To be fair, who would? It's a root cellar. Who builds into the ceiling of something that's completely underground?

Jude doesn't answer, just pounds up the stairs. He starts having to duck before he's halfway up.

I start up the stairs behind Jude, while the others mill around, mystified but curious.

But I don't even get to the top before he's yelling, "Fuck!" and heading back down.

I've never seen Jude like this, so beside himself with rage that he's barely coherent. "What's up there?" I ask, wanting to check it out myself.

But he's already brushing past me, visibly distressed.

"More jars," he says curtly.

"They're all open, too?"

"Every fucking one of them," he growls.

"You know what this means, don't you?" Remy says when we're both back on the ground.

"It means I should have killed the other three when I had the chance," Izzy answers nonchalantly. But there's a rage in her normally distant eyes that I've never seen before.

Not that I blame her. If a Jean-Jerk showed up here right now, Izzy would have to wait in line, because I'm more than ready to decimate every single one of them myself.

What they did here is unconscionable. What they did here is... There's not even a word for what they did.

"They let the nightmares out." Jude says out loud what we've all already figured out because I think he needs to hear it. "I didn't fuck up and let them escape when I was helping you. They did it."

"Yes," I tell him as I reach out to take his hand. "They did it."

He swallows convulsively, and for the first time in the ten years I've known him, there are tears in his eyes. "I didn't kill all those people."

"No," I whisper, tears pouring down my own face because his pain is as palpable as his relief. "You didn't. That's on them. They did that."

"I didn't—" His voice breaks, so he tries again. "I didn't kill Eva."

"No, Jude. No, you didn't."

He nods, then blows out a long, slow, shuddering breath as the others gather around him.

I glance at their faces, see the same devastated rage in their eyes that I feel. Because Jude doesn't deserve this—and neither did any of the people who died.

Remy puts a supportive hand on Jude's shoulder and says, "So what do you want to do?"

Jude doesn't even have to think about it. "I want to fix that fucking tapestry, capture the monsters, and then feed the Jean-Jerks to them."

Luis nods, then opens the tapestry and spreads it on the table in the center of the room. "Well, then, that's what we'll make happen."

CHAPTER EIGHTY-SIX

SHOOT FOR THE JARS

"**W**e should probably get the jars ready," Simon suggests, bending over to pick up a few of the ones on the floor. He's right, so we spend the next five minutes setting them up so Jude can funnel the nightmares into them.

When that's done, I look at him. "You can do this," I say.

"Oh, I know I can." He's more in control, more focused, and more confident about his powers than I've *ever* seen him. He's also incandescent with rage, so this should be one hell of a show.

"Okay, then. What do you need from us, man?" Simon asks, shuddering a little. I assume that's because he's brushing against a witch from the past who is currently mixing her own herbal elixirs.

"Just make sure nothing gets away, I guess," Jude answers, though he doesn't sound all that concerned—like he knows he's got this. Which I absolutely know he does.

I watch as he reaches for the tapestry and starts to pull the thread at the corner.

Nothing happens.

"Maybe you need to pull harder?" Mozart suggests from where she's peering over Luis's shoulder.

"I'm pulling pretty hard," Jude tells her, then tries again, and it's obvious that he's putting some serious muscle into it.

Nerves jitter through my stomach, and a little voice in the back of my head wonders what will happen if I'm wrong. But I ignore the doubts, because I'm not wrong. I *know* we need to unravel this tapestry, even though Jude is currently having a difficult time with it.

"Try a different corner," Izzy suggests.

But that doesn't work, either.

A glance at Jude tells me he's still trying—that he still believes I'm right. But it's obvious the others are starting to doubt, even before Luis quietly asks me, "Are you sure about this?"

"I was," I answer. But I can't see the glowing tapestry anymore, or all of the dots in space.

I close my eyes, hoping to be able to see something—anything— and there it is. The tapestry and all the many, many threads.

I move my hand over it, and the whole thing ripples. I do it again, this time with my hand several inches above it, and it does the same thing. Only it starts to glow again as well. And that's when it hits me.

"Don't touch it," I tell him. "Use your mind instead of your hands."

"My mind?" he asks. For the first time, there's a shred of doubt in his voice. "I'm not telekinetic."

"You don't have to be. But nightmares aren't tangible, right? I mean, you can't *actually* touch them. So maybe you can't touch them here, either. Maybe you just have to use your imagination to access them," I say. "Close your eyes. Picture the tapestry as thousands of little threads—"

I break off, because *he's already doing it.* In front of our shocked gazes, he pulls one long, feathery, silver thread from the tapestry.

"Oh my God..." Mozart exclaims in awe.

"He needs a jar!" Simon comments, and Luis shoves one down the table to Jude.

But Jude has already sent the nightmare floating toward a different jar and has turned his attention back to the tapestry, where he starts pulling a second thread.

Except there's a problem.

"Hey, Jude," Luis says nervously. "The nightmare isn't going in."

Jude stops mid-pull, a dark-purple nightmare in his hand. He uses his other hand to wave the first nightmare toward the jar a second time. It moves at his command, but it doesn't go in like it's supposed to. Instead, it wraps itself around the glass container.

"They've never done that before." Jude narrows his eyes in concentration and tries a third time. Once again, the nightmare follows his directions in all ways except it still doesn't slide home like it's supposed to.

Jude looks annoyed, and this time when he flicks his hand, the nightmare winds itself around his forearm before settling into his skin.

I suppose that's one way to solve the problem.

Jude goes back to harvesting the second nightmare, but it does the same thing when he tries to store it in a different jar. It flat-out refuses to go.

"Well, this is going to get interesting," Izzy says, eyeing Jude up and down. "Good thing you're tall."

Jude ignores her and keeps going. And going. And going.

Within fifteen minutes, he's pulled about five hundred nightmares off the tapestry. The only problem is he's used up nearly every centimeter of available skin on his body and he still has about three quarters of the tapestry left to go.

In fact, the next nightmare he pulls off—a bright-gold one—circles him, looking for a place to land. When it doesn't find one, it starts spinning and twisting its way around the room. Simon jumps out of its way, Mozart ducks when it twirls near her, and Luis dives under the table.

"Seriously?" I say, ducking down to look at him.

He doesn't even look embarrassed. "No way am I eating someone's face off."

"Is that another one of your nightmares?" Izzy asks. "Wicked."

"Not wicked," he tells her. "Disgusting."

Unfortunately, the nightmare is still at large and looking for a home. Plus, Jude has already pulled off another one, which I'm sure will be circling soon, and the last thing we want is for it to slip out of some crack in the door or something.

Not that I think Jude would let that happen, but these things are slippery.

Although I have no idea what I'm going to do with it if I *can* grab it, I still reach a hand out for it. But, unlike the others, it doesn't come near me. In fact, it gives me a wide berth.

I wonder what that's all about?

But Jude is currently holding two wiggling nightmares in his left hand as he continues to pick the tapestry apart with his right, so I know I've got to figure something out.

I have one more idea, but it's completely outrageous. Then again, everything about the last few days is outrageous. What's one more thing?

I walk up to him and lay a hand on the center of his back. The second I do, the nightmares in his hands start straining toward me.

Not only that, but the gray one floating around the room makes a beeline toward me, as well.

Maybe this idea isn't as outrageous as I thought. I glance up at Jude. "Do you trust me?" I ask.

In a moment that I will remember forever, Jude—who doesn't trust *anyone*—doesn't even have to think before he says, "Yes."

And just like that, something snaps taut inside me.

The sudden tug is so powerful that I stumble back—and into Jude, who also just lost his footing.

Our eyes meet, and the moment they do, a warmth like nothing I've ever felt blooms in my chest before fanning out to my entire body. It's a warmth that feels exactly like Jude when he's holding me, his big body and beautiful soul sheltering me from the world. And in that moment, as I feel his strength and determination and steadfastness and power deep inside myself, I figure out what just happened.

Our mating bond has snapped into place.

CHAPTER EIGHTY-SEVEN

WELL WORTH
THE MATE

For a moment, I'm too shocked to do anything but stare at Jude in awe. He must feel the same way—in fact, I know he feels the same way, since I can sense it deep inside myself. Also, he's gazing right back at me with the same awestruck look I'm sure I have on my face.

"Clementine," he whispers. "Did we just..."

"Did you just what?" Luis asks, poking his head out from under the table to check out what's going on. When we don't answer, he turns to the others. "Did they just *what*?"

I ignore him because right now I have something much more important to do. "I think we did," I whisper to Jude.

His whole face softens in that way I've only seen once before, in the dance hall. And then he reaches for me.

When he takes my hand, several of the nightmares on his skin crawl off of him and straight up my arms.

Jude tries to grab them back in alarm, but something tells me I have nothing to be worried about, so I shake my head at him. "Just wait."

We watch—Jude a lot more warily than I—as they make their way up my forearm to my biceps. They don't settle on my skin like they do with him, but they also don't try to arrow inside me like they did with some of the others.

Instead, they wrap themselves around me like a hug, spinning and twirling until they find their perfect spot.

Jude's eyes go wide as he watches the whole thing unfold. Once they finally settle, he murmurs, "They can't hurt you anymore."

"I don't think they want to hurt me," I counter, and I realize that I'm leaning into him. That just his presence alone is a magnet I have no desire to resist.

"Holy shit," Luis says as he finally figures out what just happened. "You're mated!"

"We're mated," I agree.

"That's totally badass," Mozart breathes, her eyes wide and starry. I recognize it because I feel the same way.

And though we're in the middle of an important, save-our-asses activity, we take a second to accept congratulations anyway. Because a moment like this only happens once in a lifetime, and it deserves to be acknowledged.

Remy's the last one to congratulate me, and when he leans in for a hug, he murmurs, "See, Kumquat? I told you you were going to be just fine."

"You knew?" I ask, surprised.

But he just shrugs in that mysterious way he has as he steps away.

I narrow my eyes at him, wishing that I could see useful things about the future like he obviously does, instead of this bizarre past, present, and future thing I've got going on.

What good does it do me to have to figure out who is with me in the present day and who in the room is actually from the past or future? Like the witch making her potions over— I freeze as I realize the witch is gone.

Which isn't a big deal, in and of itself, but so is the hotel employee putting jam on the shelves. Not to mention the teen vamp from the future who likes to use this as a make-out spot. They're *all* gone.

I turn back to Jude, who smiles at me as he goes back to sorting nightmares. There's only one of him—but there's only ever been one of him. Not to be sappy, but I can't help wondering if it's because he's my mate. He's my past, my present, and now my future in a way that no one else is or ever will be.

He hands me several more nightmares, and I slide them up my

other arm as I turn to look at Luis. And nope. He's still got three people—baby Luis, present Luis, and a very dim future Luis. For a second, I flash back to that moment at the dorm, when I saw him bleeding out from that chest wound. But I tamp it down, block it out. Because there's absolutely nothing I can do about that right at the moment, so I have to let it go.

"You okay?" Jude asks as he pulls two more nightmares out of the tapestry and passes them to me.

I loop them around my biceps as I answer, "Yeah. I'm actually really good."

After the last few days—the last few years—it's a strange feeling. But it's a nice one.

A couple of minutes later, Jude hands me close to a dozen more nightmares—now that he's been doing it for a while, he's really getting the hang of it. But the faster he goes, the faster I run out of room on my body, too.

But then I remember the idea I had earlier, right before the mating bond kicked in. I don't have a clue if it will work or not, but considering how well the nightmares are currently responding to me, I'm inclined to try.

I turn back to Jude and closely watch what he's doing to unravel the tapestry. After I have a pretty good handle on it, I take two of the nightmares he's given me and hang them in the air in front of me. And do my best to weave them together.

They bind to each other, but it's not easy, and it's definitely not pretty.

"What are you doing?" Mozart asks, getting close enough to watch but still leaving a wide gap between her and the nightmares.

"We're running out of space. I'm trying to weave them back together—and doing a shit job of it."

"Want some help?" Remy asks, moving close enough to actually touch the nightmares.

"I don't know if they'll respond to you," I tell him.

"It's worth a shot." He waves a hand, and I watch in amazement as the two nightmares weave perfectly together.

"How'd you do that?" I ask, shocked. Even Jude pauses what he's doing long enough to check out—and obviously approve of—Remy's handiwork.

Remy shrugs. "Nightmares and dreams exist outside of time," he explains. "So people who can exist in the spaces between time tend to be able to handle them a lot more easily than people who don't."

"Is that what you do? Exist in the spaces between time?"

He grins. "That's what *we* do, Clementine. It's not just me."

"Yeah, well, I think I'm going to have to disagree considering you can weave nightmares a hell of a lot better than me."

"Maybe." He reaches to take a nightmare from Jude, but in what may be the strangest thing I've seen today—which is saying something— it literally races away from him so fast that it ends up slamming into the wall across from us. "Or maybe we just have different roles to play here."

He nods to the two strands he's already woven together. "Pop a couple more nightmares up here and let's see what we can do."

I do as he asks, then watch in astonishment as he weaves them together as easily and better than any tapestry artist. But when Jude moves to hand him several more nightmares, they run away from him and circle me instead.

Remy shoots me an *I told you so* look as I grab them and hand them to him.

"What picture are you weaving?" Izzy asks from where she's keeping a safe distance—whether from Remy or the nightmares, I'm not sure.

"I'm not," he answers. "It's doing that itself."

"You're not making the picture?" I ask, surprised.

"I'm a time wizard, not an artist."

His answer only makes me more curious, because it reminds me of what the tapestry could do before it broke. I've never seen anything that could change pictures at whim like that.

"Hey!" Mozart says suddenly. I glance her way and realize she looks completely relieved. "That creepy feeling I've had since we got here is gone."

"What creepy feeling?" Simon asks, looking confused.

"Like someone's walking on my grave." She shudders. "Gave me the heebie-jeebies."

"There was a teenage vamp in here for a while," I tell her. "He's been bringing a different girl here every five minutes since we showed up. You're pretty much standing on his favorite make-out spot."

She jumps about ten feet to the left. "What the hell? Why didn't you tell me?"

I take a couple of bright-turquoise nightmares from Jude and pass them through to Remy, who adds them to the tapestry. For the first time, I understand why the chricklers are so many different colors. Because every nightmare is a different hue.

I want to ask Jude what some of the really fun-colored nightmares are. I imagine they're the milder ones—walking out of the house with no pants on or being attacked by a chipmunk—but I'm afraid he'll tell me it's the opposite, and I don't want him to ruin it for me.

So I take a yellow one and slide it over to Remy, who weaves it with a pink one that's already in the tapestry as I answer Mozart's question.

"Because it's crowded in here and there's nowhere else you could have gone. Plus, he disappeared a little while ago, so I figured you were solid."

"How long ago was that?" Remy asks.

I take several more nightmares from Jude and wrap them around my waist as my arms are getting full. "A few minutes ago, I guess."

He raises a brow. "How many minutes ago?"

"I don't know. Why?"

He doesn't answer, just watches me steadily. And then it hits me. "You think Jude's and my mating—" It's still so new that I trip a little over the word. "You think that somehow did something?"

Again, he doesn't answer, just takes the black-and-green nightmares I hand him and weaves them into the tapestry.

"I don't know, Remy. That's pretty egotistical, isn't it? Thinking our relationship can affect time and space like that?" I ask as Jude hands me a beautiful scarlet-colored nightmare. "I mean, it's important to us. But to the world? I don't think—"

"I guess that depends on what your powers are, doesn't it?" he interrupts, waving a hand at the tapestry he's weaving. Instantly, the colors rearrange into a more pleasing array.

"I mean, Jude's the Prince of Nightmares, so maybe what he does is important. But I'm just a manticore."

"Do you know any other manticore who sees ghosts?" Remy

shoots me a mild look as I hand him more nightmares. "Or who can see the past and the future the way that you can? Or who—"

"What are you trying to get at?" I ask, because I'm exhausted and have a bunch of nightmares draped all over me. While I really want to know what Remy thinks, I also want to get this show on the road.

"He's trying to say that you're not *just* a manticore," Jude says, resting a comforting hand on my shoulder before going back to unraveling. "There's something else going on with you."

"That doesn't make any sense."

Remy lifts a brow, a wicked gleam in his forest-green eyes. "Remind me again, Clementine. Who's your daddy?"

"What the fuck did you just say to her?" The nightmare Jude was in the middle of unraveling suddenly shoots across the room, sending everyone else into duck-and-dive mode. And just when we'd finally gotten Luis out from under the table...

Remy laughs, holding up a hand in a no-offense-meant gesture. "I'm just saying, your DNA comes from two different sources, Clementine. Half is manticore, half is..."

CHAPTER EIGHTY-EIGHT

WEAVE ME OUT OF IT

My stomach flips over even as I retrieve the nightmare Jude sent flying. Because I don't even know my father's name, let alone what kind of paranormal he is. I used to ask about him when I was younger, but no one in the family would tell me anything.

Carolina used to promise we'd figure it out some day, that she'd find a way to get me the answers I needed. But then she was sent away and Jude broke my heart, and for a long time I was too sad to worry about anything but getting through the day.

"Do you really think I broke time?" I ask, reeling under the implications as I hand him a dozen or so more nightmares—including the one Jude set loose after Remy's daddy comment.

"You didn't break anything," he answers, sliding them effortlessly into the tapestry. "But you definitely caused some time slips—you *and* Jude."

"Are you talking about time travel?" Mozart asks, eyes wide, and I realize everyone else in the room is as spellbound by this conversation as I am.

Then again, it is pretty wild.

"No." He pauses for a second, nightmares hanging half in and half out of the tapestry as he contemplates her question. "I mean, there *are* multiple schools of thought. But that's not what *I* think is happening here."

"So what exactly *do you* think is happening?" I ask as Jude hands me several more nightmares.

He starts to give me another mysterious look, and something inside me snaps. "Look, enough with this Jedi-master-you-must-figure-it-out-by-yourself bullshit that you're pulling. My brain feels like it's about to explode. I haven't slept, I haven't eaten, I've spent days seeing triple and being attacked by flickers, two of my best friends have died in the last forty-eight hours, I'm bruised and battered and bitten, and I just mated with the Prince of Nightmares while in the middle of helping unravel a tapestry to save the whole damn island from the most disgusting monsters in existence. So, if you could spell it out, that would be *great*."

"Attacked by what?" Luis stage-whispers.

"She said flickers," Mozart answers the same way. "But I don't know what those are."

"Ghosts from the future!" I snap at them just before Jude stops unraveling the tapestry and pulls me into his chest.

And though I want to say I've got this on my own—and I probably do—it still feels really nice to rest against his big, solid body for a few seconds and just breathe. Even still wet from the rain, he smells like honey and leather and sweet, sweet spices, and I let myself breathe him in as I listen to the steady beat of his heart beneath my ear.

The last half hour has been a lot, and I barely keep my thoughts straight. Between the flickers' bombshell about my mothers and now Remy's bombshell about time and also the whole mating bond thing, I'm amazed I still remember my name.

Jude gets it, too, because he murmurs, "We're almost there," in a voice so low it's almost inaudible.

I nod against his chest. "I know."

And take one more deep breath so I can pull his comforting scent all the way inside me before turning back to Remy.

"Sorry," I mutter begrudgingly.

"Me, too." He smiles in that way he has that makes you feel better for no reason. "I just feel like you can answer some of these questions better than I can—you just don't know it yet."

"I'm not so sure about that," I grumble.

"I am." He inclines his head. "But—that said—flickers aren't ghosts from the future. They're time slips."

"Okay, I've been attacked by time slips." I throw up my hands in exasperation. "What does that mean?"

Remy goes back to weaving. "It means all time exists simultaneously, we're just in different timelines. So something about you and Jude—"

"I vote for the fact that they refused to get their shit together for three fucking years," Izzy interjects from her seat on the rickety old steps.

Remy rolls his eyes at her as he takes a few more nightmares from me. "Sometimes it just takes the time it takes, Isadora."

"So, while they figure it out, Ember gets yo-yos tossed at her?" Simon asks, brows raised.

Ember glares at him. "To be fair, I don't think it was *at* me."

He and Mozart exchange a *yeah, right* look. "Oh, it was at you," Mozart teases her, while Jude hands me more nightmares.

He's almost done unraveling the tapestry, and Remy is almost done weaving the new one. There's obviously a picture in it—it already looks a million times better than the broken one—but for some reason, I can't distinguish what it is. It's almost like it's deliberately blocked.

"Either way"—Remy rolls his eyes at the group of them—"Jude has the nightmare thing going on, and everyone knows dreams exist out of time. You've got past, present, and future at your fingertips. Put those things together and you get a hundred-year-old yo-yo flying at your shins."

Shock reverberates through me at his words, and I'm suddenly very glad Jude was just holding me, because I can still feel his warmth even though a chill is shooting up my spine.

"But they just mated twenty minutes ago," Luis questions. "How the hell could that have messed up all this other stuff?"

"Because our mating didn't break anything." Jude sounds adamant about that, his hands flying as he unravels the last bit of tapestry. "It fixed what was broken."

He's right. It did. Including the two of us.

I think back to all the times over the last few days when weird shit happened.

Jude and I got paired up for the Keats project, and I saw my first flickers.

He kissed me, and the forest went batshit crazy.

He told me he loved me, and I started seeing the past, present, and future all together.

And through it all, these little time slips were happening, getting worse and worse each time we walked away from each other. Each time our mating bond didn't snap into place.

Because we've always been meant for each other.

Just a few days ago, I thought Jude was the puzzle that I was missing a bunch of pieces to. But now I realize the puzzle is so much bigger than I first thought. Because all the pieces of the last few days— everything I've seen, everything I've learned, everything I've done— are all spread out in front of me. I just need to put the picture together. And something tells me this tapestry will help.

Jude hands over the last nightmare strands to me, and I pass them to Remy. Then he comes over and wraps his arms around my waist as we watch it all come together.

But no matter how hard I study it, I can't see that picture.

Until, suddenly, I can.

Remy finishes weaving the last thread, and as he steps back, we all stare at the picture of a smiling man, right in the center of the tapestry.

"Who do you think that is?" Simon asks Remy.

"I have no idea," Remy answers, shaking his head. "He looks a little sleazy, though."

"More like a lot sleazy," I tell him.

"So what now?" Ember asks. "How do you want to try to catch the—"

She breaks off, eyes widening as the man in the picture suddenly steps right out of the tapestry and into the cellar with us. He's got shaggy brown hair, a long beard, a deep-purple smoking jacket that has seen better days, and the oldest, most run-down pair of slippers I've ever seen.

He's also, apparently, got an attitude because the first thing he says to us is, "Well, it's about time. It certainly took you guys long enough."

CHAPTER EIGHTY-NINE

ALL IS NOT FLOSSED

A bove us, the sky gives one more giant burst of thunder and then everything goes quiet. The rain stops. The wind grows still. And the lightning and thunder cease in an instant.

"What the fuck?" Luis exclaims. "Did the storm just...stop?"

"My bad," says the man from the tapestry. "My friends can be a little overly enthusiastic, and they've been looking for me for a while."

"What does that mean?" Ember demands.

"You didn't actually think that was a hurricane, did you?" He tsk-tsks, then turns to Simon. "I thought a mermaid would know better."

Simon's teeth clench. "Siren."

The man waves his hand. "Tomato, to-mah-toe," he says as he breezes by us.

"Umm, excuse me," Mozart starts, but the man ignores her.

So Izzy steps in, putting herself right in his path and demanding, "Who the fuck are you?"

"Come now, Isadora." He shakes his head, looking to all the world like a disappointed father. "A difficult childhood is no excuse to be profane."

"Yeah, well, jumping out of a tapestry is no excuse to be a dick, but that doesn't seem to bother you any," she shoots back.

He just laughs. "You always were quick on the uptake."

I wait for him to say something else, but instead he just crosses to the table in the middle of the room and picks up Luis's backpack. Then he pulls out the bottle of water he's got tucked into a side pocket and drains the whole thing in one long gulp.

"I apologize." He gives Luis a rueful look. "It's been ten years since I had a glass of water. Or anything else, for that matter."

"Ten years?" I repeat. "Is that how long you've been trapped in that tapestry?"

His face grows contemplative as he looks me over from head to toe. At first, I think it's because of the question I asked, but then he steps forward, hand extended. "There you are, my darling Clementine. I've been waiting to meet you for a long time."

"Ten years, perhaps?" I ask dryly. But I make no move to shake his hand. Call me suspicious, but shaggy-haired men who pop out of tapestries definitely don't rank high on my list of people to trust. To be fair, it's never been a long list, and it was shrinking even before this guy showed up.

"Perhaps." He scans the faces of everyone else, but his gaze lingers longest on Jude. "It's good to see you, my old friend."

I expect Jude to be as flummoxed as the rest of us, but he actually seems the most chill. Or maybe a better description would be the least disturbed. "That picture of the manticores playing poker was genius," he tells him.

"Wasn't it?" The man laughs. "Too bad I can't take credit for it. That was all Clementine's idea. She is a clever one." He beams at me like a teacher with a star pupil.

I don't even know how to respond, so I just keep watching him. To be fair, we all do.

Though, after a minute, he does say, "Will you excuse me for a moment, please?"

"It's a one-room cellar," I tell him. "There's not a lot of places to excuse yourself to."

He just smiles at me before walking into the corner and disappearing. Well, not really disappearing. It's more like he's hiding himself behind a blurry curtain.

Seconds later, the sound of him turning on a faucet fills the room. "What. The. Fuck?" Simon looks back and forth between the blurry corner and Jude. "Who the hell is that guy? And why the fuck is he gargling in here?"

"Beats me," Jude answers.

"What do you mean? He just called you 'old friend'!" I tell him.

"To be fair, it looks like we've shared this cellar for the last ten years. As for who he is? I have no clue. I'm guessing he's the guy who's been controlling the tapestry all along. When I was little, he'd make funny pictures in the tapestry to make me laugh. When I got older, they weren't so funny." He shrugs. "Other than that, I have no idea who he is or what he was doing in there."

"I can tell you one thing he wasn't doing," Ember says as a shower turns on behind the blurry curtain. "He wasn't showering."

True freaking story.

"And you never thought to ask him?" Mozart sounds as incredulous as I feel.

"To be fair, I never saw him. All I've ever known is that the tapestry changes regularly. For all I knew it was a bunch of nightmares making the pictures."

"You know what? I'm out," Izzy says, walking to the bookshelf and pulling the jar that opens the top part of the cellar. "Call me when the grooming routine is over."

"I'm coming with you," Mozart says.

I watch as Luis walks up the stairs after them and try not to freak out at how faint future Luis is looking now.

"Hey," Jude asks as everyone but Remy files upstairs. "What's wrong?"

I don't want to say it out loud—certainly nowhere Luis might overhear—so I just shake my head. "This seeing-in-triplicate thing is a giant pain, sometimes."

"I can probably help you with that," Remy says. "When I was first able to see the future, I couldn't block it out, either. It was there, all the time, which—as I'm sure you know—makes it hard to do anything."

"Really hard," I tell him. He definitely has my attention.

And Jude's, too, judging by how intently he's listening to our conversation. Remy nods like he understands because, apparently, he does. "I do this thing now that helps block what I don't want to see. I could show you how to do it if you want."

"Show me how to not see everyone in this room three different ways all at the same time?" I ask. "Yes, please!"

He nods, then pulls me into the corner opposite the blurry curtain. "I like to think of it as building a door between me and all the future," he tells me. "One that I can open whenever and however I want."

"Okay." That sounds reasonable. "How do I do it?"

He laughs ruefully. "I've never actually taught anyone how to do it before, so bear with me. But I'd say you start by picking something—or in your case, someone—that you're seeing in the past, present, and future."

"That's pretty much everybody in here, except for Jude."

"Okay, then. You can start by focusing on me." He steps back a little so I can get a better view of all three versions of him—Remy about fourteen, again in the present, and then finally at what I'd guess is about thirty.

"Now, once you can see all three versions, I want you to imagine closing a door on either the past or the future one."

I start to do what he says—it seems easy enough. But after four or five attempts, I still haven't gotten anywhere.

"It's not working," I tell him, frustrated.

"Yet," he says with a grin. "It's not working yet."

"Same thing."

He laughs. "Start smaller—"

"I am starting smaller. It's still not working."

He tilts his head to the side for a moment, studying me. Then asks, "What kind of door are you picturing?"

"I don't know. A door."

"That's not good enough. If this is going to work, you need to really know what the door you're closing looks like. Is it black with ornate molding? Brown wood with a peephole? White with a little wreath hanging on it? How can you expect to actually be able to close a door if you can't see what it looks like?"

I think about what he says for a minute, then close my eyes and try to do as he asks. But every time I try to picture a plain white door, my mind replaces it with a window—and not just any window, a stained glass window with three distinct colors. Red, purple, and green.

It doesn't take a genius to know that each of the colors is supposed to correspond with a time period, so I randomly assign them—red to the past, purple to the present, and green to the future.

And then I try my hand at closing all of Remy behind the window.

It takes a few different times, but eventually it gets to the point where I don't see him at all—like I can block the present Remy just as easily as the past or future Remy. And anytime I want to see one of them again, I crack open the corresponding window.

"You've got it!" Remy says when I try to explain to him what I did. "That's brilliant."

"Thank you," I tell him, just as the shower finally stops.

Jude calls up to the others, and as they start coming down the stairs, I turn to them and try to do the same thing I just did with Remy. It takes a little more doing—each one requires his or her own window—but eventually I've got it down until I only see the present version of each of them.

It's the most amazing feeling in the world, like a giant sensory overload has just been turned off. I've never been more grateful to anyone in my life.

After thanking Remy again, I lean into Jude just as the sound of an electric razor starts up.

"What the actual hell?" Luis says, looking baffled.

"Hygiene is very important," Jude says with a grin—an actual grin—that sends electric sparks dancing along my nerve endings.

Yes, I could very definitely get used to this Jude.

I turn toward Remy, wanting to thank him again for teaching me how to stay focused in the moment—with Jude and with the rest of my friends. But when I turn toward him, he's not the only one there.

CHAPTER NINETY

HERE COMES
THE SON

A flicker has shown up just behind Remy, a guy, about seventeen, dressed in jeans and a worn black shirt. He's tall—as tall as Jude, but not as heavily muscled—with spiky black hair, studs in his ears, and a scattering of freckles across his nose.

When he notices me looking at him, he grins widely.

Instinctively, I step closer to him, and as I do, I can't help but notice that he's got different-colored eyes—one blue and one green and silver. And that's when it hits me—he's in full color, unlike most of the flickers who are in black and white. And not only that, I realize I've seen him before, twice. He's the boy in the dungeon and the one in the T-Rex pajamas on the center mall in the rain, all grown up.

I raise a hand to wave to him, and his grin gets even bigger. "Looks like you found him," he tells me with a quick lift of his brows.

"Who?" I ask, confused.

"Dad, obviously." He gives a little nod toward Jude and the tapestry man, who has just stepped out from behind his blurry curtain.

Shock holds me immobile for a second, and I whisper, "What's your name?"

If possible, his grin gets even bigger. "It's Keats. I'm named after the poet. You know, from the class that started it all." Then he gives a little wave and disappears.

"Sorry, it's been a while since I've been able to take care of all that. And let me tell you, my skin is wicked dry," the guy from the tapestry says as I stare after Keats, reeling. "Do any of you have any lotion? I could really use some of the good stuff."

I kind of want to tell Jude what just happened, but I know there'll be time. So I turn to the guy and blink in surprise, because he looks a million times different than the man who walked in a couple of minutes ago.

Gone is the wild, shaggy hair. In its place is a sophisticated, slicked-back taper. His dirty, faded smoking jacket has been replaced with a three-piece pinstripe suit, complete with a bright-pink paisley tie. Even his shoes have been replaced—the old house slippers have become a pair of inlaid leather brogues. Oh, and the beard is completely gone.

I'm not sure how he managed all that in fifteen minutes in a corner, but magic is magic for a reason.

"Thank you for your patience," he tells the group of us with a benign smile, though I have the uncomfortable feeling that he's looking mostly at me.

I'm not the only one who notices that, either. Jude definitely picks up on it, and though he doesn't make any overt comments, he does position himself just a little bit in front of me.

The guy realizes Jude's doing it, too, and seems to grimace ever so slightly. Which makes me more inclined to appreciate Jude's protectiveness. If the guy is full of good intentions, why does he care where my mate stands?

Izzy gets fed up with the silence and demands, "So are you ever going to tell us who you are or we just supposed to guess?"

"Not to mention why your friends thought sending a storm like this to find you was a good idea?" Mozart adds.

"No guesswork necessary," he tells her with a small grin. "I'm Henri, the Oracle of Monroe."

"Oracle?" Remy speaks up for the first time. He sounds doubtful, but when I glance at him, his face is blank in a very un-Remy-like way. "You're an oracle?"

"I am, indeed." He doffs a sophisticated men's hat that appears out of nowhere before settling it back on his head. "And if I forgot my manners earlier, please forgive me. It's been a while since I've been around people. As for why my friends sent a seeker storm after me? I've been missing for seventeen years. I think they got tired of looking."

"Seventeen years?" I ask, eyes narrowed in suspicion. "I thought you were in the tapestry for ten?"

"It's a long story, one I'm not quite ready to talk about just yet. Needless to say, your aunt Camilla was involved." He shakes his head sadly.

"Aunt?" Luis repeats, looking confused. "I'm not sure you're much of an oracle, man. Camilla is her mother."

"Is she now?" Fury flashes across his face but is gone so fast I'm not certain I didn't imagine it.

I want to ask him how he knows when I just figured it out myself. But I'm not in the mood to have the conversation with the whole room—especially since I haven't even told my mate yet—so I bite my tongue, even as Henri steps closer.

"Would you mind indulging an old oracle for just a moment, Clementine?"

"I'm pretty sure that depends on what the indulgence is," I answer, brows raised.

"Can I shake your hand?" He holds his out for me in what is either a gesture of goodwill or a trap. But considering he didn't ask for anything and didn't try to make a bargain with me, I'm going to assume it's the former. Maybe.

But the moment my palm slides against his, an image of my mother—my birth mother—fills my consciousness. She's very pregnant and has a hand resting on the side of her stomach as she steps back and admires a mural she just painted on a bedroom wall.

The mural is my name, and each letter is filled with magical, fantastical things. I know the mural well; it was on my wall for nearly ten years before we finally painted over it. I had no idea my birth mother had painted it for me.

My lip trembles a little, but I bite it until it's steady again. No way am I breaking down about this now—not in front of a total stranger.

"I apologize for showing you the truth so harshly," he tells me. "But oracles need to face their own baggage before they ever try to be effective for anybody else."

"How is this *your* baggage?" I ask. "She was my mother."

"Good point," he says with a tiny little nod. "Makes you wonder, doesn't it?"

Any other time, absolutely. Right now? I'm tired of trying to figure things out and even more tired of learning stuff that turns my world upside down. So instead of making a guess as to what he's talking about, I settle for the one thing I know. "I'm not an oracle," I tell him. "I'm a manticore."

"Are you sure about that?" He tilts his head in question. "Because—"

He breaks off as a loud, high-pitched screech sounds from just outside the cellar doors.

"Shit!" Jude immediately leaps into action, grabbing the tapestry. "Remy, we need to get out of here now."

But Remy's already on it. He opens a portal just as the insane snake monster Luis and I had to fight in the dungeon rips the cellar doors off their hinges.

"Wait! Don't we need to fight it?" Ember asks, looking confused. "I thought that was the whole point of fixing that damn tapestry to begin with."

"We do," Jude agrees as he hustles everyone into the portal—including Henri. "I just don't think a tiny root cellar is the place to do it."

I have to agree with him. There's nowhere to go in the cellar to get away from it—if it stands in the middle of the room, its snake fingers can reach all four corners and everywhere in between.

I dive into the portal just before one of those snake fingers gets me, and I'm practically giddy with relief when I walk out into the center of the dance hall two seconds later. At least until I plow straight into Luis's back.

"Hey, what's—" I break off as I realize what he's staring at. What everyone is staring at.

The dance hall is crawling with monsters, each one more terrifying than the next.

CHAPTER NINETY-ONE

CAN'T KEEP A GOOD MANTICORE DOWN

"Am I wrong, or is that Kafka's worst nightmare?" Izzy growls as we walk out of the portal straight into Hell.

Now that the storm has passed, it's a direct contrast to the weather outside where the air is sweet, the sun is setting, and hermit thrush song fills the skies.

"Forget Kafka," I snarl as I scramble backward in a desperate attempt to avoid a giant eight-foot-tall cockroach-type monster with giant pincers at the end of each of its legs and two giant needles coming out of its mouth.

It's the needles that horrify me the most. What exactly is in them and what can they do to me? I scream bloody murder when it skitters across the floor headed straight for me.

"Shift, Clementine!" Mozart yells as she takes off running. Black wings sprout from her back as she does, and then she's launching herself into the air just in time to avoid two giant chricklers that have her in their sights.

She doesn't shift all the way—the room doesn't exactly lend itself to a giant dragon flying around it—but, then again, she doesn't have to. She's almost to the ceiling now and shooting fire toward various monsters in the room, being careful not to hit the chricklers, obviously. The last thing we need is an SUV-size chrickler. But the other monsters don't seem to have the same leveling-up capability that the chricklers do, and when she hits Cockroach Kong, it rolls over with a hiss.

At first I think it's injured, but then I realize its stomach is made of some fire-deflecting metal. Because that's exactly what the world needs from a giant cockroach: to be even harder to kill. Talk about a total nightmare.

In the meantime, Simon is running in a zigzag pattern through the ballroom, knives borrowed from Izzy in each hand. The chricklers start to swarm him, and he slams the knives into them, one after the other.

They pop like balloons.

"Do you think that will work on the other monsters?" I shout to Jude as we race toward the front of the dance hall, where Izzy and Remy are fighting back-to-back against two of the same massive monsters.

At first glance, they look like a cross between giant spiders and centipedes. They've got huge, hairy legs and a million eyes all over their long, skinny bodies. But then they turn, and I realize they've got wings, mouths full of jagged-edged fangs, and antennae made of some kind of sharp material that they're using to stab at Remy and Izzy over and over again.

As we get closer, I take Mozart's advice and shift into my manticore on the run. I'm not as smooth at it as Mozart—this is only my third time—but I get the job done.

So, while Jude jumps into the middle of the fray with Izzy and Remy, I race toward a disgusting lizard-type thing that's currently got Ember and Luis cornered on the left side of the dance hall. It's spewing some kind of noxious black goo all over them, and they definitely look like they can use some help.

Ember's in her phoenix form, and she keeps diving down, trying to go for its eyes. But apparently the monster doesn't care about its eyes because it doesn't appear bothered by her attack in the slightest.

Luis—who has shifted into his wolf—keeps going for its bony, skinny legs in an effort to bring it down. But every time he gets close to it, the goo comes flying at him like a projectile.

Figuring my best chance is to take it by surprise, I swoop down from above and grab it with my claws. Or, more specifically, *try* to grab it with my claws. Because the second I get close, a bunch of huge spikes pop out all over its back. It's like a porcupine straight from Hell.

I'm coming in fast and hard and nearly impale myself on them before I'm able to pull up at the last second. One does get me, however, slicing a long gash down my belly.

I gasp in pain as blood gushes out of me. The only plus side is the blood falls on the creature's face, blinding it just long enough for Luis to dive in and grab ahold of its front leg in his powerful jaws.

It freaks out, starts thrashing around and screaming in this weird, high-pitched chittering that makes my entire body cringe. And then it buries Luis beneath a continuous stream of its disgusting black slime.

I circle back around, a lot more confident coming in now than I was a minute ago. But with Luis out of the way, it's reached up and grabbed Ember in its sharp, crocodile teeth. It chomps down, and she screams loudly.

Panicked, I drop down beside it when it whirls around to confront me, Ember still in its mouth, so I skewer it with my tail, which—for once—is actually doing what I want it to.

I shake it around, and I can feel its body tearing as my tail makes a bigger and bigger hole through it. But it doesn't dissolve like the chricklers, and now I'm stuck, attached to this thing.

It finally lets Ember go, and she half flies, half falls several feet away from it. It takes advantage of its suddenly free mouth to twist around and spew tons of that noxious goo onto me as well.

I gasp as it hits me, because it burns like acid, even through my manticore fur. Desperate to avoid another round of the stuff coming at me, I flick my tail and send the thing flying several yards away from us.

Then I drop down to the ground to check on Ember, who's shifted back to her human form and is dragging herself along the ground as a new bunch of chricklers gets her in their sights.

I throw myself in front of them, determined to keep them from attacking her when she's in such bad shape. But I can barely see to fend them off as the goo currently feels like it's burning my eyes out of their sockets.

I wave my tail around, trying to keep the chricklers at bay, but they know I can barely see them. So they take instant advantage, going for my jugular while the lizard monster, acting seemingly unharmed, circles around to have another go at Ember. I wonder if it has the lizard ability to regenerate body parts.

Two of the chricklers leap at me at the same time, and I go down. Sharp teeth tear at my arms as I throw them up to protect my face and throat.

I can't help but smirk at the irony that after everything that's happened in the last two days, I'm going to end up dying at the hands of the same creatures that have spent the last three years tormenting me.

Apparently, fate has a really shitty sense of humor.

I tear at the chricklers with my teeth in a last-ditch attempt to save myself, but they're too far gone to notice. They're in a frenzy, their entire focus on tearing me and Ember to pieces. I try to get my tail out from under me so I can at least try to stab them, but I can't move well enough to do it.

Ember screams again, only this time it sounds a lot like a bird call. I turn my head, watch as she starts to fly up again, her phoenix determined to rise from the ashes. I try to follow her with my eyes, to make sure she escapes, but things start to go black, and all I can do is think about Jude.

Losing one's mate is one of the most agonizing experiences a paranormal can go through, and the idea of putting him through that devastates me even more than the real possibility of dying. He's been through too much. He doesn't need any more pain. I have to try to fight, but the emptiness is starting to spread through my body.

All of a sudden, an infuriated roar rips through the dance hall above me. Seconds later, the chricklers go flying backward, and then a shirtless Jude is crouching down in front of me.

His face is covered in scratches, his shoulder dripping blood from a series of bite marks, but his eyes are filled with concern and love as they search my face. "You okay, Kumquat?" he asks, voice fierce and eyes livid with rage.

Okay is a stretch. I nod and start to tell him to check on Ember, but he's already turning around to face the monsters. And for the first time ever, I realize I'm not just looking at Jude. I am most definitely looking at the Prince of Nightmares.

CHAPTER NINETY-TWO

IF YOU CAN DREAM IT, YOU CAN KILL IT

The first thing he does is let out a roar that commands the attention of everyone in the place, human *or* creature. Then he moves to stand directly in front of me—his way of protecting me from any more attacks.

Jude holds himself loosely, his legs spread and braced beneath him and his arms held out from his sides. The tattoos on his chest and arms start to glow and undulate, twisting and turning and sliding over his skin until his entire torso is alight with the magic and the power of a thousand nightmares. A flick of his fingers calls a gust of wind to him out of nowhere. It whips the air around him into a frenzy, and the entire room drops twenty degrees in an instant. And that's when Jude sends the nightmares spinning, twirling, flying off his body into the room around him.

He never would have done this before everything that happened at the cellar, never would have trusted himself to wield the nightmares like the weapons they are. But something happened the moment he realized what the Jean-Jerks had done, something switched inside him, and I know this incredible display of power and strength is the direct result of it.

The monsters must see it, too, because they back away, screeching and bellowing their displeasure. But it's already too late for them.

Jude has them in his sights, and it's obvious he's determined to settle this once and for all.

Like a conductor at a macabre symphony, he uses his hands and arms to weave a complicated pattern—a safeguard—with the nightmares into the air around us.

I expect them to flow out into the room immediately, even brace myself for whatever will come from that. But instead, they form a feathery barrier spinning around the two of us, gaining speed and power with each twist and turn, until they glow so brightly they light up the whole room.

And that's when Jude strikes.

A flick of his wrist, a quick spin of his hand, has the nightmares scattering in a hundred different directions. They cover the entire ballroom—and every monster in it—wrapping themselves around the creatures like full-body manacles.

The creatures thrash and scream, claw and gnash their teeth in frantic attempts to escape their astral shackles. But the nightmares hold them fast. Then Jude circles his hand in the air and jerks it backward. Within seconds, the nightmares start slowly, inexorably dragging the monsters closer to Jude.

The tapestry lies in the corner of the room. Remy makes a run for it and sprints it over to Jude. Simon and Mozart, looking very worse for wear, take it from him and unroll it on the ground at his feet.

And even though every muscle in my body aches and I want nothing more than to stay where I am, I force myself to stand up and move to join Jude. My mate.

He doesn't look at me—his concentration is too fierce for that as he continues to drag the bunch of snarling, furious, ferocious monsters straight toward himself.

But he manages to ask, for the second time, if I'm okay.

Like I've said before, 'okay' is a relative term—especially since I'm pretty sure I have a few broken ribs. So instead I respond with the only thing that's true.

"I'm fine," I tell him, and watch his eyes darken with concern.

"What can I do?" he asks.

"Get the monsters in the tapestry so we can finish this," I answer. "Do you know how to do it?"

"Not a fucking clue," he answers grimly.

That's what I was afraid of. We can't risk the chance that even one monster comes at us again or escapes—so I do the only thing I can think of.

I walk up to the nearest monster, ignoring Jude's startled objection. It's the squid monster that Izzy and I fought. I go inside my mind and find the stained glass window my brain has created for it.

I open the green window first, but the creature's future is completely absent.

So I move onto the second window—the red one that covers the past. Maybe if I can see how it was made, I can figure out how to get it back into the tapestry.

I brace myself for seeing our fight from its point of view. I scroll backward, past the gym. Definitely past the attack on Izzy and me in its cell. Past days and days of blood hunger and nothing else, until I finally spot my mom.

I slow down and let what works a lot like a video play back slowly as I try to find the moment when the monster came into being.

I pause for a second, try to assimilate what—and who—I just saw on the screen. My mother, yes. The squid thing, yes. But also a person who I'm pretty sure is *Jean-Luc's father.* He's definitely fae, definitely mafia, and has the same orange eyes as Jean-Luc.

But what the hell would he be doing at Calder Academy? And what the hell would he be doing with the monsters? It doesn't make any sense.

I wave a hand, and the video of the past starts playing again. I watch as he and my mother open a briefcase full of money, watch as seconds before, Jean-Luc's dad hands it to her, and then seconds before that, when they shake hands.

Suddenly, all of the snippets I've seen before start to make sense.

Except...instinct has me fast-forwarding a little past the handshake. And that's when I see Camilla catch a glimpse of Carolina hiding in the shadows as the dark deal unfolds.

I watch as the woman I thought was my mother doesn't flinch, doesn't let on by so much as a sideways glance that they're not alone. But I can see the fury in her eyes—and the fear.

But something is off. Carolina is off. I pause the "video." Look closer and closer and closer still. And then I see it—the strange glitter that trails behind every flicker. My mother isn't seeing Carolina. She's seeing a flicker of a future where she might have seen Carolina.

And that's when I know.

This is the night Jude kissed me in ninth grade. The night he was so afraid that a nightmare got loose. But there was no nightmare—and no mistake.

At least not on his part.

We kissed, and time cracked just for a moment. I saw my birth mother. And Camilla saw something she never should have seen, something that may never have even happened. And Carolina paid the ultimate price.

Everyone wants control—over themselves, over their lives, over the school they go to and the world they live in. But there's a fine line between control and chaos, and where you end up can often take you by surprise.

Tears well up inside me—sorrow, rage, pain. I beat them back, at least for now, because another vision is playing out in front of me.

Because everything is happening in reverse, I back the memories up further into the past and watch straight through as the squid creature is taken away. And how right before that, it's wrapped in a straitjacket-type garment.

Then I do it again, just to make sure I'm seeing what I think I'm seeing.

By the time I've seen it twice, I realize a few things. One, the creature I'm watching isn't the creature in front of me. I'm actually seeing things through this creature's eyes. Which means my mother made more of these squid things. Two, I've been very naive—and so has Jude. And three—my mother has been lying. A lot.

Because she didn't put these monsters back in the tapestry at all. No, from the time Jude was a little boy, she's been conning him into letting her make these monsters with his nightmares and selling them to the most dangerous paranormal organization in the country, maybe even in the world.

My stomach roils at the realization, and it takes every ounce of strength I've got not to throw up right here, right now.

So I swallow down the sickness that's destroying my insides and focus on the problem at hand. Namely that we have a whole hell of a lot of monsters here and no idea of how to get them back into the tapestry. We don't know if they can even *go* into the tapestry. I realize now that could have been just one more lie my mother told Jude.

Not knowing what else to do, I scroll back further and further, but I find no other clues.

"Did you find anything?" Jude asks, and for the first time I realize he's aware of what I've been doing.

"No," I answer, because now is not the time to explain what I just saw. "Except I don't think the monsters go into the tapestry fully formed."

"What do you mean?" He glances at me then, eyes filled with confusion. "That's how it's always been."

"No, that's how they always told you it was. But that's not how it actually is."

He starts to ask more, but as soon as his concentration slips, the monster in front of him starts to break free.

"So what do we do now?" he asks as he jerks his attention back to the monsters he's holding in thrall.

"I think we do what you did with the tapestry," I tell him, because I've got no better ideas. "I think we unravel the monsters, one nightmare at a time."

Jude's shoulders droop a little at my words, and I think it's because he's figuring out that something is very wrong here. That even if we manage to vanquish the monsters, there's a lot more to unpack here than just what's happened today.

I place a comforting hand on his back—though the truth is I don't know if it's him or myself that I'm trying to comfort.

Jude nods and says, "Okay. Let's try it."

I glance over to see Simon is sitting by Ember. I'm glad to see someone is taking care of her. But everyone else steps forward to join us. Once everyone is in place, I ask Jude, "Ready?"

The look on his face says that he is not remotely ready. But then he gives me that tiny little grin of his, and I know he's going to be okay.

He starts with the squid monster, loosening the nightmares wrapped around it but keeping them close if he needs them. But when he tries to unravel the monster like he did the tapestry, nothing happens.

He tries a second and a third time and still nothing.

"We could try stabbing them," Izzy suggests with a shrug. "It worked with the chricklers."

"I think I've got a better idea," Jude tells us. "But you might want to get behind me."

None of us has to be asked twice, not after what we've seen in the last forty-eight hours.

We angle ourselves to also provide cover for Simon and Ember, and when we're all safe behind him, he closes his eyes. Takes a deep breath. And flings his arms out.

As he does, every nightmare in the room unravels—including the ones wrapped around the monsters. The second they're free, they freak out and charge straight for us, blood in their eyes.

"Was this your big plan?" Luis asks skeptically. "Because I have to say I liked them better the other way."

Jude ignores him as he pulls all the nightmares back to him with one clench of his fist. But the monsters are closing in, too, racing for us like their very existences depend on it—because they do.

"We should run," Mozart says. "Right?"

"These aren't enough," Jude tells us, and for the first time he looks a little sick. "I need more."

"There aren't any more!" Luis tells him. "And if we wait much longer, those monsters are going to turn us into flesh spaghetti."

"Take mine," I tell him.

Jude turns shocked eyes to me. "What—"

"Take my nightmares!" I say again.

Remy joins in. "Take all of ours."

Jude stares at us for a second, as if gauging our seriousness.

"What are you waiting for?" Luis demands. "We sure as shit don't need them."

Jude nods and then holds out both his hands and closes his eyes again, despite the fact that the monsters are bearing down on us.

"Hurry!" Mozart urges.

Jude nods, and then he starts to pull. He pulls and pulls and pulls, and I watch in wonder as nightmares flow out of us and into the glowing ball of nightmares he has spinning in front of him.

Even after everything that happened in the cellar, I'm still astonished at how beautiful the nightmares are. I assumed they would all be dark, scary shades. But they're not. So many of them are brightly colored and shiny, and I realize that this is what Jude was talking about.

These are nightmares in their purest form, and they aren't scary at all. No, it's not the nightmares themselves we have to fear. But the monsters that we create from them.

Once Jude's harvested them all, once he has collected every last nightmare the room has to offer, he flicks his fingers, and the huge spinning ball in front of him flies straight at the monsters—and not a second too soon, because they're just about to bear down on us.

The monsters scream as the nightmares hit them, then arrow inside.

And then we wait, breath held, to see what happens next. And at first, the answer is nothing. The monsters just stand there, swaying, almost like they're in shock.

"What's going on?" Izzy whispers, and I realize she's got her knives in her hands as she looks from one monster to the next.

"I don't know," I whisper back.

There's a moment of deafening silence and—the first monster explodes. And then they all do. One after the other, the thousands upon thousands of nightmares they were made of rain down on us like confetti.

CHAPTER NINETY-THREE

DO NOT GO GENTLE INTO THAT GOOD NIGHTMARE

N o blood, no gore. Just so many nightmares filling the air that it's impossible to see through them all.

At least not until Jude starts gathering them up and feeding them into the tapestry, one by one by one.

I watch, a little in awe, as he slowly, methodically, clears the room one nightmare at a time. And I can't help thinking, despite everything we've been through, just how lucky I am to have this strong, powerful, beautiful mate.

Somehow, against the odds, we've weathered the storm and made it through to the other side. We've learned how to face the monsters. More, we've learned how to face them together. And though we have wounds that will never heal, we have each other. And for now, that's more than I ever dreamed we'd have.

Eventually Jude feeds the last nightmare into the tapestry, and we all kind of watch it for a second, waiting for the next Henri to appear. But it seems that was a one-time occurrence.

Thank God. Because I don't think I can handle more than one of that man. As it is, he spent the entire fight hiding out on the balcony and is only now coming down to join the rest of us. There's nothing quite like an oracle afraid to live in the present.

The coward.

I turn back to Jude to see if he's okay, but he's already across the dance hall, on his knees beside Ember and Simon.

I don't know why, but the moment I see him, ice slams through me, and I take off running toward them. As I do, I fumble inside myself for Ember's window, and once I find it, I try to open up the colors. But they fade even as I reach for them—first the green and then the purple, until all that's left is the red of the past.

And I know.

Even before I get to them, I know.

Even before Simon lets out a heartbreaking cry, I know.

Ember is gone.

I sprint the last few yards, then drop to my knees beside Jude. "What happened?" I gasp.

"I thought she would do it," Simon whispers. "I really did. I mean, she was hurt—I knew she was hurt, but she kept struggling, kept trying to burn, kept trying to rise—" His voice breaks, and his gorgeous siren eyes fill with tears. "And when it was almost over, when she was only embers, she said—" This time he breaks off on a sob. I start to hug him, but suddenly Mozart is there, too. She puts a hand on his back and one on Jude's, and then the three of them crumble into each other.

And though Jude's my mate, though I love him through time and space, and dreams and nightmares, through anything this world—or the next—has to throw at us, I also know that right now he needs to be with the friends who have been his family for the last three years.

I pull back a little, start to get up so they can have their privacy. But Jude's hand flashes out and fastens onto mine like it's a lifeline.

"Stay," he whispers.

And so I do.

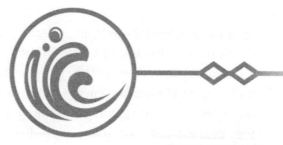

MY DARLING CLEMENTINE

- JUDE -

The thing about nightmares is sometimes they end.

Sometimes dawn breaks across the sky.

Sometimes the sun rises over the ocean.

And sometimes, if you're lucky, the girl you love finds you before you can lose yourself completely.

The wall that's kept us penned up inside the school is rubble now, and I sink down on a pile of broken bricks and wait for a still-sleepy Clementine to make her way across the debris-strewn beach to me.

The night is my domain, and I spent it the way I've spent so many nights before—harvesting nightmares while she slept. But it feels fucking amazing to watch her walk down the sand and know that she's come to find me. That she'll always come to find me and now I have the right—and the privilege—to do the same for her.

She smiles at me when she gets close, and it lights up her whole face. Makes her blue eyes sparkle and her face shine in a way I'll never take for granted. It was too fucking hard getting here—there's no way I'll ever not be grateful for her persistence, her kindness, her *love*.

Her scarred hand sliding into mine feels like a dream. And so does she when she settles next to me, snuggling into my side. Nothing in my whole fucked-up life has ever felt better than this moment, and I breathe it in—breathe her in.

"You okay?" she asks. Her voice is soft, but her body pressed against mine feels strong. Powerful. Real.

Ember's death is an open wound in a sea of scars, but somehow holding my mate makes the misery a little less raw, the grief a little more bearable.

"I'm fine," I answer, because it's true, and I don't ever want to lie to Clementine.

"Yeah," she says with a sad sigh. "Me too."

I pull her closer, try to give her back some of the strength, some of the shelter, she gives me.

I don't know if it works, but I know that I feel her release a long, slow breath as her body relaxes against mine.

"I don't want to see my mother today," she whispers. "I'm not ready."

"We'll get through it," I tell her, because I've got no fucking interest in seeing her mother, either. Between the way she hurt Clementine, what she did to Carolina, and the way she duped me into giving her the means to make monsters to sell as weapons on the black market, I'm good with never seeing her again.

But that's not a choice I get to make. One of the many, many downsides of Calder Academy is there aren't a lot we get to make. Mozart seems to think the last twenty-four hours will change that, but I'm not so optimistic.

As if just thinking about the headmaster has conjured her, a portal shimmers open just up the beach from us.

Apparently, the cavalry has arrived.

Clementine stiffens against me, and I squeeze her just a little more tightly. If I could take this from her, I would. I would take everything that hurts her.

But in a surprise move that none of us saw coming, it isn't Clementine's mom who walks out of the portal. Instead, it's Caspian, arms laden with first aid kits and food. He's followed by several Calder Academy teachers, and together they struggle their way up the beach as the portal closes.

Like everything else at this school, it's a bargain-basement cavalry. "Clementine! Jude!" Caspian yells when he catches sight of us. He tries to speed up and ends up falling, face-first, into a massive bag of dill pickle potato chips. "We've come to save you!"

"Oh, is that what we're calling this?" I ask softly.

Clementine elbows me in my ribs. "Behave, he's trying."

I roll my eyes in response, but I keep my sarcasm to myself, as requested. Besides, it's not Caspian's fault the last twenty-four hours have played out the way they have. If he wants to think he's rescuing us, far be it from me to disabuse him of the notion.

We watch as he picks himself back up, walks two steps, and promptly falls over again. "Come on," I say, pulling Clementine up. "Let's go rescue the rescue crew."

If left to his own devices, I'm afraid he'll hurt himself—not to mention we'll end up stuck here 'til the next hurricane. We make our way down the beach to her cousin, and while I help him to his feet, Clementine picks up all the supplies he's dropped like breadcrumbs over the sand.

"I'm so glad you're all right!" he gushes once we make it to the wall. "I know it's been terrible for you being here with no electricity, but don't worry. Everyone will be here soon, and we'll get everything fixed."

If what he means by fixing things is going back to the fucked-up way they were before, then they can stay broken. We sure as hell will.

"Who's everyone? And where's my—" Clementine's voice breaks, but I know what she was about to ask.

And so, apparently, does Caspian. "Your mom's totally okay. I swear," he reassures Clementine. "She'd planned on coming, but some last-minute problems kept her and my dad back at the warehouse. But you'll be seeing her soon enough. We just need to round everyone up and..."

This time it's his voice that fades off.

"We've found as many as we can," Clementine tells him, voice hoarse. "We've moved all the bodies we could into to the gym. Everyone else's location is marked. Danson has the master list."

She's trembling now, and I know she's thinking about Ember and all the others we couldn't help.

"You need to put a couple of the teachers on finding the Jean-Jerks," I tell him as I rub a soothing hand up and down Clementine's back. "They've holed up somewhere, but a lot of the deaths are their fault."

"A lot?" Caspian's eyes widen. "How many deaths were there? And what did they do?"

I don't even know what the fuck to say to that, so I just shake my head. I know I'll have to talk about it eventually, but not yet. Not when I can still see that fucking monster with Ember in its teeth.

Clementine shifts like she's about to try to answer the unanswerable, but before she can, Henri's voice travels across the air to where we're standing.

"Oooh, breakfast!" I turn to see Henri and two other men—all in velvet smoking jackets and monogrammed slippers—shamble through the wall onto the beach. They've got bloody marys in one hand and old-fashioned paper fans in the other. "By any chance, did you bring any *pain au chocolat*, dear boy?" he asks Caspian. "I'm a bit peckish after all that oracle whist. Winning so many times builds up an appetite."

The other men look deeply annoyed, and the one in the puke-green jacket snarls, "I'm beginning to regret searching for you so hard."

"So hard? I feel like you took your time." Henri sniffs.

"Oh really?" the one in piss yellow snaps. "Next time we'll leave you in that rug. And make sure it finds a home with someone who has several incontinent dogs."

"You wouldn't dare!" Henri says, looking very offended.

"Check your crystal ball," Puke Green says. "That'll tell you what we dare."

Caspian's eyes are huge as he looks back and forth between the three men. And I've got to say, if this is who the world is depending on, no wonder things are so totally fucked.

"What on earth is happening here?" Caspian demands, looking between us and them. "Who are you? How did you get here? And why would I bring you pain au anything?"

Henri looks offended at the questions, but before he can work up a retort, another portal opens just a few feet away. A puff of sparkly smoke explodes out of it seconds later, drenching Caspian with glitter.

Puke Green rears back in surprise. "What the hell is that?"

"Our biggest donor, of course," Caspian huffs. "She insisted on touring the campus after the storm. I think she wants to assess the facilities and see how big her contribution needs to be."

"Since when do we have donors?" Clementine asks, bewildered.

"How do you think we've been able to grow our beautiful menagerie so quickly?" Caspian asks. "Madame Z can't wait to see it."

Clementine glances at me out of the corner of her eye as if to say, "You want to break it to him or shall I?"

I nod at her to do the honors. But before she can break the news that the menagerie has menagered its last menager, an array of that fucking sparkly Z-shaped kibble we used to feed the monsters flies out of the portal.

"Come to Madame, my darlings!" says a low, rich voice. "Madame is so excited to see you!"

Out of nowhere, the three remaining Jean-Jerks come running down the beach and dive into the portal.

I'm not sure if she was trying to call them or some long lost dogs, but either way, I'm tempted to follow, if for no other reason than to kick their asses once and for all.

Only knowing the very special brand of hell they're in for keeps me where I am. We'll see what—if anything—is left when she's done with them. "You mean all we had to do to find them was throw some kibble?" Clementine asks, bewildered.

"Were those the Jean-Jerks?" Simon asks as he and the rest of our friends come up behind us. "Should we go after them?"

"Something tells me they'll show back up soon enough," I answer.

"What's going on?" Mozart asks.

"This island is finally getting someone with some class, obviously," Piss Yellow answers, straightening up and smoothing a hand over his shiny, bald head.

"Maybe she brought the profiteroles," Henri suggests hopefully, but I know better.

Because that very distinctive voice can only belong to one person, and she's not the profiterole type.

I turn to Clementine. "I'm sorry," I tell her.

She looks confused. "Sorry for what?" But she squeezes my hand in a very definite I-got-you-no-matter-what gesture. I don't have a chance to answer before a tall woman in a silver sequin jumpsuit emerges from the portal.

Apparently, she's currently known as Madame Z. But I used to know her by another name. Zelda, aka Mommy, aka my mother.

The very mother I haven't seen or heard from even once in the ten years since she dropped me off at this place with the tapestry and instructions not to kill anybody else. It was exactly as awkward—and as awful—as it sounds.

I can't say that I've missed her.

I look her over as she closes the distance between us. Aside from her blond hair going completely silver, she's exactly the same, right down to the sequins and the self-absorption.

She pauses a few feet from us to get the lay of the land. Her gaze goes from me to Clementine to Henri. And the first thing she says to me in ten years is a very wry, "I didn't realize it was time for the parents to meet."

At first, I don't know what the fuck she's talking about. But then Henri sighs and says, "Looks like the cat's out of the rug." He throws his arms open. "Come to Papa, my darling Clementine."

Clementine stiffens against me, her gaze going back and forth between Henri and my mother like she's watching a ping-pong match.

"What are you talking about?" she finally squeaks out. She's grabbed onto my hand and is squeezing hard enough to cut off circulation, but I don't blame her. We thought all the shit ended with the storm, but it looks like we need to brace for another whole round. But then suddenly a look of understanding comes over her eyes. "Wait a minute…"

He sighs heavily. "That's right, Clementine. I'm sorry you had to find out this way. I had planned on being more delicate, but some people"—he shoots my mother a dirty look—"don't have a delicate bone in their body."

Henri holds out a hand to Clementine, but instead of moving toward him, she backs up. Not that I blame her. She still hasn't had time to deal with everything she just figured out about her mom. This is the last thing she needs.

It's my turn to squeeze her hand. "It's going to be okay," I say for her ears only. "We'll get through this."

She shakes her head, like she's not so sure. But she stops retreating. "How could you possibly be my father?" she asks. But I can tell she believes him—as do I. Being the daughter of an oracle definitely explains her ability to see the past and future.

"It's pretty simple, really. Your mother—your real mother, not Camilla, obviously—and I had a..." He pauses, at a loss for words.

"Fling," Puke Green says, taking another sip of his bloody mary. "They had a fling, she got pregnant, it didn't work out between them. And here we are."

"It's a little more complicated than that." Henri shoots him a dirty look, too. "Once I knew I had a daughter, I came looking for you. Camilla refused to let me see you, and when I told her I would fight for access to you, she imprisoned me. Your mother died giving birth to you because her mind exploded under your power to see the past and the future. Camilla has been terrified ever since that if you left the island and got your powers, the same would happen to you. I'm pretty sure you know the rest."

Clementine makes a low sound in her throat as she sags against me. I hold her tight, keep her on her feet when I think she might have otherwise gone down.

"Get me out of here," she whispers to me.

"Already on it," I answer as I propel her up the beach. Our friends follow, Luis falling into step with us on Clementine's other side. He looks about as pissed as I feel.

"Aren't you even going to say hello, Jude?" Madame Z or whatever the fuck she's calling herself these days yells after us.

I don't bother to answer. Because fuck her and whatever she hopes to achieve by this little farce.

"I guess we're doing this the hard way, then." She claps her hands, and the sound of a couple dozen feet hitting the sand echoes down the beach.

We turn around just in time to see more than a dozen fae guards storm out of the portal.

"What the fuck?" I step in front of Clementine, braced for a fight.

But apparently, we're not the targets. Instead, the guards seize Henri and his two friends—none of whom look exactly surprised. Then again, they probably saw it coming.

"Hey!" Clementine shouts, pushing past me. "Let them go!"

"Now that I have a matched set?" my mother asks, brows raised.

"I don't think so, dear."

A wave of her hand has the guards dragging the oracles toward the portal. "So nice of you to find Henri for me, Giuseppi and Fernando. And kudos on your little storm—I did so enjoy the waves. Now, if you will excuse me. This sand really is wreaking havoc on my pedicure."

I lunge for her, but she disappears into the portal before I can even get close.

"No need for violence, dear man!" Henri says to the guard dragging him along. "I just want to say goodbye to my daughter first."

When the fae pays him absolutely no mind, I grab him by the arm—and get several fists to my face and body for my trouble from the other fae guards.

In the confusion, Henri reaches out as if to grab Clementine. But the guard jerks him away at the last second, and his hand bumps Simon instead.

"I'll be fine!" he calls as they shove him into the portal. "But remember! The future is just a flip of the cooooooooooin."

His voice echoes as he disappears.

I race toward the portal—we all do—but the last fae guards beat us to it, and just like that, it closes.

"What the fuck just happened?" Izzy asks, looking as bewildered as I feel.

"Nothing good," Clementine answers.

"You want me to build a portal?" Remy asks. "We can follow them."

"We don't even know where they went," Izzy tells him. "Just because they have the Fae Guard with them doesn't mean they returned to the Fae Court. And if they did, they'll definitely be waiting for us when we get there."

"She's right," Clementine says grimly. "We need to figure out what's going on before we do anything else."

"Yeah, well, maybe you can start with me," Simon says, and he sounds stranger than I've ever heard him.

Mozart must think so, too, because she whirls around. "What's wrong?"

"I think I have a problem," he answers. "Everything suddenly looks really weird. And I'm pretty sure it's because Clementine's dad left me a gift."

"What kind of—" Clementine breaks off in horror as he reaches into his pocket and pulls out a large gold coin and holds it up for us to read.

One side says Loves Me, the other side says Not.

"What do you think that means?" he asks.

I'm not sure what the words imply, but I do know what the coin means. "That we are totally fucked."

Can't get enough?

*Keep turning pages to read an excerpt of **Crave** by Tracy Wolff!*

If You're Not Living on the Edge, You're Taking Up Too Much Space

I stand at the outer tarmac door staring at the plane I am about to get on and try my hardest not to freak out.

It's easier said than done.

Not just because I'm about to leave behind everything I know, though up until two minutes ago, that *was* my main concern. Now, though, as I stare at this plane that I'm not even sure deserves the dignity of being called a plane, a whole new level of panic is setting in.

"So, Grace." The man my uncle Finn sent to pick me up looks down at me with a patient smile. Philip, I think he said his name was, but I can't be sure. It's hard to hear him over the wild beating of my heart. "Are you ready for an adventure?"

No. No, I am *not* the least bit ready—for an adventure or anything else that's about to come my way.

If you had told me a month ago that I would be standing on the outskirts of an airport in Fairbanks, Alaska, I would've said that you were misinformed. And if you had told me that the whole reason I was in Fairbanks was to catch the tiniest puddle jumper in existence to what feels like the very edge of the world—or, in this case, a town on the edge of Denali, the highest mountain in North America—I would have said that you were high as a freaking kite.

But a lot can change in thirty days. And even more can get ripped away.

In fact, the only thing I *have* been able to count on these past few weeks is that no matter how bad things are, they can always get worse…

1

Landing Is Just Throwing Yourself at the Ground and Hoping You Don't Miss

"There she is," Philip says as we clear the peaks of several mountains, taking one hand off the steering column to point to a small collection of buildings in the distance. "Healy, Alaska. Home sweet home."

"Oh, wow. It looks…" Tiny. It looks really, really tiny. Way smaller than just my neighborhood in San Diego, let alone the whole city.

Then again, it's pretty hard to see much of anything from up here. Not because of the mountains that loom over the area like long-forgotten monsters but because we're in the middle of a weird kind of haze that Philip refers to as "civil twilight" even though it's barely five o'clock. Still, I can see well enough to make out that the so-called town he's pointing at is full of mismatched buildings randomly grouped together.

I finally settle on, "Interesting. It looks…interesting."

It's not the first description that popped into my head—no, that was the old cliché that hell has actually frozen over—but it is the most polite one as Philip drops even lower, preparing for what I'm pretty sure will be yet another harrowing incident in the list of harrowing incidents that have plagued me since I got on the first of three planes ten hours ago.

Sure enough, I've only just spotted what passes for an airport in this one-thousand-person town (thank you, Google) when Philip says, "Hang on, Grace. It's a short runway because it's hard to keep a long one clear of snow or ice for any amount of time out here. It's going to be a quick landing."

I have no idea what a "quick landing" means, but it doesn't sound good. So I grab the bar on the plane door, which I'm pretty sure exists for just this very reason, and hold on tight as we drop lower and lower.

"Okay, kid. Here goes nothing!" Philip tells me. Which, by the way, definitely makes the top five things you don't *ever* want to hear your pilot say while you're still in the air.

The ground looms white and unyielding below us, and I squeeze my eyes shut.

Seconds later, I feel the wheels skip across the ground. Then Philip hits the brakes hard enough to slam me forward so fast that my seat belt is the only thing keeping my head from meeting the control panel. The plane whines—not sure what part of it is making that horrendous noise or if it's a collective death knell—so I choose not to focus on it.

Especially when we start skidding to the left.

I bite my lip, keep my eyes squeezed firmly shut even as my heart threatens to burst out of my chest. If this is the end, I don't need to see it coming.

The thought distracts me, has me wondering just what my mom and dad might have seen coming, and by the time I shut down that line of thinking, Philip has the plane sliding to a shaky, shuddering halt.

I know exactly how it feels. Right now, even my toes are trembling.

I peel my eyes open slowly, resisting the urge to pat myself down to make sure I really am still in one piece. But Philip just laughs and says, "Textbook landing."

Maybe if that textbook is a horror novel. One he's reading upside down and backward.

I don't say anything, though. Just give him the best smile I can manage and grab my backpack from under my feet. I pull out the pair of gloves Uncle Finn sent me and put them on. Then I push open the plane door and jump down, praying the whole time that my knees will support me when I hit the ground.

They do, just barely.

After taking a few seconds to make sure I'm not going to crumble— and to pull my brand-new coat more tightly around me because it's literally about eight degrees out here—I head to the back of the plane to get the three suitcases that are all that is left of my life.

I feel a pang looking at them, but I don't let myself dwell on everything I had to leave behind, any more than I let myself dwell on the idea of strangers living in the house I grew up in. After all, who cares about a house or art supplies or a drum kit when I've lost so much more?

Instead, I grab a bag out of what passes for the tiny airplane's cargo hold and wrestle it to the ground. Before I can reach for the second, Philip is there, lifting my other two suitcases like they're filled with pillows instead of everything I own in the world.

"Come on, Grace. Let's go before you start to turn blue out here." He nods toward a parking lot—not even a *building*, just a parking lot—about two hundred yards away, and I want to groan. It's so cold out that now I'm shaking for a whole different reason. How can anyone live like this? It's unreal, especially considering it was seventy degrees where I woke up this morning.

There's nothing to do but nod, though, so I do. Then grab onto the handle of my suitcase and start dragging it toward a small patch of concrete that I'm pretty sure passes for an airport in Healy. It's a far cry from San Diego's bustling terminals.

Philip overtakes me easily, a large suitcase dangling from each hand. I start to tell him that he can pull the handles out and roll them, but the second I step off the runway and onto the snowy ground that surrounds it in all directions, I figure out why he's carrying them—it's pretty much impossible to roll a heavy suitcase over snow.

I'm near frozen by the time we make it halfway to the (thankfully still plowed) parking lot, despite my heavy jacket and synthetic fur-lined gloves. I'm not sure what I'm supposed to do from here, how I'm supposed to get to the boarding school my uncle is headmaster of, so I turn to ask Philip if Uber is even a thing up here. But before I can get a word out, someone steps from behind one of the pickup trucks in the lot and rushes straight toward me.

I think it's my cousin, Macy, but it's hard to tell, considering she's covered from head to toe in protective weather gear.

"You're here!" the moving pile of hats, scarves, and jackets says, and I was right—it's definitely Macy.

"I'm here," I agree dryly, wondering if it's too late to reconsider foster care. Or emancipation. Any living situation in San Diego has got to be better than living in a town whose airport consists of one runway and a tiny parking lot. Heather is going to die when I text her.

"Finally!" Macy says, reaching out for a hug. It's a little awkward, partly because of all the clothes she's wearing and partly because— despite being a year younger than my own seventeen years—she's about eight inches taller than I am. "I've been waiting for more than an hour."

I hug her back but let go quickly as I answer. "Sorry, my plane was late from Seattle. The storm there made it hard to take off."

"Yeah, we hear that a lot," she tells me with a grimace. "Pretty sure their weather is even worse than ours."

I want to argue—miles of snow and enough protective gear to give astronauts pause seem pretty freaking awful to me. But I don't know Macy all that well, despite the fact that we're cousins, and the last thing I want to do is offend her. Besides Uncle Finn and now Philip, she is the only other person I know in this place.

Not to mention the only family I have left.

Which is why, in the end, I just shrug.

It must be a good enough answer, though, because she grins back at me before turning to Philip, who is still carrying my suitcases. "Thanks so much for picking her up, Uncle Philip. Dad says to tell you he owes you a case of beer."

"No worries, Mace. Had to run a few errands in Fairbanks anyway." He says it so casually, like hopping in a plane for a couple-hundred-mile round-trip journey is no big deal. Then again, out here where there's nothing but mountains and snow in all directions, maybe it's not. After all, according to Wikipedia, Healy has only one major road in and out of it, and in the winter sometimes even that gets closed down.

I've spent the last month trying to imagine what that looks like. What it *is* like.

I guess I'm about to find out.

"Still, he says he'll be around Friday with that beer so you guys can watch the game in true bro-mance style." She turns to me. "My dad's really upset he couldn't make it out to pick you up, Grace. There was an emergency at the school that no one else could deal with. But he told me to get him the second we make it back."

"No worries," I tell her. Because what else am I supposed to say? Besides, if I've learned anything in the month since my parents died, it's just how little most things matter.

Who cares who picks me up as long as I get to the school?

Who cares where I live if it's not going to be with my mom and dad?

Philip walks us to the edge of the cleared parking lot before finally letting go of my suitcases. Macy gives him a quick hug goodbye, and I shake his hand, murmur, "Thanks for coming to get me."

"Not a problem at all. Any time you need a flight, I'm your man." He winks, then heads back to the tarmac to deal with his plane.

We watch him go for a couple of seconds before Macy grabs the handles on both suitcases and starts rolling them across the tiny parking lot. She gestures for me to do the same with the one I'm holding on to, so I do, even though a part of me wants nothing more than to run back onto the tarmac with Philip, climb back into that tiny plane, and demand to be flown back to Fairbanks. Or, even better, back home to San Diego.

It's a feeling that only gets worse when Macy says, "Do you need to pee? It's a good ninety-minute ride to the school from here."

Ninety minutes? That doesn't seem possible when the whole town looks like we could drive it in fifteen, maybe twenty minutes at the most. Then again, when we were flying over, I didn't see any building remotely big enough to be a boarding school for close to four hundred teenagers, so maybe the school isn't actually in Healy.

I can't help but think of the mountains and rivers that surround this town in all directions and wonder where on earth I'm going to end up before this day is through. And where exactly she expects me to pee out here anyway.

"I'm okay," I answer after a minute, even as my stomach somersaults and pitches nervously.

This whole day has been about getting here, and that was bad enough. But as we roll my suitcases through the semi-darkness, the well-below-freezing air slapping at me with each step we take, everything gets superreal, superfast. Especially when Macy walks through the entire parking lot to the *snowmobile* parked just beyond the edge of the pavement.

At first, I think she's joking around, but then she starts loading my suitcases onto the attached sled and it occurs to me that this is really happening. I'm really about to ride a snowmobile in the near dark through *Alaska* in weather that is more than *twenty degrees below freezing*, if the app on my phone can be believed.

All that's missing is the wicked witch cackling that she's going to get me and my little dog, too. Then again, at this point, that would probably be redundant.

I watch with a kind of horrified fascination as Macy straps my suitcases to the sled. I should probably offer to help, but I wouldn't even know where to begin. And since the last thing I want is for the few belongings I have left in the world to be strewn across the side of a mountain, I figure if there was ever a time to leave things to the experts, this is it.

"Here, you're going to need these," Macy tells me, opening up the small bag that was already strapped to the sled when we got out here. She rummages around for a second before pulling out a pair of heavy snow pants and a thick wool scarf. They are both hot pink, my favorite color when I was a kid but not so much now. Still, it's obvious Macy remembered that from the last time I saw her, and I can't help being touched as she holds them out to me.

"Thanks." I give her the closest thing to a smile I can manage.

After a few false starts, I manage to pull the pants on over the thermal underwear and fleece pajama pants with emojis on them (the only kind of fleece pants I own) that I put on at my uncle's instruction before boarding the plane in Seattle. Then I take a long look at the way Macy's rainbow-colored scarf is wrapped around her neck and face and do the same thing with mine.

It's harder than it looks, especially trying to get it positioned well enough to keep it from sliding down my nose the second I move.

Eventually, I manage it, though, and that's when Macy reaches for one of the helmets draped over the snowmobile's handles.

"The helmet is insulated, so it will help keep you warm as well as protect your head in case of a crash," she instructs. "Plus, it's got a shield to protect your eyes from the cold air."

"My eyes can freeze?" I ask, more than a little traumatized, as I take the helmet from her and try to ignore how hard it is to breathe with the scarf over my nose.

"Eyes don't freeze," Macy answers with a little laugh, like she can't help herself. "But the shield will keep them from watering and make you more comfortable."

"Oh, right." I duck my head as my cheeks heat up. "I'm an idiot."

"No you're not." Macy wraps an arm around my shoulders and squeezes tight. "Alaska is a lot. Everyone who comes here has a learning curve. You'll figure it all out soon enough."

I'm not holding my breath on that one—I can't imagine that this cold, foreign place will ever feel familiar to me—but I don't say anything. Not when Macy has already done so much to try and make me feel welcome.

"I'm really sorry you had to come here, Grace," she continues after a second. "I mean, I'm really excited that you're here. I just wish it wasn't because..." Her voice drifts off before she finishes the sentence. But I'm used to that by now. After weeks of having my friends and teachers tiptoe around me, I've learned that no one wants to say the words.

Still, I'm too exhausted to fill in the blanks. Instead, I slip my head in the helmet and secure it the way Macy showed me.

"Ready?" she asks once I've got my face and head as protected as they're going to get.

The answer hasn't changed since Philip asked me that same question in Fairbanks. *Not even close.* "Yeah. Absolutely."

I wait for Macy to climb on the snowmobile before getting on behind her.

"Hold on to my waist!" she shouts as she turns it on, so I do. Seconds later, we're speeding into the darkness that stretches endlessly in front of us.

I've never been more terrified in my life.

2

Just Because You Live in a Tower Doesn't Make You a Prince

The ride isn't as bad as I thought it would be.

I mean, it's not good, but that has more to do with the fact that I've been traveling all day and I just want to get someplace—anyplace—where I can stay longer than a layover. Or a really long snowmobile ride.

And if that place also happens to be warm and devoid of the local wildlife I can hear howling in the distance, then I'm all about it. Especially since everything south of my waist seems to have fallen asleep...

I'm in the middle of trying to figure out how to wake up my very numb butt when we suddenly veer off the trail (and I mean "trail" in the loosest sense of the word) we've been following and onto a kind of plateau on the side of the mountain. It's as we wind our way through yet another copse of trees that I finally see lights up ahead.

"Is that Katmere Academy?" I shout.

"Yeah." Macy lays off the speed a little, steering around trees like we're on a giant slalom course. "We should be there in about five minutes."

Thank God. Much longer out here and I might actually lose a toe or three, even with my doubled-up wool socks. I mean, everyone knows Alaska is cold, but can I just say—it's freaking *cold*, and I was *not* prepared.

Yet another roar sounds in the distance, but as we finally clear the thicket of trees, it's hard to pay attention to anything but the huge building looming in front of us, growing closer with every second that passes.

Or should I say the huge *castle* looming in front of us, because the dwelling I'm looking at is nothing like a modern building. And absolutely nothing like any school I have *ever* seen. I tried to Google it before I got here, but apparently Katmere Academy is so elite even Google hasn't heard of it.

First of all, it's big. Like, really big...and sprawling. From here it looks like the brick wall in front of the castle stretches halfway around the mountain.

Second, it's elegant. Like, really, really elegant, with architecture I've only heard described in my art classes before. Vaulted arches, flying buttresses, and giant, ornate windows dominate the structure.

And third, as we get closer, I can't help wondering if my eyes are deceiving me or if there are gargoyles—*actual gargoyles*—protruding from the top of the castle walls. I know it's just my imagination, but I'd be lying if I said I didn't half expect to see Quasimodo waiting for us when we finally get there.

Macy pulls up to the huge gate at the front of the school and enters a code. Seconds later, the gate swings open. And we're on our way again.

The closer we get, the more surreal everything feels. Like I'm trapped in a horror movie or Salvador Dalí painting. *Katmere Academy may be a Gothic castle, but at least there's no moat*, I tell myself as we break through one last copse of trees. *And no fire-breathing dragon guarding the entrance.* Just a long, winding driveway that looks like every other prep school driveway I've ever seen on TV—except for the fact that it's covered in snow. Big shock. And leads right up to the school's huge, incredibly ornate front doors.

Antique doors.

Castle doors.

I shake my head to clear it. I mean, what even is my life right now?

"Told you it wouldn't be bad," Macy says as she pulls up to the front with a spray of snow. "We didn't even see a caribou, let alone a wolf."

She's right, so I just nod and pretend I'm not completely overwhelmed.

Pretend like my stomach isn't tied into knots and my whole world hasn't turned upside down for the second time in a month.

Pretend like I'm okay.

"Let's bring your suitcases up to your room and get you unpacked. It'll help you relax."

Macy climbs off the snowmobile, then takes off her helmet and her hat. It's the first time I've seen her without all the cold-weather gear, and I can't help smiling at her rainbow-colored hair. It's cut in a short, choppy style that should be smooshed and plastered to her head after three hours in a helmet, but instead it looks like she just walked out of a salon.

Which matches the rest of her, now that I think about it, considering her whole coordinating-jacket-boots-and-snow-pants look kind of shouts cover model for some Alaskan wilderness fashion magazine.

On the other hand, I'm pretty sure my look says I've gone a couple of rounds with a pissed-off caribou. And lost. Badly. Which seems fair, since that's about how I feel.

Macy makes quick work of unloading my suitcases, and this time I grab two of them. But I only make it a few steps up the very long walk to the castle's imposing front doors before I'm struggling to breathe.

"It's the altitude," Macy says as she takes one of the suitcases out of my hand. "We climbed pretty fast and, since you're coming from sea level, it's going to take a few days for you to get used to how thin the air is up here."

Just the idea of not being able to breathe sets off the beginnings of the panic attack I've barely kept at bay all day. Closing my eyes, I take a deep breath—or as deep as I can out here—and try to fight it back.

In, hold for five seconds, out. In, hold for ten seconds, out. In, hold for five seconds, out. Just like Heather's mom taught me. Dr. Blake is a therapist, and she's been giving me tips on how to deal with the anxiety I've been having since my parents died. But I'm not sure her tips are up to combatting all this any more than I am.

Still, I can't stand here frozen forever, like one of the gargoyles staring down at me. Especially not when I can feel Macy's concern even with my eyes closed.

I take one more deep breath and open my eyes again, shooting my cousin a smile I'm far from feeling. "Fake it till you make it is still a thing, right?"

"It's going to be okay," she tells me, her own eyes wide with sympathy. "Just stand there and catch your breath. I'll carry your suitcases up to the door."

"I can do it."

"Seriously, it's okay. Just chill for a minute." She holds up her hand in the universal *stop* gesture. "We're not in any hurry."

Her tone begs me not to argue, so I don't. Especially since the panic attack I'm trying to fend off is only making it harder to breathe. Instead, I nod and watch as she carries my suitcases—one at a time—up to the school's front door.

As I do, a flash of color way above us catches my eye.

It's there and gone so fast that even as I scan for it, I can't be sure it ever really existed to begin with. Except—there it is again. A flash of red in the lit window of the tallest tower.

I don't know who it is or why they even matter, but I stop where I am. Watching. Waiting. Wondering if whoever it is will make another appearance.

It isn't long before they do.

I can't see clearly—distance, darkness, and the distorted glass of the windows cover up a lot—but I get the impression of a strong jaw, shaggy dark hair, a red jacket against a background of light.

It's not much, and there's no reason for it to have caught my attention—certainly no reason for it to have *held* my attention—and yet I find myself staring up at the window so long that Macy has all three of my suitcases at the top of the stairs before I even realize it.

"Ready to try again?" she calls down from her spot near the front doors.

"Oh, yeah. Of course." I start up the last thirty or so steps, ignoring the way my head is spinning. Altitude sickness—one more thing I never had to worry about in San Diego.

Fantastic.

I glance up at the window one last time, not surprised at all to find that whoever was looking down at me is long gone. Still, an inexplicable shiver of disappointment works its way through me. It makes no sense, though, so I shrug it off. I have bigger things to worry about right now.

"This place is unbelievable," I tell my cousin as she pushes open one of the doors and we walk inside.

And holy crap—I thought the whole castle thing with its pointed archways and elaborate stonework was imposing from the outside. Now that I've seen the inside... Now that I've seen the inside, I'm pretty sure I should be curtsying right about now. Or at least bowing and scraping. I mean, wow. Just...wow.

I don't know where to look first—at the high ceiling with its elaborate black crystal chandelier or the roaring fireplace that dominates the whole right wall of the foyer.

In the end I go with the fireplace, because *heat*. And because it's freaking gorgeous, the mantel around it an intricate pattern of stone and stained glass that reflects the light of the flames through the whole room.

"Pretty cool, huh?" Macy says with a grin as she comes up behind me.

"Totally cool," I agree. "This place is..."

"Magic. I know." She wiggles her brows at me. "Want to see some more?"

I really do. I'm still far from sold on the Alaskan boarding school thing, but that doesn't mean I don't want to check out the castle. I mean, it's a *castle*, complete with stone walls and elaborate tapestries I can't help but want to stop and look at as we make our way through the entryway into some kind of common room.

The only problem is that the deeper we move into the school, the more students we come across. Some are standing around in scattered clumps, talking and laughing, while others are seated at several of the room's scarred wooden tables, leaning over books or phones or laptop screens. In the back corner of one room, sprawled out on several antique-looking couches in varying hues of red and gold, is a group of six guys playing Xbox on a huge TV, while a few other students crowd around to watch.

Only, as we get closer, I realize they aren't watching the video game. Or their books. Or even their phones. Instead, they're all looking at *me* as Macy leads—and by "leads," I mean "parades"—me through the center of the room.

My stomach clenches, and I duck my head to hide my very obvious discomfort. I get that everyone wants to check out the new girl—especially when she's the headmaster's niece—but understanding doesn't make it any easier to bear the scrutiny from a bunch of strangers. Especially since I'm pretty sure I have the worst case of helmet hair ever recorded.

I'm too busy avoiding eye contact and regulating my breathing to talk as we make our way through the room, but as we exit into a long, winding hallway, I finally tell Macy, "I can't believe you go to school here."

"We *both* go to school here," she reminds me with a quick grin.

"Yeah, but..." I just got here. And I've never felt more out of place in my life.

"But?" she repeats, eyebrows arched.

"It's a lot." I eye the gorgeous stained glass windows that run along the exterior wall and the elaborate carved molding that decorates the arched ceiling.

"It is." She slows down until I catch up. "But it's home."

"Your home," I whisper, doing my best not to think of the house I left behind, where my mother's front porch wind chimes and whirligigs were the most wild-and-crazy thing about it.

"*Our* home," she answers as she pulls out her phone and sends a quick text. "You'll see. Speaking of which, my dad wants me to give you a choice about what kind of room situation you want."

"Room situation?" I repeat, glancing around the castle while images of ghosts and animated suits of armor slide through my head.

"Well, all the single rooms have been assigned for this term. Dad told me we could move some people around to get you one, but I really hoped you might want to room with me instead." She smiles hopefully for a second, but it quickly fades as she continues. "I mean, I totally get that you might need some space to yourself right now after..."

And there's that fade-out again. It gets to me, just like it does every time. Usually, I ignore it, but this time I can't stop myself from asking, "After what?"

Just this once, I want someone else to say it. Maybe then it will feel more real and less like a nightmare.

Except as Macy gasps and turns the color of the snow outside, I realize it's not going to be her. And that it's unfair of me to expect it to be.

"I'm sorry," she whispers, and now it almost looks like she's going to cry, which, no. Just no. We're not going to go there. Not when the only things currently holding me together are a snarky attitude and my ability to compartmentalize.

No way am I going to risk losing my grip on either. Not here, in front of my cousin and anybody else who might happen to pass by. And not now, when it's obvious from all the stares that I'm totally the newest attraction at the zoo.

So instead of melting into Macy for the hug I so desperately need, instead of letting myself think about how much I miss home and my parents and my *life*, I pull back and give her the best smile I can manage. "Why don't you show me to *our* room?"

The concern in her eyes doesn't diminish, but the sunshine definitely makes another appearance. "*Our* room? Really?"

I sigh deep inside and kiss my dream of a little peaceful solitude goodbye. It's not as hard as it should be, but then I've lost a lot more in the last month than my own space. "Really. Rooming with you sounds perfect."

I've already upset her once, which is so not my style. Neither is getting someone kicked out of their room. Besides being rude and smacking of nepotism, it also seems like a surefire way to piss people off—something that is definitely not on my to-do list right now.

"Awesome!" Macy grins and throws her arms around me for a fast but powerful hug. Then she glances at her phone with a roll of her eyes. "Dad still hasn't answered my text—he's the worst about checking his phone. Why don't you hang out here, and I'll go get him? I know he wanted to see you as soon as we arrived."

"I can come with you—"

"Please just sit, Grace." She points at the ornate French-provincial-style chairs that flank a small chess table in an alcove to the right of the staircase. "I'm sure you're exhausted and I've got this, honest. Relax a minute while I get Dad."

Because she's right—my head is aching and my chest still feels tight—I just nod and plop down in the closest chair. I'm beyond tired and want nothing more than to lean my head back against the chair and close my eyes for a minute. But I'm afraid I'll fall asleep if I do. And no way am I running the risk of being the girl caught drooling all over herself in the hallway on her very first day...or ever, for that matter.

More to keep myself from drifting off than out of actual interest, I pick up one of the chess pieces in front of me. It's made of intricately carved stone, and my eyes widen as I realize what I'm looking at. A perfect rendition of a vampire, right down to the black cape, frightening snarl, and bared fangs. It matches the Gothic castle vibe so well that I can't help being amused. Plus, it's gorgeously crafted.

Intrigued now, I reach for a piece from the other side. And nearly laugh out loud when I realize it's a dragon—fierce, regal, with giant wings. It's absolutely beautiful.

The whole set is.

I put the piece down only to pick up another dragon. This one is less fierce, but with its sleepy eyes and folded wings, it's even more intricate. I look it over carefully, fascinated with the level of detail in the piece—everything from the perfect points on the wings to the careful curl of each talon reflects just how much care the artist put into the piece. I've never been a chess girl, but this set just might change my mind about the game.

When I put down this dragon piece, I go to the other side of the board and pick up the vampire queen. She's beautiful, with long, flowing hair and an elaborately decorated cape.

"I'd be careful with that one if I were you. She's got a nasty bite." The words are low and rumbly and so close that I nearly fall out of my chair. Instead, I jump up, plopping the chess piece down with a clatter, then whirl around—heart pounding—only to find myself face-to-face with the most intimidating guy I've ever seen. And not just because he's hot...although he's definitely that.

Still, there's something more to him, something different and powerful and overwhelming, though I don't have a clue what it is. I mean, sure. He has the kind of face nineteenth-century poets loved to write about—too intense to be beautiful and too striking to be anything else.

Skyscraper cheekbones.

Full red lips.

A jaw so sharp it could cut stone.

Smooth, alabaster skin.

And his eyes...a bottomless obsidian that see everything and show nothing, surrounded by the longest, most obscene lashes I've ever seen.

And even worse, those all-knowing eyes are laser-focused on me right now, and I'm suddenly terrified that he can see all the things I've worked so hard and so long to hide. I try to duck my head, try to yank my gaze from his, but I can't. I'm trapped by his stare, hypnotized by the sheer magnetism rolling off him in waves.

I swallow hard to catch my breath.

It doesn't work.

And now he's grinning, one corner of his mouth turning up in a crooked little smile that I feel in every single cell. Which only makes it worse, because that smirk says he knows exactly what kind of effect he's having on me. And, worse, that he's enjoying it.

Annoyance flashes through me at the realization, melting the numbness that's surrounded me since my parents' deaths. Waking me from the stupor that's the only thing that's kept me from screaming all day, every day, at the unfairness of it all. At the pain and horror and helplessness that have taken over my whole life.

It's not a good feeling. And the fact that it's this guy—with the smirk and the face and the cold eyes that refuse to relinquish their hold on me even as they demand that I don't look too closely—just pisses me off more.

It's that anger that finally gives me the strength to break free of his gaze. I rip my eyes away, then search desperately for something else— anything else—to focus on.

Unfortunately, he's standing right in front of me, so close that he's blocking my view of anything else.

Determined to avoid his eyes, I look anywhere but. And land instead on his long, lean body. Then really wish I hadn't, because the black jeans and T-shirt he's wearing only emphasize his flat stomach and hard, well-defined biceps. Not to mention the double-wide shoulders that are absolutely responsible for blocking my view in the first place.

Add in the thick, dark hair that's worn a little too long, so that it falls forward into his face and skims low across his insane cheekbones, and there's nothing to do but give in. Nothing to do but admit that— obnoxious smirk or not—this boy is sexy as hell.

A little wicked, a lot wild, and *all* dangerous.

What little oxygen I've been able to pull into my lungs in this high altitude completely disappears with the realization. Which only makes me madder. Because, seriously. When exactly did I become the heroine in some YA romance? The new girl swooning over the hottest, most unattainable boy in school?

Gross. And so not happening.

Determined to nip whatever this is in the bud, I force myself to look at his face again. This time, as our gazes meet and clash, I realize that it doesn't matter if I'm acting like some giant romantic cliché.

Because he isn't.

One glance and I know that this dark boy with the closed-off eyes and the fuck-you attitude isn't the hero of anyone's story. Least of all mine.

Vampire Queens
Aren't the Only Ones
with a Nasty Bite

Determined not to let this staring contest that feels a little like a show of dominance go on any longer, I cast around for something to break the tension. And settle on a response to the only thing he's actually said to me so far.

"*Who's* got a nasty bite?"

He reaches past me and picks up the piece I dropped, holds the queen for me to see. "She's really not very nice."

I stare at him. "She's a chess piece."

His obsidian eyes gleam back. "Your point?"

"My point is, she's a *chess* piece. She's made of *marble*. She can't bite anyone."

He inclines his head in a *you never know* gesture. "'There are more things in heaven and hell, Horatio, / Than are dreamt of in your philosophy.'"

"Earth," I correct before I can think better of it.

He crooks one midnight-black brow in question, so I continue. "The quote is, 'There are more things in heaven and *earth*, Horatio.'"

"Is it now?" His face doesn't change, but there's something mocking in his tone that wasn't there before, like I'm the one who made the mistake, not him. But I know I'm right—my AP English class just finished reading *Hamlet* last month, and my teacher spent forever on that quote. "I think I like my version better."

"Even though it's wrong?"

"Especially because it's wrong."

I have no idea what I'm supposed to say to that, so I just shake my head. And wonder how lost I'll get if I go looking for Macy and Uncle

Finn right now. Probably very, considering the size of this place, but I'm beginning to think I should risk it. Because the longer I stand here, the more I realize this guy is as terrifying as he is intriguing.

I'm not sure which is worse. And I'm growing less sure by the second that I want to find out.

"I need to go." I force the words past a jaw I didn't even know I'd been clenching.

"Yeah, you do." He takes a small step back, nods toward the common room Macy and I just walked through. "The door's that way."

It's not the response I'm expecting, and it throws me off guard. "So what, I shouldn't let it hit me on the way out?"

He shrugs. "As long as you leave this school, it doesn't matter to me if it hits you or not. I warned your uncle you wouldn't be safe here, but he obviously doesn't like you much."

Anger flashes through me at his words, burning away the last of the numbness that has plagued me. "Who exactly are you supposed to be anyway? Katmere's very own unwelcome wagon?"

"*Un*welcome wagon?" His tone is as obnoxious as his face. "Believe me, this is the nicest greeting you're going to get here."

"This is it, huh?" I raise my brows, spread my arms out wide. "The big welcome to Alaska?"

"More like, welcome to hell. Now get the fuck out."

The last is said in a snarl that yanks my heart into my throat. But it also slams my temper straight into the stratosphere. "Is it that stick up your ass that makes you such a jerk?" I demand. "Or is this just your regular, charming personality?"

The words come out fast and furious, before I even know I'm going to say them. But once they're out, I don't regret them. How can I when shock flits across his face, finally erasing that annoying smirk of his?

At least for a minute. Then he fires back, "I've got to say, if that's the best you've got, I give you about an hour."

I know I shouldn't ask, but he looks so smug, I can't help myself. "Before what?"

"Before something eats you." He doesn't say it, but the *obviously* is definitely implied. Which only pisses me off more.

"Seriously? That's what you decided to go with?" I roll my eyes. "Bite me, dude."

"Nah, I don't think so." He looks me up and down. "I'm pretty sure you wouldn't even make an appetizer."

But then he's stepping closer, leaning down until he's all but whispering in my ear. "Maybe a quick snack, though." His teeth close with a loud, sharp snap that makes me jump and shiver all at the same time.

Which I hate...so, so much.

I glance around us, curious if anyone else is witnessing this mess. But where everyone only had eyes for me earlier, they seem to be going out of their way not to glance in my direction now. One lanky boy with thick red hair even keeps his head so awkwardly turned to the side while walking across the room that he almost runs into another student.

Which tells me everything I need to know about this guy.

Determined to regain control of the situation—and myself—I take a big step back. Then, ignoring my pounding heart and the pterodactyls flapping around in my stomach, I demand, "What is *wrong* with you?" I mean, seriously. He's got the manners of a rabid polar bear.

"Got a century or three?" His smirk is back—he's obviously proud of getting to me—and for a moment, just a moment, I think about how satisfying it would be to punch him right in the center of that annoying mouth of his.

"You know what? You really don't have to be such a—"

"Don't tell me what I have to be. Not when you don't have a clue what you've wandered into here."

"Oh no!" I do a mock-afraid face. "Is this the part of the story where you tell me about the big, bad monsters out here in the big, bad Alaskan wilderness?"

"No, this is the part of the story where I show you the big, bad monsters right here in this castle." He steps forward, closing the small distance I managed to put between us.

And there goes my heart again, beating like a caged bird desperate to escape.

I hate it.

I hate that he's bested me, and I hate that being this close to him makes me feel a bunch of things I shouldn't for a guy who has been a total jerk to me. I hate even more that the look in his eyes says he knows exactly how I'm feeling.

The fact that I'm reacting so strongly to him when all he seems to feel for me is contempt is humiliating, so I take one trembling step back. Then I take another. And another.

But he follows suit, moving one step forward for every step I take backward, until I'm caught between him and the chess table pressing into the back of my thighs. And even though there's nowhere to go, even though I'm stuck right here in front of him, he leans closer still, *gets* closer still, until I can feel his warm breath on my cheek and the brush of his silky black hair against my skin.

"What are—?" What little breath I've managed to recover catches in my throat. "What are you doing?" I demand as he reaches past me.

He doesn't answer at first. But when he pulls away, he's got one of the dragon pieces in his hand. He holds it up for me to see, that single eyebrow of his arched provocatively, and answers. "You're the one who wanted to see the monsters."

This one is fierce, eyes narrowed, talons raised, mouth open to show off sharp, jagged teeth. But it's still just a chess piece. "I'm not afraid of a three-inch dragon."

"Yeah, well, you should be."

"Yeah, well, I'm *not*." The words come out more strangled than I intend, because he may have taken a step back, but he's still standing too close. So close that I can feel his breath on my cheek and the warmth radiating from his body. So close that one deep breath will end with my chest pressing against his.

The thought sets off a whole new kaleidoscope of butterflies deep inside me. I can't move back any farther, but I can *lean* back over the table a little. Which I do—all while those dark, fathomless eyes of his watch my every move.

Silence stretches between us for one...ten...twenty-five seconds before he finally asks, "So if you aren't afraid of things that go bump in the night, what *are* you afraid of?"

Images of my parents' mangled car flash through my brain, followed by pictures of their battered bodies. I was the only family they had in San Diego—or anywhere, really, except for Finn and Macy—so I'm the one who had to go to the morgue. I'm the one who had to identify their bodies. Who had to see them all bruised and bloody and broken before the funeral home had a chance to put them back together again.

The familiar anguish wells up inside me, but I do what I've been doing for weeks now. I shove it back down. Pretend it doesn't exist. "Not much," I tell him as flippantly as I can manage. "There's not much to be afraid of when you've already lost everything that matters."

He freezes at my words, his whole body tensing up so much that it feels like he might shatter. Even his eyes change, the wildness disappearing between one blink and the next until only stillness remains.

Stillness and an agony so deep I can barely see it behind the layers and layers of defenses he's erected.

But I *can* see it. More, I can *feel* it calling to my own pain.

It's an awful and awe-inspiring feeling at the same time. So awful I can barely stand it. So awe-inspiring that I can't stop it.

So I don't. And neither does he.

Instead, we stand there, frozen. Devasted. Connected in a way I can feel but can't comprehend by our very separate horrors.

I don't know how long we stay like that, staring into each other's eyes. Acknowledging each other's pain because we can't acknowledge our own.

Long enough for the animosity to drain right out of me.

Long enough for me to see the silver flecks in the midnight of his eyes—distant stars shining through the darkness he makes no attempt to hide.

More than long enough for me to get my rampaging heart under control. At least until he reaches out and gently takes hold of one of my million curls.

And just that easily, I forget how to breathe again.

Heat slams through me as he stretches out the curl, warming me up for the first time since I opened the door of Philip's plane in Healy. It's confusing and overwhelming and I don't have a clue what to do about it.

Five minutes ago, this guy was being a total douche to me. And now...now I don't know anything. Except that I need space. And to sleep. And a chance to just breathe for a few minutes.

With that in mind, I bring my hands up and push at his shoulders in an effort to get him to give me a little room. But it's like pushing a wall of granite. He doesn't budge.

At least not until I whisper, "Please."

He waits a second longer, maybe two or three—until my head is muddled and my hands are shaking—before he finally takes a step back and lets the curl go.

As he does, he sweeps a hand through his dark hair. His longish bangs part just enough to reveal a jagged scar from the center of his left eyebrow to the left corner of his mouth. It's thin and white, barely noticeable against the paleness of his skin, but it's there nonetheless— especially if you look at the wicked vee it causes at the end of his dark eyebrow.

It should make him less attractive, should do something— anything—to negate the incredible power of his looks. But somehow the scar only emphasizes the danger, turning him from just another pretty boy with angelic looks into someone a million times more compelling. A fallen angel with a bad-boy vibe for miles...and a million stories to back that vibe up.

Combined with the anguish I just felt inside him, it makes him more...human. More relatable and more devastating, despite the darkness that rolls off him in waves. A scar like this only comes from an unimaginable injury. Hundreds of stitches, multiple operations, months—maybe even years—of recovery. I hate that he suffered like that, wouldn't wish it on anyone, let alone this boy who frustrates and terrifies and excites me all at the same time.

He knows I noticed the scar—I can see it in the way his eyes narrow. In the way his shoulders stiffen and his hands clench into fists. In the way he ducks his head so that his hair falls over his cheek again.

I hate that, hate that he thinks he has to hide something that he should wear as a badge of honor. It takes a lot of strength to get through something like this, a lot of strength to come out the other side of it, and he should be proud of that strength. Not ashamed of the mark it's left.

I reach out before I make a conscious decision to do so, cup his scarred cheek in my hand.

His dark eyes blaze, and I think he's going to shove me away. But in the end, he doesn't. He just stands there and lets me stroke my thumb back and forth across his cheek—across his scar—for several long moments.

"I'm sorry," I whisper when I can finally get my voice past the painful lump of sympathy in my throat. "This must have hurt horribly."

He doesn't answer. Instead, he closes his eyes, sinks into my palm, takes one long, shuddering breath.

Then he's pulling back, stepping away, putting real distance between us for the first time since he snuck up behind me, which suddenly feels like a lifetime ago.

"I don't understand you," he tells me suddenly, his black-magic voice so quiet that I have to strain to hear him.

"'There are more things in heaven and hell, Horatio, / Than are dreamt of in your philosophy,'" I answer, deliberately using his earlier misquote.

He shakes his head as if trying to clear it. Takes a deep breath, then blows it out slowly. "If you won't leave—"

"I *can't* leave," I interject. "I have nowhere else to go. My parents—"

"Are dead. I know." He smiles grimly. "Fine. If you're not going to leave, then you need to listen to me very, very carefully."

"What do you—?"

"Keep your head down. Don't look too closely at anyone or anything." He leans forward, his voice dropping to a low rumble as he finishes. "And always, *always* watch your back."

ACKNOWLEDGMENTS

Writing this book, the first in a new series, has been both a challenge and a joy, and now that it is ready to go out into the world, I have a lot of people to thank who helped me along the way.

Justine Bylo, the most amazing and intrepid editor a girl could ever ask for. Thanks for all your help and patience and guidance as I worked to get *Sweet Nightmare* right. You are exceptional.

Emily Sylvan Kim, you are truly the best in all the ways. Thank you for everything.

Liz Pelletier, for pushing me to get it right—and for everything that led up to this moment. You are incredible.

Brittany Zimmerman, for everything you do for me and for the fans of the Crave Series. I love you a lot.

Bree Archer, for the most gorgeous covers any writer could ever dream of. Sincerely. You awe me every time.

Stacy Cantor Abrams, for being the best support system and friend a girl could ask for.

Ashley Doliber and Lizzy Mason, for putting up with more than one hysterical phone call and for always having a plan. You are wonderful and I'm so excited to work with you!

Curtis Svehlak, for putting up with me for all these years and somehow making everything work. You're the best!

And to everyone else at Entangled—Meredith Johnson, Rae Swain, Jessica Meigs, Hannah Lindsey, Britt Marczak, LJ Anderson, Hannah Guy, Heather Riccio, and my Entangled Buddy Readers— who have taken such good care of me with this book from the start. I am so grateful. I truly do work with the best team in publishing and I know just how lucky I am.

A special thank-you to Veronica Gonzalez, Liz Tzetzo, and the amazing Macmillan sales team for all the support they've shown this series over the years, and to Beth Metrick, Lexi Winter, and Emi Lotto for working so extra hard to get these books into readers' hands.

Eden and Phoebe Kim, for being the best!

Jenn Elkins, for being my ride or die. Here's to thirty more years!!!!!

Stephanie Marquez, thank you for all your love and support for two of the worst years of my life. You are a marvel, and I'm so grateful you found me.

For my three boys, who I love with my whole heart and soul. Thank you for understanding all the evenings I had to hide in my office and work instead of hanging out, for pitching in when I needed you most, for sticking with me through all the difficult years, and for being the best kids I could ever ask for.

And finally, for my fans—thank you, thank you, thank you for all your support and enthusiasm and love through the years. I have the most amazing fans in all the world, and I am grateful for you every single day. Welcome to Calder Academy—I hope you love it as much as I do. xoxoxoxoxo